FATE
HAS ITS
Favorites

Eralides E. Cabrera

Gotham Books

30 N Gould St.
Ste. 20820, Sheridan, WY 82801
https://gothambooksinc.com/

Phone: 1 (307) 464-7800

© 2025 *Eralides E. Cabrera*. All rights reserved.

No part of this book may be reproduced, stored in a retrieval system, or transmitted by any means without the written permission of the author.

Published by Gotham Books (February 25, 2025)

ISBN: 979-8-3484-9410-0 (P)
ISBN: 979-8-3484-9411-7 (E)

Because of the dynamic nature of the Internet, any web addresses or links contained in this book may have changed since publication and may no longer be valid.

The views expressed in this work are solely those of the author and do not necessarily reflect the views of the publisher, and the publisher hereby disclaims any responsibility for them.

From under any rock, a frog may suddenly leap out.

—Cuban Proverb

Cover by Julio Martinez

Table of Contents

CHAPTER 1 1
CHAPTER 2 5
CHAPTER 3 8
CHAPTER 4 11
CHAPTER 5 13
CHAPTER 6 23
CHAPTER 7 27
CHAPTER 8 31
CHAPTER 9 34
CHAPTER 10 36
CHAPTER 11 48
CHAPTER 12 52
CHAPTER 13 56
CHAPTER 14 60
CHAPTER 15 63
CHAPTER 16 69
CHAPTER 17 74
CHAPTER 18 77
CHAPTER 19 92
CHAPTER 20 94
CHAPTER 21 96
CHAPTER 22 110
CHAPTER 23 112
CHAPTER 24 117
CHAPTER 25 125
CHAPTER 26 128
CHAPTER 27 132
CHAPTER 28 135
CHAPTER 29 137
CHAPTER 30 146

CHAPTER 31	148
CHAPTER 32	150
CHAPTER 33	157
CHAPTER 34	160
CHAPTER 35	163
CHAPTER 36	167
CHAPTER 37	169
CHAPTER 38	172
CHAPTER 39	175
CHAPTER 40	178
CHAPTER 41	187
CHAPTER 42	189
CHAPTER 43	194
CHAPTER 44	198
CHAPTER 45	200
CHAPTER 46	203
CHAPTER 47	205
CHAPTER 48	207
CHAPTER 49	211
CHAPTER 50	215
CHAPTER 51	226
CHAPTER 52	233
CHAPTER 53	236
CHAPTER 54	240
CHAPTER 55	243
CHAPTER 56	250
CHAPTER 57	253
CHAPTER 58	256
CHAPTER 59	259
CHAPTER 60	262
CHAPTER 61	265
CHAPTER 62	269
CHAPTER 63	271

CHAPTER 64	277
CHAPTER 65	280
CHAPTER 66	285
CHAPTER 67	288
CHAPTER 68	290
CHAPTER 69	297
CHAPTER 70	299
CHAPTER 71	302
CHAPTER 72	305
CHAPTER 73	310
CHAPTER 74	314
CHAPTER 75	317
CHAPTER 76	320
CHAPTER 77	324
CHAPTER 78	327
CHAPTER 79	330
CHAPTER 80	334
CHAPTER 81	341
CHAPTER 82	346
CHAPTER 83	352
CHAPTER 84	355
CHAPTER 85	360
CHAPTER 86	363
CHAPTER 87	371
CHAPTER 88	375
CHAPTER 89	378
CHAPTER 90	382
CHAPTER 91	387
CHAPTER 92	392
CHAPTER 93	396
CHAPTER 94	401
CHAPTER 95	404
CHAPTER 96	411

CHAPTER 97	416
CHAPTER 98	419
CHAPTER 99	421
CHAPTER 100	423
CHAPTER 101	425
CHAPTER 102	428
CHAPTER 103	435
CHAPTER 104	437
CHAPTER 105	441
CHAPTER 106	444
CHAPTER 107	446
CHAPTER 108	449
CHAPTER 109	451
CHAPTER 110	458
CHAPTER 111	462
About the Book	464

CHAPTER 1

On a stormy night at the end of the month of March, the eighteen-wheeler driven by Carlos Figueroa was moving slowly on Route 95 North, now in the outskirts of the city of Jacksonville. An intense rain made the road slippery and dangerous. Mixed with ghostly winds, the curtains of rain swayed across the road as if driven by some invisible hand that pulled them back and forth. Carlos felt that the storm was intensifying, and he slowly switched lanes, moving the truck to the extreme right, preserved for the slow traffic. His caution would no doubt cost him additional hours on the road, but because of the bad weather, he thought to himself that "it was better to be cautious than have regrets later," as they said where he came from. To rush in this bad weather would be suicidal.

He slowed down until his speedometer read 45 miles per hour. He heard the sound made by splashing water on his wagon and saw a long SUV trying to overtake him in the center lane. It seemed reckless to even try in this weather. It was clear the vehicle would not make it. As soon as the driver was able to push past Carlos's truck, he struck the incoming rain head on, and for a moment, he seemed to lose control of his vehicle. The impact of the heavy rain on his front wheels was enough to make it swerve, and the driver had no choice but to pull back and ride side by side with Carlos's wagon, which protected him from the waves of rain.

"I wish I could guard you, friend," Carlos murmured to himself, "but I am going west. Better slow down if you want to make it."

Carlos took the exit to Route 10, heading west, and drove his truck through the elevated road that made a half-moon turn from Highway 95. Carlos always took this road when going on long trips to Texas, Arizona, and some of the other western states that he frequently visited and that he would have rather not. But the money was good, and he had no family to answer to, so he had agreed with his boss on this trip to Phoenix; then he would move on to the northeast before returning home to Miami, to rest for whatever was left of the week at that point.

Carlos was not a long-time driver. He had been doing it now for almost four years, and he was happy driving, although not particularly fond of the routes his employer chose for him. They were always the toughest ones. Gordon, his boss, seemed to value his work ethic and his driving skills. But he put enormous pressure on him to work more hours. Every week Carlos had to play a cat-and-mouse game with his boss, trying to evade another run out of state. By the end of the week, Carlos could feel the pressure as his cell would light up with another phone call from an unfamiliar number. It was his boss again, trying to persuade him to go on one quick trip: a quick trip to upstate New York or to Chicago. When Carlos pointed out that his hours on the road for the week were too close to the limit of the federal guidelines, his boss would try to box him in. If he drove five miles faster, he'd answer, he would be at least two hours below the limit. He had done the math.

"No," Carlos would answer, "it was too risky." Besides, there was no such thing as a quick trip in interstate driving. A trip to New York could last an eternity.

Carlos maneuvered his truck past the elevated highway and went into the smooth road ahead, leaving the city of Jacksonville behind. The weather showed no improvement, and the windshield wipers were going full speed. It was in this area of the beginning of Route 10 that always brought him the memory of his friend Alfredo Fuentes. He was a happy-go-lucky young man who loved motorcycling and spent weekends traveling with his gang of friends, all riding Harleys like him. While going east on Route 10, nearing Jacksonville, an eighteen-wheeler passed them at an unusually high speed. The other bikers scrambled quickly to the right lane, some on the shoulder of the road, yelling profanities at the speeding trucker. Alfredo did not move fast enough. His bike was too close to the truck's wagon, and the draft created by its bulk was the last thing he felt. He lost control of his bike, which went immediately straight into the ditch, past the shoulder of the road. Alfredo survived the accident, but he lost movement in his right shoulder and arm. Despite the therapy, he never could ride again. Nowadays he was a disabled thirty-year-old who spent most of his time hanging by the service windows of local Miami restaurants, drinking his espresso coffee and telling stories with the locals.

Excessive speed was a killer in this business, and Carlos knew it. This was the moral of the story, and he kept it alive in his mind. He was one of the last Cuban *balseros* who trickled through the ninety-mile stretch of water between Havana and Miami on the eve of President Obama's ominous order cancelling the old wet foot-dry foot policy, which revised the Cuban Adjustment Act of 1966. The new policy was justified by the administration as one more step towards normalizing relations with the island. Its effect was evident immediately, as it stopped the flow of rafters coming from Cuba.

Carlos was processed by the immigration authorities, gaining status two years later. He was barely seventeen at the time of his arrival in late 2014. As soon as he obtained his legal permanent status, he set his goal on obtaining his commercial driver's license. One year later, he graduated from trailer driving school, and immediately after he began driving for a living.

Carlos had just turned twenty-four years old. He had been a driver now for five years, and so far, he had a clean driving record. He lived in a small apartment in southwest Miami. But for a cousin, he had no relatives in the US, and he considered himself a lucky man. He had challenged the treacherous Caribbean waters, all for the sake of freedom.

To his surprise, during the trip he had encountered tranquil waters that allowed him and his two companions to sail through them during the night. In the early dawn, he and his friends sighted land. They hesitated rushing in, thinking they might have somehow been pulled back towards the island by the sea currents during the night. For Carlos, that had been the tensest moment of the trip. The three men argued about their bearings and what to do next. One of them had a compass which had been steadily pointing northwest throughout the trip. They all had made sure of that, and the raft had been moving steadily forward the entire time. It would be impossible to find themselves back in their place of origin. Finally, all three men decided to move forward and carefully skirt the coastline. The silhouette of a tall building and the brown tiled roofs of the surrounding homes, visible now in the first light of dawn, assured them that they were in America.

Reaching the shore this early proved to be an advantage, as there was nobody around. The three walked ashore, leaving the remnants of the raft behind. They were too exhausted to consider that leaving the raft afloat would immediately tip the Coast Guard that refugees had sneaked in.

By late morning, all three had been apprehended. They were taken by the local sheriff into the big courtyard of one of the last surviving stucco homes from the previous century. Carlos remembered to this day how the structure seemed familiar to him from old pictures he had seen in Cuba. Yes, there was no doubt. They were in America. But it felt like heaven opened up when a sheriff's officer pointed towards a table in the middle of the courtyard stocked up with watermelons. They all hesitated for a moment but the officer pointed towards the table again. Then they all went for it and grabbed the round slices that had been cut up in the middle of the table and devoured them. Thirst was man's worst enemy, Carlos thought. It was worse than hunger, and it could drive a human into desperation like nothing else. After feasting for fifteen minutes or so, Carlos was the first one to drop on the ground, holding his belly and passing out. They were in the Florida Keys. God bless America.

CHAPTER 2

About three in the morning Carlos had made the TA truck stop in Grand Bay, Alabama, a good place to park and sleep until late morning. He had traveled well, about seven hours on Route 10 and six hours on 95 since he left Miami, some in bad weather, and he was reaching his limit of driving hours on the road. He tried to find a spot where he could hook up to power and get internet service to view a movie on his laptop, but suddenly he felt so tired that he could not think about anything else but sleep. He logged himself out of the system and wrote the time on his worksheet. He went outside and found a public bathroom. He urinated, washed his face, and brushed his teeth. He then went back outside and looked around for any truckers, but they all seemed to be inside their haulers with the engines running. He went inside his truck's cabin and fell onto the narrow bed that ran from window to window. Before he had lifted the covers to tuck himself underneath them, he was sleep.

By sunrise, Carlos was awakened by the familiar sound of tractors making their way out of the parking lot. He turned and went back to sleep. He needed to stay off the road for ten hours, so he slept till the afternoon. He was more of a night driver anyway, so he took his time. He went to the food service in the middle of the parking lot and chose Roy Rogers for a burger and some juice. Coffee was out of the question. He could not tolerate regular coffee. If it wasn't espresso with a drop of milk, or *cortaito,* as the Cubans called it, he would go without it until he returned to Miami. It was one of the few things from his culture that he could not shake off. Sitting at the table he felt for his cell phone, still clipped to his belt, and checked the time. It was fifteen past twelve.

"I really overdid it this time," he said to himself. "I need to run."

His phone vibrated, and he picked up.

"Hello," said the voice from the other end.

"Hello," Carlos responded somewhat groggily.

"Have you signed in yet?" the male voice asked. "I've tried reaching, and no one answered. Phoenix is waiting for that load. When do you plan to get there?"

Carlos knew it was his boss. As usual, Gordon's sarcasm was more recognizable than his voice. Carlos had always marveled at the man's ability to change the sound of his voice from call to call. That was his strategy to disguise himself; otherwise, his drivers would never pick up his calls.

"I need to sleep to get there in one piece," Carlos replied.

"I need the load delivered," the man insisted. "That's what I pay you for."

"You haven't discovered America, Gordon," Carlos grudged back. "Because you pay me doesn't mean I stop sleeping. Listen, I gotta go. The longer you keep me on the phone, the longer I take."

"What time will you get there tonight?"

"Tonight? No way. Late tomorrow maybe. I can only drive for fourteen hours straight, and I have twenty-one left. Those are the federal rules."

"Ah, rules can be bent."

"No, I bend nothing. It's my license that's on the line."

"Get going then."

After fueling, Carlos exited the cabin holding a bottle of water and looked around. He always planned his trips mentally. He figured he could drive his allowed time of fifteen hours straight.

Carlos got back on Route 10 West and sat comfortably on his seat. He had delayed to comply with the ten-hour rest that was required for interstate drivers, but he had overdone it the night before. He should have stopped earlier. But he went on until almost 3:00 a.m., and now he felt trapped. He needed to use his allowed time straight, which meant he would end up well after midnight, and then he would start late the next day. It had all been because of that storm the night before.

Now the road ahead seemed flawless, and he visualized reaching mid-Texas tonight before getting rest again. It would be a long, lonely trip. The Midwest hauls would have to stop, he thought. Sitting behind the wheel motionless for so many hours dried the fluid out of his body. There must be a better way. This was it, he resolved. When he got back to Miami later in the week, he would lay his cards on the table in Gordon's office. He would not travel farther west than Louisiana.

CHAPTER 3

Nearing 3:00 a.m., Carlos was parked at Love's Travel Stop #542 in Fort Stockton, Texas. He was approximately seven hours from Phoenix; it was a good time to stop. He had been driving for nearly fourteen hours since he left Alabama. He was pushing for El Paso, but time just ran out, and he could not stay on the road any longer. He came into the wide parking lot and pulled next to another truck with its engine running. Carlos waved at the driver from the window, not sure whether he was asleep or awake, but a light movement of his hand let him know he had spotted him. Carlos turned his engine off and went out of the cabin. He walked to the service center and greeted the night attendants. They knew him now by name after his frequent stops.

"Hey, Carlos," said the young woman at the counter. "You are late today."

She had a slight Middle Eastern accent and wore a head scarf.

"I've been running late now for two days after I got out of Florida. I hit bad weather."

She smiled slightly at him.

"I need to use the shower," Carlos said.

"I don't think anyone is there. Go ahead."

Carlos returned to the counter a few minutes later, looking fresh with his hair combed straight back. He bought a ham sandwich and an orange juice, and winked at the cashier as she gave him his change back.

"Are you going to stay the rest of the night?"

"Yes. I am going to sleep in the cabin. I'm dead tired."

"So, I guess I will see you on the way back?"

"I am not sure yet. I will try to come back the same route, but I am not sure where they will be sending me. It may be too far north."

She waited for him, and after a pause he spoke again.

"It's not goodbye, but I will see you later," Carlos said.

They both laughed. Carlos grabbed his sandwich and juice, and went outside. He had come to know several young Middle Eastern women at some of the stations. He still could not make up his mind whether he found them attractive. He thought the head garb did not do them justice and hid some of their beauty.

"Well, how goes it, friend?" asked a man standing right by the front door of the store, obviously a driver. "Where are you headed?"

"Phoenix," Carlos replied.

"Oh, I haven't been there in two weeks. I kind of miss it."

"Yeah," Carlos said. "It's pleasant this time of year. I'm going to get some sleep. I was on the road for almost fifteen hours."

"Good to see you," said the man, turning back to go inside.

Carlos went in his truck's cabin and sat to eat his sandwich, but he ran through his telephone cursor to check on his phone calls first. There were two calls with the 305 area code. One was from his boss, and the other one was unfamiliar to him. He read the number several times, trying to recognize it, but he felt the fatigue on the lower part of his neck from his many hours on the road and gave up.

He sent a short text to his boss telling him he was about to go to sleep and gave his location, not that the company would not know it already. But knowing his boss's character, he understood that a text would fall short in appeasing him. He imagined the man waking up and dialing his number to check up on him. Did he ever sleep? Carlos thought it was so unnecessary for a business owner to follow his employees around so ferociously.

He put the remnants of his sandwich in the same bag the store had given him and gulped the rest of his drink, placing the empty bottle in the bag. He laid down in the truck's narrow bed, already pillowed up from the night before. He thought about how he would run a truck company if he ever came to own one but quickly put these thoughts away. For now, he was content holding a job and saving his money. His deepest desire was to bring his parents to America. He imagined them in the island right now at this early hour, probably already awake trying to figure how to find food for the day. Then he was not able to hold another thought as he fell fast asleep.

CHAPTER 4

The vibration of his phone woke him. Before picking up, he tapped the phone screen to get a glimpse of the time. It was nearly one o'clock. He took the call.

"Carlos here," he said.

"You on the road yet?"

"I'm about to."

"Well, let's get going. We don't pay you for sleeping."

"You know the rules," Carlos replied. "I can't get on the road until ten hours of rest."

"That's what it's been, ten hours."

Carlos felt like answering in kind but stopped. What good would it do? He had been down this road before. The only solution was to leave the job. He had offers from other outfits, but now was not the right time.

"I gotta go."

Carlos had his tank filled and ran to the store to grab some juice for the road. He was planning to drive straight to Phoenix and make his drop-off in time. He figured he could make it before 10:00 that night, drop his box, and get a decent meal before going to bed again. He knew of a place.

"Get enough sleep?" the cashier asked as he checked out.

She was wearing a more lively colored head scarf this morning. Not red or pink but certainly brighter than the usual gray. She was glad he noticed her as she handed him his change and smiled at him.

"I did sleep. You're here kind of early, aren't you?"

"I just started at 1:00. I had to cover for the regular cashier."

"So you're on overtime. You don't mind that?"

"No, not during the week," she said. "Are you leaving now?"

"I am," he replied. "The engine is running."

"Phoenix again?"

"Yes," he said, now making eye contact. "Sounds like routine, right?"

"What is it like there?" she asked. "If you were to bring someone a token to let them remember the city, what would it be?"

Carlos looked past her. What was she asking him? Was she proposing?

"Nothing like a key chain or a T-shirt but maybe a fake cactus. It is very dry there. Would you like one?"

She suddenly hesitated, perhaps feeling she had leaped too far, farther than expected of a young girl from her culture. But it was too late.

"Yes," she answered.

"Okay," Carlos said. "I will bring you one."

He grabbed the bag with his two bottles of Tropicana juice and waved at her as he went out the door. He had chatted to her almost on reflex while his mind reflected on the rest of his trip. He had already decided that he would be at his drop station no later than 8:00 p.m. It would be a smooth drive, all of it on Route 10.

CHAPTER 5

Carlos's prediction on his time of arrival was almost on target. His drop-off location was in Chandler, Arizona, west of Phoenix. Carlos reached the gate just in time. The company did not have a night shift, and they closed the entrance at 9:00 p.m. sharp. Carlos signed the log at the entrance shack and handed it to the guard inside.

"We had you scheduled for tomorrow morning," the guard said, taking the logbook back. "How did you make it so fast?"

"I just drove west on Route 10," Carlos said, smiling. "You can't go wrong."

"No kidding," said the guard. "Practically every truck that comes through here travels on Route 10."

"There aren't many other options."

"There are but not for heavy trucks. There are local roads."

"So where shall I take the box?"

"Oh, yes. Go to gate six."

It was one of the gates on the side of the building, and Carlos knew of it. He had brought in cargoes to this building twice in the past week. He made a right and drove to the end of the building and then turned left. There were trucks and trailers parked in all the gates. Number six was empty, but the next slot was also taken.

Carlos stopped right in between the two. Backing up the trailer in such a narrow space and without room to maneuver in the front would be a challenge. But this is why he had chosen to drive tractors. The skill needed to achieve miracles in tight situations was what fascinated him.

He took his time. He had to position the tractor just at the right spot to be able to back up and arch the trailer at the right angle so it would start coming in at the designated spot, leaving the same space size on both sides. He only had to try three times. The trailer went in straight as an arrow until Carlos felt the light jolt of the rubber stoppers as the trailer made contact with the gate. He viewed the mirrors on both sides and satisfied himself that the space between the trucks was equal. He took his log with him and went inside the warehouse to check in. Moments later he made a call to his company to let them know the box was in. A bearded man with a baseball cap came outside with him.

"Your people said you'd be taking a box to Atlanta," the man said.

"Yes, in the morning."

The man paused for a few seconds. Carlos could sense that he would have wanted for him to take another trailer out tonight, but because he understood drivers' regulations and their need to have their rest, he had no choice but to wait until the morning.

"Well, can you be here by 7:00 a.m.? We are late with this cargo. You are one of your company's best drivers, and we really need you to take this load out as early as possible."

Carlos resigned himself to the fact that sleeping late was not an option for him. He would need to come back for the trailer early and find a rest stop before he could get back on a highway.

"Fred, I will be here by 7:00," Carlos said. "Let me unhook the tractor. I have to find a place to eat and somewhere to spend the night."

"You're not far from downtown Phoenix," Fred said. "There are many Hispanic restaurants off Route 10 that have your kind of food."

"And what kind of food is that?" Carlos asked curiously.

"Well, you know, Spanish food. Mexican, Central American."

"Hmmm. It is getting late, so I will grab what I can find."

"All right, then," Fred said, holding his clipboard close. "See you in the morning."

"Good night," Carlos said.

Carlos got to work quickly; he stood in back of the tractor and disengaged the cables connected to the trailer, lowering the landing gear and checking the wheels. Then he jumped inside the tractor and slowly moved it to begin the uncoupling. When he was satisfied that the tractor would clear the trailer safely, he pulled out slowly and headed for the shack, where he checked himself out with the guard. He headed for Route 10 and went east on it. He could not see anything to his liking. Several signs for Central American restaurants popped up, but he was looking for some light food like hot soup. He got off on Route 60 and made a left turn at the first intersection. There were no neon signs of any fast food restaurants on either side of the street, but suddenly in the distance, he saw the sign for Guatelinda Restaurant and Bakery.

It wasn't his first preference, but it would have to do. He parked the tractor off a way from the cars in the lot, got off the truck, and made his way into the restaurant. He noticed the small garden on both sides of the walkway, right before the main door, and he had to look again. It seemed impressive, he thought, slightly overdone for an eatery like this. Some landscaper had taken the time to really crowd the sides of the walkway with flowers.

As Carlos walked in, he surveyed the tables, most of which were taken. It was middle of the week, but at nighttime, traditional restaurants like this one seemed to flourish. He was not a fan of Central American food, but he had been on the road now long enough to learn how to select from their menu. When ordering, he was meticulous, sometimes even ordering outside of the menu. He sat at one of the few unoccupied tables, near the counter, where several men sat on stools. He reached for the menu, placed between the salt and pepper shakers with the sugar dispenser at the middle of the table. He had just begun reading the entries in Spanish when a young woman with long black hair that she wore in a long braid approached him.

"Are you going to order?" she asked him in Spanish.

Carlos was momentarily stunned by her beauty. Her intense black eyes had a shine about them, as if they reflected light. Her thin black eyebrows reminded him of an actress from an old-time movie. Her lips formed a perfect cupid's bow, and without lipstick they seemed a pleasant contrast to those of any young girl today.

"There is not much left," she said. "The kitchen is about to close."

Carlos realized she was waiting for him, and he quickly gazed through the entries on the short menu.

"What's in a *tamal?*" he managed to say, raising his eyes. "Besides corn, what else is in it?"

"There are many ingredients," she answered shyly. "They have flour, bell peppers, raisins, olives, some *chipilin*. Some others too. It depends on how you want them. We have some left if you want to order."

"Why are they wrapped in banana leaves?" Carlos asked cautiously. He did not want to insult her, although he was still unsure whether she was Guatemalan.

She smiled at him gently. It was evident by now that he was not a local and even more clear that he was not Guatemalan.

"It helps to preserve them," she answered him.

"No, I want to eat something solid with some meat in it. I drove almost the whole day and have not eaten since early; do you think they could cook me a steak?"

"Ah, a steak," she said, somewhat baffled.

Carlos sensed her hesitation and tried to be suave.

"Could you help me? I can't find a place to eat this late."

She smiled at him again.

"You only want a steak?"

"Do you have any rice to go with it, or maybe some potatoes?"

"Would you like beans?"

"No, I would rather have some salad."

"All right," she said, smiling again. "I will try. What about something to drink?"

"I can get some juice from the fridge," Carlos said and stood up to go to the refrigerator by the wall, near the counter.

It was only when she turned that he became aware of the length of her hair. The tip of her braid reached down to her waist. She was unusually tall for a girl from Guatemala, and Carlos froze as she walked around the counter towards the kitchen area. She had wide hips and a lean body. There was nothing in her at the moment that he could not find attractive. He rolled open one of the doors of the refrigerator and grabbed a plastic bottle of Tropicana juice, almost without thinking, and went back to his table. Everyone in the restaurant seemed to be Spanish, mostly couples with children. Just then he felt his cell phone vibrate, and he headed back to the table and sat down. He did not have to guess who was on the other end.

"Hello," he said.

"Are you heading back yet?"

"No, I'm not heading back. I need my ten hours rest."

"You mean to tell me you did not hitch up the other load yet?"

"No, I unhitched my load, and now I'm eating supper."

"You could have picked up the other load and started moving east."

"No, I'm out of time. I will pick it up in the morning and then start heading back. I need to sleep."

"I'm counting on you to get that load to Atlanta before the weekend. It's needed there."

Carlos took the phone off his ear in frustration. He saw the waitress walking back to his table and spoke softly into the phone.

"Gordon, you know I brought that tractor here in record time. I gotta go."

17

Carlos clicked off the call and set his phone on the table. The waitress came towards him, smiling again.

"They will fry a steak for you. How do you want it done?"

"Well done," he replied. "Burned, even."

"We only have rice with beans."

"That's okay," he said. "I'll eat them tonight."

"I can have them make you a lettuce-and-tomato salad. It will be dry, but we have some dressing."

She pointed to the glass receptacle on the table.

Carlos's mind was not even on the food anymore but wondering how much more beautiful the attractive young girl would look if she undid her braid and let her hair down. He could care less about salad dressing at this point, and the odor emanating from the glass holder on the table made him nauseous anyway. Carlos belonged to a culture that for the most part, whether fairly or unfairly, did not think much of the Central American cuisine and rejected it as unrefined and untamed. Yet, the young girl striving to serve him appeared as fine and gracious as any waitress at any Cuban restaurant in Miami.

"I will take it dry," Carlos replied. "I never put dressing on it."

That was a lie, and Carlos knew it, but he felt compelled. He could not tell her that the dressing on the table smelled horrible.

"Okay. I will bring it now."

She stepped back towards the rear, and Carlos followed her with his gaze. He found her so beautiful: her eyes, her hair, her posture, even her walk. She was wearing a long light dress, and he could not see much of her body, but her curves were noticeable even through her clothes. Carlos could not take his eyes off her. He took a sip from his orange juice bottle and looked around him. A man at one of the tables was trying to get the waitress's attention, and he kept his left hand raised. Carlos saw her bend to get something from behind the counter and turn around towards him. She still had not noticed the customer at the other table calling her.

"Here's your salad," she said, handing him a plate.

Carlos took the plate from her and placed it on the table. He was able to get a look at her up close. Her skin looked so soft and smooth. It was brownish, and Carlos felt like he was looking at a wheat field caressed by the wind. It was then that he remembered the customer's raised hand in the back.

"There's a man at a table near the entrance who is calling you."

She turned to look.

"Oh, I see him," she said. "They're starting to leave."

Carlos still watched her as she walked through the middle aisle of the room, towards the rear table. Another hand went up, and a man from one of the other tables called her.

"Hey, pretty Yasmin, come get your tip."

She seemed unaffected by his voice, as she handed the other customer his bill. But the other man's voice kept getting louder, affected by the effects of alcohol. From his table, Carlos began to get fidgety, trying now to keep his balance and not jump to intervene prematurely in a situation that the waitress could probably handle quite successfully on her own. There was no need. But still, the raucous sound of the man's voice, insisting on getting Yasmin's attention, disturbed him. He watched as the waitress worked her way over to him and handed him his bill. He did not make a sound.

She worked through each table with finesse, exchanging pleasantries with the guests and handing them their checks. As she returned to the kitchen area, most of the customers were approaching the cash register to pay their bills. She also handled that function without any help. There was no one else helping her, and she worked her way through each customer, taking their cash and giving them change back.

After the rush, she came to Carlos's table, carrying two plates. She set them down on the table.

"Are you done with your salad?"

"Yes, it was great," he answered.

She smiled at him, but it was a closed smile, just a slight stretching of the lips and a coy, quick look at him as she took his empty plate. She then served him the two other plates she had brought in.

"I had the cook prepare you a steak," she said, "and I was able to find a few grains of rice with steamed beans. It is not much, but there was nothing else left. I will discount the price since we were unable to give you a full order. Unless you want to order something else."

"No, thank you. I appreciate your taking the time," Carlos said. "Your name is Yasmin, right?"

She nodded her head in agreement as she got ready to return to the rear. Carlos watched her walk back, admiring her silky hair and easy gait. He had no idea what to do next, how to ask her the many questions that were crossing his brain right now.

He began to slice his steak into small pieces. The meat felt hard and dry, but it looked burned as he liked it. He could tell she had taken the time to give the cook careful instructions on preparing his order. That meant he had impressed her. Well, maybe. There was hardly anybody left in the room now. It seemed as if all the customers had suddenly agreed to leave at once, or perhaps they were traveling in groups together. Maybe they had sensed his need for privacy with Yasmin, he thought amusingly.

She returned from the rear a few moments later to ask if he needed anything else, and he said no. She stood there silently, as if she had expected him to go on speaking.

"Where are you from, Yasmin?"

The question just seemed to slip out of his lips. He had not wanted to ask it, but it just flowed out of him. She stared at him for a fleeting moment, and he was riveted by her beautiful eyes. It was so unexpected, he thought, to look into them and find their shine, as if they were lightning.

"I'm from Guatemala," she answered.

"What part of Guatemala?"

"Jutiapa," she replied.

"I thought that was a state."

"Yes, I am from the city of Jutiapa."

"So what is Jutiapa?"

"It is the capital of the state."

"Have you been here for a long time?"

"More than a year now."

"And you live in Phoenix?"

"Yes."

"I only found this place by chance. I drive for a living, and I dropped my trailer not far from here and came off the highway, trying to find a place to eat. This was the first one I found."

Carlos sensed her shyness. He was inviting her to join him in conversation, but she gave no inkling that she was willing to engage. He couldn't decide whether it was shyness or lack of interest. Perhaps she was married and had a long line of kids. His mind was now giving into preconceptions fueled by his own culture, which looked down upon Central American nationalities as intolerable people who knew nothing better than to breed in excess. He felt ashamed for a moment.

"Can I take your plate?" she asked.

"Yeah, I'm all done. I have my truck in the parking lot, and I have to find a place where I can hook onto power and sleep for the night. Do you know of any nearby?"

"I think on the road," she said. "The big highway."

She took the plates in one hand and placed them on a tray. She placed his bill on the table and turned to finish with the only other table still occupied. He wanted so much to ask her if she was with someone. She did not look older than twenty-one or twenty-two, but in Central America people aged fast. The sun was unforgiving there, and that meant she could be younger but not likely.

At the cash register he tried to make conversation again. He told her how he would be heading east after 7:00.

"Will you be here at that time?" he asked.

"Yes," she answered. "I have to open the restaurant."

"I will be back then. Maybe you could have them make some espresso coffee in the morning?"

She smiled at him and nodded, giving him the first real sign that she was receptive to his comments. He smiled back. Now he did not feel so alone. He clipped off the keys from his belt and said good night. She answered the same.

Carlos got his truck started and headed for Highway 10. He drove a couple of miles east until he found a good rest spot, where he could hook into power and sleep. He lay on the bed of his compartment and watched the latest news of the day. There was something different about tonight. He had met Yasmin, and somehow everything seemed different. He did not feel as tired after being energized by that bolt of emotion that had touched him after meeting her. He had felt the need to ask her more questions but realized it would have been too intrusive. He checked the time on his phone once more and then laid his head back on his pillow and went to sleep.

CHAPTER 6

The next morning, Carlos was up by 6:00 a.m. He sat on the bed and quickly sorted out his movements. He must wash his face, grab a bottle of juice to drink on the way, and then drive to Chandler, pick up his load, and get himself some breakfast. That was where he was planning to see Yasmin again, and just the thought of it made his heart jump. He must hurry. He jumped from bed, grabbed his toothbrush and paste, and raced for the men's room at the station store. He picked up a bottle of juice on his way out and then climbed inside the tractor and turned the engine on.

On his way to Chandler, it dawned upon him that he could not make it into the restaurant area carrying his rig. No, that was out of the question. Driving into a local street while dragging a trailer on your back could be catastrophic. He had made a mistake in his plans.

He got off the highway at the exit for the Guatelinda Restaurant. As he pulled into the parking lot, he noticed only two cars parked side by side and doubted whether he would see Yasmin again. It was not even 7:00 yet. She would probably be sleeping still, or even worse, she could be tending to the children that she inevitably mothered, getting them ready for school or preparing their breakfast. Now, he thought, he needed to get ready for a Central American breakfast. He had never ordered one before. Whatever they included, he thought, it would different.

In a downcast mood, he got out the truck, hanging his carabiner key chain around his neck and crossing over to the walkway at the entrance of the restaurant. The variety of flowers sparkled in colors that had not been visible the night before, and right by the door was the figure a young woman leaning over and spraying water from a watering can into the flowers. Carlos almost came to a stop, but to his surprise she turned towards him to greet him.

"Hello," she said, smiling.

"Good morning," Carlos answered. "Are you watering the garden so early?"

"Yes," she said. "I have to do it early. Later, I will be too busy."

He opened the door to go in, and she quickly put the watering can on the ground and came up behind him.

"Do you think I could have some espresso coffee? That is all I want for breakfast. Then I have to get back on the road."

They both stopped in the middle aisle. The restaurant was empty, and only one person was at the counter.

"Yes, I made the coffee already. Don't you want some fried eggs and toasted bread maybe?"

"I will take a bread roll if you have one for the road and the coffee. I have to pick up a load and then drive very far east. I am running a little late."

She seemed disappointed, and Carlos was surprised that he had made an impression on her. He wanted more, and he followed her to the counter, sitting on a stool. She came back quickly with a cup of coffee in a small styrofoam cup, as espresso is typically served.

"I will wrap up a bread roll for you. Would you like butter?"

"Yes," Carlos said.

Carlos took a sip of his coffee and watched her as she moved about in the rear, working on his toast. When she returned, she handed him a wrap.

"It's probably going to be a week before I can come back this way."

Carlos hesitated to see her reaction.

"Do you think I could call you at your cell?"

She was taken aback a little, but without saying anything, she wrote her number on the wrap.

"Where will you be traveling to?"

"Atlanta, Georgia," Carlos said. "Very far from here."

"How far?"

"All the way across the country to the east," Carlos replied. "Atlanta is in the state of Georgia. About two and a half days' drive from here."

"You always drive that far?"

"Yes, but I always come back this way. I come to Phoenix almost every week, delivering and picking up. Now, I'm on my way to pick up the trailer, and then I deliver it in Atlanta."

"And then you come back to Phoenix?"

"Not right away," Carlos said, taking another sip from his coffee. "I have to go home first. I live in Miami. Gee, this coffee is really good. You did great."

She smiled at him.

"I don't know how good it came out. I think it's my first time. Is that the coffee you always drink?"

"Yes. Only that they usually add a bit of milk to it."

He took another sip.

"Sorry about that. I did not know," she said. "It's very strong."

"That's why I drink it in the morning," he said. "It keeps me awake. But I only drink one cup a day, or two at the most."

Carlos took a gulp and stood up, ready to leave.

"How much is it?" he asked.

"No. It was going to be my treat."

"No," he said. "I should be the one treating. You work very hard."

Carlos put a five-dollar bill on the table and waited for her to return.

"Somehow, I planned this very badly. I was supposed to be at the factory where I pick up my load already, so I am late. I wish I could stay longer."

She nodded at him.

"I will bring your change," she said.

"No," Carlos replied. "It's supposed to be a tip. I will call you on my first stop tonight, which will be close to midnight. Will that be too late for you?"

"No," she answered him and smiled again.

This time, Carlos smiled back. He wanted to ask her so many questions, but time was running out. But they had made a connection, and that had made his day. He took one last look at her braided hair and grabbed the wrapped roll.

"Your braid is beautiful," he said.

He did not hear her say anything back, but as he hurried out to the front door, he could feel her eyes on him. He thought Yasmin was an unusually shy girl for the times but rather typical of her culture. He could not decide for certain whether she was part indigenous or whole. But in the end, it did not matter. She was beautiful.

CHAPTER 7

Carlos drove straight back east on Route 10 and then merged into Route 20. He drove nonstop for as far as he could. That evening, he was in Dallas, where he finally made a stop. He was still a good ten hours from Atlanta, but he could not push on anymore. He was bordering his limit of allowed driving time, and he had to stop. He found a Pilot center in Monahan, a few minutes short of his eleven hours driving time. He found a spot for parking next to another trailer. The driver in the cabin gave him a hand salute, and Carlos responded in kind. He logged himself off and prepared for the inevitable call from Gordon.

"Where are you?" said the grumpy voice from the other end.

"In Monahan," Carlos replied. "I should be in Atlanta by midday tomorrow."

"It's an important load," Gordon reminded him. "You're playing with fire."

"What fire would that be, Gordon? I've gone as far as I could within my allowed time. Why don't you find someone else to bother?"

"Because I need that load there. Can't take my eye off the ball."

"Don't you have other drivers?"

"I follow them all. It's my business."

"I gotta go. I need to wash up and eat supper. Goodbye."

Carlos did not wait for his response. He disconnected the call. He headed for one of the showers and freshened up. He did not take his time, as he usually did, but hurried back to the truck to put his dirty clothes in the small hamper at the foot of the bed. The cabin was almost like a small apartment. Then he grabbed his phone and hastily walked to the restaurant, where he bought a sandwich and an orange juice. Then he sat at a table, and before taking a bite, he dialed Yasmin's number. He expected the phone to ring a few times and was not even sure that she would pick up. But to his surprise a hello came right after the second ring.

"Hello, Yasmin," he said.

"Hello," she answered, a tiny bit of waver in her voice.

"I am sorry that I did not get to even tell you my name. I'm Carlos. I hope we have more time to talk in person the next time."

"All right," she said, agreeing.

She gave out a soft laugh, sounding shy.

"I know it's late, but I wanted to call you before going to sleep."

"Where are you?"

"I'm in Texas. I drove the whole day today. Tomorrow I should be in Georgia."

"And then where will you go?"

"Then I will have to bring the truck back home to Miami."

"And that is home?"

"Yes, I've always lived in Miami."

"Where are you from?"

"From Cuba," he answered. "I've been here for seven years now."

"When will you come back here?"

It was a pleasant question to hear, Carlos thought. He had suspected that she would ask him more details about his roots, but it seemed that she was focused on his return and wanted to know when he would return. Something between them had been born last night.

"I will probably leave Miami again by Monday," he said. "I will be in Phoenix by the middle of the week."

Their conversation then turned into family history and how they had gotten to America. Gradually, Yasmin told Carlos about her background and how she crossed the border on her own. She came from humble roots, something that Carlos had already imagined. Although she did not say it, he knew she was probably of indigenous roots, something common in Guatemala. The fact that she came from a relatively big city meant only that her family probably had broken out of the chain of dependence and muted compliance of an ancient culture overtaken by conquerors. Her modesty and meekness were typical traits of her people, but there was something different about her. Something daring and bold.

Carlos returned to the truck's cabin with the image of Yasmin's face from twenty-four hours earlier, thinking only of the moment when he would see her again. He sat on the bed of his cabin, wondering about her living conditions and how she managed in her daily living, having apparently no close family. In many ways, he thought, she was his equal. He considered himself a simple man, but his accomplishments made evident a thirst for progress, the desire to succeed and embrace freedom, something that he had learned to nourish as a young boy in his homeland. He had luckily found freedom at a young age. He wondered if Yasmin had similar hopes and thoughts as he did. Why was she in America? Was it not the poverty and miserable conditions of a life in a third world country, destined to live malnourished and in danger of being harmed? What had made her leave her family and come alone across the border to an unknown land?

Carlos stopped asking himself questions. He thought about the familiar comments that he heard in Miami, showing the speed with which people judged others. He came from a country where certain assumptions were made. Assumptions about people, about their way of life, and there was no need for deeper search. The idea was that Latin America was still only partially conquered. The scattered leftovers of the Maya culture were vibrant, and their tentacles still imprisoned their members. That is why their lives were so miserable. But Carlos could not adhere to such thinking. He was different than any other man from his community. He thought everyone, no matter what their origin, deserved a fair chance, a fair chance at life, opportunity to advance, and opportunity to love.

He sat on his bed and stared at himself. The life of a trucker was harsh, but he had chosen it primarily to bring variety into his life. He hated monotony, and he came from a system where life was incredibly boring and scarcity was a daily hardship. Small things like toothpaste that were taken for granted in America were of great need there. He considered himself a lucky man to have been able to break away from such wretchedness. He had risked his life to be a free man. He had picked up the language quickly and could speak it with only the trace of an accent. That in itself was a big accomplishment, considering the community where he was living. Very few immigrants who had been in America for as long as he could even speak English.

Carlos lay on the bed but did not cover himself. He was afraid to fall asleep. He wanted time to reflect on how he had met Yasmin and how it had affected him. He needed to know why his reaction had been so spontaneous. He needed to know why the timid brunette with the long braid had overwhelmed him. He kept going over the scene at the restaurant the night before and then this morning. It was somewhat of a miracle. He wanted to hold on to this thought, but he could not do it for long, and then he fell asleep.

CHAPTER 8

Carlos arrived in Atlanta early the next evening and dropped off his load at a manufacturing plant in northeastern Atlanta. Half an hour later, another load was ready for him to take to Jacksonville, Florida. He chose not to wait and drove south on Route 75. His due time was a little bit over four hours. He made it to Jacksonville by 9:00 p.m., and Gordon instructed him to pick up another load from Orlando to be delivered in Miami. Carlos hitched up the new load and got under way but made his stop for the night at a truck stop a few miles south of Orlando on Route 75. As soon as he parked the trailer, he dialed Yasmin's number, and she answered him on the first ring.

"Hello," she said in a soft, low voice.

"It's me, Yasmin," he said. "How are you?"

"I was waiting for you," came the bold answer that bolted Carlos.

He needed time to recover after hearing her say it. Her answer seemed out of character, he thought, or had he misread her? Perhaps she was not the timid young girl he had thought her to be. Or perhaps she felt the same about him and had in fact been waiting for his call.

"I am now in Florida," he said. "I wanted to call you earlier, but I had to drop off the trailer in Atlanta and be on my way home. I am now about three hours from Miami. But I had to stop. I can't go beyond fifteen hours driving. It's against regulations. I miss you. I wish I was back in Phoenix."

"Me too," she said.

Again the same short answer, straight to the point and causing him an anguish that made him shake. How wrong he had been, he thought. Yasmin had fooled him. She had fallen for him as much as he had fallen for her. Could it be possible?

"I did not think that you missed me," he answered her, and he was honest. He really didn't.

"You were wrong."

"I will be back soon," he managed to say.

"When?" she asked.

He felt the same anxiety, a rush of adrenalin to the brain, felt disarmed that startled him a little. Was she daring him? Was this really Yasmin?

"I will be back early next week, and you will be my first stop after I drop off the load. Where will I meet you?"

"Wherever you want. I will be waiting for you."

"Yasmin," he started to say and then paused. "I wish I had not gone so far from you, but I could not help it. I had to finish my route. I wish I could go back now."

"I know," she said. "But you will be back next week?"

"Yes; if I could, I would go earlier. I wish I could see you now."

"Me too."

"Do you have a camera in your phone? We could do a video call."

"I am not that good with the phone."

"It's the easiest thing in the world," Carlos said. "Do you have a camera? Can you take pictures in your phone?"

"Yes."

"Then we can video call. Look on your screen, look for video. I will hang up. Call me back."

It only took her one try. Carlos saw her picture in the screen of his phone. Even at this hour, she seemed radiant; her black eyes had a glow about them, and her hair was pulled back, packed tightly into the long braid in the back. They talked about everything in their lives and how different life was in America. Carlos had more time in the US. Yasmin had been in the country for about one year and a half.

She was still getting adjusted. She had crossed the border through the desert and had managed to avoid La Migra, as the immigrants nicknamed the border patrol.

Her story was as harsh as that of any other immigrant who had dared make the trip, except that she was a beautiful young girl, coveted by coyotes and gangs that crowded all known passages into the north. Yasmin gave Carlos all the details. No, she had not been raped. She had been lucky enough to follow the right group of people who used a smuggler to get them through the long way, across the desert, the least patrolled area but also the most dangerous to life.

In exchange, Carlos told her about his daring escape from the island and how he and his companions had managed to navigate a raft through the night that landed them almost magically in the Keys. She wanted to know more, how he had been able to learn to drive a trailer, and most of all, how he had managed to learn the English language so well. Carlos told her everything about his life in Miami, his struggle with the language at first, and what he considered his biggest accomplishment, his getting a commercial driver's license. Slowly, the two disclosed to each other the most important aspects of their lives right now. Neither one of them was married, and each one lived alone. They had found each other by twists of fate.

CHAPTER 9

There was a spot after the toll on Route 95 that always gave Carlos the jitters. He had memorized the sign, and psychologically, it helped him know that he was home. He had returned. He watched the sign for Miami Gardens off Route 95 and felt better, elated that he was in his familiar neighborhood. But there was something different this time. He rolled the window down and heard the buzzing sound made by the afternoon traffic, traveling smoothly on the highway, and thought about how soon he would see Yasmin again.

Carlos planned ahead, as he always did while driving. He would drop the trailer at the warehouse and then unhook that tractor and drive to NW 22nd Street, home base to his company, and maybe, just maybe, he might escape Gordon. But he did not have high hopes. If anything, Gordon would try to convince him to go back on the road tonight, which was unthinkable; well, no, unless there was a trip to Phoenix.

Carlos did just as he planned. After dropping off the box, he drove the tractor to his home base, handed the keys to the foreman, and dashed out the door to get his car. His phone was vibrating by the time he opened the driver's door.

"Why are you in such a hurry? We got other loads."

"Not tonight, Gordon. I need some rest."

"We really have an emergency with New York. We could use your help."

"No, not tonight, sorry."

"I am really short of drivers tonight. I really could use you."

"The only way you'd get me back on that road tomorrow is if you have a trip to Phoenix."

"Phoenix, eh? Got a girlfriend out there or something?"

"No. I just like being far away."

"Well, I could switch a couple of drivers here and there. I could have sent you this afternoon, but you don't have the hours."

"That's right. It would have to be tomorrow. The clock says I need rest."

"I will call you later," Gordon said. "Pick up."

Carlos wondered if he had not just made a big mistake, agreeing to go back on a long trip so soon. But Yasmin's face kept coming back to him. It would all be worth it. For tonight, he would have to settle for a video call and watch her face on the screen.

CHAPTER 10

That evening, after freshening up in his apartment and napping, Carlos drove off into SW 40th Street, or Bird Road, as it's commonly known among the locals. The road was wide, and both sides were a mega of business activity: restaurants, strip malls, clothing stores, and various other shops where buyers could find anything to their heart's delight. The evenings attracted the working crowds, with an appetite for a soft drink, a smoke, or the coveted cortaito, a miniature espresso that got its name from curdling the small milk content in the cup with a thick shot of coffee and usually one spoonful of sugar, sometimes two. The end result was a disposable tiny cup with foam up to its rim that people savored while engaged in conversation about the daily events.

Carlos stood next to the counter at a local restaurant. Next to him several men and women were getting served coffee and the popular *guarapo,* which was an abstract from sugar cane popular among the Cuban population. A group of men and women were chatting and exchanging views on the latest events.

"Carlos," the man next to him asked. "Are you back or leaving somewhere tonight?"

"I'm back," Carlos replied. "I came in this afternoon, and that was since four days ago. I need a good night sleep. How about you?"

"I'm about to go tonight. In a few more hours."

The man was one of the local truckers, well known to Carlos.

"Where to?" Carlos asked.

"They're sending me to Texas. I've never been out of state before. I'm a little worried."

"Really? Oh, don't worry. Don't think about it, and do what you do best: drive."

"Yeah, I guess you are right. But you know the roads are not easy to handle out of state."

"No, it's just the opposite," Carlos corrected him. "You drive on a straight line. There's hardly ever any heavy traffic. The problem is local, Ralph. That is when you run into roadblocks and clogged-up roads. Interstate is a breeze."

"Yeah, but I worry about the speed."

"Well, you don't have to speed. You are an experienced driver. You know what you're carrying in your back. You're not driving a car. Speeding is deadly."

The crowd behind them began to build up, and they retreated a couple of steps. They were at the edge of the sidewalk, and several motorcycles were parked in the slots behind them. A police car slowly pulled over and parked horizontally to the sidewalk, taking part of the next parking space. Two police officers got out of the patrol car and came over to shake hands with Carlos and Ralph.

"Simple men travel fast, they say," one of the two officers grunted. "Did you just get back from Texas today, Carlos?"

"Yeah, that is one of the states I got back from, also Arizona, Georgia, and even northern Florida."

"You know your way around," the other officer said.

Carlos took a sip of his coffee and nodded to the high-booted men.

"Do you guys want some coffee?"

"Thanks," the officer said and patted Carlos on the shoulder. "We are actually gonna get some now. We're taking a short break."

"How were the roads in the West?" the other officer asked, following his partner, both men squeezing themselves among the crowd that had built up in front of the counter.

"The roads were clear," Carlos replied out loud. "No accidents. It was smooth."

Ralph turned to Carlos again. Stress was written all over his face.

"So, you always go on Route 10 to Texas, right?"

"Mostly, yes," Carlos replied, "but you can't depend on just one road when you're traveling far. If you're going out of state, you have to have options. You never know when you are going to run into a jam, especially with a truck to handle. You have to have a second way."

It felt a little odd to Carlos to assume the role of advisor to a man who appeared several years his senior. He was not the type to eagerly provide it either. He was more on the side of modesty, but Ralph had openly requested it. It seemed like he really needed it.

"Carlos," a man's voice called behind him. "When did you get back?"

Carlos turned and shook hands with an overweight man with a protruding belly, probably in his forties, who greeted him cheerfully. A woman with wavy pixie-cut hair and long-sleeve white shirt standing next to him also reached out to shake hands. The early evening atmosphere at the local restaurants was always pleasant, reminiscent of a holiday and drawing a crowd thirsty for conversation.

"I came back this afternoon," Carlos replied. "I went home and relaxed a while, and I'm here for some coffee. This is Ralph," Carlos said, pointing to his companion. "I guess you know him."

"Of course we do," the man answered, extending his hand to shake Ralph's.

"Ralph, this is Roberto and his lovely wife, Amelia," Carlos said.

"*Un placer*," Ralph said.

"Do you also drive?" Roberto asked.

"Not as far as my friend Carlos here, but yes, I drive."

"You came from the West, right, Carlos?"

"Phoenix," Carlos replied. "And then I made two stops on the way back."

"I've never been to Phoenix," Roberto said. "That's Indian country."

"Some, I guess. There is a large Latin American population."

"All Indians too," Roberto quickly quipped, smiling towards Ralph. "Mostly Central American."

"I love the women's hair," Carlos said as if Roberto's comment had never been made.

"Well, they have to have something," Roberto countered. "I'll give you that some have some hair. But can you live with hair only? The women are all half the height of one of ours, and the men are lucky if they go past five feet. It's a midget population."

"What makes you an expert in height, Roberto?" Carlos asked.

"I'm not," he shot back. "But it's undeniable. This is why I refuse to leave Miami. Right, darling?"

He turned to his wife, who quickly nodded.

"*Ay, sí,*" she added. "After you live here, there is nowhere else to go."

"There's life beyond the Miami freeways," Carlos said. "It's a whole world out there waiting to be discovered. People like anyone else who feel and think."

"You are talking like a bleeding heart now, Carlos. It's time that we get off that way of thinking, especially in this town."

"I actually don't know that you can put a label on it," Carlos said.

"If you are going to be doing any rediscovering," Roberto said, "you are heading the wrong way. The most civilized societies are north of here. You will find nothing but misery and ignorance in any Latin American country."

"It doesn't mean there aren't any good people around."

"No, but this is what you find: a family of at least ten when they can't support even half of them."

"A sign of poverty," Carlos corrected him.

"Also stupidity," Roberto added.

"People cannot be judged for what they do not know, Roberto."

Amelia pinched Roberto in the back of his arm so discreetly that no one could see it.

"My point is they should know by now. It's only been six centuries since they were conquered."

"All right," Carlos said, tossing his empty cup into a nearby garbage can. "Let me order you some coffee. We'll debate a little more about that issue once you've had some caffeine."

Carlos waded through the crowd that had grown even larger by the open counter. He asked to be excused as he managed to slide in between two men conversing as they held cups filled with their precious hot liquid.

"Carlos," both of them said as Carlos made his way in between them. "You're back."

"I am," Carlos answered. "Pardon me, guys. I just want to order some coffee for some guests."

Behind the counter, it was all business. Two women worked the coffee machines, running steadily at this time. Others squeezed orange juice from a big juice maker, another one slid sugar cane stems through a high-powered juice extractor. It was hard to get service, and one had to speak loudly over the machines to be heard.

"Ma'am," Carlos said, raising his hand, "two cortaitos and two guarapos, please."

He had to repeat himself twice before they finally took his order. He headed back to Roberto and his wife carrying four cups among familiar faces, all trying to make conversation with him. Roberto, Amelia, and Ralph had sat down at a table outside.

"There you go," Carlos told them, putting down all four cups at the center of the table. "Grab what you want."

"So, how is Phoenix, Carlos?" Roberto asked.

He smiled tongue-in-cheek. He knew well that Carlos was in Phoenix every week. Perhaps this trip was different.

"I met someone nice," Carlos replied. "A beautiful Guatemalan girl."

"We kind of knew that. Your face says it all," Amelia answered, grabbing one of the coffee cups. Her husband took the other one.

"Guatemala, ah?" Roberto commented.

"A beauty," Carlos said again and took a seat.

"Does that mean we can no longer talk about the indigenous people who inhabit the Americas?"

"No, it does not mean that at all. You can talk about whoever you want. I may just not be able to be impartial."

Carlos took a seat across from him and next to Ralph.

"It's no fun without impartiality," Roberto explained. "You need it in any discussion."

"Well, that's funny, Roberto. You don't strike me as being very impartial. Your views on indigenous people or any minorities seem to have been lodged in you long ago."

"You know, Carlos, you are a very smart young man, and you have to call a spade a spade. Let's be frank, the people who are migrating to this country are not what they used to be. I came to Miami when I was a boy. Everyone who was coming here at that time was looking only for work and to get ahead. But look at it now."

Carlos sensed his bias, but although young, he was not quick to make conclusions about people. He'd rather wait. He had seen Roberto's good nature at a personal level. Despite his race bashing, if an indigenous person magically appeared at this restaurant right now, Roberto would be the first one to ask him to join them at the table. Was it just pride? Was it just a manner of speaking that he adhered to? There were no easy answers, Carlos thought. Roberto was a complex person.

"You'd be surprised to find that most Latinos from Central America are only here to work. That is why they risk life and limb to cross over the border to America."

"Have you seen the gang element that they bring along?"

"No, I haven't. They come fleeing from gangs. They are looking for safety. Children go to work before they are ten years of age in their countries. Women go from house to house to be a maid for somebody just so they can feed their families."

Roberto began to wrap his napkin, first in one half then into a quarter of it. He pushed his index finger firmly into each fold and then dragged it along the edge to make a deep crease.

"The gangs were born here," Ralph muttered suddenly.

"How's that?" Roberto asked.

"They were actually boys who had grown here in the States and who were deported back to their countries and then continued being in gangs there."

"So, what are you saying, Ralph?" Roberto asked, sounding surprised as he finished folding his napkin into a small square. "Do you mean that we are to blame for their activities here?"

"I mean that the gangs were born in America. They were exported to Central America by the immigration authorities here."

"Oh, come on, Ralph," Roberto said, looking irritated. "Where were all those boys from?"

"Mainly from El Salvador," Ralph replied.

"So, there!" Roberto exclaimed, setting down his empty cup and lodging his folded napkin inside. "They came from El Salvador, right? So how can you say that the gangs were American?"

"Hold it," Carlos said interrupting them. He had so far listened carefully as the conversation unfolded. "No matter where they came from, the point is that they learned to be gangsters right here, in America. They were a product of American society. They brought gang warfare into the Central American countries where they were sent to."

"They did not," Roberto insisted. "They brought that here themselves, in their genes. It's something they carried with them from their native countries and brought it here as one carries a disease. Those boys should have never been allowed to cross. They poisoned our environment. Another failure of our immigration system."

Roberto turned to toss his empty cup into a garbage can but found none. Carlos looked towards Amelia, expecting her to do the same, but she took her time savoring her coffee.

"I guess the system did fail," Carlos said. "Those kids should not have been sent back to their home countries. They should have been given long prison sentences here first."

"No, send them back," Roberto argued. "Send them all back. They should have never been allowed to be here to begin with."

"We know who would have been allowed into this country if Roberto was president."

"You know it," Roberto said.

Carlos leaned forward as the two troopers stopped by the table on their way back to their patrol cars.

"Well, what have we here?" one of them said.

The two of them took turns shaking hands with Roberto.

"Are you coming or going?" Roberto asked.

"We are going back on duty," the other one said. "Anybody driving out tonight?"

"Ralph may be," Carlos said. "He's going out of state for the first time."

"Really? Where to?"

"Texas," Ralph answered modestly.

"Driving an eighteen-wheeler?"

"Yeah," Ralph answered.

"This is your first time?"

"Out of state, yeah."

"Best advice we can give you is, stay off the shoulder unless it's a true emergency," the other officer said, lifting his coffee cup as a sign that they were leaving. "See you guys."

Everyone at the table said goodbye.

"These guys deserve our respect," Roberto said. "But you see how unappreciated they are."

"I wouldn't want their line of work," Ralph said, agreeing.

"Some of them are quite nice," Carlos said. "It's the ones that have an attitude that get me."

"What do you mean, an attitude?" Roberto said, lifting his gaze. "These guys risk their lives for us."

"You gotta get on the road more often, Roberto. Your odds of being stopped then increase, and you will remember me."

"I actually drive through the turnpike a lot. I never get stopped."

"Do you ever leave Dade County?"

"No, I must say, not very often, but Amelia and I just got back last week from Tampa."

He turned to his wife, and she nodded.

"Yes, it was lovely," she said. "I was thinking the same as you, Carlos. Here we were along a busy state road with plates from another county. Curiosity arises right away. Why not stop these folks, an interstate trooper might say."

She smiled coyly at Carlos and Ralph.

"I actually don't think it's that bad, Amelia. I do not think they sit there just picking shots at people, but if they see you make a slight infraction, the fact that you are from another county may be enough for a trooper to stop you."

"Oh, come on," said Roberto. "You must have been watching one too many liberal shows on your trips across the country, Carlos. I can't remember the last time I was stopped by a trooper. This is just another media frenzy that we are living today. They are always picking on the police, and police are only doing their job, that is all."

"Actually, I don't watch any TV except when I am in Miami."

Carlos and Amelia exchanged smiles.

"Well, doing nothing may be just as bad. Somebody needs to speak about this and challenge the left."

"What are you, Roberto, an activist now?"

Two men wearing the ubiquitous *guallavera* came by the table.

"Carlos," one of them said, and both put out their hands to shake his.

Carlos stood up and shook their hands.

"I want you to meet my friend Ralph," Carlos said. "Of course, you know Roberto and his wife."

"We all know each other very well," the man commented. "I've known Roberto for quite some time."

"Yes, you are daily visitors at this café."

"Yes, that and more," the man replied, leaning forward to shake Roberto's hand. "This café holds many secrets." The man held onto Roberto's hand. "Don't you agree, Roberto? Sinister plans were made here. Political maneuvers were created. Decisions were made here. If these tables only had ears, what wealth of information they would give us. My name is Sergio Moza, as you know. The man behind me is Antonio Prieto. We are friends from way back. And I know this lovely lady."

His slim hand, with rings on almost every finger, moved cautiously towards Amelia, waiting for her own hand to meet his, but she kept hers cuddled up around her small coffee cup until Moza's hand was so close to hers that avoiding it would have required an explanation.

"As always, it's a pleasure to see you, Mr. Moza," Amelia said, shaking his hand.

"The pleasure is all mine," Moza answered. "And here is Antonio."

The burly man behind him moved forward to greet Amelia.

"We need more men like Carlos, don't we, Roberto?"

Roberto glanced at him and nodded.

"He's honest and a hard-working man, young but willing to learn, never stubborn, and as long as there is hunger for knowledge, there is hope for all of us. Youth is a divine treasure, Carlos," Moza said. "One does not realize it until it's past. Isn't it so, Roberto?"

"Speak for yourself, Mr. Moza," Roberto replied.

Amelia covered her mouth in a fake attempt to show embarrassment.

"It's no secret," Mr. Moza agreed. "I'm well past my time. But I've decided to wait until someone much more powerful than me decides to make that fateful call."

"It's only a number," Antonio added behind him.

"So what is the plan ahead?" Mr. Moza inquired.

He was a man of years, slim, fair skinned, and with totally gray but copious hair. His appearance, like that of his partner behind him, was exceedingly neat. Both men came from a forgone era, the one which Roberto had referred to in his comments, as if he had been part of it when, in fact, he had been merely a boy when it was in full force. Now Roberto took pleasure in chastising one of its most prominent members.

"The plan is to stick with the agenda," Roberto answered. "The more liberals we allow in power, the closer we get to the abyss. Communism is watching us like a panther in the night, just waiting for its turn, and if we let it happen again, there will not be a need for truck drivers in that world."

He glanced down Carlos's way, a gesture that Carlos picked up as he stood up to allow Mr. Moza to have his chair.

"Sit, Señor Moza, sit."

"Thank you," Mr. Moza answered and slid sideways to sit down. "Can you get another chair?"

"I'm all right," Carlos said. "I will be going back home in a little while. I may get called in tonight for work."

"Oh, that's not fun."

"Yeah, life's tough."

Carlos sensed that the other men wanted privacy, probably to discuss political issues of the day. He got ready leave.

"Carlos, stay," Roberto said. "You need to hear this too."

"There are some men by the counter I need to speak to. I'll be back."

Carlos headed for one of the garbage cans to dump the empty cups of coffee and went by the counter to exchange one last laugh with two men he recognized as haul truck drivers from the area, just what he needed to release the stress of the last half-hour. He placed an order of fried chicken and French fries and talked to the men until his got his order to go. He bid goodbye to Roberto and the others, apologizing for his fast getaway, but he had to travel out West tonight.

47

CHAPTER 11

Carlos's apartment was not far from the restaurant. But there was an unspoken code of conduct in Miami that discouraged walking the streets, much less the highways, and driving was the preferred method of transportation, even if home was only a block away. Carlos got inside his Chevrolet Sonic and turned the engine on. He preferred small vehicles, and after driving an eighteen-wheeler all day, driving a regular car felt like such a relief.

He went across Bird Road and turned into one of the back streets, two blocks away. His apartment was in a duplex with a driveway on the side. The porch was half-fenced in with white window boxes on both sides and an assortment of multicolored daisies. He paid a woman to maintain the apartment for a reasonable weekly fee, which included watering the flowers. Carrying his laptop and his wrapped dinner, Carlos went inside. His apartment was small: living room, dining room, kitchen, and bath. He spent too much time on the road to have a big place. He preferred it this way for now. He had few expenses and saved most of his money.

Carlos sat on the living room sofa, put his laptop and food on the center table, and turned the TV on. It was 5:30 p.m., and he knew Phoenix was three hours behind. Yasmin must be working now, but he was afraid he might fall into a deep sleep and miss her call. He dialed her number, and she picked up on the second ring.

"It's me, Yasmin."

"Hello, Carlos. Are you resting?"

"I am, yes. I just came back from the restaurant, and I'm going to eat some dinner now. I might leave for Phoenix again tomorrow."

"I hope so."

He felt a tingle inside. It was reminiscent of his teenage years on the island. Not even. It was at that time when puberty had just begun, and he would hide in between buildings on the way to school, waiting for his favorite girl to pass. He was planning to tell her about the passion he felt for her, his endless love, and if she showed a sign of interest, he would go on. Yasmin had just given him the sign he needed. He would call Gordon and tell him that yes, he would drive to Phoenix tonight.

"Really?" he asked her in a low voice. "You really want me back?"

"Yes," she replied. "Very much."

"I was going to rest tonight and go back tomorrow, but I will call my boss now and book for a trip back."

"Can you? Will you be all right driving?"

"Yes. But I'm limited to eleven hours of driving. After that, I have to stop and rest for ten hours. And there's no cheating. The truck is connected electronically to the agency."

"Come only if it's safe. I can wait."

"Knowing that you want me is all I need. Nothing can keep me away."

Carlos heard the crashing sound of silverware. Had Yasmin dropped her plate?

"Are you working? I heard a crash."

"No, it's nothing."

"Yes, it is. Let me call you back later."

"No, stay."

Again, Carlos felt jolted. The sound of her voice even affected him. It was shattering, disarming to him. He heard the sound of clattering silverware again.

"Call me when you are free. Let the phone ring a few times in case I fall asleep. I will try to wait for you."

She did not respond, waiting for him to say goodbye.

"I'll be waiting, Yasmin."

There still was no response from her when Carlos ended the call. He realized she was too sweet to let him go, even at the cost of getting in trouble at work. He had to end it. He began to pick French fries from his order as he watched the news on his TV. There were hard critiques about the administration's handling of the American economy. Miami was part of Dade County, a nest for Republicanism, conservatives who are radical in their beliefs. He clicked on his monitor until he found a movie that caught his attention: *News of the World*, a new Western by Tom Hanks. Carlos considered Western movies one of the wonders of America, and after he arrived, he began devouring the old Westerns that he had seen as a kid and then the new ones. But he lagged in the language at first and was forced to study to gain control. He was a fast learner, and in two years he was well ahead of his compatriots, some of whom did not learn the language at all.

After finishing his dinner, now well into the movie, he laid his head back in the sofa, and fatigue overcame him. He was out like a light until the vibrations of his phone woke him up. He placed the phone on his ear without even looking at the screen.

"Hello."

"I've got a run for you early tomorrow," Gordon said, his voice sounding hoarse. "Ready?"

It took Carlos a few seconds to wake up. He was expecting Yasmin, but here he was listening to his boss again.

"Ready? How can I be ready? I haven't even slept yet."

"Four in the morning. You can get plenty of sleep between now and then."

"Where to?"

"Phoenix."

"Wow."

"Yes, wow. Are you in or what?"

"Yeah," Carlos answered.

He pressed the screen to put out the call. The movie was going midway through, and Carlos watched as Tom Hanks rode in a wagon with a young girl he had found by the hanging body of her caretaker. It was a heck of a movie, he thought. Then he leaned his back again and felt for his phone. Yasmin would call at some point. But he decided he would not tell her. He would surprise her.

CHAPTER 12

Yasmin must have made the call, Carlos thought as he got up without an alarm by 4:00 a.m. The phone call from Gordon woke him up. So he would be a little late. There were plenty of times when he had waited for hours for a rig to be loaded. It would not kill them to wait for him for a few minutes. The first order of things would be to call his Yasmin and apologize for having missed her call last night.

He went inside the small bathroom and brushed his teeth. He put on jeans and a short-sleeve shirt, picked up his laptop, and headed out the door. It was pitch-dark, no sign of dawn yet, and he jumped in his car. He had parked head on last evening, and there was no room to maneuver a U-turn with everyone home at this time, so he backed out the driveway and into the street. There were no cars out this early, so he checked for traffic as he made a 90 degree turn in reverse. He braked for half a second and then drove forward, gaining speed as he went down the block. If anyone was up they would have heard the sound of a forced engine that stopped briefly and turned a corner, fading away in the distance.

Carlos felt the vibrations of his phone on his lap. Gordon was at it again. Didn't this man sleep? There was a reasonable explanation for his goading. Carlos knew about his background. Gordon had been a truck driver before, and he ran his company as he had driven his truck in the old days, before the age of the internet and before the government regulated a driver's time on the road, limiting his hours behind the wheel.

"I'm on my way," Carlos spoke into the screen of his dashboard that linked to his phone.

"Where the hell are you?"

"On my way. Why don't you go to sleep?"

"Get over to the loading site and pick up that rig right now. You're late!"

"The trailer is probably not even loaded yet."

Carlos ended the call. He was already on Bird Road and took Route 826, also known as the Palmetto Expressway, heading north to his home base to pick up his truck. In less than an hour, he was already inside his cabin, his laptop and phone connected to the truck's internet system and his rig hooked up. He headed for 95 North, planning to go on Route 10 West by Jacksonville as usual. Dawn was breaking when he touched the screen in the dashboard to dial Yasmin's number.

She picked up on the second ring.

"Pretty Yasmin," he said, "I'm on my way to you. Dawn is breaking, and the sky looks so beautiful. It's orange, almost red."

"It means a new beginning," she said softly, groggy after waking up.

She had waited for him all this time, dozing on and off.

"How do you know such things?"

"I know because my folks always said that."

Carlos could only imagine, although they hadn't really talked about it. By folks, she probably meant her elders, parents and grandparents, who came from a very rural area and were set in their indigenous ways. Maybe nature's secrets were passed on from generation to generation, and they were no longer legends but true.

"Did you learn that in Jutiapa?"

"No, it happened in the village where I come from, before Jutiapa."

"Where is your village?"

"It's the village where I was born. Jutiapa came later."

"Why did you move?"

"I went to the city to study."

"How old were you then?"

"About ten. I finished primary school in the village, then went to stay with an aunt in Jutiapa."

"At ten years old?"

"Yes."

"You must have been really smart. What is the name of your village?"

"Xococ."

"Xococ," he repeated.

"It's pronounced *shokok*."

"Hmm. How far is that from Jutiapa?"

"Very far. My family wanted me far from there, and she wanted me to learn to speak Spanish well."

"Something tells me that your parents saw you were special, and they sent you to the city for a good education."

"Yes, and to get away from the past."

"What past?"

"They were survivors from the Rio Negro massacres. There aren't many of them."

"Oh. What happened there?"

"The Achi people were massacred by government troops during the guerrilla wars."

"When did all this happen?"

"A long time ago. My parents came from there when they were small with their parents. The government moved them to Xococ."

Carlos felt Yasmin was finally opening up to him, but there was still some hesitation in her voice. She seemed to stop too short in her sentences, as if holding back. It was perhaps a sign that Spanish was not her first language.

After passing the Dade County line, Carlos told Yasmin he had to get off line. There were calls coming in, and it might be his home base calling him in. He would call her later. He rolled down his window a bit to let some fresh air in. The day was now well under way, and he could only drive till about 4:00 p.m. before he would be forced to stop for the night. If he could make Louisiana, he would be happy.

CHAPTER 13

Carlos did not reach the outskirts of Phoenix until late during the third day of his trip. The limit placed by regulations on his allowed time to drive put a dead end to his plans to make fast timing. It was really impossible. Speeding up was not an option. The dangers of traveling with a trailer behind you at a higher rate of speed were hardly worth the risk to gain a mere few hours in arrival time. Instead, Carlos chose to concentrate on the road and not divert his attention from the most important issue, safety.

It was early evening, the sun had just set down, when he finally made the turn off Route 60 and instinctively drove his tractor into the restaurant's parking lot, using three spaces to park. There were several cars but not as many as the last time he was here. He walked at a normal pace towards the door, his inside burning with anticipation, and would have rushed right in if not for the discovery he made midway through the walkway towards the main door.

At both sides of the walkway, the rows of flowers seemed to beam with radiance, stars in the early night. He smelled the freshness of the water dripping from them, a sign that someone had just watered them. As he opened the door, Yasmin's was the first face he saw. She was standing by one of the tables, holding a tray and tending to a customer. She looked straight at him, smiling, as if nothing else mattered to her at the moment and she had been secretly waiting for him.

Carlos walked in the direction of the counter, skirting the group of tables and stopped only when he was at a straight line from her. He stopped, and she hastily came towards him. Without saying a word, she threw her left arm around him and pulled him close. He held her and made face contact with her cheek but then pulled back and kissed her on the lips. Suddenly, everyone became silent in the room, watching the unexpected scene. Carlos finally pulled back, and Yasmin rested her head on his shoulder for a brief moment.

"I told you I'd be back, pretty woman. Your hair got longer."

They both looked at each other and laughed, and then they heard the gradual, growing applause of the customers at each table. Many of them knew Yasmin from their patronage with the restaurant. Those who didn't joined in the cheering.

"Is there a table for me?" Carlos asked.

"By the wall, same as last time," she said. "I saved it for you."

"How did you know I'd be here tonight? I never said the time."

"The sky told me," she answered.

She walked him to his table, holding hands, and he sat down with his side against the wall, just as he had done that first night when they had met.

"Dinner for two," he said. "What will you have?"

"Anything," she answered. "As long as I am with you."

"Me too. I will even have tamales made the Guatemalan way, wrapped up in banana leaves, if it means being with you. Is that what we are having?"

"No, I made you rice and beans, a filet mignon steak with onions, and ripe plantains."

"Yasmin, how did you know? That's my favorite dish."

"I knew. I knew it was your favorite dish."

"Yes, it is a favorite. But who did you ask? How did you find out?"

"I found it in my recipe book," she said smiling. "Steak, *congrí*, and ripe plantains is the favorite dish in your country."

"You could say that, yes. Cooking the rice can be tricky if you've never made it before. I cook a little bit. I will cook you a meal one of these days."

She smiled at him, and he reached out with his left hand and grabbed a strand of her hair. She was not wearing the braid.

"I let it loose to show you," she said.

"It's beautiful."

"Shall I bring you the food?"

"Yes, whenever you can. There will be a big tip for you."

They both laughed together, and she turned to go to the kitchen area.

"I will be right back."

"There are some customers calling you."

Carlos pointed to the second group of tables, past the middle aisle, where a man had raised his hand.

"Yasmin," he called.

"He can wait," Yasmin said to Carlos in a low voice.

She raised her index finger towards the table as a sign that she was coming.

"What shall I bring you to drink?"

"I will get it," Carlos said. "Take care of the customer first. They are always right, and I am in no hurry. Go see him first, Yasmin."

Yasmin went to help the customer while Carlos rose and went to retrieve a bottle of juice from one of the refrigerators. Yasmin joined him later when she brought him his order. She had added a salad that she had prepared herself.

"I hope you like it," she said. "I added a bit of sugar to the lettuce. I read that they do that in Cuba."

"Yasmin, you know so much about Cuba. Thank you for doing this, but you don't have to. All I want is to be with you. Please don't stand, sit down."

"I have learned some things in the last few days," she said smiling. "How long will you stay this time?"

"I don't have to leave until the afternoon. I arranged it that way so I could spend time with you."

She looked shyly at the table, and Carlos kissed her cheek. It was unexpected. A customer raised his hand from one of the tables in the back.

"Yasmin, they don't give you a break. When does it end?"

"It's dinner time now. I will be back."

Carlos held onto her hand as she got up to leave, and she turned and waited until he let go.

"The food is great, Yasmin. Everything looks great."

"I made it," she said. "I asked them to let me cook it since they do not know this dish. They let me use one of the stoves, and I made it."

She went towards the back of the room to help the customer, and Carlos waited for a moment before he began cutting the meat. He felt so humbled. It seemed like a dream to him that she had cooked him a special meal.

CHAPTER 14

Carlos realized quickly that Yasmin was a victim of her status (or lack thereof). She was obviously undocumented, and the people who ran this restaurant were using her as an attraction to draw new customers in. But if that wasn't enough, they made her work until late hours to clean the dishes and to get everything ready for the next day. She was not allowed to carry on conversations with anyone who was not a customer. Someone must have admonished her in the kitchen because she did not stop by his table when she came back with an order. So he waited until she returned from one of her trips from the rear and raised his arms, as the other customers did to gain her attention.

"When does your shift end?"

"I have to stay after the customers leave and do some clean up. Can you wait for me?"

"Yes, of course I will wait. I hope they pay you for all these hours."

"No, they don't," she whispered.

"I will wait all night if I have to, darling. Can I pay for my order now? I will go wait in the tractor. I don't want to cause you any problems."

"Stay here," she said. "I will be back."

For the next three hours, Carlos waited at his table. Yasmin crossed words with him every now and then, as often as she could, on her way to one of the tables or back to the kitchen area. She could not stop to chat but only a passing word. There were only two tables occupied when she came to his table and stood there holding an empty tray and looking anxious.

"What is it?" Carlos asked.

"They're telling me to have you wait outside."

"Who's telling you that?"

"The cook in the back. He is the manager. He can see everything from there."

"Is he mean to you?"

"No," she said quickly, looking down.

"Yes, he is," Carlos said. "Yasmin, you don't have to be afraid. He can't do anything to you. He is just a person like you and me. He does not have any powers over you."

Yasmin looked at him quietly with tender eyes.

"I don't know. I'm afraid."

Carlos stood up, leaned over, and kissed her on the cheek.

"I am going to go inside my tractor and turn the radio on. I will be waiting for you. I may fall asleep because I am very tired, but you can just tap on the window glass, and I will wake up. Don't rush. I will wait."

"Do you want to take some coffee?"

"All right, I'll take some. What kind is it?"

"It's the kind you like. I made it."

She went back to the kitchen and brought him a Styrofoam cup of espresso. He asked for the bill, but she wouldn't give him one. He told her that if she didn't, he would leave money anyway, so he left a twenty and a five-dollar bill, which was probably twice the real price. He touched a strand of her hair again and held onto the coffee cup.

"I will be waiting for you in my truck," he said.

He touched his lips with two of his fingers and then placed them on her lips as the symbol of a kiss. Yasmin was teary eyed as she watched him walk around the group of tables, heading for the door. She had no desire to tend to anyone and would have followed Carlos outside if it wasn't for the hissing sound made by the cook as he showed his blemished face through the low window from the kitchen as a sign for her to hurry and get busy. For once, she ignored him and went about her business serving the customers.

CHAPTER 15

Carlos went inside his tractor through the rear door and turned on his laptop. The evening was young, and he guessed he would be here a good two hours, waiting for Yasmin. So he made himself comfortable and stacked up two pillows at the head of the bed. He placed his laptop on his lap and searched the web for a movie. Even though the cabin was equipped with a small screen TV, he preferred to watch movies through Xfinity on his computer, which he usually never got to finish watching because he fell asleep. He looked at the time. He barely had two hours left to drive his tractor to a safe place for the night or risk a fine. There were lots of motels nearby. He dozed off in just a few minutes.

***

Inside the restaurant, Yasmin began to get anxious. She knew about Carlos's driving limitations. She must hurry and leave. But how? There were still customers occupying tables, and they showed no sign of leaving. She thought about asking the cook to let her leave for the night. But it was useless. He would never agree. She had already figured out that it was more than just work discipline. He looked at her with hungry eyes, the eyes of a man filled with lust, and she could feel him watching her incessantly through the small window from the kitchen. He knew her every move. She finally worked up the nerve to talk to him.

"I really need to leave," she told him in one of her trips to the kitchen. "I cannot stay late tonight."

"You don't say," he replied without looking up.

He was moving pots and pans away. Most leftovers could not be saved for the next day. It was too risky with the city inspectors, who could show up unexpectedly for an inspection. Besides, the restaurant had gained a good reputation, due in large part to his skilled cooking and the restaurant's fresh food and cleanliness. He could not afford to lose a clientele for which he had worked so hard. Now his only waitress, cashier, and janitor wanted to leave early, leaving him without any help.

"Yes," Yasmin insisted. "I have cleared most of the tables. There are only three customers left. I have been here all day, and I have to leave."

"Your work is not done. The tables have to be cleaned, the floor has to be mopped. There is a lot that needs to be done yet."

"But I can't stay tonight. I will do it in the morning."

"You are not going to do it in the morning. You are going to sleep with that young guy that came to see you. That's where you're going."

"But I will," Yasmin said, putting her tray down on one of the kitchen tables. "I have to go now."

"Yasmin," the cook warned her. "If you walk out that door, you're not coming back."

Yasmin could not hear him anymore. She went through the double doors out into the main parlor and headed out the front door without looking back. She did not turn around once to look back, and once outside, she stopped to look for Carlos's tractor. It was parked by the end of the parking lot, parked horizontally across three parking spaces and barely visible in the darkness. She walked towards it at a fast pace, and once near it, she looked through the driver's window and saw no one inside. Maybe Carlos had gone somewhere. But then she noticed a dim light, coming through the cracks of the door in back of the driver's seat. She tapped on the driver's window with her house key. She heard some movement inside. A door behind her, on the side of the truck, opened.

"Yasmin," Carlos said, stepping out of the truck through the side door. "I fell asleep."

"I got in trouble at work. I think they will not take me back tomorrow."

"Why? What happened?"

"I knew you were waiting outside. I could not let you down."

She broke down and covered her face.

***

Carlos stood still for a moment, as if reality had struck him for the first time. Yasmin had just showed him an act of unselfishness. She was willing to risk her own livelihood all on account of him.

"So what happened? What did they say?"

"The cook said if I walked out not to come back."

Carlos hugged her. For the very first time he smelled her perfume, now fading after her long day at work. Her hair brushed against his arms as her body swayed from the strength of his embrace. He felt the wetness of his tears by his neck.

"He's just saying that because he was afraid you would leave. But think about it, darling, who is he going to get to replace you tomorrow morning if you don't show?"

"No, he really means it. They have gotten rid of people before. They don't care. They will just get another immigrant like me and pay her nothing like they do with me now."

She sobbed, and Carlos grabbed her by her shoulders.

"Yasmin, don't worry about anything. Come with me. We will go to your place and pick up your things and leave. You don't need that lousy restaurant."

"I can't do that," Yasmin said, still with her head laying on his shoulder.

"Why not?"

"Because it's not decent to do that. I can't just run away with any man like some unchaste woman."

"I thought I was not just any man to you."

"You are not. But we just met practically a week ago."

"So what? Don't you believe in love at first sight?"

"I do. But it's not right to do it like this."

"Do you have any place to go right now?"

"I just have my room in an apartment that I share with other women."

"I only have forty-five minutes left in driving time. I have to park the truck at a truck station and rest; otherwise, I can get in trouble. Will you come with me? We can rent a room at the hotel."

"I have no change of clothes with me."

"It's all right," Carlos said. "You can wear one of my T-shirts and my baggy pants."

She looked down and held her lips together to break a smile.

"All right," she said. "Let's hurry then. Do you know where to go?"

"Yes, there are several rest areas off Route 10, but I have to hurry."

Carlos took her hand and went to the other side of the truck, opened the door for her, and let her in. He held her arm high as she stepped on the ladder and climbed into the front of the cabin. She had never seen the inside of a tractor trailer cabin before.

"Are you okay now? Comfortable?" he asked from below.

She nodded, and he closed the passenger door, went to the other side through the front of the truck, and climbed inside the cabin.

"I've got to hurry," he said. "I can't be on the road past my time. Put your seat belt on."

He had to lean over to strap her and then kissed her. It was a passionate kiss, and she put his arms around him for a moment until he moved back behind the wheel and clicked the engine on. The noise vibrated in her ears, and she felt somewhat frightened but she reached out with her left arm and held his.

"You won't go fast?"

"No, darling, I won't go fast," he replied with a laugh. "You've never been in a truck before?"

"No."

"There is nothing to worry about. You have your seat belt on, and you'll get used to it. It feels a little bumpy at first, but once we get on the highway, it will be smooth. How far is your room from here?"

"About ten minutes up this road."

"Do you want me to stop so you can get your clothes?"

"No, we have to hurry, but it's okay. I carry all my papers with me in my backpack."

He couldn't imagine that she could keep her things in the small light-green bag she was carrying in her lap, but such was the life of an immigrant. You must be ready to move on at any time and take what you have with you. Yasmin had it right; your documentation and some essentials was all you needed.

Carlos got on Highway 10 East and stopped at a Walmart Super Center, where he gassed and parked the truck. He clicked the engine off.

"We can get a room at the motel behind us, and then we can shower," he said. "Why don't we get something to eat first? There's a small restaurant inside. I am starved."

"I will only have something to drink, but I will watch you."

The two kissed, and he unplugged her seat belt. Then they kissed again, and he looked at her close, their faces touching.

"Let's go," he said.

She carried her backpack in her left hand and held Carlos's hand with her right one. They carried a conversation as if they had known each other for years. They later sat at the restaurant and ate, still talking and laughing. They had finally been able to sit next to each other without apprehension, enjoying the moment together, he curious about her life as an infant in Guatemala, and she answering his inquiries without a hint of reserve. She seemed to out glow herself tonight, and Carlos discovered that she could be quite chatty when exposed. Perhaps her happiness had overwhelmed her usual shyness.

They carried on for a good hour until it suddenly became uncomfortable for them. The ceiling lights were turned off, and only the glare of the store lights kept them from the dark.

"Someone is sending us a message," Carlos said, smiling.

"They are closing?"

"Is that how you do it with your customers?"

"No," she responded. "I announce it."

"Yes, it's much better mannered like that."

"The customers will always come back if you are decent to them. It's not even the food so much."

"That is why I do not think they would fire you."

"I do not know if I want to go back," she said.

Carlos stared at her, surprised by the resolve of her comment. He kissed her on the cheek, and she kissed him back.

"Why don't we buy something for you to wear at the store? We still have time."

"I won't be wearing your baggy pants anymore?"

"You will, but you will need other clothes."

"I can wait till we are in Miami. I heard they have nice stores there."

"We will do that too, but you still will need clothes for the trip. Come on, let's go pick out some things."

They held hands and walked through the main store alley towards the female section to look around while they carried on their conversation from the table as if they had never been interrupted.

CHAPTER 16

It was past nine when Carlos opened his eyes. They had rented a double room the night before, as Yasmin would not sleep on the same bed with him. She could not articulate a thorough reason. She just said it was not proper, not yet. They slept in separate beds, but when Carlos looked towards his side and noticed the bed empty, he jumped. Where could she had gone? The bed was perfectly made, not a sign that someone had slept in it.

He quickly ran to the door and opened it. They were on the first level, and a few cars were in the parking lot, including his truck. Just then, he heard his phone vibrate, and he ran back to bed. As he touched the screen to take the call, he noticed the many calls from Yasmin's phone. Was everything all right?

"Hello," he said.

"I have been calling you and calling you. I waited for you to wake up, but you must have been really tired. I found a place that has espresso. I'm getting it now."

"Yasmin, you scared the living daylights out of me. Don't ever do that to me again. I thought something happened."

"I did not want to disturb you. I wanted to surprise you."

"Come right back now, please. You almost gave me a heart attack."

"I am sorry. I walked many blocks to find your coffee. I will be there now."

"Thank you, Yasmin. You are very sweet, but darling, come on back, come on. I will wash up and put the TV on."

She arrived a good half-hour later, walking at a fast pace and carrying a two-cup plastic carrier with two cups in it. She was sweating from her long walk back to the motel, despite the early hour. She opened the door and found Carlos sitting on the bed with his back against a stack of pillows. She placed the cup holder on the night table and leaned over to kiss him. He held her with both hands on her cheeks and brought her back to his lips and kissed her again.

"Do you want your coffee now? You should have it before it gets cold."

"And where did you go to find this coffee?"

"There aren't many places that make it this way around here. But I found one."

"How far, darling?"

"About half-hour walk."

"Yasmin! Thank you, my pretty girl, thank you, but don't ever do that again. Look at you, you're sweating."

"It's all right," she said and pulled his coffee cup from the cup carrier, removing the lid.

"Thank you," he said, reaching for the cup. "I can't believe you did that, darling. Had I known, I would not have let you go."

"It's only a surprise. I wanted to make you happy."

"You don't have to walk twenty city blocks to make me happy. Just being here with you makes me happy."

She removed the other cup and took a sip.

"Look, I am drinking your coffee too."

He smiled at her.

"So, you did not just walk for me. You walked for you too."

"No, darling, I just want to try everything you do."

"And me too. It's only those tamales that I have some trouble with."

They both laughed.

A morning show was on TV. The host was interviewing a government official about inflation and the condition of the American economy. Carlos thought this must be a talking point from the Miami area. There'd be endless discussions in Miami about this. The prospect of catching a Democratic president mishandling a sensitive situation would prove too tempting for the Cuban population.

"If you want, Yasmin, I can put on a Spanish channel for you. This is just a talk show."

"No, I want to learn English well."

"But you speak pretty well now."

"I studied it in Guatemala. But I did not have a lot of practice."

"Do any customers in the restaurant speak to you in English?"

"I've had maybe ten in the entire time I've been there. I did not know what they were saying at first, but I asked them to repeat it, and then I did."

"I will teach you. You need to learn the language fluently. It's important. Oh, by the way, you would have been working at the restaurant right now if it wasn't for me. Do you realize that? Do you miss it?"

"No."

She shook her head. Her eyes sparkled with joy, as someone who has found a lost jewel or discovered a new way to decipher a puzzle. He smiled back, grabbed the monitor, and went through the channels until he found one in Spanish. The heavy Hispanic population in the city made a mandate for Spanish channels. It was also a talk show.

"There is nothing else on in the morning but talk shows. No *novelas* at this time. Do you watch them?"

"No."

"Do they watch them in Guatemala?"

"Yes. But not everybody, some people. Many don't have TV."

"How was it where you lived? Did you have TV?"

"I had to work before and after school. I could not watch anything."

"Where did you work?"

"I was my aunt's maid. I had to pay her back for feeding me."

"Oh, God."

He leaned forward from the pillows and kissed her again. This time she held him with her arms around his neck, but then suddenly, she pulled back.

"Do you want to have some breakfast?"

"Yes," he agreed. "Let's go. After breakfast, we have to get going. I have to pick up my load and head back East."

"Where will we be going?"

"We'll be going to Atlanta, Georgia."

"Same as the last time you traveled."

"Yes."

He drank the rest of his coffee and took her hand. She still was drinking hers, and she held onto his hand. They left the room and headed for the restaurant on the grounds of the motel. There was no waitress, so they got a table and looked over the menu. Then they went to the counter to place their order but stayed back for a moment.

"Your top looks beautiful on you," he said. "Do you like it?"

"I like anything you like," she answered.

He had picked the T-shirt she was wearing among other things the night before. It was gray with medium-sized letters in white that said "Florida." He had seen it when the two were looking for clothes for her to wear. He thought it was appropriate for the occasion and wanted it for her. It was the future. He did not want her to think about Phoenix anymore.

"It does not have to be like that, Yasmin. You have to like it too."

"But I do. This is where I am going with you. Don't you want me to go?"

"Of course, darling. Of course I want it. I chose it."

"Do you folks want to order?" the man behind the counter said.

They approached, and Carlos placed the order. They both ordered the same: scrambled eggs, bacon, and toast with butter and orange juice. They skipped the coffee. They did not let go of their hands until Carlos had to go in his pocket to retrieve cash and pay for the order. They both laughed at each other as they waited as if they were kids who had just met.

CHAPTER 17

Carlos and Yasmin left Phoenix around 11:00 in the morning after picking up a trailer from Chandler. He would have liked to make Dallas tonight but knew it was impossible. So he planned on getting as close to it as possible. Time would go fast now that he had Yasmin as his traveling companion. As they got well into the road, he began to feel the difference. The distance shortened, and those familiar names that he knew along the highway seemed to sneak up on him fast, as if somehow the distance had gotten shorter all of a sudden. It was the magic that Yasmin had made in his life. In a matter of days, everything had changed for him, and although he had no idea what the next day would bring, right now, at this moment, he felt happiness like he had never felt it before.

The calls from Gordon did not stop. They seemed to always come as his break neared the end. He tried to keep from him that he was traveling with Yasmin, but Gordon was an old dog that knew all the tricks. As they reached the outskirts of Atlanta two days later, Gordon asked him the inevitable question that Carlos knew was coming.

"By the way," Gordon said. "Did I ever tell you I charge rent for any roommates you keep in my truck?"

"No, I did not know. But did I ever tell you that I only pay rent to my landlord?"

"Who is traveling with you?"

"I am looking at the most beautiful black eyes I've ever seen," Carlos answered. "They are mesmerizing."

"I knew it," Gordon shot back. "Do not take your eyes off the road, and we will settle our account when you are back in Miami. Black eyes will cost you."

Carlos laughed softly. He had totally predicted Gordon's reaction and looked straight into Yasmin's eyes with his soft smile.

"This is Atlanta?" she asked him.

Carlos nodded and disconnected Gordon's call from the phone system in the truck's dashboard.

"We are going to drop the trailer at a factory, and then we can stop and eat some supper. We have to find a good place because we have to stay the night. We could leave early in the morning and be home in the afternoon. Do you want to do that?"

"Whatever you want," she said smiling.

Carlos wanted to kiss her, but he held back, and she understood. The perils of taking your eyes off the road when driving an eighteen-wheeler were immense. She leaned towards him and kissed him on the cheek. Now they were a pair, she thought. A pair that flew together always.

"We are almost at the place for our drop-off," Carlos said. "My boss could not fit a load to take back from this location; we will have to pick up another trailer on our way to Miami. But that will give you a chance to get to know another city, and then after that, we will drive straight through to Miami."

"Okay," she answered.

She listened to him attentively when he spoke. She focused her glance on him, showing that serene look that Carlos now understood. It was not shyness but concentration.

They got off the main highway and fed into another road that was quite busy with traffic. There was a long line of trucks in front of them, and they sat at the same spot for a half-hour.

"Accident up ahead," Carlos said.

Slowly, they made their way into a single lane, and when they reached the accident scene, Carlos pointed to the carcass of what was once a truck, unhinged from its trailer. Firemen were at the scene, and black smoke was still spewing from the cabin. Yasmin reached out and touched Carlos's arm.

"What happened?" she asked.

"That was an eighteen-wheeler. That is what can happen in the blink of an eye if you're not looking."

"Maybe you should not do this anymore."

"You can do it if you are careful, very careful."

They were in an industrial area, and they got off the highway and into an empty road. They made their way into a large building and checked in at the security shack. Carlos drove the trailer into a narrow spot in between two other trailers. A man came by the driver's window as Carlos was unhitching the trailer. He had to get out of the truck to open the trailer's back door for someone to check the load. Just as Carlos was getting ready to get back on the road, Gordon's call came on his phone, checking up on him. Then they were off again, this time with no trailer behind him. They made a stop in Orlando, same as his last trip, picked up another trailer, and headed south to Miami.

CHAPTER 18

There was a touch of cheeriness in the air, and Yasmin felt it as Carlos entered the Miami area with a trailer in the rear. Perhaps it was the busy traffic or the proximity to the ocean, but something struck her as if she had arrived at a new beginning. After paying the toll, they stayed on Highway 826 for only a few miles until Carlos got off to drop the load. Traffic was heavy this late afternoon, but Carlos made it seem easy, she thought. He got off in Hialeah to drop off the trailer, and then they were back on the highway again. After reporting to his home office and parking the truck, they got inside Carlos's car and headed for his apartment. They entered the mutual driveway he shared with his neighbor. As they came onto the porch, Yasmin pointed to the flower boxes of multicolored daisies.

"Hmm, you did not tell me you had flowers. How pretty."

She got close and ran her fingers through one of them tenderly, as if touching a newborn.

"I pay a lady to maintain them."

"Why?"

"Because I'm never here. They need care."

They looked at each other, and Carlos slid his key in the lock and opened the front door. He took her by the hand and pulled her gently inside.

"It's a small place," he said. "It makes no sense for me to have a big house if I am not around enough. Let me show you."

He showed her each room, turning the lights on as he went in. Then they sat together in the living room and watched TV together and rested from the long days on the road. They each took a shower and then talked about dinner. She wanted to cook for him, her feminine instinct telling her that she should.

"You have to get to know the area. I want to show you around. I never cook at home. I eat out all the time."

"There's nothing like a home-cooked meal, Carlos," she answered.

"We will have time for that, darling. Let's enjoy for now. We can go eat at the restaurant I told you about, and then we can go to Miami Beach later. It is beautiful at night."

"I always wanted to live near the sea."

"But you spent a lot of time near the ocean."

"In the summer. I went to the beaches far away on the west coast of the country. That's how I got to be such a devoted swimmer."

"You will see the ocean here tonight. Come on, let's go."

Carlos grabbed the car keys, and the two of them hopped in the car and drove across Bird Road to reach Carlos's local hangout at La Carreta, a restaurant. They held hands as they left the parking lot and came around the restaurant to reach its main door, which was a few yards from the counter, where people gathered to drink their coffee, smoke, and tell stories. Carlos was not going there this evening. He was going inside with Yasmin to have dinner and a passionate conversation. If any of his many friends discovered him and came to lure him to go outside, he would tell them no, not this evening. He had brought his very special girl to dine. Perhaps later, when they had caught up in their talks, he would stop at the counter and request a cortaito coffee, and he would take a sip and then pass it to his Yasmin. He wanted her to be part of every aspect of his life.

Carlos eyed a two-seat table at the end of the large room where numerous other tables were spread out, a reminder of the preventive measures of the COVID-19 virus . He waved to one of the waitresses and signaled the table he had chosen. He and Yasmin walked down to the end of the room and sat.

"Good evening, Carlos," said the waitress, a pretty brunette, as she came close to their table. She handed each of them a menu inside a plastic folder. "Who do we have the pleasure of having here?"

"This is Yasmin," Carlos announced.

"Hello," said Yasmin, barely stretching her lips in a soft smile.

"A pleasure to meet you," the waitress responded. "Would you like anything to drink while you wait for your order?"

"We will just have water," Carlos said, cutting in.

The waitress winked her eye at him and went back to the front to get their drinks.

"This is the restaurant that you told me about?"

"Yes. The food is great, and I come here almost every day when I am in Miami. Let's see now, what are you thinking of having? They have very typical Cuban entries here, but there is some variety too. The chicken soup is great. The broth is very thick, and I always have it at night."

"I will have one too."

"Okay. And what are you going to drink?"

"Just water."

"Let me order some juice for you. If you do not like it, you don't have to drink it. It's called guarapo, and it is sugar cane nectar. There is nothing in it except for the juice that comes out of the stem of the plant. They make it right in front of you. Do you want to try it?"

"I will try anything you have."

"You are sweet, Yasmin. What about the main course? What will you have?"

"I don't know. What about rice?"

"How do you want your rice?"

"I will have it the way you do."

"Well, I am going to have a steak and white rice with fried, ripe plantains. But you don't have to have that. You can look at the other entries. You want to go over them?"

"No, I will have what you have. I know about the plantains. I made them for you, remember?"

"Yes, of course I remember. I love them, and they are so easy to cook. All you need is a little oil and some salt."

Yasmin smiled at him, and she held his hand over the table just as the waitress came back. She noticed their hands intertwined on the table.

"Your friends are all outside," the waitress said. "I think they are following me. They are looking for you."

"Yes, I see them."

Roberto was right in front, his hair looking wet and combed back, with his wife Amelia behind.

"Is this a private party?" Roberto asked.

"No, of course not," Carlos answered. "You are welcome to join us."

Roberto asked the waitress for some help setting them up together.

"The only way I could fix you up is if Carlos moves to a bigger table," she said.

"Come on, Carlos," said Roberto. "Be a sport."

"Of course, we will join you. This is Yasmin," Carlos said, introducing her. "We just got here from Phoenix."

"Well, hello," Roberto said, extending his hand.

Amelia quickly followed. The waitress then waved them to follow. She had found a bigger table for them on the other side of the wooden divider that split the aisle from the dining room, where a few more tables had been set up out of necessity. They sat at a table with space for four.

"How was Phoenix?" Roberto asked.

"I hardly had anytime. I stayed in the outskirts of the city and came right back."

"Have you been to Miami before?" Roberto asked Yasmin.

"No," she said.

"You will love it here. Summer is coming."

Yasmin nodded, and Amelia stared at her with curious eyes.

"This is the best time to come," Amelia said. "June, July, and August are prohibited unless you like to be fried."

"You must like hot weather," Roberto added. "You live in Arizona."

"She has lived there by necessity, not because she likes it," Carlos said. "She had even considered moving to New Jersey."

"Oh, New Jersey," Roberto said. "No, that's too cold. Stay here. This is where everybody wants to be."

Yasmin smiled at him and nodded. Carlos came to her rescue.

"Arizona is hotter than here. But it's less humid."

"Well, this is what everyone says, but look, when you hit 120 degrees, I don't care that it is less humid. What difference does it make? Heat is heat. Amelia and I have been there. There are times when you can't even turn your doorknob. You'll burn your hand."

"It's true," Yasmin said.

"Where are you originally from?" Roberto asked.

"She's from Guatemala," Carlos said, cutting in.

"Where in Guatemala?"

"From Jutiapa," Carlos replied.

"Well, it is a pretty country. It's a shame what's going on with crime and the gangs. But it is pretty."

"Just bloody," Amelia added.

The waitress passed water to everyone and got ready to take their orders on her tablet.

"Are you ready, or do you need some more time?"

"We are ready," Carlos said.

"Carlos, could you give me a few more minutes?" Roberto asked softly, raising his gaze.

"Maybe," Carlos replied in jest. "Just don't go to sleep on me."

"Gee, he thinks he is still on the road, Amelia."

The two exchanged glances and laughed.

"No, we're just hungry."

"You did not eat on the road?"

"Yeah, of course. Last time was this morning with a light breakfast that we ate while I gassed the truck."

"Oh, that's a long time. Man, I don't know how you do it. Yasmin," he said shifting eyes to her. "Are you sure you want to hang out with this guy? He lives on the road."

"I like traveling," she said.

Both Roberto and Amelia turned to her.

"Really? You like living on the road?"

"The money is good," Carlos cut in. "And it's an honest living."

"I still don't know how you can cope, Carlos. I'd be going nuts."

"I think I know what I want," Amelia said, pointing to an entry in Roberto's menu.

"That?" Roberto said, pointing. "You want that?"

"Yes, it's not heavy. Don't forget, it's evening now."

"All right, so it will be a tamal with salad. Amelia, that is really light. Well, I am going to have *vaca frita* with rice."

"Roberto, that is too heavy of a meal at this time of day," Amelia said. "Get something lighter. Order a soup like Carlos. He's got the right idea."

"Carlos is a soup guy. He lives on soup."

"Carlos," Amelia said, "what are you having?"

"A large chicken soup."

"What did I tell you?" Roberto said.

"All right, Carlos. You have to eat some solid food with all those hours you are putting on the road."

"I'll follow up with a steak with French fries."

"Now we're talking. And what will you have, Yasmin?"

She looked towards Carlos, unsure as to how to answer.

"I'd like to try one tamal."

"That's okay, Yasmin, but it's not like your tamal. You should add something more solid."

"A steak? Some rice?"

"That's better, darling."

The waitress approached and took their orders. They all added soft drinks. Carlos ordered two guarapos. Roberto ordered a beer, and Amelia asked for a cup of wine.

"So, Yasmin," Roberto said, "how long have you been here?"

"Almost two years," she replied.

Roberto nodded and was ready to fire another question, but Carlos got ahead of him.

"She has been living in Phoenix all this time, where she has some friends. She has no immediate family though. She has a high school education from Guatemala, and she has been working as a waitress. She is a terrific swimmer."

"Oh, that's a match for you," Roberto said. "You seem to have given me her resume. I just asked her how long she was here. But thanks, Carlos."

"Yasmin is not very talkative. I thought I'd jump ahead."

"And what do you have planned tonight?"

"We are going to Miami Beach."

"Any place in particular?"

"The beach," Carlos said laughing.

"Really? At this time?" Amelia said.

"They are a couple, Amelia," Roberto said. "They want to sit on the beach and watch the waves."

"If we get lucky, there might be a full moon tonight reflecting on the water," Carlos added.

Roberto and Amelia looked at each other. There was no doubt about it. These two were lovers.

"Sergio Moza and his friend Antonio Prieto are in the house. Hang in here for a little while longer."

The waitress came in holding a tray and began serving everyone. Carlos took his drink and passed the other one to Yasmin.

"This is that sugar cane juice I told you about. Try it, and tell me if you like it."

He held the paper cup for her, and she took a sip from the straw.

"Do you like it?"

She nodded and took another sip.

"It's very sweet," she said. "I had it in Guatemala."

"Yasmin, if you're going to make a habit of hanging out with Carlos, you will have to learn to like guarapo and espresso coffee. Carlos," he asked, looking towards him, "why can't you drink a beer like normal men?"

"I have no use for beer."

Yasmin held on to Carlos's hand.

"Please don't," she said to him, almost in a whisper.

"Yasmin," Roberto uttered. "This is your advice to my friend? No beer?"

She nodded.

"Yasmin is a nondrinker like me," Carlos commented. "If you drive for a living, you must learn not to touch alcohol."

"Who says?" Roberto insisted. "All the truck drivers I know cannot sit without a beer in front of them."

"They won't be drivers for long."

Carlos cut the steak for Yasmin while Amelia and Roberto sat there mesmerized.

"How nice," Amelia observed. "When will you do that for me, Roberto?"

"Does he take good care of you, Yasmin?" Roberto asked, ignoring his wife's remark. "He is good, isn't he?"

"Leave her alone," Carlos said. "This is a new menu to her."

"How is that? She's never had steak before?"

"She has but not like this, Roberto. She is used to another menu."

"Hmm. So how do they make a steak in the Guatemalan menu, Yasmin?"

"We make it several ways. If it's fried, it's greasier. But we also have other ways. There is the *salpicón* that is made with onions, tomatoes, pepper, and mint, and not as well cooked as this."

"You guys are big on spice, right?"

"Yes, we use spice, but not everyone does."

"That is the part I don't like. I don't like too much spice."

"There is actually more variety in the Guatemalan menu than in ours," Carlos pointed out.

"Are you turning Guatemalan on me, Carlos?"

"Not yet, but I'm learning," he answered smiling.

Carlos ate half of Yasmin's steak after his soup and then ordered coffee for everyone.

"Have you tried our coffee yet?"

Yasmin nodded.

"She's even made it," Carlos said.

The two of them crossed glances, and then Roberto and Amelia stared at them.

"How's your soup?" Yasmin asked him, getting close to him.

"It's delicious, my Yasmin, do you want to try it?"

He took a spoonful from his plate and brought it to Yasmin's lips. She let herself be fed and made a happy gesture.

"Hmmm."

"Wait a minute," Roberto said, truly alarmed. "What are we watching here?"

"Two love birds feeding each other," Carlos said.

"Oh, no," Roberto grunted. "But we are not at a park or at a lover's concerto. Cool it down."

"There's no law against feeding each other," Carlos replied. "In fact, we are doing what we should do at a restaurant and that's to eat. We are eating."

Yasmin laughed. It was her turn to feed Carlos, and she managed to pick a slice of her tamal for him. Carlos took it open mouthed.

"You must have known what she was going to order," Roberto said. "It was really for you and not her."

"Of course, why else would she have ordered tamal? We ordered for each other. I ordered the soup for her."

"Oh, my God. Amelia, what is this?"

"It's love at first sight, Roberto."

"We were in love once, and we are again, Amelia. We never fed each other."

"Pigeons do."

"I gotta get Moza over here. This is too much," Roberto said, getting up.

"If you do, remember that we are leaving right after dinner," Carlos said. "Yasmin and I gotta get to the beach."

"A little darker will not harm you."

"Darkness by the water is beauty. You and Amelia ought to try it sometime."

"I am going to bring Moza, just to say hello," Roberto said, getting up.

"Yeah, of course," Carlos replied. "You might as well tell the waitress that we need more room. Moza will not just say hello."

Roberto pointed at the waitress with his index and walked towards her.

"So, you're going to the beach," Amelia commented, looking towards Yasmin. "A real nice place for a romance. Have you ever been to a beach, Yasmin?"

She smiled cunningly at her as she waited for an answer.

"Amelia," Carlos said, acting surprised, "did you know that Guatemala has two coastlines? The Pacific on the south and the Caribbean on the north. You can pick where you want to swim, not to mention the waterfalls and lakes. It puts us to shame."

"Well, I would not go that far, Carlos. Cuba had beaches in every which way."

"No doubt. I'd say Yasmin had plenty to choose from, though."

"Carlos," Yasmin interposed, "the beaches are not that many in Guatemala, and they are far from each other. I was far from the coast."

"But you swim," Amelia observed.

Yasmin nodded. No matter how pressed, she maintained her composure. It was Carlos who fought her battles, and Yasmin had begun to adhere to this role.

"She swims beautifully," Carlos answered.

"Have you guys been to the beach yet?"

87

"No, tonight is our first time. We might get to swim together tonight. She might have to save me. I'm a poor swimmer."

"Carlos, how can you say that, having been born on an island?"

"Because I lived deep in the countryside. Going to the beach was a torturing trip."

"So how did you get to be such a good swimmer?"

Their conversation was interrupted by Roberto, who had brought Mr. Moza and his aide with him. Both Mr. Moza and Prieto dressed in the typical garb of guallavera and wide dress pants. Mr. Moza came forward and shook Carlos's hand, and Mr. Prieto followed. The waitress moved quickly to accommodate them, bringing two more chairs and squeezing them between Roberto and his wife.

"And who is this beautiful young lady?" Mr. Moza said. "How is it that I have not had the pleasure of seeing her before?"

"Her name is Yasmin," Carlos responded, "the name of a flower which she already is."

"Ah, she is that and much more," Mr. Moza added, extending his hand to her. "She reminds me of those beautiful *jasmines* from my old home, long green stems and beautiful white buds. She's exactly like one, and it is right that she be named like one."

Yasmin hesitated then moved her hand forward and let Mr. Moza grasp it gently.

"Yasmin and I arrived today from Arizona. We are eating dinner and then we are going to head out to the beach."

"Oh, well, I think that is a splendid idea," Mr. Moza said. "It's a warm evening, clear sky, and there will be a beautiful moon out. It's a lover's dream. I am glad you are taking a good night rest after such a long trip. You and Yasmin might get so relaxed that you might fall asleep on the sand and wake up tomorrow morning."

Carlos and Yasmin both laughed. They had stopped eating their meal in deference to Mr. Moza and his friend. It was common courtesy in Cuban culture to invite new arrivals to join those at the table in their meal, so Carlos beat Roberto to the chase.

"Will you and Mr. Prieto join us for dinner, Mr. Moza?" Carlos asked.

"Oh, I thank you. I think we will both pass on that. We are only going to order a coffee each, and then Mr. Prieto and I are going to talk business with Roberto as usual."

"Carlos, you and Yasmin are welcome to stay," Roberto said.

"No, thank you," Carlos replied. "We will get going once we are done."

Carlos and Yasmin had stopped feeding each other. Yasmin seemed a slow eater, savoring her steak and slicing thin pieces of her tamal. Mr. Moza veered the conversation towards politics.

"It's a sad day watching how the economy seems to be disintegrating," Mr. Moza commented. "It's a really bad situation. What a tragedy."

"Some people do not agree that that is the case, Mr. Moza," Roberto commented.

"Well, perception makes it evident, and the polls show that," Mr. Moza added.

"What can you expect?" Mr. Prieto asked. "It's politically unwise for those in power to admit it."

Carlos gazed towards Yasmin. He began to drink his soup steadily, a spoonful at a time. The conversation seemed to take its usual political tone; that was a sign to him that it was time to leave. Yasmin kept looking at him, indecisive as to what his intentions were, but eventually she followed his pace and finished the slices of her steak.

"*Caballeros*," Carlos said, "we are going to get going. We will run into you tomorrow, I'm sure."

"How long will you be around?" Roberto asked.

"A couple of days, and then we go back, maybe to Phoenix or up north. I'm not sure yet."

"Does Yasmin want to stay with us while you're gone?" Amelia asked. "We'd be happy to have her."

"No thanks. She's coming with me."

"Oh, no. You're going to put this poor girl through the hardships of truck traveling. What is it?"

"Nothing is with me," Carlos answered. "We don't think of it that way."

"That is a gentleman for you," Mr. Moza observed. "He will not leave his sweetheart behind."

"You should learn from that one, Roberto," Amelia said, cutting in. "I always wanted to go with Roberto on his long drives," she added, as if talking to everyone. "But he would only take me on the short trips. Go figure."

"Amelia, that is a sign of protection. I did not think it was safe to take you into unfriendly territories."

"Unfriendly? What's unfriendly?" Amelia insisted.

"Texas, Oklahoma, New Mexico. All those western states I used to travel to. They are dangerous places, not to mention the hardship. Anyway, my days as a driver did not last long."

"I hated to stay behind."

Carlos and Yasmin got up from their seats. Carlos shook hands with Moza and the others, and Yasmin followed.

"Take good care of that Yasmín," Mr. Moza said. "Flowers need to be watered."

"I will. I will water her."

"Let me know if she needs company while you are gone, seriously," Amelia repeated. "I can take her out and show her the city while you are gone."

"Well, thanks. It's true. There may be trips when she can't accompany me."

"Just call, and we'll be there," Amelia said.

"Good night, everyone," Carlos said and waved.

Yasmin waved and followed him. The two of them turned and headed for the waitress by the middle of the aisle to pick up the bill and pay at the counter. They got out through the front door and turned left to avoid being spotted by the crowd at the outside counter. Holding hands they walked up to Carlos's car. Carlos clicked the doors open and held the passenger door open for Yasmin. Night had fallen, and a pleasant fresh breeze was blowing.

CHAPTER 19

Yasmin could not be more amazed. Holding onto Carlos's arm and watching the ocean split in two by the road, the scene was more beautiful than she ever imagined. Darkness had fallen in the night sky, and a sharp brightness reflected on the waters. The moon was out as Mr. Moza had predicted, and it was working its magic again. What impressed her the most was that the water was all around them, on both sides of the road, immediately raising questions in her mind as to how this highway could have possibly gotten here. Afar into the horizon she could make out the tall buildings of Miami Beach.

"How did this road get here?" she asked Carlos gently.

"I've wondered about that myself. How did they build it? Isn't it incredible? I don't know but when you see it, it makes you want to be here. It's such a beautiful place."

She held his arm tighter.

"Are you afraid?" he asked.

"No. I'm with you. But what happens if your car breaks down?"

"You pull onto the shoulder," Carlos said.

"There is not much room."

"It's tight in some areas. That's true. But road service is quick here. It's never happened to me."

"It's such a smooth ride. It seems like we are traveling so fast."

"But we are not. Looking at the ocean gives you that impression."

Carlos could see her smile from the multicolored reflection in the dashboard. He too never failed to be impressed by the beauty surrounding them. They exited through Alton Road and eventually worked their way onto Collins Avenue. All the way through Yasmin was mesmerized by the bright streetlights and the freshness and novelty of everything. They worked their way into Mid Beach and dashed into a parking lot.

"The beach is there," Carlos said, pointing ahead. "There will be few people at this time. Maybe just us."

They held hands and went into the sand with the ocean ahead of them and the hotel lights behind them. Carlos took his shoes off, and Yasmin followed. They suddenly stopped as they got near the water, both touched by the booming sound of the waves as they emptied onto the shore.

"Do you want to go in?" Carlos asked.

"Not yet," she said smiling.

He pulled her close to him and kissed her, and she embraced him and held onto his shoulders. It was a magical moment. Carlos looked at her and saw tears in her eyes. Then they stepped back a little and sat on dry sand, watching the water run towards them and then slip back, giving them that false sense of movement.

"Ah!" she gasped feeling it.

He laughed and held her close to him. It was more than any living soul could ask for, and they both felt a burning passion for each other come to life, as if they had just met and had no memory of ever seeing each other before except here.

"Where were you all this time, Yasmin?"

"Right here," she said, "waiting for you."

They were lost in themselves, inside a boundless romance that had been born on the immensity of interstate highways and blossomed amid the silent beauty of nature.

CHAPTER 20

By late morning the following day, Yasmin was busy arranging the daisies on the porch of Carlos's apartment. They had returned late from the beach, but Yasmin was up before Carlos. She made him breakfast, which she had now quickly mastered, buttered Cuban bread with café au lait. She was careful not to disturb him and left the steaming cup of coffee with a cover on the table. She left two long slices of the bread on a plate that she covered with a napkin. Then she searched for tools she needed for the garden. All she could find was a small garden shovel and water hose outside. She got right to work inside the window boxes, turning the dirt and pulling the weeds. Carlos surprised her in the middle of things as she was watering the boxes with a dripple from the hose.

She put the hose aside and came to kiss him at the door.

"Good morning, angel," he said as they hugged. "You know, it's been a few hours, and you are turning this place upside down. How did you get the bread, the milk, the coffee?"

"I walked to the shopping center by Southwest 40 and bought it at a convenience store."

"Yasmin, be careful with the traffic here. I need to teach you how to drive. You can't go walking around here on foot."

"Aren't we going back on the road again?"

"Yes, as a matter of fact my boss was already calling me. That's what woke me up, but I didn't answer. We have to find ourselves some time."

"It's okay," she answered. "We can go back on the road when you are ready."

"You don't have to do any gardening either. I pay someone to do that."

"Well, she must not come very often," Yasmin said. "There was more weed than daisies in those boxes."

"All right, maybe you can take over. Let's go inside and eat breakfast. Come on."

She went to the kitchen and poured herself some coffee and milk, and sat by him at the table.

"Yasmin, you're drinking Cuban coffee?"

"I'm learning," she said smiling.

"Very fast. Much simpler than Guatemalan breakfast, right?"

"Yes. In Guatemala, we eat tortillas, beans, and eggs. It's breakfast like lunch."

"What would you like to do today? We could go to an amusement park. They are open now. Dancing tonight."

"Whatever you want."

Carlos's phone vibrated again, and Yasmin pointed to it.

"It's only Gordon, my boss," Carlos said. "I think I have to get you a phone. Then we can multiply our problems, but you really need one."

She smiled and took a sip of her coffee. Together, just the two of them, she felt a feeling of peace that made her feel so secure. He, likewise, felt relaxed and secure, knowing that for the first time he had found someone who truly filled him with pleasure, a sense of knowing that she was with him not just for a little while, ready to follow him wherever he went, through all the interstate highways, through all of life's paths. Could it be that he had found his dream girl? And what about her timid ways, her lack of words? Wouldn't that hamper his way of life? She would probably not gain the liking of the Robertos and Mozas of the world. They would probably already have labeled her as a peasant girl, limited in her ways of communication. But Carlos did not care what anybody thought. If his friends could not accept her, he will cease being popular in some of the stomping grounds of Miami.

CHAPTER 21

In the coming weeks, Carlos and Yasmin traveled together as a pair. They were seen together in every truck stop on the highway, and others soon assumed that the couple were married. Life on the road can be hard and inconvenient, but it is also a medium of intimacy that could only be equaled by those very few moments at home for a couple. The romance between Carlos and Yasmin grew and flourished into a passion that could no longer be stopped. In their truck cabin, they came to know love as they never did before, and neither one of them could imagine being away from the other any longer.

"We are going to take 95 off Route 10," Carlos said on their return trip to Phoenix. "I do not have to make any other stops but Orlando. This hardly ever happens. It's the first time since we've been traveling together."

Yasmin looked ahead at the signs and noticed the one for Route 10 East. Carlos took that one.

"So we are going back empty to Miami?"

"No, Gordon would never let that happen." Carlos laughed. "He would die if I came back empty. We were just lucky that we made our delivery in Louisiana and can come down this way. But he just told me to stop in Orlando and make a pickup."

Yasmin laughed. She recently talked to Gordon on the phone for the first time. Carlos had introduced her after his boss demanded to know who was traveling with him in the truck. After all, he had reasoned, it was him who was responsible for any mishap, and he would rather just know. He was pleased with Yasmin, he later confessed to Carlos. Despite not having seen her in person, he just knew. A lot could be said about a person only by her voice. Gordon was a man of voices. His business had been trucking for a lifetime, and he had learned to gauge people's qualities by sound. The voice of a woman was no different, he had said.

As the truck reached Jacksonville, Carlos told Yasmin the story of Alfredo Fuentes, his biker friend who had lost control of his motorcycle in that area, caused by the draft created by a passing tractor trailer. Such heavy machinery could cause damage without even making contact. This was why one could never be too careful. The road was owned by careful drivers, Carlos had said more than one time, and Yasmin agreed.

It was late spring, and the heat was beginning to make itself known, even this far north in the state of Florida. Carlos got off on Route 95, heading south, and threw a laugh.

"We made great timing," he said. "Orlando is a breath away."

"A hot breath," she said.

They both laughed.

"When I was a boy," Carlos began, "I thought the weather was hot all over the world. I could not imagine that there was cold weather anywhere, except the South Pole or something like that. I only saw snow in Christmas cards, if I could find one. The world was supposed to be all sunny and hot all the time. Until I came here, and I traveled north. I saw snow for the first time there."

"I never saw snow either," Yasmin said. "It's only in the mountains."

They made a pickup in Orlando and then headed south on 95. They dropped the trailer at the warehouse and went to the home base to leave the truck. Then they got into Carlos's Chevy and were off home.

"What would you like to do? Do you want to pick up coffee or go straight home? But it's kind of too hot for coffee."

She gave him an eyeful.

"It's never too hot for coffee."

"Yasmin, you've gotten really hooked on coffee. I would have never guessed that you would like it so much."

"It calms my nerves."

"What are you nervous about?"

"I am anxious about our date tomorrow."

They both looked at each other, and she reached for his right hand as he drove. They did not want to say it, just feel it. But in the morning, they had an appointment with City Hall. They were going to be married. They had not yet arranged for the witnesses, and a stop at La Carreta would be wise so they could round up two of Carlos's friends.

They parked the Chevy in the back of the building and made for the front terrace and both asked for a cortaito. A slight soft breeze in the open porch made the afternoon heat a little more bearable. Even at this early hour, there were people by the counter, drinking the hot espresso coffee.

"Do you see anyone you know?" Yasmin asked.

"No, it's too early, angel. But do not worry. I think I will call Roberto and tell him to meet us here later."

"Do you think he will mind? I do not think he will be pleased when he hears the news."

"Despite his attitude, Yasmin, he can't help but be a human. He will not mind."

She hesitated.

"I don't think he will approve."

"Then we won't ask him. He does not have to approve. I can call lots of other people."

"No," she said. "Let's give him a chance."

They drank their coffee and got back in their car and then drove home. While he undressed and showered, she was watering the daisies outside. She suffered from an issue with waste, not to let time pass by unattended. Time was the only luxury she had. By the time Carlos got out of the shower she was waiting for him. She kissed him and went inside the bathroom to clean up.

"Do you want to go somewhere tonight? I mean, other than our usual restaurant?"

He was standing in front of the open door to the bathroom while she picked up his clothes from the hamper.

"No," she answered. "We have to get up early tomorrow."

"Yasmin, honey, can you stop acting like a maid? Come on, stop cleaning."

"Okay, my Carlos. Give me a few minutes, and I'll be ready. You dress up while I shower, okay?"

"Yes, deal."

"Deal."

She showered and put on a new pair of jeans. She knew Carlos loved to see her wear jeans, and she was anxious to please him. She wore a T-shirt for a top and low-heel shoes.

"I'm ready," she said, stepping into the living room.

Carlos took her hand, and they both went outside and got in the car. They arrived at La Carreta, and Carlos was able to get a space in one of the slots at the front of the restaurant. The weather had freshened up, and they went inside as Carlos exchanged hellos with several men. They sat at the table at the end of the large room and asked for a menu from the waitress.

"We always sit at the end but end up in the front later," Yasmin said.

"You are right," Carlos said laughing. "But at least we get a few minutes of privacy."

"Yes," Yasmin said, looking straight towards the entrance. "Here comes someone."

"Oh, that would be Ralph."

"Well, hello, stranger," said Ralph.

He seemed to have changed since he started driving, and he had grown a goatee.

"Ralph, how are you?"

"You changed your mind about eating outside with the rest of us, or what?"

"No, not at all. I was only sitting with my fiancée for a little while. May I introduce you? This is Yasmin."

"A pleasure meeting you, ma'am. My name is Ralph, and I am Carlos's friend."

"Nice to meet you," Yasmin said.

"Well, can I see you later then? I will be outside."

"We will join you shortly."

Ralph tipped his baseball cap in deference to Yasmin.

"Shall we go through the menu?" Carlos asked as he sat down.

"I think I am going to have chicken soup," Yasmin said.

"Yasmin, you are hooked, honey. You really have come around to the Cuban menu."

"It is so thick. It's different."

"Yes. I think the critics have that right, Yasmin. I am sorry about that, but the soups from Central America are really very watery. You drink this soup, and you will never drink any other one."

"It's true, Carlos. I want no other one."

"Anything to drink?" said the waitress, approaching.

"I will have a guarapo," Carlos said.

"I will have the same," Yasmin said.

It was at that moment that Carlos raised his head and saw Roberto and Amelia heading his way. Roberto raised his hand to the waitress, asking her to wait.

"Can we join you?" Roberto asked.

"Sure," Carlos answered. "We were wondering what had taken you so long."

"I saw Ralph coming inside, and that's how I knew you were here."

They exchanged pleasantries and followed the waitress, who set them up at a table in the next room.

"Tell me, Yasmin, how did it go for you in this last trip? Will you finally give in and stay with me for the next one?"

Yasmin smiled shyly and shook her head.

"Leave her alone, Amelia," Roberto said. "Do not worry. The day will come when she will beg you to come over."

"She enjoys being with me," Carlos said. "There is nothing strange about it. This is the way it should be."

"Okay, what do we have here? Machismo? Not you, right?"

"It's not machismo," Carlos replied. "It's called love."

"Oh, did you hear that, Ralph? He is in love."

"What will you have to drink?"

"One guarapo for me," Carlos said. "What will you have, Yasmin?"

"One guarapo also."

"I will have a cup of white wine," Roberto said and pointed to Amelia and Ralph in deference.

"Wine for both," Amelia said.

"Did you ask Ralph first, Amelia?"

"Oh, my! Ralph, will you join us?" Amelia asked, and Ralph nodded.

"So," Roberto said, looking at Carlos, "where are you going tonight?"

"Nowhere," Carlos said. "As a matter of fact," he began, eyeing Yasmin, "we wanted to ask you two and Ralph also if you could join us at City Hall tomorrow. Yasmin and I will be getting married."

"What?" Amelia screamed, making some of the heads turn at the other tables.

Ralph stood up and gave Carlos his hand.

"Congratulations," he said, "now I really want wine."

"That's what you should have said instead of yelling, Roberto. How crude can you be?"

"When did you guys decide this?" Roberto asked, ignoring Amelia's comment.

"So long ago I can't remember."

"It couldn't be so long ago. You met only a couple of months ago. Not even."

"We knew before then."

Yasmin assented, nodding her head.

"Oh, come on."

"So, what is the answer? Can you join us? We need witnesses."

"At what time?"

"Our appointment is at 10:00."

"Oh, boy. I will have to finagle that with work. Why in the world did you not tell us?"

"It's true, Carlos," Amelia said. "We could have prepared."

"We have so little time," Carlos explained. "We have to get on the road again."

"It cannot all be about work," Amelia explained. "You have to plan these things, right, Yasmin?"

"We tried to," she replied. "But it's better like this."

She smiled, leaving Amelia wondering what she had meant.

"The answer is yes, of course," Roberto finally answered. "We will all be there."

The waitress came back with the drinks. Roberto led the others in a toast to the about-to-be newlyweds. Carlos and Yasmin looked at each other. All was well after all.

"Mr. Moza is coming," Amelia said.

"Have you guys resolved anything yet?" Carlos asked.

"About what?"

"The Republicans, the Democrats, the conspiracies in America."

"You keep living in darkness, Carlos. I hope marriage makes you a wiser man."

"It might, but it will never turn me into a freak."

"Good evening, ladies and gentlemen," Mr. Moza said, followed by Mr. Prieto.

Both men wore white *gaballeras*. Mr. Moza leaned on the table with both hands and spoke to Yasmin and Amelia first.

"Ladies, you look lovely this evening, just lovely. Now shall I ask? May we join you?"

"Of course," Roberto replied. "We reserved two seats for you. Sit down, Mr. Moza."

"I think it's good in this spot. Was it your choice, Roberto?"

"No, there's your man," Roberto said, pointing to Carlos.

"Oh, Carlos. That's good, Carlos. I can understand why you'd choose to be inside. You have to preserve the beauty of your lady. Flowers need care."

Yasmin smiled at him. Despite all the fanfare, she sensed something delightful about the old man. Perhaps it was his excessive complimentary attitude that felt awfully fake. Perhaps something deeper.

"Carlos has some news for us," Roberto said. "Tomorrow is a big day for him."

"Oh, Carlos." Mr. Moza shifted his gaze to him. "Could it be what I suspect?"

"That is exactly what it is," Roberto said. "Those two are getting married tomorrow."

"Well, I think that's wonderful. I could not agree more. You have chosen a *jazmín* for a wife. And what does the lady have to say about that?"

Everyone remained quiet, and Yasmin felt she had no choice but to answer.

"I am very happy."

Carlos held her hand. The waitress came in between them with a big tray that she rushed to put down.

"I did not realize there were two more of you. I'm sorry about that."

She pulled her tablet from her apron pocket.

"Sir, can I get you something to drink?" she asked, addressing Mr. Moza and Pietro.

"Water will be fine," Mr. Moza said. "What will you have, Mr. Pietro?"

"Same. Water," Mr. Prieto said.

"Take your time," Mr. Moza said. "You may serve them. We won't make them wait. It's our fault for arriving late."

"No, we will wait," Carlos interposed. "Take your time. We are in no hurry to eat."

The waitress stood by Mr. Moza and took his order and that of his companion.

"So, we have a wedding tomorrow morning," Roberto added.

"You have everything ready?" Amelia asked Yasmin.

"Sure," Carlos said. "We are ready now."

"What will you be wearing?" she asked.

Carlos eyed Yasmin.

"We will be casual," Yasmin said.

"Come on, Carlos," Amelia insisted. "It's your wedding day. It's a day to remember. Pictures will be taken."

"It is their choice," Mr. Moza said. "They are the youth of today."

"You mean to tell me that Yasmin will not be wearing a wedding dress?" Amelia asked.

"No," Carlos said. "We will be casual. That's our choice."

Amelia nodded.

"That is absolutely right," Mr. Moza said.

The waitress came back with drinks for Mr. Moza and Mr. Prieto.

"Please serve them," Mr. Moza told her. "Their food is going to get cold. We wouldn't want that."

"I could take your orders back to keep them warm if you decide to wait," the waitress explained.

"All right," Roberto said. "Why don't you do that?"

The waitress picked up the tray and headed back inside.

"Well, that's that," Mr. Moza said. "Can you give me any good news, Roberto? What do you think about our man?"

"Oh, no," Carlos muttered to himself. "Politics again."

"He will prevail," Roberto said. "This is not politics, Carlos. This is the world we live in."

"You are trying to engage me," Carlos pointed out. "It won't work. I'm not into this game that you guys play."

"Now, Carlos, you are an interesting young man," Mr. Moza began. "I am not usually wrong about judging characters. Very seldom, actually. And I see something in you, great potential in that world that you refer to as 'politics.' I would invite you to reconsider. You have great potential. Many more men like you are needed. We can start with the city of Miami. What would you care to diagnose as wrong in the city of Miami? What do you think we need here that we don't have right now?"

"More impartiality to begin with."

"Well, Carlos, that is a funny word, son. You cannot achieve anything if you are impartial, you see? Nothing gets done unless you take a side. You cannot achieve sitting on the fence."

"That may actually be true, Mr. Moza, in the dirty game of politics. What is the name of that song that says, 'I would rather drive a truck'?"

"'Garden Party,' my boy, by Ricky Nelson. He batted a home run with that one. I remember it like it was yesterday. I was a young man like you back then. People ridiculed him for trying to be different. They mocked him, and he took it in stride. He wrote it all down and said it with music. He made a million dollars off them later, as he told them their own story, and the song went to number one on the charts. 'But if memories were all I sang, I'd rather drive a truck.' That's what he said."

"I never knew that, Mr. Moza. I don't even know the song."

"I've heard of it," Roberto said. "But I did not know the story."

"It's a hard-earned lesson," Mr. Moza said. "It is what they call in Spanish a *moraleja*. It means a moral story from which a lesson is to be learned. People will not always be in agreement with what you do, but you must always do what you feel is right. That is what it means, and that is precisely what's going on in our country right now. You must do what is right, no matter how unpopular."

Carlos seemed as if he was going to answer, but Mr. Moza put out his hand.

"Carlos, I know," he said. "I know how you feel about the whole thing, son. I know. But hold that thought for a moment. Hold it. Just think. You could make it all come true, Carlos. Your dreams, your hopes for the future. There's room in the city of Miami for you. It desperately needs men like you."

"Mr. Moza," Carlos said. "I am not a Republican. I'm not even a politician."

"That's just a word, son. It's just another word that you must adhere to, but not really. It's a term that will serve you well. You have a young and pretty wife there, Carlos. You're going to have a family now. You need this word."

"Mr. Moza," Roberto interrupted. "I like Carlos too, but aren't you seeing a little bit too far in him?"

"Now, Roberto, do not feel threatened. You must learn to recognize bare talent, my boy. It is the secret to success in life. Why do I say that? You can't do everything yourself. You need other hands. This young man is not to be wasted."

"So where could we put him exactly?"

"Commissioner, councilman, someday mayor, someday congressman, and who knows what else someday? The point is, we need him. We need him very badly."

The waitress returned with Mr. Moza's order and that of his companion. She also brought the others' tray and began to distribute the plates. Two couples who had gotten off their tables stopped near Mr. Moza and said hello. He waved back at them.

"It's a hard sale, Mr. Moza," Roberto said. "Carlos is apolitical."

"That will change," Mr. Moza said.

"The tamales are great," Carlos commented. "Yasmin and I always eat them."

"A lot of work goes into making them," Mr. Moza said. "Imagine that a crop is turned into flour by bare hands. That is how it used to be made many moons ago, before there were machines to grind them. Deep in the countryside of Cuba, peasants would spend a full day beating the corn to seed it into a pulp."

"Mr. Moza," Carlos cut in. "I remember that being done in my house way after there were machines to grind the corn. Actually, it is still being done like that in the countryside of Cuba today, where time has stood still."

"Well, I'm sure that is true," Mr. Moza said, "but that is another side of the story. The peasants there know how to survive without today's technology. Miracles still happen there, but not that many. Your family is one of the good ones. The hard-working families that have kept their customs alive or have been forced to in order to survive. Corn is a very important staple, a product of the New World, I might add."

"Mr. Moza," Carlos said, "your food is getting cold, sir."

Roberto laughed out loud.

"Mr. Moza can get ahead of himself sometimes," Roberto said.

"You are right," Mr. Moza answered. "Mr. Prieto, let's join our friends and supper."

Mr. Moza and his partner ate similar entries, white rice, ripe fried plantains, and shredded beef. They ate slowly and sipped wine as they went along. The conversation seemed to have reached a plateau, and it was Roberto's turn to shift it back.

"Where do we meet tomorrow, Carlos?"

"City Hall," Carlos answered. "Yasmin and I will be there early."

The two looked at each other and smiled. The moment was theirs, and they both were eager to be alone.

"I'd like to make a toast," Roberto said. "Carlos, let's get you and Yasmin a drink."

"I have to drive, Roberto," Carlos said, grabbing his glass of water.

Yasmin joined him.

"To a great friend and his bride," Roberto announced.

They all lifted their glasses, and Mr. Moza followed the announcement.

"May time rain happiness on the two of you," Mr. Moza said. "Congratulations," everyone at the table echoed Roberto. Carlos nodded.

"Thank you," Carlos and Yasmin said in unison.

"We are going to leave you to your discussions," Carlos said. "Yasmin and I are headed for the beach."

"Again?" Roberto asked. "What is it with you and the beach?"

"It's about Yasmin and me."

Roberto nodded, never once looking at Yasmin. Carlos and his bride went around the table, shaking everyone's hand. Mr. Moza grabbed him by the arm to get his attention.

"One of these days you will have to stay and hear us," Mr. Moza said. "It's a prerogative."

"I will keep that in mind," Carlos replied.

CHAPTER 22

Carlos and Yasmin laid on the sand so close to the water that the incoming waves would sometimes touch their bare feet. It did not matter to them. It made them feel ecstatic, a feeling of warmth and passion for each other as they hugged and rolled on the sand. Then they sat a ways back from the rolling waves, watching the distant boat lights on the dark horizon and softly whispering to each other.

"What if the two of us could go to Guatemala?" Carlos asked. "Would you take me there?"

"Yes," she replied softly.

"Where would you take me?"

"We would go to Jutiapa and Xococ to see where I lived."

"Why not to see where you were born?"

"It's very poor there. You might not like it."

"You'd be surprised about how poor it is where I come from."

"Yes, you told me, but this is more than poor. It's dirt poor."

"Still, Yasmin, you should not be embarrassed about your roots, no matter how humble. It's not a sin to be born poor."

"I know."

"We have to see a lawyer after we marry and start your paperwork to make you legal. You cannot be without immigrant status."

Yasmin nodded.

"I can't wait till tomorrow," she said.

"Neither can I."

"I'm happy Roberto is going to be our witness."

"Yeah, and his wife Amelia."

"Do you think she is sincere when she offers me company?"

"I don't know. Why, you think she's not?"

"I can't be sure."

"You'd rather not have them as our witnesses?"

"No, I think it's okay."

"I think they are the kind of people who talk too much. They have their set ways, but they can actually be very loyal."

"I think so too."

They kissed and hugged close, watching the dark waters ahead.

CHAPTER 23

The next morning was a typical sunny one in Miami and already hot even at an early hour. Yasmin was up early. It had been well established between she and Carlos that she would be the early riser of the two. She watered the plants outside and prepared breakfast. She retrieved the wedding dress from the closet and hung it on the louvered doors. Then she headed for the bedroom to wake up Carlos.

She whispered in his ear that it was time. He jumped, hearing her voice, and quickly sat on the edge of the bed.

"What time is it?"

"It's past 8:00."

"Oh, boy, I must get ready quick."

"Come and eat breakfast first."

"I will be right there."

He went inside the bathroom to brush his teeth. Yasmin placed breakfast on the table, and the two ate together. Then she carried the dress to the bedroom and dressed. It was a high-neck embroidered shoulder top and conventional skirt below the knee. As she came out of the room wearing it, Carlos suddenly stepped back.

"Yasmin, you look beautiful," he said.

She did not answer him but came close and kissed him.

"I will fix my hair, and then we can go. We don't want to be late."

She rearranged her braid, and looking at herself in the mirror, she decided to wear it outside the dress. She had contemplated tucking it inside, but no, that would not look right, not to mention it would feel uncomfortable. She seemed younger after she released it down, packed so tight to the roots of her hair that you would not notice that she wore a braid at all, unless she turned her back. Carlos seemed stunned again as she walked into the living room. He had quickly put on a brown suit and tie and sat down waiting. She came close and fixed his tie. Then the two walked to the car hand in hand. Clasping her small soft pebbled pink purse and wearing her silver peep-toe short heels she looked astonishingly beautiful.

Carlos stopped at the flower shop, where he had ordered flowers. It was a small white peony bouquet that he had ordered two days back, and the girl at the shop counter fetched it for him as soon as he entered. Carlos carried it in his left hand, hidden behind him as he opened the passenger door, and handed it to Yasmin. He was too choked up to speak, and she became mute as he laid the flowers on her lap.

"Oh, Carlos! How beautiful!"

They headed for City Hall at Pan American Drive, a short distance from the wharfs where the smell of salt water permeated their surroundings. They went inside the building through the double glass door and checked with a clerk.

"Your bride looks beautiful," the clerk said from inside. "Just beautiful."

Carlos thanked her, and he and Yasmin sat down in one of the row seats in the main lobby to wait.

"I do not see Roberto yet," Carlos said.

"What happens if he does not come?"

"We can't marry without witnesses," Carlos said.

One of the side doors opened, and a familiar figure walked towards them. Wearing a beige suit and his hair meticulously combed back, Mr. Moza leaned over to kiss Yasmin.

"You look fantastic, dear," he said to Yasmin. "Precious."

"Mr. Moza, what a surprise," Carlos said. "How did you know?"

"I work here, remember?" he said. "Well, not exactly. I am a county officer, and I know my way around. I would not miss a friend's wedding for the world. We even have a judge here for you. I made sure of that."

"But your office is not here, right?"

"Technically not, but I made it a point to be here."

"We thank you," Carlos said.

"Yes, thank you," Yasmin repeated.

"It's my pleasure, dear, totally a pleasure. We will wait until Roberto and Amelia get here, and then I will get you inside to see the judge in no time. Are you maybe a little nervous?"

Yasmin nodded her head and smiled at him slightly. She was surprised by his presence, feeling a little guilty for having misjudged him. Mr. Moza seemed like a wise older gentleman who knew all the tricks. He seemed to be everywhere at the right moment.

"Your flowers are precious. Could that be Carlos who chose them?"

"Yes," she said, glancing passionately at Carlos.

"It was a surprise," Carlos said.

"Those are the ways of a true gentleman," Mr. Moza said. "True, Yasmin?"

She nodded her head, and he patted her on the shoulder.

Right through the front door at that very moment, Roberto and Amelia came in. Amelia walked towards Yasmin, noting how beautiful she looked. Yasmin stood up, and the two women embraced. Roberto shook her hand.

"Well," Mr. Moza said. "This means we now have a full crew. I will get them to call you."

He went inside through the same door. Carlos handed Roberto his phone and asked him to take pictures of him and Yasmin. It was Amelia who surprised the couple the most when she approached them.

Fate Has Its Favorites

"I need to tell you that Yasmin looks exceptionally beautiful," she said. "She reminds me of a doll I got one time for Kings' Day. What did you do to your braid? It's hardly noticeable today."

Yasmin smiled gently.

"I think she should show her braid more. It's beautiful."

"No, I like this way better," Amelia said. "She looks so much younger, like a little girl. Are you sure you're eighteen?"

"Twenty-two," Yasmin replied.

"Hold it," Roberto said, snapping a few pictures. "Amelia, move in the middle of them."

The young girl behind the window called them through a microphone, and they all moved towards the door, where a buzzer rang out, and they went inside. The aide led them into a room where a judge and a clerk were waiting for them behind a desk. Mr. Moza sat on a chair in a corner of the room, legs crossed. He smiled happily at them.

Judge Stevens introduced himself and explained the procedure. Mr. Moza got up just as the judge was about to begin with the questions.

"Excuse me, Judge," he said. "They need to line up properly."

He signaled Roberto to move next to Yasmin and Amelia next to Carlos.

"Now, pay attention," he whispered to Carlos and Yasmin."

"Thank you, Mr. Moza," the judge said.

The judge proceeded to ask the questions. Carlos answered quickly, having the advantage of knowing the language. Yasmin was slower but still answered adequately. Then Carlos placed a ring on Yasmin's finger, and they kissed. Then the judge thanked the newlyweds and the witnesses.

Mr. Moza opened the door for the wedding party to come through. He nodded to the court's staff and the judge.

"Let me be the first one to congratulate you," Mr. Moza said.

He shook their hands, and Roberto and Amelia came next.

"Well, can we go somewhere to have a toast?" Roberto asked.

"Can we do that tonight?" Carlos asked.

Roberto seemed unsettled at his refusal.

"Let them have their time," Mr. Moza said. "They have earned it."

Amelia elbowed her husband discreetly.

"We are just going to walk by the piers together," Carlos said. "But we promise we will meet you at the restaurant tonight. I really appreciate your coming here for us. That was a gesture we will never forget."

"Congratulations," Amelia said.

Carlos and Mr. Moza shook hands. The old man stayed with Roberto and Amelia as Carlos and Yasmin drifted away holding hands.

"It sure is hot wearing this suit, Yasmin. I think I want to take off my tie."

They stopped walking, and she handed him the flowers. She undid his tie, and he clumsily took his jacket off. She took the flowers back, and they walked through the piers, admiring the boats that swayed near them. Carlos's phone vibrated, and he picked it up.

"What's up, Gordon?"

"I wanted to be the first to congratulate you. I called as soon as I knew."

"Thanks, Gordon, but you are actually late, even though you call every minute, every hour of the day."

"Congrats anyway," Gordon said. "Where will I find you tonight? Oh, I guess you'd be at that wagon restaurant, right? You won't make an exception even on your wedding night?"

"My wife actually likes it as much as I do."

"Good, I will see you there tonight."

CHAPTER 24

Carlos and Yasmin stayed at the Fontainebleau Hotel in Miami Beach after the wedding. Neither one of them wanted company. They needed time alone. They went for a splash swimming at the beach in the early evening to avoid the sun. Then they came back and showered. They both knew they could not avoid their date with Roberto and the others at La Carreta. There would be a toast and music there for them. Besides, who could say no to Carlos's boss, Gordon?

Yasmin wore an over-the-knee baby blue dress they had bought for the occasion. She again stole her husband's heart as she uncoiled her braid and let it down to her waist.

"Is this a new look you are purposely wearing now? You look the same as this morning. It's like the lights come on as you walk around the room."

She kissed him and held his hand.

"Let's go. Our friends will be waiting."

"We'll keep them waiting," he said, hugging her.

"Really," she said. "We should not keep them waiting."

They went to the lobby, and Carlos asked for their car from the valet parking attendant. The sun was setting, and a golden aura had set in between the two tall buildings of the hotel. They went to the check-in area, and a young woman asked how she could help them.

"We are in room 405. We are going for dinner in the southwest area and will be back late," Carlos said.

"That is fine, sir. We will hold any calls that come for you. Drive safely."

She gave them a cheery smile, and they both stepped out to the hotel's front driveway, where their car was waiting. Carlos tipped the attendant and eased slowly onto Collins Avenue. Traffic was busy, and they went with the flow until they found an exit to turn around and come up the opposite way to pick up 195 and 836 and eventually Bird Road, where unknown to them a crowd was awaiting them.

Carlos did not park in the rear as he usually did. It was a special evening. He and Yasmin had been married. But it seemed highly suspicious that a parking space would be available right in front of the window service counter, or *ventanita,* at this time. Nevertheless, Carlos took the spot thinking that he and his bride had merely gotten lucky.

They exited the car and passed unsuspectingly by the few scattered patrons sipping coffee and chatting by the window. They went inside, and Carlos told the cashier they would choose a table by the far end of the room.

"Go ahead, Carlos," she said. "The waitress will be there in a few seconds."

Carlos and Yasmin went to the very end of the room and picked a table. Carlos was aware that Roberto and the others would be coming, so they picked the larger table of two. An unusual number of tables were vacant around them. They sat down and began discussing how much they would enjoy the beach tonight, sitting on the sand near the water and getting their toes wet by the incoming waves.

A nearby chatter made them look behind them. It was a large group of people, Roberto and Amelia leading the way. They were all known faces to Carlos, some truck drivers, some regulars who came to the restaurant on a regular basis, and there was of course Mr. Moza and Mr. Prieto but wearing suits tonight. There were also women in the group, spouses of some of the men.

"Congratulations," they kept saying.

Carlos and Yasmin stood to receive them, and slowly, everyone hugged Yasmin. Most of them were meeting Yasmin for the first time. She hugged everyone who came to her, and after the last one had given his embrace, there were tears in her eyes. Carlos drew her close, trying to ease her emotion.

"We had no idea," Carlos said. "We did not know."

"Please, everyone sit down," Roberto called. "We are all here to honor our friend Carlos and his lovely wife, Yasmin. Yes," he said, pointing towards Yasmin. "This lovely lady is now Yasmin Figueroa. Can we all wish them a big congratulations?"

"Congratulations!" everyone yelled in unison.

"In a couple of minutes, our favorite waitress is going to go around your tables, and she will be pouring some champagne in your cups, and we will have a formal toast to our dear couple here. Let's give our waitress, Marlene, a chance to get through, please. Then you can choose your favorite dish from the menu, all in honor of our wedding party here tonight."

Roberto walked by Amelia, who was sitting at the same table as Carlos, circled by Mr. Moza, Prieto, Ralph, and others. He waited until the waitress filled everyone's glasses. The group had grown to well over twenty, occupying half of the tables in the room. Some onlookers who had strolled in came towards Carlos and Yasmin to congratulate them. Roberto stood up again, cup in hand, and waited for silence.

"I will pass on the torch to Mr. Moza, who will make the toast for our friend," Roberto said getting up.

Mr. Moza left his seat and stood near Carlos, addressing all four tables.

"You might say that this was a rushed meeting, but not really. When you look at the bride you know the answer. How could Carlos not rush to marry such a beautiful bride?"

There were soft smiles among the tables.

"Our couple is young, resolute, and smart. We are honored to have them as our guests tonight. Carlos is our dear friend, our compatriot, one of our future leaders, and now we know his lovely bride. We have them here tonight, for the first time appearing as Mr. and Mrs. Figueroa, and tell me, ladies and gentlemen, don't they look a lovely couple? We are the first ones to lay eyes on them as a married couple."

Mr. Moza paused to allow for the inevitable applause. He then lifted his hand holding a full cup of champagne.

"Let's drink to Carlos and Yasmin's health and happiness. Carlos and Yasmin," he said, "we wish you a long and healthy life together."

Mr. Moza took a sip of champagne, and everyone followed. Then he approached the couple and shook each of their hands. He stepped back to allow the others to congratulate the couple.

A burly-looking man, wearing a short-sleeve summer shirt and dress pants, stood in queue to congratulate the couple. He approached the table and looked straight at Yasmin.

"Are you the lady who stole my driver?" he asked in English.

Yasmin smiled at him, not understanding.

"Yasmin," Carlos said in Spanish, "this is Gordon, my boss."

"Oh, so we are going to play the language game to evade me, ah? Well, I can speak Spanish too. You stole my driver," he repeated in Spanish.

"He's kidding you," Carlos said.

"No, I am not," Gordon said, handing her an envelope. "Congratulations."

"Find a seat and stay a while," Carlos told him.

"I see a few of my drivers here. I will find a seat and remain incognito."

"I can be back on the road in a couple of days. We just need till the weekend."

Gordon nodded and smiled mischievously. Behind him came a man walking with a limp and accompanied by a woman who held his arm.

"Congratulations," they both said to Carlos.

"Alfredo!" Carlos responded. "How are you doing?"

"I am well. This is my wife," the man said pointing to the woman next to him. "Are you still driving by Route 10 near Jacksonville?"

"Yes, all the time."

"Be careful."

They shook hands with Carlos and exchanged other pleasantries. After meeting everyone, Carlos and Yasmin left their seats to converse with some of the guests, going from table to table, ending at the last seat of the first table where Gordon sat, surrounded by drivers.

"I will give you a break tomorrow," he said to him. "I think you and your beautiful bride need some time. But the orders are stocking up. I will be begging you to make a couple of long trips up north. I am struggling with the orders."

"Gordon, I just got back from a long trip for you. How busy could it be?"

"I can't send many other drivers on these trips, the company here excepted, of course. These are long trips that need experienced drivers. You may even have to haul two trailers. That's the kind of market that we have out there now. And the thing about it is punctuality. When I send a load out, I need to be sure that delivery will be made at the time I promised, or else I'm out of business."

"Gordon, we are having a wedding, please."

Carlos turned to Yasmin and put his arm around her shoulders.

"You two look great, by the way," Gordon said smiling. "You have to thank me for creating the opportunity for you to meet. You met in Phoenix when I sent you there on a trip."

"I was on my own time when it happened."

"I put you there. Yasmin, what do you say about that?"

"I thank you," Yasmin answered in Spanish.

"So, you understand English more than I thought, right?"

"I understand more than I can speak," Yasmin said.

"Ah, you will be speaking English in no time. Carlos will teach you."

"I need someone to teach me," Carlos replied.

"Hold it now," Gordon said, raising his hand. "I have to tell you, Yasmin, that Carlos learned a lot of his English driving my trucks."

"That's not so true. I was fluent before I took the job."

"You could only say 'water' in English," Gordon said. "You learned the language while being on the road. I remember worrying about it after I sent you on a trip."

"I had a good handle on the language, but I did learn more after I went on the road. I owe you that," Carlos said.

"Good. Can we all have a drink now?"

"I can't drink, Gordon. I'm driving."

"Don't you live around here?"

"We are staying in Miami Beach."

"Oh, way to live."

"Yeah, right," Carlos said, patting him on the shoulder.

Carlos and Yasmin went back to their seats, as supper was now being served. Roberto, Amelia, and Mr. Moza were sitting at their table.

"May I ask where your honeymoon is going to be?" Mr. Moza asked.

"At the beach," Carlos replied. "We have a room at the Fontainebleau."

"Oh, splendid. Yasmin, how do you like the hotel?"

"It's beautiful," she nodded.

"Wow, Carlos, you surprise me," Roberto added. "You went all out."

"You are staying at the Fontainebleau?" Amelia asked. "Yasmin, isn't it beautiful, honey? Have you ever seen anything like it?"

"No," Yasmin replied. "Never."

The waitress came by their table, bringing their orders.

"I do not recall ordering," Carlos said.

"It's okay, Carlos," Amelia said, laughing. "We took care of it ahead of time."

"Did anybody else order?"

"We all did, except for you and Yasmin. It's our treat. We know your taste."

The waitress was standing right next to him, holding a tray.

"Congratulations," she said to them. "You look just gorgeous, honey," she said to Yasmin. "Can you tell me your secret?" she asked her in a whisper, as she placed a plate of *moros* and tamales before her.

Yasmin shook her head, smiling.

"She was born beautiful," Carlos said and smiled at her.

The waitress served Carlos a bowl of chicken and noodle soup, steaming slightly.

"We all know how much you love soup, even in 90 degree weather."

"Soup is like a medicine to me. It relaxes me. It reminds me of my mother. She used to make an unbelievable soup."

"Do your parents know?" Roberto asked.

"We both told our parents last night. They are expecting our calls tonight, both Yasmin's parents and mine."

"That's very appropriate," Mr. Moza commented. "You must never forget, Carlos."

Two police officers came to their table and congratulated the couple. They were regulars at the restaurant. They turned to Mr. Moza and tipped their hats. They were followed by a man in a gray suit.

"This is Judge Stevens," Mr. Moza said. "He is the judge who married you today."

The judge stretched out his hand to Carlos, and then he leaned over and embraced Yasmin.

"Congratulations," he said. "You both look lovely."

Mr. Moza got up to shake hands.

"Thank you so much for coming, Judge. It's greatly appreciated. Will you stay for a drink?"

"I thank you. I am actually on my way home from work. I had late court."

"I understand," Mr. Moza said. "This is Roberto, as you know, and his lovely wife."

Roberto and Amelia stood up to shake the judge's hand.

Carlos gazed at Yasmin.

"I've never seen a more beautiful bride," he said.

She smiled at him.

"Drink your soup," she said.

Carlos took a large spoonful, suddenly wondering how Mr. Moza had managed to get the judge to attend their ceremony and for what purpose, if not only to show his influence. That Mr. Moza was some character.

CHAPTER 25

Late that evening, after the swimmers had left the beach and the music was playing loudly at the hotels, Carlos and Yasmin walked barefooted towards the oncoming waves. They were wearing shorts and did not stop when a wave bathed their feet but held hands and went on. They kept walking until the water reached their chests. Carlos suddenly swam under, got in between Yasmin's legs, and lifted her over his shoulders. She screamed and quickly held on to his shoulders.

"Ready for a splash?"

"No, not really."

She screamed again as he tilted her forward. Carlos knew she was a good swimmer, but he had yet to try her skills. Out of caution he reached out, grabbed her, and straightened her body.

"We are not that far away," Carlos said. "Do you want to swim farther out?"

"No," she said, shaking from the splash.

"So, let's swim sideways towards the other beaches. Watch for the incoming waves. They will drag us if we don't move along."

They began to stroke, the two moving parallel to each other, and Carlos kept close. He was a skilled swimmer and swam at a steady distance from Yasmin. They were sluggish at first but then began to pick up a steady pace. Under the reflection of the lights of the hotels, their bodies could be seen gaining ground as they stroked forward, by now almost in perfect unison, with Yasmin gaining a few inches ahead on Carlos and he quickly catching up. He was so close to her that he would touch her back on occasion as they moved forward.

There were hardly any bathers at the beach. A small group of youngsters gathered near the glare of the hotel's lights, siting in the sand, telling each other stories. They could not help but notice Carlos and Yasmin swimming freestyle in long strokes so well timed that they seemed to be made by the same person. Some in the group yelled out to the couple.

"Great show!" someone said. "You are the perfect pair!"

Carlos gave them a wave with one arm up.

"Fantastic!" someone else yelled.

Slowly, Carlos and Yasmin passed them by, each second stroking the water at the same exact moment, turning their faces to their right to breathe. They kept moving in a straight line, unaffected by the swaying movement of the waves that rocked them.

They stopped after a good half-mile, standing up with the water reaching their chests and holding each other. Yasmin laid her head on his shoulder, turning sideways.

"I love how we swim together, Carlos. I can't believe we had such coordination. I love how we do everything."

"We are two halves put together, Yasmin. There are no other ones like us."

"Promise?"

"Yes, forever."

They kissed and began swimming back, again passing the small crowd that cheered them on."

They reached the spot where they had left their towels and dried off. Then they sat in front of the ocean watching the distant lights of the boats that had anchored in.

"Wouldn't you like to go on a ride in one of them?" Carlos asked.

"Only if you are with me," she answered.

"Where else would I be?"

She kissed him, and he held her hand.

"What did you think of our party?" she asked.

"They really got us, didn't they?"

"Yes, very much. It was such a surprise."

"Even our judge came."

"How did he know to come?"

"I think Mr. Moza did it."

"Where does Mr. Moza work?"

"He's some type of commissioner for the city. He's an elected official who pulls strings."

"Well, it was nice."

"Yes, I think you won him over. You won all of them over."

They embraced, and she rested her chin over his shoulder.

"I only want to win you over."

CHAPTER 26

Carlos and Yasmin returned back late to their hotel room. They owed it to themselves to spend their first married night in the way they desired, and for them, that was the ocean. It was past midnight when they arrived, finding their room tidy and clean. Then, to their surprise, they saw the several bouquets of flowers in the night table along with gift boxes and wedding balloons that reached up to the ceiling. Carlos and Yasmin were stunned.

"How did these get here?" Carlos asked.

"I don't know, darling. Who sent them?" Yasmin asked.

Carlos read some of cards attached to them.

"Someone must have delivered them to our room while we were at the beach. How thoughtful. This one is from Gordon, my boss," Carlos observed. "How do you like that? Gordon can actually be a gentleman. Have you noticed that he has not called me?"

"He wants to give us time alone."

"But make no mistake, after tomorrow he will start."

"No, not so fast."

"The man does not rest. He does not sleep. He's amazing."

Yasmin held her open hand to her mouth to hide her chuckle. She went instinctively to one of the bigger boxes with a bigger than usual balloon and turned the card open.

"This is from Mr. Moza," she said.

Carlos looked at it and wondered out loud.

"What could it be? Shall we open it?"

"Yes."

The box was covered in white paper, which she easily unwrapped and then slowly pulled the box out and opened it. There, before their eyes, was a folded dark red garment with designs in yellow and blue. Neither Yasmin nor Carlos had any idea what it was.

"I don't know what that is," said Carlos.

"Let me unfold it to see," she replied.

She went from the size of a napkin to a vast glossy sheet decorated busily throughout.

"I think it is a tablecloth," Yasmin said.

"It's beautiful," Carlos commented.

"It is. It's gorgeous."

"It's made in Hungary," Carlos said, reading from the card.

"You can only use that on certain occasions. The cloth is very thin and can be spotted easy."

"What detail," Carlos added.

"Sure, very detailed. Does he come from Hungary?"

"No," Carlos said laughing. "He comes from where I come from. He probably traveled there."

"Should we open everything?" she asked.

"We can take them home tomorrow. Why don't we call our parents now?"

"Which ones first?"

"Can we call yours first?"

She dialed her parents' number. It was a long-distance call, and she placed the call on speaker. The groan of an older woman was heard at the other end. Yasmin told her that she and Carlos had just married. She paused and then congratulated her, giving her a blessing. Yasmin asked for her father, but she said he was sleeping. They lived in a village, near a rural area. If there were any news, it was expected that the caller would have them. Yasmin said that Carlos was a sweet man and that he wanted to meet them. Did she want to speak to him?

She said yes, and Yasmin handed the phone to Carlos. They exchanged pleasantries, and Carlos said he was anxious to meet her and her husband.

It was then Carlos's turn, and he called his parents' number. The reception was livelier. The woman who answered the phone was cheerful, showing anticipation in her voice.

"Carlos, why haven't you called me? I've been waiting."

"We needed some time, Mom. Yes, we did it, and here she is to talk to you."

Carlos passed the phone to Yasmin. The voice at the other end was going even before Yasmin had the phone.

"Yasmin, is this you? Are you real?"

"Yes," Yasmin answered. "How are you?"

"I'm fine, *mija*. I'm fine, just waiting for the two of you all day."

"We had the ceremony late in the morning and then—"

"I know, I know. But tell Carlos to call me. I was waiting all day."

"Is your husband home?"

"She is, mija. But he is sleeping. He has milking to do. He'll be up in three hours. I can't wake him up."

Yasmin looked at Carlos and smiled. She knew she was in for a long one. Evelia was her name, and she went on for ten minutes describing her day, occasionally interrupting herself to say how happy she was that Yasmin had married her son. And when could she see her? When could they have a video call?

It was Carlos who finally ended the call, promising a video call the next day and much more time, but tonight they were newlyweds, and this was only their first night. They must use their time together wisely. Surely, she must understand. Reluctantly, she let him go but not before making him repeat his promise to call her back during the day tomorrow.

Finally, Yasmin and Carlos laid in bed, still in their bathing suits, their bodies feeling heavy from the salt water. The two showered together and then laid in bed again, watching their TV set. There were no words spoken, just kisses and caresses that took them away into another world, a world of passion and ecstasy that they themselves created.

CHAPTER 27

It was late Friday, two days after their wedding, and now at home in their apartment, Carlos saw Gordon's name pop up on his phone screen. He hesitated before picking up and showed Yasmin his phone. She laughed and nodded, agreeing that he should pick up.

"What's up, Gordon?"

"How is married life?"

"It's great. We barely got going yet."

"You will get acquainted. Give it time."

Carlos would have wanted to keep going. He wanted to tell the world that Yasmin was the lightning bolt that had struck his boring life of driving through the empty highways, never reaching an end. She was what had suddenly awakened a desire in him to engage, to reach for the unknown. But Gordon was bringing him back to the mundane, the world of timely deliveries and punctual pickups.

"I need a big favor, Carlos. It's a matter of life or death."

"Gordon," Carlos said, as if to warn him.

"I hate to do it to you but—"

"Then don't, Gordon. I'm busy."

"Carlos, I wouldn't ask if it was not an emergency. I have no one else to go to. You're the only one."

"Gordon, what is it?"

Carlos looked towards Yasmin, who only smiled back at him as if she knew what Gordon was about to ask, but she would not be bothered by it. She would follow him in whatever he decided.

"I have to get a load to New York City and bring one back by the end of Monday. I had committed myself, but my driver quit on me. Carlos, you can take off all the time you want after that. I know you are on a honeymoon but I really need your help."

"Calm down, Gordon. I will do it tomorrow."

"I owe you my life," Gordon said.

"More than that," Carlos replied ending the call.

Yasmin came towards him and hugged him.

"When are we leaving?" she asked him.

"Tomorrow morning."

"I will get everything ready."

"No," he said holding her by her hand. "Let's go outside for a moment, come."

Carlos stepped onto the porch and pointed to the window boxes. They had changed dramatically. The daisies that had grown sparingly were now surrounded by yellow buttercups, white alyssums, and white cuckoo flowers.

"Yasmin, where did all these flowers come from? How did they grow so fast?"

"I got them as we went shopping, little by little. I wanted to surprise you."

"Darling, I am beyond surprised. I am shocked. How did you do it so fast? And what kind of flowers are they? I've never seen anything like them."

"They are simple little flowers. They are small and grow well in boxes."

"They are magnificent. I just cannot believe it."

He came close to her and kissed her.

"I am so glad you liked them. I tried to mix the colors."

"Darling, you must have the hand of God."

"What time do we leave tomorrow?"

"Oh, I don't know, by six maybe."

"So, I will fix some sandwiches for the road."

"No, darling. We'll buy something off the road."

Carlos sat on one of the chairs, and Yasmin sat next to him. They were about to start their working lives together. It was their first day on the road as a married couple.

CHAPTER 28

Carlos went north on 95. The long stretch of road between Miami and the state border with Georgia was always the longest when traveling north. Carlos had compartmentalized the trip in his mind, and he felt like he was making progress on the road after he entered Georgia. He knew it even if he missed the signs. The springs in both sides of the road and the marsh lands gave it away. It was the first time he and Yasmin traveled this way, going north all the way to New York City.

"We are out of Florida," Carlos said. "This is Georgia."

"Do you want to stop and eat?"

"I wasn't planning to, but we can if you want."

"You have to rest, Carlos. You've been driving more than six hours now."

"I have to make fourteen hours straight. Gordon really needs this load delivered. We can rest for ten hours straight after. We can do the same on the way back."

"You can still take a break though."

"All right, darling. What do you prefer? Wendy's is your favorite, no?"

"I like anything that you like."

There was no use in contradicting her. They each wanted to please the other so much that there was no point in asking. Their desires blended together.

Carlos pulled over at a rest stop at a Wendy's. They went inside, and both got a burger, French fries, and juice, and sat down to eat. The human traffic in and out of the place was relentless. They both sat in front of each other and conversed, as if no one was there.

"We have to get help for your immigrant papers. You cannot go on like this."

"Why?"

"Not having a green card. We have to get some help to do that."

"Does that take a long time?"

"I am not sure. I know someone in Miami who can help us with that. He is the lawyer who helped me get mine. Did you ever try doing any applications when you came?"

"No."

"No one ever told you what to do?"

"No. I heard rumors from different people. Some said to go see a lawyer. Others told me not do anything, that it was dangerous."

"Why?"

"Because they could send me back. I do not want them to take me from you."

"No, Yasmin. Never."

They fueled the truck's tank at the pump and got on Route 95 North again. For Yasmin, it would be the first time seeing such a big metropolis, an impressive sight to anyone. In days to come, their relationship would strengthen even more, reaching new heights in an unprecedented spike of passion.

CHAPTER 29

"Your passion for driving must give way to other avenues in your life," Roberto commented as Carlos and Yasmin sat across from him and his wife in La Carreta, a few days later.

"It is so powerful that it has dragged your wife right into it. There are other modes of life."

"I only love driving as much as you love your job," Carlos answered. "It's the only thing I know to earn a living."

"Oh, baloney. You just haven't tried."

The spring weather had given way to the early summer that had arrived across the tropics. Sitting under the sun proved unbearable for most in the midafternoon, but now in the early evening, some of the customers sat under the umbrellas covering the tables near the entrance. A few feet away from them, the open counter served cup after cup of espresso to the crowds that arrived relentlessly.

Carlos gazed towards Amelia, smiling.

"You still do not want to stay home, Yasmin?" Amelia said.

"No, I am fine traveling with Carlos."

"I can't believe you are still doing that," Roberto said. "You are trapped in that cabin for so many hours."

"We are together," Carlos replied. "This is why we got married."

"But you should spend more time at home."

"We are going to see a home tomorrow."

"What?"

"Yasmin and I are going to look at a house tomorrow."

"Oh, really?" Amelia remarked. "You are going to buy a house? Where?"

"We are looking," Carlos said. "Yasmin likes Miami Springs."

"Carlos, you are shocking me," Roberto said. "I did not know you were looking for a house."

"It's time. I've been saving."

"I know that. You are a hoarder. But a house? That's major."

"Why is that a problem? Don't you have your own home?"

"Yes, of course, but Carlos, that is a tremendous achievement."

"We all need a home."

Roberto glanced at Yasmin quietly. The waitress came to stand by the middle of the table, behind Yasmin, with her electronic tablet, ready to take their order.

"I will have chicken soup," said Carlos. "Yasmin, what are you having?"

"I am going to have a tamal with salad," Yasmin said.

"How about a steak that we both can share? Some *yuca* on the side?"

"Okay."

Carlos gazed at the waitress and nodded. She then turned to Roberto, who seemed to ignore her.

"So where will you be looking?" Roberto asked.

"We were in Miami Springs today. We are going to see another house in South West Miami tomorrow."

"Where in South West?"

"It's on 125th Street. It's a high number, but we drove by it, and we liked it."

"Sir," the waitress interrupted. "What will you and Amelia like?"

"Oh, yes." Roberto turned to Amelia. "What are we having, Amelia?"

"Let's go light, Roberto," she said. "How about some soup, first?"

"No, let's eat solid food. Leave that for Carlos."

Roberto gazed at Carlos, then at the waitress.

"We will have the *vaca frita*," he said. "We'll have some wine too."

"Roberto, you have to drive," Amelia scolded him.

"One cup, Amelia, one cup. Bring it on," he said, looking at the waitress.

"All right," she answered and turned away.

"Where exactly on 125th Street is this house?" Roberto asked, turning to Carlos again.

"Can't remember the number. We have a picture. Darling, can you show him?"

Yasmin retrieved her phone from her purse, tapped on the screen, and passed it to Roberto.

"Oh, yeah, that is elegant," Roberto said, nodding in approval. "We're going to be close."

"Let me see, let me see," Amelia said, reaching for the phone.

"Does it have a pool?" Roberto asked.

"Yes. That is a must for us."

"Yes, you guys are swimmers."

"We are more of salt water swimmers, but we have to think of the future, you know, kids."

"Kids?"

"Hey, hey, hey!" Amelia suddenly shrieked. "This house is gorgeous, Carlos. Who found it? You or Yasmin?"

"Carlos did," Yasmin replied.

"No, not quite. We have a Realtor, and we are working with her. She suggested it. We are just following. But we are going to see it tomorrow."

"We did not know you were looking for a house," Amelia said.

"Well, we need to find a place to live."

"Yes, you need to stop living in a truck."

"Where is Mr. Moza?" Carlos asked. "It's strange here without him."

"No need to worry about that one. He'll pop out any minute."

The waitress returned and brought their orders on a cart. She served Carlos and Yasmin first then turned to Roberto and Amelia and placed their dishes, covered with stainless steel tops to keep the meat warm.

"Roberto, what am I going to do with all this food this late in the day? This is too much."

The waitress poured wine into their glasses. She turned towards Carlos and Yasmin and pointed to the wine bottle as an offer.

"No, thanks," Carlos replied. "We could take one bottle home. Yasmin?"

"Do you want this label?"

"Yes, that would be fine," Carlos answered.

Some distance behind her, Carlos noticed Mr. Moza's familiar figure, wearing his white guallavera and followed by his close ally, Mr. Prieto.

"Good evening, gentlemen," Mr. Moza said, quickly moving to shake everyone's hand.

He leaned forward to kiss Yasmin on the cheek.

"Mr. Moza, there is room for you on the other side," Roberto noted. "Won't you take a seat? How about dinner?"

"Thanks, but we will pass. My wife is waiting for me tonight."

He and Mr. Prieto went around Amelia and Roberto and sat at the table.

"It's an eventful day," Roberto said.

"Do you mean the hearings on the attack at the Capitol?" Carlos asked.

"Attack? What attack?" Roberto asked in surprise.

"So what else would you call it then?" Carlos replied.

"A protest. Protected speech under the First Amendment."

"You could have fooled me. Last I heard, incendiary speech and assaults are not protected."

"You're a very smart man," Mr. Moza commented, broadly smiling.

"Only because I married my wife," Carlos said smiling back.

"That too, of course. You hit a home run when you did that, but it is remarkable that a young man such as you, having lived in this country only a few years, has already a sharp knowledge of the American Constitution. Not to mention your grasp of the language. Ah, yes, the First Amendment. What shall we say about it?"

"We can talk about it all you want, but it is plain to see that it does not apply to what happened that day."

"Yes, it does," Roberto said. "This is what the left claims about protests by Antifa or Black Lives Matter. What's different in this case?"

"This was an attempted coup, supported by the defeated president."

"Hold it now," said Mr. Moza. "Hold it. Think about it. Why would our president do that?"

"We can't wonder about the president being logical. Such a concept does not exist for someone like him."

The waitress returned to inquire from Mr. Moza and Mr. Prieto whether they wanted to order. They declined and thanked her.

"You must not rush, Carlos," Mr. Moza advised. "You must not rush."

"I'm not rushing. I am calling a spade a spade."

"And it's good to do that on certain occasions."

"This is one."

"It's not," Roberto said. "Those people had a right to express themselves."

"Maybe the next time they decide to express themselves, they could do it at your house, Roberto," Carlos went on. "Let's see how much you like them breaking your windows and pounding your walls."

"That's not what happened."

"Watch the tape."

"Oh, those tapes. That's the leftist media, fake news."

"Since when are people's cell phones fake?"

"Wait, Carlos," Mr. Moza said. "Let's talk about the facts first."

"Mr. Moza," Carlos replied dismissingly. "We all know the facts. How can you argue about live images? Why do we need to talk about the facts? We all know the facts."

"What's come over you today, Carlos?"

Roberto gazed at him as if in awe. Carlos did not give in an inch, but then he dropped the discussion with a funny note.

"My soup is hot."

Everyone laughed.

Mr. Moza insisted.

"But wait a minute," he added. "Let's talk about what happened."

"No," Carlos replied. "We can't discuss wannabe facts. Stick to the truth of what happened, and then we can have a discussion. There was an attempted coup on the nation, and a committee is reviewing it. That is what happened."

"I don't agree that's what happened," Roberto added.

"I know you don't agree," Carlos said. "That's why we cannot have a discussion, until we agree on the facts."

"Oh, but I'm afraid that's not correct, Carlos," said Mr. Moza. "This is America after all. Why can't we discuss issues? That is what it's all about. It would be a shame to pass on this."

"Mr. Moza, until you see the attack for what it is, what good would it do for us to have a discussion? You've already thrown a monkey wrench in our discussion that will trip us. So, what's the sense in talking about it? Let's talk about yuca, a staple from our culture."

"And truly, it is a marvelous staple, one that sustained large cultures in the islands such as the Tainos, and it also serves as a source of starch. I am well aware of its many benefits."

The waitress returned with a bottle of wine and handed it to Carlos.

"It's on the house," she said.

"Oh, thanks so much. Yasmin, they gave us the bottle."

Yasmin thanked her.

"You're setting conditions to a discussion," Roberto argued. "A condition to force us to conclude a fact that is not there. Plus making the discussion a failure before we even start."

"Well, I think it's the other way around. No one can tell me that what I saw in the news that day was not a violent attack at the Capitol; that's where it happened. So, you want to bulldoze me into believing what plainly did not happen. I don't want to be forced to negate the obvious."

"This is how wars begin between countries."

"It could be. All you have to do is rely on common sense. What you see is what you get."

"Very well put," said Mr. Moza. "Now, let's go a step further."

"No, Mr. Moza, we can't do it this way. Let's first agree to the facts."

Roberto shook his head in disagreement.

"The facts are being altered by the media," he added.

"Which media, yours?"

Carlos laughed out loud. Then they heard someone's voice shout out from the table behind them.

"That's the left's media!"

This was different. Whoever had said it was not part of this web of friends, and even Roberto became agitated. But then the man continued on.

"What hypocrisy for them to say that it was an attack. And you are crazy," he said, pointing to Carlos. "You are just crazy."

Carlos stood up and turned to the intruder.

"If I am crazy, it's none of your fucking business, man. And who the heck let you in this conversation? Eat your food and choke."

"What's a Democrat like you doing here?"

"Like I said, it's none of your damned business."

"Why do you guys hang out with him?" the man said, turning to Roberto, but Roberto cut him off.

"It's like he told you, none of your business. Eat your food and shut up."

The man looked down at his plate just as the waitress came around, asking if everything was all right.

"Everything is fine," Carlos replied, taking his seat again. "I think they put too much spice in his food."

Carlos pointed to the table behind and laughed. Yasmin took his hand and held it tight. He kissed her.

"Everything is fine," Roberto said. "Too much spice."

Everyone laughed, and Mr. Moza gazed towards the intruder. Whatever the discussion might be, there were lines you could not cross. He nodded approvingly towards Carlos.

"This is what politics does for you," Carlos said.

"It's not even politics," Mr. Moza commented. "There is no excuse for uninvited intrusion. Let us continue our conversation another time."

"I actually want to have it now," Carlos replied.

"No," Mr. Moza said. "Stubbornness is not the way, Carlos."

CHAPTER 30

Several weeks later, Yasmin and Carlos sat at a long table in a legal office downtown, where the purchase of their house was being completed. Carlos had insisted that Yasmin's name be included on the deed of their property, despite her lack of immigration status.

"Not a wise move," their attorney said. "This could have complications in the future if something should happen."

"I want her interest in our property to be protected."

"I understand that. But it could go against you two if your wife does not gain status."

"So what do I have to do for Yasmin to gain status?"

"You have to petition for her."

He was a middle-aged man with copious gray hair that grew from the contours of his temples, and he leaned forward as he handed Carlos a document to sign then leaned back in his chair.

"So, when can we start that?"

"I do not do that kind of work, Carlos. You'd have to contact an immigration attorney."

"Can you recommend someone?"

"I'll give you the name of a friend of mine before you leave."

Carlos handed him the document back, and his attorney then shuffled through some papers and retrieved a few forms.

"These are for Yasmin to sign."

Yasmin was sitting next to Carlos, and he passed the forms over the table to Yasmin.

"What is she signing?" asked Carlos.

"You asked that she be allowed on the title, and the bank had agreed to it, provided she is also on the mortgage. So, we added her to the mortgage."

"They sure don't miss a beat," said Carlos.

"No, they can't, and you can imagine why. They need to protect their interests too. She cannot be on the title if she is not on the mortgage."

Carlos nodded. They had been sitting at the table for more than a half-hour, and he was anxious to receive the keys for the home which he had been told would be his at the end of the session. A woman carrying a tray came in the room, and she went past each of them offering small cups of espresso coffee. All three of them accepted one each.

A man wearing a suit held the door open for a couple to enter the room. The suited man announced them as the sellers, and Carlos's lawyer introduced them to Carlos and Yasmin, who stood up to shake their hands. The midafternoon sun shone through the shuttered windows of the room. Carlos and Yasmin remained standing, anxious to leave and see their new home.

"We are pretty much done," said Carlos's lawyer, handing him the keys. "Congratulations."

He handed them a set of keys in a ring with an emblem bearing the name of the city of Miami.

CHAPTER 31

As the sun was setting down, Carlos and Yasmin arrived in a rented pickup loaded with furniture and some essential clothes. They turned the key in the door and entered their home for the first time. They walked through a long living room with the gleaming parquet floor and sat by a bay window holding hands.

"We are the owners of all this entire property, Yasmin, do you realize this?"

"I do," she said. "And it's you who did it."

"No, it is not. We both did it. Let's go see the pool, darling."

The pool was visible from the Florida room on the left side of the large kitchen and accessible from that room.

"Wow, that water is gorgeous, isn't it?"

"Doesn't it remind you of a still beach in the early morning?"

"It does. I guess you will be swimming laps in the early morning while I am still sleeping."

"No, I will not. But I can see myself drinking a cup of coffee at the edge of the pool, waiting for you to wake up."

"And that's how you see our daily living, Yasmin, right? You will be always the early riser, and me the later sleeper."

She nodded and smiled. They were now standing at the edge of the low end of the pool. The turquoise-colored water looked still and beautiful, now darker with the fall of the evening. Carlos looked around for a utility room and found it in a shed at the far end of the yard.

He grabbed Yasmin by the hand and went inside the shed. He found the switch and flicked it. The entire body of water in the pool was flooded with brightness that came from the sides and the bottom of the pool.

"Wow," he said. "They really got a lot of lights in this pool."

"Maybe we can go swimming in it later on," said Yasmin.

"It would be nice. But we first got to unload some of our furniture, or we'll be sleeping on the floor tonight, and that's hard tile we got there."

"Let's go then," she said. "We can get the bed out first, then shower and go for a light meal."

"We could just order in if you want."

"But we have nowhere to sit. Let's get the bed in and then we can go to La Carreta for a fast meal, no?

"Yasmin, you are hooked, darling. You don't miss a day of La Carreta."

"It can be addictive. I can't deny that I love their tamales."

"And the coffee and the rice and the steaks. Shall I go on?"

"Well, yes, other things too."

The two smiled and hugged each other and went inside the house to turn the lights on. It was a new world for them. The future seemed bright, and they went outside to the pickup to bring some of the furniture inside. This was the beginning of a new era for them.

CHAPTER 32

Carlos and Yasmin got back on the road two days after the purchase of their home. Carlos's boss was relentless in his exigencies and insisted that Carlos cover even longer runs. There was even a call from him to cover a trip to Sacramento, California, which Carlos turned down. There were other requests immediately after until Carlos could not ignore his boss anymore. Carlos and Yasmin found themselves on a trip up north to New York again. It was a straight drive through Route 95 without any turns until reaching New York City. But as it happened occasionally, they were held up near Jacksonville.

"An accident on the road," said the officer directing traffic, looking up towards Carlos as he signaled for him to go forward but then flagging him down again. "Pull up on the shoulder," he said.

Carlos did as he asked. Of course he had no other choice, and not complying with the officer's request would have been unthinkable, and there was no reason why. Carlos drove slowly to the side of the highway, entering the shoulder.

"Hey!" yelled another officer farther up the road. "Where are you going?"

Carlos could not answer him. The traffic was moving fender to fender in a single line past him. To brake suddenly with a loaded wagon could have been disastrous. He slowly pulled over to the shoulder and brought the truck to a dead stop.

"Hey, what's the deal, buddy?" the trooper now yelled, walking up hastily to catch up to Carlos's truck in the shoulder of the highway that had been shut to traffic because of the accident.

A battered vehicle lay right in the middle of the closed two other lanes.

The officer stopped the traffic from moving forward so he could cross the lane. He walked hastily across and came to stand by the driver's door of the truck cabin.

"Step out of the truck," he said, taking a step back to allow Carlos room to open the door. "Come on, step out. I need to see license, registration, insurance, and documents regarding the load you are carrying."

Carlos stepped down from the cabin.

"I need the passenger to step out also."

"What is wrong?"

"Sir, just do as you are told. Are you carrying any weapons?"

"No."

The officer took Carlos's credentials and looked them over. Yasmin came out of the driver's door and stood next to Carlos.

"I need you to keep your hands where I can see them. No hands in pockets. Madam," he said, turning to Yasmin, "I need to see some identification."

"She doesn't have any identification. She's not driving."

The officer uncapped the radio from his left breast and identified himself then reported his location and asked for backup.

"I did not say she was driving," the officer replied. "And it makes no difference. I still need to see identification."

"She is my wife. She keeps me company in my runs, and she does not have a driver's license. She has a passport."

"That'll do."

Carlos asked Yasmin to give him her pocketbook, and with her shaking hand, she passed it on to Carlos. Carlos retrieved Yasmin's passport from inside and handed it to the officer. He turned it around and back.

"What country is this?" asked the officer.

"Guatemala," Carlos replied.

"Guatemala," the officer repeated to himself. "Does she speak English?'

"She speaks a little," Carlos said.

The officer gazed at Yasmin as if trying to decide for himself whether she understood.

"*Habla Inglés?*" he asked.

"A little," Yasmin answered.

"A little," he repeated.

Two state trooper vehicles now pulled over behind them. The second one drove down towards the ditch and parked midway down for lack of room. The officer got out and began redirecting the traffic around Carlos's truck to move forward.

The other two troopers moved slightly away from Carlos and began talking. One of them got on the phone. The other one came straight to Carlos. He was carrying all of the documents Carlos had given him. He seemed older than the other one, and he removed his sunglasses as he got close.

"Everything seems to be in order with your papers, son," he said. "Do you mind if we take a look inside your trailer?"

"No, not at all."

"Ok. Come on, let's go in the back, and you can get the door open for me. Bring her along," he said, pointing to Yasmin. "You should not be standing so close to traffic anyway. Let's go."

The officer let them go first as the two other troopers watched. At the rear of the truck, Carlos yanked the door's handle and opened the door. The trailer was packed to the roof with midsize boxes that seemed identical. The trooper asked Carlos to hand him a box from the trailer. He ripped the tape holding the flaps and tossed the fillers aside until the contents were visible.

"What are these?" the trooper asked. "Do you know?"

"I think it's electronic equipment, according to the papers."

"You don't know what you are carrying?"

"I go by the papers they hand me. I look at the load before I leave and again when I deliver."

"Very good," the trooper said. "That's fair."

At the trooper's signal, Carlos grabbed the box, put it inside the truck, and then closed the door. He was feeling somewhat leery about this stop. He had been stopped by the highway patrol many times before, mostly for weight checkups and equipment, but this was different. It felt different. He noticed the other two officers coming towards them now. The one who had stopped him came up to him and handed him his license back.

"Congratulations," the trooper said. "I think it's the first driving record I've seen without a blemish. A seven-year period and not one ticket. That's something to be proud. How'd you do it?"

"I drive like an old man with a torpedo behind me."

"You mean your trailer?"

"Yes."

"Well, that's understandable. I see that. Your passenger is gonna have to come with us."

"What?"

"She will need to come with us. We have to hold her at the Jacksonville station until ICE comes for her."

"What? She's my wife, sir!"

"She may be but she's also here without immigration status. They'll deal with that."

Carlos grew alarmed. He fidgeted with his hands and then held Yasmin's arm.

"We will take her from here, sir."

"No, she's my wife. I can't let her go by herself."

"You can't interfere, sir. This is technically an arrest. If you interfere then we will have to place you under arrest and take you too. You don't want to do that."

"But wait, how can you do this? What has she done?"

"She is here illegally. She's wanted by Homeland Security."

"But we just got married. We are hoping to build a family."

"You'll have to take that up with them, sir."

The officer put out his hand towards Carlos as a sign for him to stop. Meanwhile the other trooper accompanying him got behind Yasmin and in a heartbeat got her hands behind her back and handcuffed her. Yasmin kept trying to turn her head, but the trooper had grabbed her forearm and moved her forward. That was when Carlos became irate and was about to charge forward, but the older trooper behind him stopped him. He grabbed his arm and got in front of him.

"Son, don't make that mistake," he said softly. "You cannot interfere, or else we will have no choice but to arrest you, and you don't want that to happen. Your wife needs you now more than ever. This is not the way. Hold back."

The other two officers had taken Yasmin away. She had not even been able to say goodbye. Carlos broke down in tears.

"How can this be? We were doing nothing wrong."

"She is undocumented. She should have never been on an interstate highway."

"But still," Carlos said. "We were doing nothing wrong."

"Listen up, son. She is being taken to the Jacksonville local jail. From there, the ICE personnel will come and pick her up and take her to a federal facility. You will have to contact them to find out where she is, and if I may say so, you should get a lawyer. Not any lawyer but an immigration lawyer."

Carlos watched as the troopers crossed the highway, carrying Yasmin by the arm, and he felt an urge to run after them and snatch Yasmin away from them. The older trooper next to him saw it in his eyes.

"Don't even think about it, son. Don't wreck your life. It's not the end of the world. You can fix this."

Carlos was on the verge of tears. He saw how they placed Yasmin in the back of the trooper car and then shut the door. Yasmin searched for him through the window, but Carlos knew she could not see him. Tears streamed down his face.

"She is my wife," Carlos muttered. "We were so happy, and they are taking her from me."

"Has she ever had any dealings with the law in this country? Anything wrong?"

Carlos shook his head. He saw the trooper's car come up from the ditch, where crews were working on the accident scene. It stopped near the outer lane and turned its overhead lights to allow it passage, and the oncoming traffic stopped.

Carlos could no longer make Yasmin's figure at the rear window of the trooper's car. His whole world came crashing down at that moment, and he, oblivious to the friendly trooper standing next to him, leaned against the side panel of the truck and covered his face with his hands and cried. He cried like never before, more than when he said goodbye to his parents on his way to America, more than when he lost himself in the woods one time near his parents' farm. More than he ever would have imagined he could.

"Son," the trooper said. "You have to get going. You need to move your truck. We are blocking traffic here. Come on."

Carlos lifted his head and looked at the trooper, his eyes red and puffy from the tears.

"You gotta go, son. You need to move your truck."

"Move my truck?" Carlos asked bitterly. "How can I move anything? You guys have just destroyed my life, and you want me to move on?"

"Is this the kind of a man your wife married? One small bump on the road, and you are just gonna give up? You need to move on. Your wife needs you. You need to see a lawyer, get your life together. Come on. Let's go."

The trooper grabbed Carlos's arm and helped him straighten up. Nothing anybody else would have said at that moment could have bolstered Carlos's defenses as the trooper just had. In a daze, Carlos walked by the side of the trailer with the trooper behind him. Carlos climbed into the cabin in silence and shut the door behind him. He needed time, but the trooper was right; he needed to get moving, not just on the road but with his wife. He needed to save Yasmin.

He took a couple of minutes to focus. He was on the road driving an eighteen-wheeler. He needed to remember that. He must seek help to save Yasmin. Who would he call? He did not know yet but whoever it was would need to be faithful. The trooper flagged the traffic to stop and give Carlos room to pull out of the shoulder. He waved him to merge onto the road. Slowly, the trailer started to move forward, gradually merging into the lane.

CHAPTER 33

Carlos did not know how he got to the Carolinas. It was barely one o'clock in the morning. Everything seemed a fog, and he had no recollection of having traveled through Georgia. That was a dangerous thing to do for an eighteen-wheeler driver. What had happened in the past four hours? He had just driven, knowing what he did best, and now he found himself at South of the Border, almost halfway the length of his trip north. He had entered the South of the Border stop wedged at the border line between the two Carolinas, and it was weird that he had almost unconsciously made the stop. It was as if his mind knew exactly where he needed to stop to get his mandatory rest. He was near the fourteen-hour deadline. He was parked at the lot where he had slept so many times in other trips. He looked sideways and noticed the empty space next to him. Yasmin's red backpack was lying there, as if she had just left. Then it all came back to him, and the tears slid down his checks He abruptly unclipped his phone from his belt and dialed Gordon's number.

"Gordon, I need your help," he said.

"Where are you?" Gordon asked.

"South of the Border," Carlos replied. "They took Yasmin."

He let out a couple of sobs, and Gordon seemed to go on high alert.

"They took Yasmin? What do you mean they took Yasmin? Who took Yasmin?"

"Troopers stopped me by Jacksonville, and when they found out she was undocumented, they took her. What do I do?"

"Oh, boy. I was afraid this might happen. I thought of it but never told you. It's a high risk when you travel interstate with someone who has no status. Gee. All right, well, you've got to get a lawyer, Carlos. We need to get her out fast; otherwise, they could take her. But hang on, hang on. Don't get desperate. You concentrate on driving and getting there. I will take care of it here. Tell me exactly from where they took her. Where in Jacksonville?"

"At the outskirts of the city. Maybe ten minutes north."

"Past the A1A exit or before?"

Carlos hesitated a moment. Although he had been distressed, he had realized that he needed to mentally photograph the spot where it all had happened. Yes, he had seen the notorious sign for A1A, which led to Highway I-301 past Ocala. He had seen it before.

"Okay, where are you now?"

"I just stopped at South of the Border. My fourteen hours are almost up."

"I'm gonna get on the phone, and I will call you. Get some rest."

Carlos thought it odd that Gordon would be worried about his rest but that was precisely the reason he had called him over any of his other friends. Gordon was a hard shell, but inside was a true friend who appreciated loyalty above all things, and if you had him on your side, the battle was half won. He wanted to relax. He knew there was no other way to face the crisis than by first gaining control of himself. Nothing could be accomplished with a run-down body. For now, he could settle down. He had made the right choice. Gordon would take care of it.

Carlos sat on his bed at the rear of the cabin. It felt like a bunk today and not exactly a bed. It did not feel like home, although it was. It felt like he was on this faraway trip where he found it hard to believe that his wife was not with him. It felt like a strange trip, a trip he should not have undertaken. If he had stayed home a couple of more days, it would have been all right. But now it was too late. They had taken his bride. They had handcuffed her and taken her away as if she were a criminal. When would she be back? How would he live without her?

He finally lay down and sunk his head in the pillow, staring at the ceiling, which was nothing more than the roof of his tractor, which he had seen and wondered at on so many lonely nights. Today was one of those nights. It felt miserable, and he felt so insecure. He missed Yasmin's long braid, her almost solemn stare, her energy. Where was she? What would he do without her? He went through these thoughts methodically, as if his brain created them, and then lodged them at him, one by one, for him to answer. What was he going to do? Gordon was working on it. He need not worry. He was in good hands. Yasmin would be out in no time. In a daze, he fell asleep.

CHAPTER 34

The vibrations of his phone, lying next to him on the bed, woke him. He sat up abruptly on the bed, not remembering anything at first, and then suddenly all of it appeared to him in a flash. He held the phone with his right hand and brought it to his ear.

"Hello."

"We've located Yasmin," Gordon said. "She is in Jacksonville."

"Oh, where is she?"

"ICE has her. That is Immigration and Customs Enforcement. She's detained locally in Jacksonville. She will probably be transferred to another jail tomorrow, where she will be assigned to an Immigration agent and scheduled to see a judge. I got a lawyer working on it. The attorney I hired for her is the best in Miami. He already got in touch with the jail and asked them to let her know he is on the case. This way she won't feel abandoned. You know, she is probably in shock right now, not knowing what will happen, so I tried to move fast. You settle down now, you hear me? You go on north and make this delivery and then get back. I got you stopping in Atlanta on the way back."

"Gordon, wait a minute. Where can I go to see Yasmin? When will they let her out?"

"It's probably going to take a few days, I'm told. Provided she has a clean record, a judge will let her out on bail. As far as seeing her, we won't know until tomorrow, when they transfer her to an Immigration jail."

"And where is the jail going to be at?"

"The attorney tells me that it will probably be somewhere in Orlando or even southern Florida. We don't know for sure."

"I've heard of many people being taken to Louisiana. Is that possible?"

"I know just as much as you, Carlos. I've no idea what they do with people once they are detained by Immigration. This is new to me, but we got a great legal mind working on our side. He knows what he is doing, and he's in the driver's seat already. We will have to wait till tomorrow. You go back and get some sleep now."

"Gordon, who's the lawyer we got?"

"His name is Norman Kline, a namesake of the old days, before the Spanish people invaded Miami. He has an office in Coral Gables. He's an immigration specialist, and he's in control. We have to let him do his job."

"Gordon, I thank you so much for helping me. You don't know what it means to me."

"I do know. All I have to do is look at your face when Yasmin is around you, and I know."

"Gordon, I don't care how much this costs. Whatever I have to pay I will. Even if I have to go drive for the rest of my life to pay for what you've done, I will."

"All you have to do is get that load to New York City, and we are even for the moment."

"No, I mean it, Gordon. Whatever it costs I am prepared to pay. She's bigger than my soul. She's my life."

"I know. That's why I'm on the case. I will call you in six hours. Your time will be up by then. Get that load to New York City and then get back."

"Please try to find out where they took Yasmin."

"Sure thing."

For as far as Carlos could remember, Gordon had never before been the first to end the call. He understood why. Gordon was all about business, and today he was busy. He had taken Carlos's situation to heart and probably was on his way to calling one of his contacts to stir some action. He would find out how to reach Yasmin, among other things.

Carlos laid back down and looked at the time. He had another four hours left of rest. There was no doubt, he thought, that he had made the right choice in choosing Gordon. He felt so sure about it that he closed his eyes and was deep in sleep immediately.

CHAPTER 35

Carlos's trip to the Bronx seemed like another hazy experience. He was painfully aware that his mental awareness was obstructed by the recent events, and he paid more attention to detail than usual. He let his GPS do the driving by guiding him, even though he was well familiar with the Webster Avenue area in the Bronx, where he was now traveling. What he needed was to deliver his load and head on back south past the George Washington Bridge as soon as possible, unless there was a change of plans triggered by Gordon's computerized mind. He held his breath as he saw his boss's name on the phone screen.

"Hello."

"Don't leave the Bronx yet," Gordon said.

"How did you even know I was here?"

Gordon ignored the comment.

"I have a load available at Riverdale. It's half an hour drive from you. Can you make it?"

"Yes, I'm empty already."

"Go for it, kid. Directions are being emailed to you right now."

"Wait, Gordon, wait! Do you know where they're holding Yasmin?"

"I'm working on it. I'm waiting for a phone call."

"Can you call me as soon as you know, please?"

"I'm on it, Carlos. I'm on it."

"Okay, I will go get your load now. I want to go see Yasmin on my way back."

"Don't worry, Carlos. You will see Yasmin."

Carlos felt glad about the tone of the conversation. Gordon's assertive ways gave him an assurance that he needed at this moment of weakness. He was not the usual self-assured eighteen-wheeler driver who drove east and west throughout the country. Perhaps by some strange coincidence, he found himself in New York City today when more than ever, he wanted to be near Jacksonville, close to Yasmin. When he arrived at his next pickup, he got his truck past the gate and felt immediately lost, not knowing where to go. There was no gate to check in. He dialed the number that showed up in his computer screen in the message he had received from Gordon.

"I'm here for a pickup," he said to a female voice that answered. "I'm outside in my truck. Where do I go?"

"Where are you from? What company?"

"Sailor Trucking from Miami," he answered.

Carlos gave her the load number, and she guided him to one of the gates around the building. He backed his truck to the trailer at the gate. He left it running while he went inside the building through a side door to check in. No one was in charge inside. A steady flow of human traffic came and went, and Carlos stood there patiently, waiting till someone heard him.

"Are you here for that trailer?" said a young man wearing a baseball cap; Carlos immediately realized this was not the person he needed to see.

"Yes."

"I will get someone for you."

Carlos watched him run in the direction of the front of the building. It was odd for him to be rushing, but the present situation called for action. He had already computed in his brain the hours he would need to get to Orlando. That's where he was hoping to see Yasmin. He was sure that they would send her there. There was no doubt in his mind. There could not be. But then there was that small darkness of doom. What if they sent her to Louisiana? He had heard of the stories about people being transported there for a final stop before they were sent to their countries of origin. The word was that when someone went to Louisiana, he was gone.

"Hello," said a man holding a clipboard.

He was lean and tall and wearing sunglasses despite the fact that they were inside the building.

"I'm here to hook up the trailer and move on."

"Are you in a hurry?" the man asked somewhat haughtily, with a smirk of a smile.

"When is a driver not in a hurry? I am supposed to deliver this load tomorrow in Atlanta."

"That's not gonna happen," the man said. "It's already afternoon."

"Is there a problem with the load?"

"There sure is. It's not quite ready."

Just then Carlos felt his phone vibrate. He picked up.

"Where are you?" said Gordon.

"I'm here picking up the trailer, but it's not ready," Carlos said.

"What do you mean it's not ready?"

"I'll pass you to the supervisor. Might as well not repeat myself. Here," Carlos said to the man with the clipboard."

From the moment that the man took the phone to his ear, his face became pale from the barrage of insults that Gordon lodged at him. It was obvious that he had been totally unprepared and grabbed the phone, thinking that it would be a routine phone call, another faraway hauler inquiring about an estimated time of pickup so he could get his driver back on the road. But after a couple of head nods, the man was about to lose it, and Carlos came to his aid.

"Give me the phone," Carlos said. "Try to get me out of here and do the best you can. I will talk to him."

Carlos grabbed the phone and tried to control his boss.

"Gordon, it's okay. They're going to get me out of here now. No worries."

"Who is that silly son of a bitch? What purpose does he serve in there?"

"He's all right. He's gonna get me out now."

"Come straight to Atlanta. I will possibly have another load for you in Orlando on your way down."

"How about Yasmin, Gordon? What do you know?"

"I will know before you get to Atlanta."

"Okay, I will be waiting."

"Get out of there as soon as you can."

Carlos clicked the phone off and looked for the man with the clipboard. He was gone, but he noticed a sudden burst of activity at the gate. One man opened the back door of the trailer, and two others went inside to straighten some boxes. They hurried to get the load ready for the road.

CHAPTER 36

On his way south, Carlos kept reminiscing about his new spouse. Her long braid, her silent eyes that seemed to be speaking to him all the time, and her soft manners came to him in images that he could not drive away, even while driving. Perhaps he should not be on the road, he wondered. Perhaps just the breeze would blow him away, that's how fragile he felt, and he did not know what to do next, what his life would be without his Yasmin. Would it all end? Is this what it came to? He was way past the Delaware River when he heard the ring of his phone. He had switched it from vibrating to the ring because he was afraid to miss a call from Gordon. He touched the call option on his screen.

"Yes, Gordon, what news do you have?"

"I have great news, Carlos. She is in Orlando. She's at the women's detention center on John Young Parkway. You probably know where it is."

"Do you have the full address?"

"I will text it to you in a minute. I called you as soon as I knew. She will be all right, Carlos. There will be some bail, but as long as she can be released, the money is not a problem. You have to get down here so you can talk to the attorney in person. There are some papers you have to sign."

"I am getting close to DC now. I probably won't make the drop till the afternoon tomorrow, and then I will head straight down to Orlando to see Yasmin. She must be so anxious, my poor Yasmin."

"You want to know something, Carlos? Yasmin is a tough kid. She may be even tougher than you."

"I don't know about that, Gordon. It was so gruesome how they took her, and we were just married. I'm even afraid for her safety."

"Yasmin is not the breaking type. Yasmin is tougher than you think. She may even call you. The attorney managed to speak to her. He gave her your number. Be on the lookout for her call. It will be a collect call, I'm sure. Listen, you may have to bring me a load from Orlando. I will let you know in a few hours."

"I will bring anything, Gordon, but tell me, what does the attorney think about our case?"

"He's concentrating on getting her released. He thinks he will get her out since she's married to a US citizen. The hard part will come later, after she is out."

"Why is that?"

"I think because of the applications. He'll talk to you about that. Don't worry. Everything is looking good. You just drive, okay?"

"Okay."

Carlos cut the call off, but he would have liked to stay on. He wanted to know what would come next. He wanted to hear assurances that Yasmin would be able to get out and then what he could do to stop them from taking her away again. His eyes got cloudy from the tears, and he thought maybe he should pull over, but that would be a recipe for trouble with an eighteen-wheeler. He knew that. He checked for signs of a rest stop but that was not an easy catch in the DC area. No, he must keep on. Nothing like a real rest stop could be made until Virginia.

He bit his lip as he increased speed from the middle lane. He must be careful. Now was not the time to crumple. He needed strength and clarity to reach Atlanta. That was his goal at the moment. From there he would head on to Orlando, and there was his love, Yasmin, his beautiful wife. He must keep on. He must make the drop in Atlanta and then head off to Orlando. He must keep his sights on Orlando because that is where he would find Yasmin.

CHAPTER 37

The truck moved fast on 95 South, past the boundary line with Georgia and Florida. Carlos had dropped the trailer in Atlanta and pushed himself; he got back on the road immediately, traveling awfully close to the speed limit. He felt like he had a date with Yasmin. All he needed was to get to the detention center in Orlando. But there was that business of the phone call. Gordon had said that Yasmin would call him, and she had not.

The sun was setting, and Carlos must have missed the "Welcome to the State of Florida" sign, but he was fairly confident that he was by the boundary. The silver-plated lakes on both sides of the highway and the uprooted grass islands, growing in scattered bundles on marshy ground, left no doubt that he was about to leave Georgia. Traveling through this area would never be the same for him. He would always remember the spot where the officers had stopped him for reasons that still remained obscure to him. What traffic violation had he made? Why wasn't he ticketed? These things weighed on him because he saw himself as the possible cause for police action that took his wife away. He had gone over those moments before the stop in his mind, any error in his driving habits that may have led that one trooper to order him to pull over. What had he done? The thought that he could have been the reason for his wife's arrest had haunted him since he had gotten behind the wheel, slowly eating him inside, and now that he was in the area he was hoping to reconstruct the scene again.

He looked for the exit for A1A that connected into Route 301. That was the mark he needed. The troopers had pulled him over before that sign, not more than a mile on the north side of the highway. That meant he needed to pass it on the south side. He was on guard, and his heart skipped a bit when he saw it coming up. There it was. A relatively small number in the middle of two As. He knew then that he was close. He switched to the right inner lane of the highway and slowed down and kept eyeing the other side.

All traces of the accident were gone. There were no cones on the road, and all lanes were open. Carlos could not quite make out the exact spot as he drove by slowly in the right lane. He would try to find it in his next trip, coming north. Suddenly, he was startled as he heard his phone ring. He did not know what to do for one slip of a moment, but then he quickly pressed the screen on the truck's dashboard to accept the call. He heard a recorded voice, asking him if he would accept the charge for a call.

"Yes," he said quickly.

"Your account will be charged," said a woman's pleasant recorded voice and then a pause.

"Yasmin, is that you?"

"Yes," said Yasmin's soft voice, hardly being heard.

"How are you, my angel? How are you? I'm coming to see you. I'm on my way."

"Carlos, my love. I miss you so much. But I don't think they'll let you," she answered, showing the slight trace of a sob. "You have to make an appointment."

"Darling, it doesn't matter what they say. I'm coming to see you. I'm already in Florida."

"But they won't let you," she said.

"Yasmin, let them tell me that. I will be at the detention center in a couple of hours. Gordon gave me the address. It's gonna be all right, darling. We have a lawyer working on your case."

"I know."

Carlos was touched by the soft tone of her voice. She must be fighting the tears. Gordon was right. Yasmin was stronger than him. He was already looking through a haze of tears, and he rushed to pull over to the shoulder.

"You will be out in no time, darling. It's gonna be over soon. You will be out."

"I know. Are you all right?"

"Kind of," he mumbled. "You can't imagine how I miss you."

"I miss you more," she said, sounding sure of herself. "What time do you think you will get here?"

"Well, depending on traffic, it will be early evening."

"There is no way they'd let you in at that time."

"I will try. If can't get in, how do I get ahold of you?"

"You can't. I have to call you."

"So, if you don't hear from me by 8:00, call me please."

"They won't let me be on the phone for more than ten minutes. I miss you so much, my husband. I don't want to live without you."

"I don't want to live without you either, Yasmin. You mean everything to me. Life's not worth living if without you."

"Yes, neither one of us can be without the other. My time is coming up, Carlos. They're going to cut me off.

"Goodbye, my love. I will talk to you a little later."

Carlos was on the shoulder of the road, and he knew this was a sign of trouble for the police. Even though he was pulling no trailer, the tractor on the shoulder would prove to be an incredible attraction to any state trooper. They would pull over behind him, and then there would be an hour of questions and checkups. He slowly began merging the truck into the driving lane. He headed south on 95 towards Orlando. Even if they would not let him see her, he would try.

CHAPTER 38

It was already dark when Carlos reached the sign for Orlando. He needed to go west on Highway 4, and he felt energetic about it. He needed to make his pickup in the morning, and then he would try to set up an appointment to see Yasmin. He knew nothing about visiting hours or how to go about setting an appointment, but he would find out. For now, he only needed to know where his Yasmin was. He needed to at least see the enclosure where she was. He could look at it in the dark and say to himself that Yasmin was there, that she was only a few steps away from him, and that she was still here, and all he needed to do was to persevere. She would be released, and they would be together again. It was only a matter of time.

Carlos fed his GPS the address Gordon had given him. It was easier to maneuver in the city without a trailer, and he was able to reach the facility off John Young Parkway in fast timing. It was past 8:00 this evening, and there were only a few cars in the parking lot in front of the building. He pulled the truck into one of the empty lanes, placed his phone inside his cell phone holster attached to his belt, and got out of the truck. He headed for the glass entrance to the lobby and went inside. There was not a soul around, but he spotted a female guard behind a desk.

"Can I help you?" she said as he approached.

"I need to find out about visiting hours. My wife is detained here."

She swept him with an inquisitive look.

"All visitations are handled by appointments. The hours are 9:00 a.m. to 11:00. Afternoon visiting hours are 1:00 to 3:00, and evenings are 5:00 to 8:00. You would have to schedule an appointment."

"Could I see her this evening?"

"No, visitation hours are over now. You'll have to schedule an appointment tomorrow."

"I'm a long distance driver, and I drive out of Miami. It's really hard for me to get here."

"You'll have to make an appointment. Who are you here to see anyway?"

"It's my wife. She just got detained two days ago. She was traveling with me on our way to New York, and we got stopped. I'm on my return now from my trip, on my way to Miami. Her name is Yasmin Figueroa."

He gave her Yasmin's married name. He did not think she would have given them her maiden name, but it was hard to tell what they would have picked up from her record when she did not have any identification on her at the time of the stop.

"I have her here," the woman said. "She's Yasmin Figueroa, right?"

"Yes."

"She's here. She just came in from Jacksonville. Unfortunately, sir, you have to make an appointment to see her. Visitations are closed now."

At that very moment, Carlos felt the vibration of his phone. Yasmin was calling a few minutes after 8:00, as they had agreed. Carlos picked up the call.

"Hi, Yasmin. I'm here. I'm right at the detention center. They are telling me I can't see you. I missed visiting hours by minutes."

"There's no way you can come in?"

"I don't know, darling. I'm trying. I'm here though. You may even see me through a window."

"I'm not allowed to look through windows," she said. "I'm pretty isolated."

"Don't worry, Yasmin; if there is a way to get in, I will do it. Call me back in a few minutes. I am going to see what I can do to get in."

Their conversation could be heard by the guard, who kept giving Carlos long looks. Carlos ended the call and went back to implore the guard to let him in. The answer was no. The visits could only be set up by scheduled appointments, after the advent of the COVID-19 virus.

"Your name has to be registered first of all," the guard said. "There is no way around it. Even if you were within the visiting hours, you could not see her. You have to be registered first."

"Can I do that now? Can I register?"

"You have to fill out forms, either in person or online. That has to be done before you can get an appointment.'

"It would be real hard for me to get here," Carlos said. "Can I try to fill them out now?"

"No, sir. You don't need to come back here to do it. You can do it online. But you cannot see her without an appointment. I am sorry."

Carlos saw no point in pushing anymore. There was no way this woman was going to let him in to see Yasmin, and somehow he had known that even before he had gotten here. This had been a test, and it was time to leave. He had to find a place to sleep and hurry up to take his load to Miami and then rush back to see Yasmin.

CHAPTER 39

Carlos reached Miami the next afternoon, and after dropping off his trailer, he went back to base and parked his truck at the usual stop. But he did not go to his car. He needed to see Gordon immediately. Yasmin was a priority to anything he envisioned right now.

He went around the bend of the warehouse and entered through the glass door in the front. He avoided coming into the building except to pick up his check, which he did usually on weekends, but now he yearned to see his boss's stern face to give him directions as to where to go to see the lawyer he had found for Yasmin. He went into the first door to the right from where Gordon ran his operation.

"I'm here, Gordon. What news do you have?"

"Did you park the truck already?"

Gordon was sitting on a high office chair, cell phone in his ear, and he waved for Carlos to sit down.

"Yes, of course I parked the truck. Where do I have to go to meet this lawyer?"

Gordon raised his index finger to tell him to wait.

"I don't want to be too late and miss him. I want Yasmin out of there as soon as possible."

"She'll get out," Gordon said, ending the call.

"When?"

"Actually, it will be earlier than I thought. She is in Miami."

"What?" Carlos asked in astonishment, getting up from his chair. "I just came from Orlando. I was there last night, and they told me how to register my name as a visitor in their records and then make an appointment. That was just a few hours ago."

"Well, be glad, Carlos. They transferred her down here this morning."

"Where is she? I want to try to see her."

"Carlos, you gotta go see your lawyer before you do anything else. He will see you now. Yasmin is at the Krome Center. You know, the one on Southwest 12th Street. But don't go there now. Go see your lawyer. He's waiting for you."

"What shall I bring with me?"

"Your checkbook. You have to give him a retainer."

"I thought you paid him some money. Don't I owe you?"

"I gave him some money just to get him started. I gave him a thousand dollars, and look how far he's taken us. He's got her to Miami. Next thing will be the hearing, and then she'll be out."

Carlos made a move as if to head for the front door, but then turned around and walked back towards Gordon. He reached out across his desk to shake his hand.

"Thanks, Gordon. I really appreciate it."

Carlos pulled his checkbook from his back pocket, wrote him a check, signed it, and slid it on to him.

"Thanks again."

"No sweat, kid. I only do this for you."

Carlos swept the room with his eyes. The dark wood paneling covering the entire room always gave him a feeling of nostalgia. Wood paneling felt more appropriate for a cold climate, but Gordon was originally from Massachusetts and had come to live in South Florida only in the early 2000s, when his trucking business signed up to transport goods from an international firm in Miami. He had gotten adjusted to the heat, but there were features that he needed as reminders of the coziness of a cold climate. An office room needed some paneling to give it character, purpose. As he shook his hand

and looked deep into his eyes, he felt he had learned something about his boss today. He had learned to respect the man who chased him all over the interstate highways.

CHAPTER 40

Norman Kline's office was located in a two-story building in the quiet and peaceful Coral Way section of Miami. Known for its wide and leafy banyan trees, the highway maintained a look of affluence in its comfortable settings while, at the same time, offering a strong business presence strewn among its surrounding suburbs. Law firms and other professional offices in the area catered to a middle-class crowd, offering specialized fields of service. Only in the last two or three decades those fields had widened, and today they included the exclusive field of immigration law.

Carlos parked his car in the landscaped parking lot behind the building. He came through a wide glass door and went up the stairs to the second floor. He found the oak door with Mr. Kline's nameplate right in the middle of the aisle and opened it. A receptionist sitting behind a partially opened glass door immediately asked how she could help him.

"I'm here to see Mr. Kline," Carlos said.

"Your name, please."

"Carlos Figueroa," Carlos answered.

"He's actually waiting for you," she answered. "I'll take you to him."

She got up from her chair while Carlos looked around the waiting area. A couple sitting behind him was chatting in Spanish. The receptionist opened the side door and waved him in. She was tall with straight black hair and a pleasant smile. She led him past a few doors to a large room in the rear; the door was open. It seemed to be the conference room. A suited man with gray hair stood up to greet him, and Carlos shook his hand.

"You must be Carlos," the man said. "My name is Norman Kline, and it's a pleasure to meet you."

"How're you doing?"

"I'm doing fine. Please sit down."

"Thank you."

"Thanks for bringing him in, Lucrecia," Mr. Kline said to the secretary, and she closed the door.

Norman Kline was in his fifties, but his face did not show it. He had started his career in a large law firm where he did criminal litigation and slowly became acquainted with the immigration field. In the decade of the eighties, there was a large push to deport people who had built a criminal record, and he began to gain interest in the field. But when he brought it to the attention of his bosses, they were not impressed. They did not like the type of clientele that the field attracted and did not want their law firm to get involved. Norman understood but disagreed. In less than a year, he was ready to hang his shingle, as they said among lawyers starting a new practice. He opened up his law office and rented a small space in this building, which was then occupied by several solo practitioners, none of whom did any immigration work. The result was as he had predicted. Word of mouth traveled fast, and crowds began to come in to consult with the young lawyer, who was known to save deportees as they were boarding a plane to their home country. The rest was history. Today, Norman owned the very same building where he had started off and headed his own law firm of three lawyers, who practiced only immigration law.

He had personally become involved in Yasmin's case when Gordon had called his cell in the middle of the night to ask for his services. The two men had known each other for decades, since Gordon still drove trucks for a living and sought his help to bring his Russian bride to America. It was hard to imagine a more unlikely match. Norman was calm and on the quiet side. Gordon was impulsive and boisterous. But the two men developed a solid friendship through the years. To Norman, Gordon was a savvy entrepreneur, just the kind of spirit that America was made of and what he saw in many of the immigrants he helped. To Gordon, Norman was a rare breed of lawyer: someone you could trust and who was not particularly driven by money.

In some early evenings when the last rays of the sun filtered in through the clouds of a hot tropical day, the two men could be found sipping cups of coffee at a restaurant in the Coral Way area. Gordon would talk about his most recently hired drivers or his plans for two replacement tractors, for a new route to Texas, and asked for Norman's opinion. Norman would give him his assessment in the latest trends of migration and how it would affect the Miami economy.

Their topics of discussions had no limits and could go from politics to such liberal themes as the terrible plight of immigrants facing bills for medical care. But invariably, the conversation would end when either of the two men would bring forth a new opportunity for a delivery route or an unfortunate stranded migrant needing legal help. Both men would dig in with their opinions and how they could help each other out.

"You are Carlos Figueroa, and you work for Gordon," Norman said smiling. "You're a heck of a driver, and you just got married, and your wife was picked up by ICE while riding in your truck. It's not a good place to ride when you're running from them. That's the first place they will look and, considering their stand now on human trafficking, not a very safe place to be if you are undocumented."

"We just got married. We wanted to be together."

"I understand that, but for as long as your wife does not have status here, there are certain places where she should not be. The key is to keep a low profile. The fact that you had a rider in your cabin was what attracted the troopers to you, and that's why they stopped you."

Carlos felt the impact of his words in his chest. Had it been his fault then? Should he had been more careful?

"So, what can be done now?" he managed to say.

"Well, the good news is that you are a US citizen, I'm told, right?"

"Yes."

"So, that means that your wife has a path towards citizenship, and that is something that the judges always look at. In fact, it is a requirement. That is what's going to help her get released. Now, let me make this clear to you, the fact that your wife is released does not mean that the case is over. The case will continue, but with her on the outside."

"And what will happen then?"

"Well, you will have to file a petition for her. There is a little bit of a hump there though. Your wife came to the US through the border, correct?"

"Yes."

"That means that your wife cannot gain status here. She will have to return to her country of origin for a consular interview. And her country is Guatemala, right?"

"Yes. But how can she return to Guatemala? She can't."

"I understand. She will need a waiver. She will need a waiver establishing that you, her husband, would suffer an extremely unusual hardship if she leaves."

"Well, of course, I need her."

"The problem is that it's more than just needing her. There has to be something unusual. How is your health?"

"Fine."

"No problems of any kind?"

"No."

"Then it's going to be hard to get a waiver, and without the waiver she cannot travel. I tell you what. We will have to go a step at a time. Let's first try to get her released. What paperwork, if any, do you have with you now?"

"I just got back from a long trip. I came here to meet you and bring you your payment."

"Okay, that's fine then. My secretary will give you a list of documents for you to bring. As I said, I am going to concentrate on what we need to do to get your wife released, and once she is out, we will begin working on the next step, which will be the petition."

"Okay."

Norman reached for the office phone and pressed the intercom.

"Lucrecia," he said to his secretary, "I will need a list of documents in Spanish." He tilted his head towards Carlos to confirm, and Carlos waved back. "Pick a list of requirements for a release, and then add another one as to a US citizen husband petitioning his spouse who entered the US without inspection."

Norman clicked off the call and turned to Carlos.

"She'll bring up a list of the requirements, things you will need for now."

"Gordon said that Yasmin is in Miami now. When do you think I could see her?"

"All right, let me see. We will try to set up an appointment for you tomorrow, but the appointment will not be tomorrow. Probably sometime next week, which, if luck is on our side, your wife should be out by then. Let's hope."

"Really?"

"Yes, I'm pretty confident she will be. You need to get us all that documentation immediately, tomorrow if possible, so that we can file a motion to have her released."

"What do I have to do?"

"Bring everything that we ask for in the morning if possible. We will have an affidavit prepared for you to sign, and we could try to have it filed with our motion to the court before the end of the day."

Lucrecia opened the door gently and handed Carlos two sets of papers.

"I really want to thank you," Carlos said, handing him the check he had prepared. "I believe this is what Gordon said would be your retainer."

"Yes, that's right," Norman said, looking at the check. "But hold on just a bit. We are going to give you a retainer agreement to sign now. Do you want it translated or is English okay?"

"English is fine, of course."

"All right, so Lucrecia will be bringing that for us to discuss while I answer any questions you may have."

He turned to Lucrecia standing by the door.

"Can you prepare a retainer now?"

"Sure thing," she answered. "A standard retainer agreement for bond?"

"Yes, and a separate one for the husband's petition. Will you be able to do that now or shall we wait till tomorrow morning?"

"No, I'll have it. Fifteen minutes?" she asked, staring at him.

"Okay, that's fine."

She left the room closing the door behind her.

"What questions do you have? I know there must be many."

"Well, first of all, pick up the check I brought, so I don't feel like I'm cheating you. Then I'll ask the questions."

Norman took the check from the table and placed it at his side.

"You really are a very proper young man, ah? Just like Gordon described you. Well, there is no need for formalities. I know this is a very hard time for you, just married and then this happens. But hang on in there; your wife will be released. Then we will deal with the rest. So, tell me, what bothers you the most? I know your head feels heavy now, but believe me, many folks wish they were in your position. You are an American citizen to start with."

"Yeah, I know that part is fine, but I am worried about Yasmin. I'm especially concerned about what you mentioned with that waiver. How are we going to get past that?"

"You are a smart young man. Most people have to be told this several times before they begin to even get a notion. It will be difficult, no question. But believe me, it is not an unsurpassable bridge. I think that for now, you should put that aside. Let's concentrate on getting your wife out of detention. Once she is out, then we can plan our strategy."

"But can I ask you something?"

"Of course, that is why we are here."

"I see no problem with my petitioning her. I was already thinking about starting the process before any of this happened. I know that part will not be a problem. We are really married, and we are really in love. We are starting our lives together, and our situation is nothing like some of those horror stories you hear. You know what I'm saying, people who fake it. Our situation is legit. We just bought a house. But this waiver business is going to make me lose sleep at night. How can we prove this unusual hardship? I think you may have said it. You asked me about my health, and my health is fine, but my question to you is that if I am healthy, then that means we can't get this waiver, right? Are there other reasons besides health, is what I am asking, I guess. I'm not even sure."

Carlos threw up his hands in frustration, and Norman stopped him and came to the rescue, as the experienced attorney that he was.

"Carlos, I know that you want assurances, but again, I tell you, let's take it step by step. You asked if there are other causes beyond health that could be used to establish a hardship. And that is a smart question, one that most people would not even think of at this early stage of the proceedings. The answer is yes, there are other causes beyond health, such as economic need, your ability to function without your wife, and ramifications from her absence. What you want to know is whether we can work with your situation as it is now. Yes, we can. And how, you may ask? I am not exactly sure yet, but you see, you are looking far ahead, and I am afraid we just cannot do that right now. We have to put all of our efforts at the moment into having your wife released from detention. And the reason for that urgency is that for as long as she is detained, she will be in danger of being removed, and even if the court allows us some time to file for some type of relief, it won't be much. Again, what that means is that it is urgent that we move quickly and get her out, and that should be our point of discussion at this moment. We have to concentrate all our efforts into achieving that. So, I am not brushing you off when I say this to you, but you need to stay calm and let me guide you through this ordeal. Our goal right now is to get Yasmin out."

The door opened slowly, and Lucrecia came towards Norman. She handed him two sets of documents. It had not even been fifteen minutes since she left the room, and she had returned with the documents requested ready to sign. Norman thanked her and asked her to stay in the room with pen and paper at the ready.

"This is the retainer agreement. This is what we lawyers use to start a case. I know that some of this language may sound foreign to you, so if you want time to read every word, you can take them home with you and return them tomorrow, and then we will have them signed. I am not supposed to even do any work without having the agreement signed by you, but in this case, Gordon explained to me the urgency of the situation. I don't know if you know, but Gordon and I go back a long time. So, I stepped in early and managed to have her transferred to the Miami detention center. Imagine how difficult it would be for you as well as me to handle her case from Jacksonville or Orlando. So, we've made some progress. How would you like to proceed then? You want to take the agreement home and read it carefully, or would you like me to go over it with you now?"

"I want to sign now and get things rolling, Mr. Kline. I don't want Yasmin to be held back."

"That's fine, Carlos. I just want you to read this first. I won't have you sign something that you haven't read. Yasmin is not going to be held back."

Norman went through the forms with Carlos and explained each paragraph. Carlos was impressed by his methodical ways. He must have done this a thousand times, Carlos thought. His language was flawless, not a chip in his sentences, and for a moment Carlos wished he could speak like him.

"I have no questions," Carlos answered to his query. "I will try to be back with these documents tomorrow as early as possible."

"Can you answer a few questions for Lucrecia before you leave? She will be the one drafting your affidavit, which we will attach to the motion papers. That way we can file it tomorrow."

"Sure, of course."

CHAPTER 41

That evening, Carlos felt the urge for a shot of espresso and perhaps a warm soup that he could only get at his favorite restaurant of La Carreta. He also missed his friends Roberto and Mr. Moza, and it had been a few days since he had seen them. But if he showed up at the restaurant, there would be many questions, many opinions that would put his judgment in doubt. No, he'd rather wait till Yasmin was out. Besides, he felt so bereaved without her that he did not know if he could handle it.

He parked the car in the driveway to the house and walked towards the porch. He noted the flowers alongside the walkway. Yasmin had brought them from the apartment and replanted them before they left on their fateful trip. They seemed a little withered from the heat. He left his papers inside the house and then searched for a hose outside to water the plants. He could not do it very well. His hands were shaking. Then he felt the vibration of his phone and unclipped it from his hip. It was Roberto calling him.

"Where have you been?" Roberto asked even before he said hello.

"I just came back," Carlos said. "I just got home."

"We've missed you. It has been so many days. Can you come over?"

"I'm scheduled to leave early in the morning. We are so backed up at work from those days Yasmin and I took off. I need to make just one more trip before I can take some time off."

"Can you stop over for a few minutes tonight? We want to see you. Mr. Moza is here."

"I am just getting in," Carlos said. "I think we might be late. We have to get back on the road early."

"Is everything all right?"

"Yeah, sure."

"All right, I'll be calling you."

Carlos wondered whether he made the right decision. These people were his friends, no matter what their faults. He could not lie to them. He went into the shower, feeling distressed as to what to do. Should he go or not? If he showed they would notice immediately that Yasmin was not with him, and he dreaded the explanation he would have to make. Then he felt guilty about appearing at the restaurant, drinking his coffee and having his dinner as if nothing had happened. Yasmin was behind bars. How could he go on having a normal life while she was jailed? He stepped into the shower and let the warm water spray his back. He began to relax and took his time washing. When he stepped out of the shower, he felt as if he was on automatic pilot, no different than driving his truck. He paid no attention to the details in his new house. None of that was important to him now.

He suddenly found himself outside the house. He had actually passed the front door and locked it and was headed for his car when he came to his senses. Yes, he would go. Yasmin would have wanted him to go and tell his friends the truth. She would be out soon, as Norman had predicted, and then the two of them would return by the weekend. He was sure. But he would have to field the questions from both Roberto and Moza, and their chagrin for him not having asked for their help. But no matter, he resolved, he must go. These people were on his side.

CHAPTER 42

Carlos walked to the counter (or ventanita, as they called it) and stood behind the crowd, all asking to be served. He felt someone pat him on the back and turned.

"Carlos, how are you?"

"Ralph, how're you doing?"

"Are you back from where?"

"It was a delivery in New York, then a pickup in Atlanta and drop in Orlando. How about you?"

"I was in Pennsylvania two days ago and back here. That was my first time."

They both edged to the counter as the people ahead of them got served.

"And how is your wife?"

"She's fine," Carlos answered. "Resting from the long drive."

"Roberto and Moza are inside," Ralph said. "I think they are waiting for you. How they know you are in town, I have no idea but they know. They can smell you."

Carlos nodded and ordered two cups of the popular cortaito. Even with the high humidity of the evening, it was a much-craved item by all the customers. Carlos did not feel a drop of hunger at the moment, and he kept touching the phone on his waist, anxious not to miss any call that might come in from Yasmin. He had not heard anything from her since the previous evening in Orlando.

"Shall we go inside?" Carlos said to Ralph. "I'm sure there will be room for the two of us."

"With Mr. Moza, there's always room," Ralph joked.

"Let's go," Carlos said, leaving a five-dollar bill on the counter. "Where are they sitting?"

"Straight on from the cashier; don't go to the left side."

They went inside, and the cashier recognized them immediately.

"Hello, Carlos," the young waitress greeted him. "You haven't been around. You've been on a honeymoon, I know. And where is she? Where is your wife?"

"She is sleeping. I'm just picking up an order for us both."

"You won't be able to leave without seeing them," she replied and pointed to a table by the end, where a hand was already up and waving at him.

"I know," Carlos said. "I wouldn't think of leaving without sitting with them first."

Carlos and Ralph walked straight to the rear and waved at everyone at the table. There was Roberto, wearing a colorful Hawaiian shirt, his wife Amelia in full makeup, with her hair carefully pinned down, giving her a flair of youth. Then there was Mr. Moza, with his impeccable guayavera and his hand, crowded by rings on almost every finger, that he extended to Carlos to grab.

"And where is that princess Yasmin that we all want to see?"

"She's fine. She was unable to come tonight."

"Oh, no. It's no fun without her. She must be here."

Mr. Prieto stood up to shake Carlos's hand.

"I can't believe it, Carlos," Mr. Moza insisted. "You are like a bird without wings at the moment."

"Can we sit down?" Carlos said.

"But of course," Moza answered.

He lifted his arm and waved to one of the waitresses. She rushed over to the table.

"We need one more chair," he said to her. "You go ahead and sit next to me. Ralph's chair is coming."

"So, where is Yasmin?" Roberto asked.

Carlos stared at them as if still unsure whether he could confide in them.

"There was a problem," he said quietly, as if to himself. "On our way to New York we were stopped by troopers near Jacksonville. They made a make-believe inspection and then asked Yasmin for her papers. She, of course, did not have any, and they detained her."

"Oh, no," Amelia gasped, and Roberto looked on, baffled.

Mr. Moza showed no reaction but was the first to make an inquiry.

"Where did they take her?"

"First to Jacksonville, then to Orlando, and this morning she arrived here in Miami. She is at the Krome Center. My poor Yasmin has traveled all the big cities of the state of Florida in shackles already."

"Carlos, we are lucky. She is here. Now, before you talk to anyone, I will call an attorney who's going to get her out right away. Speed is the key here."

"Mr. Moza, I got an attorney through my boss already. I had to. I could not wait."

"But why didn't you call us?" Roberto protested. "We would have taken care of it immediately."

"I'm sorry, my boss Gordon knows this attorney, and he jumped on it right away. I was just at his office. He's filing papers tomorrow."

"What is his name?" Mr. Moza asked.

"Norman Kline."

"Oh, yes," Mr. Moza replied. "I know him. He's excellent. It's a good choice. Now listen, Carlos, it's important that he files papers to have her released. There may be bail involved, but no matter, the important thing is that she comes out, and then we get to work on the rest. He's filing papers tomorrow, you say?"

"Yes. I have to go back in the morning and sign them."

"Have you talked to Yasmin? Is she holding up all right?"

"Yes, she's okay."

"Carlos, let's order you something to eat now. What would you like, your soup?"

"I'm not hungry, Mr. Moza. Coffee is all I wanted."

Roberto raised his hand to gain the waitress's attention. She spotted him immediately and came right over.

"It's the usual for Carlos," Roberto said. "He hasn't eaten, and he's hungry."

"So, the soup, maybe some rice and a steak? Is that right, Carlos? What do you want to drink?"

"Just the chicken soup and some guarapo."

She walked quickly back and disappeared behind the double doors leading to the kitchen. Roberto rose and walked towards Carlos. He placed a hand on his shoulder.

"Yasmin will be out in no time, Carlos. You should have called us. What are we here for if not to help you, ah?"

"I was desperate, Roberto. Gordon is on the phone with me constantly. He was my closest contact at the moment."

"You will have to file a petition for your wife as soon as she is released."

"No, hold it, Roberto," Mr. Moza said. "What does your attorney say to do, Carlos? What does he think?"

"I think he's planning to file right away."

"Good. Now, Carlos, this will pass, my boy. It is a difficult time for you, but it will pass. I promise you. Now, let's talk about it. Let's plan a strategy. You said she's at Krome Center, right?"

Carlos nodded.

"Will you be getting there sometime?"

"As soon as they let me."

"Well, Carlos, keep in mind that you must cooperate with your attorney. Do what he tells you, and if you need help, we are here. Let's get Yasmin out of there quickly. That's our goal for now."

"Thank you, Mr. Moza. Thank you for your concern."

It was now Amelia who stood up and came over to Carlos and embraced him, whispering words of encouragement.

CHAPTER 43

By midafternoon Carlos was on his way north on Route 95, pulling a tight rig destined for Phoenix. He had told Gordon that he did not want to go too far, in case he was called for a hearing on Yasmin. But after speaking with his lawyer, Norman had told him that there would not be any court hearing until at least three more days. Gordon had made a plea for him to make this trip, and after all he had done for him and Yasmin, Carlos could not say no.

It was not until that evening that he saw an unrecognizable number come up on his dashboard screen and quickly touched it to take the call.

He heard the recorded voice of the message asking whether he would accept the charges. He knew it was Yasmin.

"Yes," he answered. "Hello, hello, Yasmin, are you there?"

"Yes, darling, it's me. How are you?"

"I'm fine, my angel. I have been waiting for your call."

"I've been trying, but they don't let me. They are giving me ten minutes, they said."

"Yasmin, I signed all the papers at the lawyer's office today, and he said they would be filed with the court also today. We are asking for a hearing with the judge to try to get you released. They said it looks good."

"And where are you?"

"I'm by Jacksonville. I am on my way to Phoenix. Our lawyer said that I would not see the judge for another three days, so Gordon asked me to make this run. After all he's done, I could not let him down. But the secretary at our lawyer's office is trying to get me an appointment to see you. I might hear tomorrow about that."

"How is the road?"

"Lonely without you."

"Be strong, Carlos. I will be out soon. I spoke to the attorney today."

"Really, Yasmin? How did you manage to do that?"

"I called. They gave me a message here, and I called the number. He sounds very nice. He says he will be coming to see me either tomorrow or the next day."

"I'm sorry that I have not been able to see you, Yasmin. They arranged my appointment to see you Monday. But I guess it's easier for him because he is an attorney. But how were you able to talk to him? In what language?"

"Spanish."

"He spoke to you in Spanish?"

"Yes."

"Did he tell you about the petitions we have to file?"

"A little bit, yes. But he says we have to concentrate on my release, then we will deal with the rest later."

"Yes but—"

Carlos was going to tell her about the waiver, the one issue that was worrying him, but he thought it was best to hold back.

"I know you're worried about the waiver, I know."

"Yasmin, how did you know that?"

"The lawyer told me. But do not worry, darling. Everything will be all right."

There was a long pause. Carlos felt that their roles were suddenly reversed. He should be the one saying that. Instead, Yasmin was sensing his insecurity, his fear of the future, and she was encouraging him to be strong. He suddenly felt a true delight knowing that he had married such a brave woman. There she must be, standing near the phone, dressed in an orange jumpsuit and wearing prison-issued plastic slippers for shoes. How he had underestimated her. It seemed she had unexpectedly turned into a bastion of energy and valor. Where had it come from?

"How were you able to understand him? How did you speak to him?"

"He spoke to me in fluent Spanish. I liked him. He was very positive and made me feel so secure."

Again a pause. Carlos felt a little ashamed. Shouldn't he have been like Norman? Was he not being weak and unsupportive to his wife? He needed to emulate Norman.

"He's right, Yasmin. You will be out in a couple of days. We will work everything out once you are released. Our lawyer has already started to prepare the petition that I will file for you. I gave his secretary all the documents before leaving Miami, signed all the forms. We are going to be all right."

"I know we are. How is the house? You slept there last night, right?"

"It's beautiful, darling, but empty without you. It's not a home without you."

"You must not talk like that, Carlos. It's our home; it's both of us. This is only a temporary situation. I will be there in a couple of days, and we will swim laps in the pool together. We still did not get to do that."

Carlos fought the tears.

"I know. But we will do that right away, as soon as you get out. It will be just right, like before. Our love has never been stronger."

"No, it hasn't. It's made of steel."

"Steel and heart, darling."

"Steel and heart, honey. Tell me where you are now."

"I am about to take Route 10 West, my usual way of going to Phoenix. It's very sad, Yasmin. It's awful not having you."

"Carlos, my love, hold on tight. I will be with you in no time. Darling, I have to go. I'm out of time. They're going to cut me off the line."

Before Carlos could say anything, the line went dead. She was so right. But where did she get her strength from, he wondered.

CHAPTER 44

Going to Phoenix seemed now a dark adventure. Yasmin's absence reflected on everything. Even the getting in and out of the truck seemed arduous, as if he were carrying an extra burden on his shoulders from not having Yasmin with him. He was not two days into his trip to Phoenix, and he had stopped at Love's Travel Shop 542 in Fort Stockton, Texas. He had not been here for a good two weeks. As he entered the service center, the cashier greeted him cheerfully.

"Carlos, where have you been? It seems like weeks since the last time I saw you."

"I've been on the East Coast," Carlos said. "How are you?"

"All right, working as usual."

She moved sideways from the cash register to place herself right across from him. Carlos spotted the small artificial cactus that he had brought her from Phoenix, just before meeting Yasmin. She had placed it on top of the cashier.

"I'm going to use the shower," Carlos said.

"Go ahead," she answered. "No one is there."

Carlos thought the scarf she wore tonight was definitely brighter. It was not entirely yellow but in the neighborhood. He headed for the shower in the back and wondered how Middle Eastern women chose the colors of their scarfs. Perhaps it was their husbands who, as in everything else, seemed to have the last word. Then he thought about Yasmin and asked himself how she would look wearing one. No, of course not. It would defeat the purpose of her long braided hair. A scarf would only serve to hide her beauty. You could not understand the purpose of women's head scarfs without first understanding their culture. Carlos had always been intrigued by them, until he met Yasmin, and her long braid won him over.

He took a long shower and put on new underwear, T-shirt, and socks. He had barely showered the night before, worried from the meeting at his lawyer's office. But after his last conversation with Yasmin, he felt a boost that brought him back to his usual clarity. Yasmin would get out, and they would be together again. He would file his petition and do anything he had to do, and at the end, they would both be happy again. He got himself a cold sandwich and juice, and paid the cashier.

"When will you be back again, Carlos?"

"I am not sure if I will return the same way. I will probably be sent to the Northeast on the way back. There's no telling how it will go until I get there. My boss follows me on the phone and doesn't tell me where I'm going until the last minute."

"Are you staying over?"

"Yes, I hooked up the truck. I guess I will see you in the late morning or afternoon."

She gave him back his change.

"Make sure you get enough sleep."

Carlos went outside and entered his truck's cabin. He turned on his laptop and watched the local news. No new calls had come in from Yasmin, and although he hadn't tried, it was no use. He could not initiate the call. Yasmin had changed his life entirely, and he now knew where he was headed like never before. She was right. This was only a temporary situation. They'd soon be together again, plotting their destiny.

CHAPTER 45

Carlos reached Chandler, Arizona, a few minutes before the end of his shift. He had hustled to get to the building in time, knowing they did not have a second shift. If he did not make it in time, he would have to wait till the morning to drop off his load.

"You got lucky this time," the dispatcher said at the gate. "A few more minutes, and I could not have let you in."

"I know, and then I would have been really screwed holding the rig for the night."

"Where are you going next?"

"Don't know yet. I'm sure I will be getting a call shortly."

"Well, you know where to go for the night. It's much easier without the rig."

"Sure. I got to make a stop at a local restaurant here for dinner. I don't want them to close up on me."

"Something special, ah? Good food?"

"The food stinks there, actually. But there is someone I gotta see there."

"Oh, yeah? I bet the cook is a female."

Carlos grinned and drove off to the rear of the building to drop off the load. Some things were better left unsaid.

Carlos backed up the trailer to a gate and then rushed inside to work out the arrangement for the pickup the next morning. Strangely, Gordon had not called him to tell him that a load would be ready for him the next morning. But Carlos knew. After confirming the pickup time with the attendant, he hurried to uncouple the load and pulled his truck free. He went on Route 10 East and got off on Route 60.

He was not looking for a place to eat. He had one in mind, and when he saw the sign for the Guatelinda Restaurant, he slowed down and cut into the parking lot. He maneuvered the truck around and set it with the front facing the road. Then he got out of the cabin and went towards the front. The flowers on both sides of the walkway had withered away. He thought how saddened his Yasmin would be if she could see them. But that was part of the reason why he was here.

He went inside and did not take a table. He went straight to the counter, where a man asked him how he could help him.

"Is the cook here?"

The man behind the counter was wearing a long white apron and could hardly have passed for a cook. He made a strange grimace.

"I am the cook," he said.

"You're not the one I'm looking for."

"That one is the owner. I took over the kitchen. Is there anything I can do for you?"

"Yeah, you can tell him Carlos said that he's a lousy cook, and I'd love to break his nose."

The man looked at him with wide eyes, not quite sure he had heard Carlos right. But he slowly recovered and then spoke.

"He is gone for the day, but he will be here early in the morning. You can see him in the morning and tell him then."

"I have no time to be waiting for an idiot like him, but when I'm in town again, I will see him."

"I'm just the cook here. I don't know anything else."

Carlos did not answer him. If the man had challenged him, he would have grabbed him by the neck and pulled him over the counter like a ragdoll. But the poor devil was not at fault, and there was no point in punishing the innocent. At least his boss would know that he was here. On his way out, Carlos did not spot a new waitress. Apparently the owner had not been able to replace Yasmin. As he passed the rows of dead flowers, he became choked up. No one had cared. No one had given any thought to the lovely hands that had planted them and kept them alive.

CHAPTER 46

Carlos made it out of Phoenix the next morning, taking a new load to Atlanta, and counted the hours that had passed since he last talked to Yasmin.

His phone vibrated on the seat, and he touched the computer screen on the dashboard.

"Are you on your way?"

Carlos knew it was Gordon. In fact, he found it odd not to have heard from him earlier.

"I'm on Route 10 East on my way to Georgia. Am I traveling to Florida empty or what?"

"There will be another trailer there waiting for you. It's going to Orlando."

"Good. Anything to pick up from Orlando?"

"I don't know yet. I am hoping to get something from Orlando or near about."

"I want to get to Miami two days from now to see Yasmin."

"How are you gonna pull that? Are you flying here or something? Don't forget you need to break for ten hours. Besides, you may not have to go see Yasmin. Court is on for tomorrow."

"What?"

"That's what Norman's office just told me. See the difference between dealing with a loser and a winner? He's gonna get your wife out right there and then."

"Oh, God, but what about bail? I'm not there."

"Do not worry about bail. My guess is that he'll get her out without bail."

"Will they let her out right there and then?"

"Possibly."

"That's great, but she'll be out in the street without any money, and she can't even get inside our home. She has no keys."

"Don't worry about it, Carlos. That's the least of our problems. I'm in touch with Norman, and if he tells me that she's getting out, I'll send one of the drivers from here to help."

"Thanks, Gordon. You've done miracles for me. I will never be able to pay you back."

"You don't worry about it, Carlos. Drive carefully and concentrate on what you're doing. Yasmin will be fine."

"Okay."

Carlos ended the call and wondered about his boss. He had never before mentioned safety. It was always about how soon he could deliver the load, but he was now concerned about him driving carefully? But Carlos was always careful and now more than ever.

CHAPTER 47

It was not until after Carlos had gone through Atlanta and was on his way to Orlando that he finally heard from Yasmin again. She called on the morning of the next day.

"How are you doing, my love?" she asked, without saying hello.

"I have been waiting for you, darling. How are you feeling?"

"Missing you more than ever," she replied. "But I was already told that tomorrow I see the judge."

"Oh, tomorrow? Gordon was right then. He said that you would probably have the hearing before I got back. It's gonna be all right, darling. You'll see."

"Where are you now?"

"I'm going to Orlando, you know, the usual route."

"Oh. I was hoping to see you tomorrow."

"My love, I wish with all my heart that I could be there. But it's happened so fast. Our lawyer is really good. He has moved our case at high speed. I did not know it was going to be like this; otherwise, I would have never agreed to make this trip, but you know, Gordon has been so good to us that how can I say no to him now?"

"I know. I think you have to help him. He has helped us, so we have to help him back. What have you heard from our lawyer? What does he think will happen tomorrow?"

"Gordon seems to think bail will be set."

"And then what happens?"

"I pay the money set for bail so you can get out."

There was a silent pause. Carlos sensed Yasmin's uncertainty. He wanted to be careful in what he would say next. Building a false hope could make things even worse.

"I will get out," Yasmin said. "I need to be with my husband."

"Yasmin, I want to be with you more than anything. Nothing else matters to me other than that. I have not prayed in such a long time, and now I am praying so much that you can get out of there. I do not think I will make it there on time, darling. I have to stop in Orlando still. And then after I drop the load I can really hurry."

"Do not hurry," she answered. "Be careful my love. If they release me, I will find a way to get home."

"Gordon told me that he would send someone to take you home. But I can also call Roberto or one of our other friends. You just call me right away. You call me collect. You know how to do that."

"I know. I will be fine, my darling. Do not worry about me. You just drive carefully and stay safe. My time is up, Carlos. I have to get off the phone."

"I love you, darling. I love you so much!"

CHAPTER 48

Carlos could not drop his rig in Orlando until the next morning. He had never rushed during these procedures. Hurry was a truck driver's enemy. You needed to pay attention to detail, go over what you were doing in your mind, move slowly, checking every step. Today, releasing the wagon from his truck was mentally challenging to him. He needed to be in Miami. His wife needed him, and every time he took a breath, he felt the need to rush, to unhook his tractor from the trailer and go. But he could not. He followed his standard method except that today, he was even more careful. His mind urged him to hurry while his hands moved slowly. When he was finished with the uncoupling, he got inside his tractor without bidding goodbye to the crew inside. He checked both mirrors and made sure it was clear. Then he pulled away from the trailer slowly and drove to the shack to sign himself out.

"How goes it this morning?" said the dispatcher.

"Good, anxious to get home."

"Miami, right?"

"Yes."

"Well, that will be about a four-hour drive on 95 South," the dispatcher observed, smiling.

"There is a faster way."

"Turnpike?"

"Yes. I will see you in a few days."

Carlos got on the Florida Turnpike South. He was not pulling a rig, so he could speed up. But every time he found himself going past the speed limit, he would automatically slow down. The turnpike was flooded with troopers. He remained hovering the speed limit. He had only been on the turnpike for a few minutes when he felt the phone vibrating. He took the call without even looking at the name.

"Yasmin is out," said Gordon enthusiastically.

He did not even say hello. He did not need to. Carlos could identify his voice anywhere.

"All right!" Carlos answered.

"Norman just called me. In a few minutes she will be out."

"What about her bail? How much?"

"No, no bail. I gotta tell you something. I'm no fan of lawyers. In fact, you will never hear me say anything nice about them. My attitude towards them has always been that they are a bad plague. All they care about is how much money they will suck up from the next victim. And I forget who said it but there is some famous writer who said it best in one of his stories. He said, 'Kill all the lawyers.'"

"That was Shakespeare, Gordon," Carlos said interrupting him. "Even I know that, and I came here in a banana boat, as you have told me many times."

"All right, whoever, Shakespeare said it. But I gotta say that with Norman you have to make an exception. That man keeps his word. Look at how fast he moved and got results for you. I gotta call him tonight and maybe we can go out for supper."

"I'm on the road to Miami already. I think I have someone who can go pick up Yasmin, so you don't have to bother your drivers. I will call you if I need help."

"You sure?"

"I'm sure. I appreciate everything you've done. Let me go now."

Carlos ended the call and immediately dialed Roberto's number. Leaving Yasmin waiting for four hours outside a jail did not seem like a good thing, especially after all she had been through. But as he dialed Roberto's number, he thought that his Yasmin was tough. She could handle anything they threw at her.

The phone rang about four times before Roberto's familiar voice came on.

"Hello."

"Roberto, it's Carlos. I am calling you to ask if you can do me a favor, only if you can. I understand that it's the middle of the day, and you are probably working."

"Shoot."

"Yasmin just got released from Immigration jail. She is probably outside looking for a phone to call me, but I am on 95, heading for Miami and three hours away."

"Say no more. I understand. I am far from Miami right now, but Amelia is home. She can pick her up."

"She just needs a ride to get home. She has no money, and the judge just released her. I really would appreciate it."

"Stop. I'm glad she got released. That's great news. That means you are on the right track. Where is she exactly?"

"She's at Krome Center. That's where they were holding her. She's probably outside trying to get a call to me."

"Do not worry. I know where she is. Amelia will go and pick her up. Is she all right?"

"She seems to be all right, but I am sure she is in some kind of shock at the moment. So many things have happened to her in the last few days that you can imagine how she feels."

"I'm calling Amelia right now and will get back to you. You should have called me before. Why did you wait till the last minute?"

"I did not think she would be released so quickly."

"Well, Mr. Moza said your lawyer was a good one. He's usually right about these things. He has a lot of contacts. I'll get back."

Roberto was gone in a flash. The conversation had not lasted more than two minutes. Despite their differences, Carlos thought, he was a friend. But no sooner had their call ended when the computer screen by the dashboard lit again. It was an unknown number, and Carlos knew instinctively that it was Yasmin.

"Hello," he said, pressing the accept option.

"My love," Yasmin began.

There was not the lightest trace of unease in her voice, which Carlos found remarkable.

"Where are you, pretty girl? Where are you calling from?"

"Mr. Kline let me use his phone. He's standing right here next to me. I only wanted to let you know that I am out."

"I know. Gordon told me, and I already called Roberto for help. His wife Amelia is coming to pick you up. Please just wait by the front of the building. She's coming. Yasmin, I love you so much. So, so much."

"I love you even more," she answered. "You will see. I will wait at the house for you."

"I am still a good three hours away. Get something to eat with Amelia."

"I am not carrying any money."

"Amelia will treat you. These people are like family."

"I know. They are. I have to go. I don't want to inconvenience Mr. Kline."

"All right, darling. Tell him thanks, and don't move from where you are. Just wait there."

"All right."

Carlos heard the dial tone and realized she was gone. He looked straight ahead on the road, a long stretch that seemed to have no end, and wished he could move to the left lane and fly past all the traffic. But no, he couldn't. A Florida trooper would grab him in no time. He looked at the speedometer once more. The needle was right at 70.

CHAPTER 49

Carlos got to Miami by late afternoon. He was in a hurry, so he dropped the truck and ran inside to shake Gordon's hand. He owed him that much but then quickly turned and left. Yasmin was home waiting with Amelia. He got in his car and raced through the highway and took the exit to his house. It was the first time he was coming back to his new home from a trip. He made the turn too early to get to 125th Street so he had to make it right to go up one more block. When he got to the corner, he saw the house and noticed the blue Impala parked in the driveway. Amelia was there and maybe even Roberto.

Carlos pulled up the driveway behind the Impala and got out. Yasmin had already seen him, and she came running outside. He ran towards her and lifted her up in the air. Then he noticed that her braid was gone.

"What happened?" he asked. "What happened to my beautiful braid?"

"They chopped it off, my love. It will grow again, I promise."

"But why? Why?"

"It's for security reasons, they said."

Carlos bought her up close and saw the girl of his dreams, her hair chopped clumsily by some inmate who called himself a barber to get an inside job at the prison. What a crime, he thought. Then he kissed her, again and again, and for the first time he became aware of Amelia's presence.

"Carlos! She's home!" Amelia said in a cheer.

"Thank you, so much," he said walking up to Amelia.

He embraced her and kissed her on the cheek.

"Oh, it's no trouble. I know you are upset. It was savage what they did to her hair. But it will grow again, Carlos. It will come out stronger."

He gave Amelia a hug and thanked her again. They all went inside. The house was still not fully furnished, and they sat on the old sofa that Carlos and Yamin had brought from the apartment.

"So, how was it, Yasmin? How bad was it? Tell me."

"It was not too bad. They treated me well."

"What did you think about the hearing this morning? How did it go?"

"Mr. Kline did all the talking. There was a translator who spoke to me in Spanish."

"So what did the judge say?"

"He said very little. He only asked if my husband was a US citizen. Mr. Kline answered and then he said he had reviewed the papers and that he was releasing me."

"No bail?"

"No, no bail."

"I think that's wonderful," said Amelia. "Don't you, Carlos?"

"Yeah, of course."

"And that tells you that now she may be a legal resident through you. Right?"

"Well, I hope so. I understand it's a process."

"Oh, everything is a process," Amelia said. "Won't you show me your house? Roberto was supposed to meet me here, but I can't wait to see the other rooms. Yasmin and I just barely got here. I've only seen the kitchen and this room, and the pool. Oh, yes, the pool."

"We will need to clean it now," Yasmin said. "There's been no one here, and leaves have flown in."

Carlos turned to Yasmin and kissed her on the cheek. He turned her head slowly towards him to get a good view of her hair. It barely reached her ears, and some thin strands floated sloppily on both sides of her face.

"Who was this butcher that cut your hair?"

"It was a woman, not a man. She's the official barber of the prison."

"Man, what a criminal she is to just cut your beautiful hair like that."

"I was actually lucky, Carlos. They could have given me a crew cut or even shaved my head."

"But why? What's the point?"

"It's for safety reasons, Carlos," Amelia replied. "They do not allow inmates to wear their hair long because they can hurt themselves. They even take their shoelaces away because they could hang themselves."

"Yes, that's true."

"Well, can we see the rest of the house? I can't wait. It's beautiful."

"I hope you don't mind the empty rooms. We have not had a chance to buy furniture. So many things have happened to us in the last few days."

"Everything will be all right," Amelia said. "It's only a test, a small test."

The three left the sofa and went on a tour of the house, Yasmin leading the way. The living room floor was parquet, while the rest of house was tiled, as it was common in Florida. At every spot they made, Amelia offered suggestions with the type of furniture fit for it, lamenting its present state of affairs. Finally, after a long while, they ended at the pool, where Yasmin and Carlos received specific instruction on how best to avoid the influx of leaves falling in the water. Then she looked at them and realized she was keeping them from each other.

"I have to go home to meet Roberto. Then I believe we are going out for dinner at the restaurant. Will you meet us there?"

"I don't know," Carlos said. "I am sure Yasmin needs rest. What do you think, angel?"

"It's up to you, darling," she answered gallantly, not giving a hint of the ordeal she had just been through.

"Well, then, we will be a little late on purpose to give you time to catch up, and we'll meet you there. We missed you. I am sure Mr. Moza will be there."

"Yes," Carlos said. "And I am sure he will be on time too."

Carlos and Yasmin walked Amelia to the car. She backed up her vehicle around Carlos's to the road. She went back a few feet more then she turned and waved goodbye as she sped off. Carlos kissed Yasmin passionately on the lips, and the two went inside. They had so much to talk about.

CHAPTER 50

It was past 8:00 when Carlos and Yasmin arrived at La Carreta. He was concerned about the reception she might get from people who knew her. He felt for her. He did not want her to be hurt.

They held hands as they walked away from their car and looped around the building to go in through the front door, hoping to avoid the crowd at the ventanita. But no such luck. There was a group of men talking behind the crowd, waiting to be served, and some of them called out his name. He raised his hand as a greeting and held the front door of the restaurant open for Yasmin to go inside.

"Is Roberto here?" Carlos asked the cashier.

"Hi, Carlos," she replied, looking at Yasmin. "You cut your hair?"

"Yes," Yasmin said.

"It looks good. You look so different."

If she only knew that Carlos had to use his trimmer at home to make her ends even. He did a better job than the woman barber at the detention center, who had massacred Yasmin's hair.

"Oops, there you go," the waitress said, pointing to the rear end of the room, where Roberto held his hand raised.

"I see him, thanks."

Carlos and Yasmin waved at her and walked towards Roberto and his wife. They were sitting at the very end of the room as usual. In the next section of the dining room, in the other side of the partition wall, there seemed to be a commotion, but Carlos recognized Mr. Moza's voice, louder above all the others. It must be some political rally. Mr. Moza must be engaged.

"Well, hello," Roberto said, getting up and coming towards Yasmin. "What have you done to your hair?"

"They trimmed it for me," she answered, looking towards Amelia.

"Oh, what a shame. But you might like it this way better, Yasmin."

He finally got close enough and gave her a hug.

"We want to thank you," Carlos told him. "You went out of your way for us today."

"Oh, come on," said Amelia. "That's what friends are for."

"Sit down," Roberto said, pointing to the chairs in front of him at the table.

"Did you eat?" Amelia asked with a broad smile.

"No, Yasmin has only had some juice. She has not eaten."

"Oh, poor girl," Amelia said. "You must be hungry, honey."

"A little."

"No, not a little," Roberto corrected her. "No tamales for you tonight. You are going to eat solid food. A steak, rice, potatoes."

"This time," Carlos said, "I think Roberto is right. You have to put some nutrients in that thin body."

"What did they give you to eat when you were inside?" Roberto asked. "Was the food any good?"

"They gave us three meals a day."

"What kind of food?"

"Mashed potatoes with gravy, some vegetables. Very little meat though."

"So you felt that the diet was good? I mean you did not go hungry, right?"

"I did not. I hardly ate."

"Why? You did not like the food?"

"No, it wasn't the food. I was just not hungry."

The waitress had been standing right at the head of the table, waiting for them to end their conversation. It was Carlos who first noticed her.

"Let's not make our waitress wait. She's got other tables to tend to."

He kissed Yasmin on the cheek.

"What are you going to have, honey?" he asked her.

"Can we share a steak?"

"Yasmin," Carlos chirped, pulling himself back. "You are actually going to eat a steak?"

"One-half."

"Still. This is a diary entry."

She reached forward and kissed him.

"What will the lovers have?" the waitress said, interrupting them.

"We are going to share a steak," Carlos answered quickly. "And what else, Yasmin?" he asked his wife.

"Let's see," she said cheerfully. "Let's have the congris, ripe plantains, and some salad."

"I got it all," said the waitress. "And to drink?"

Carlos stared into Yasmin's eyes. She nodded, reading his mind.

"Let's get some guarapo," Carlos said.

"Wait," Roberto interrupted. "Bring us a bottle of red wine. Let it not be too sour. We have something to celebrate tonight."

"Sure," the waitress replied, smiling.

"But we can only have a sip," Carlos complained. "We are driving."

"You're only a few blocks away," she said.

"Well, that does not matter. All you have to do is sit behind the wheel. You know that. But actually we are going to the beach after this."

"What?" Roberto faked surprise. "Amelia says you have an Olympic pool at your house which I still haven't seen by the way, and you are going to the beach?."

"Oh, why didn't you come today?" Yasmin said.

Roberto hesitated. Yasmin's sudden affableness surprised him.

"I was too far away. I was by Palm Beach."

"Yeah, you could have helped us with that door," Amelia uttered.

"What door?"

"I told you. Yasmin had no keys to get in. We were locked out for a good ten minutes. It was hot, and I had to think fast. I figured if there's a chance of tampering with any door in a new house, it had to be the sliding door to the pool. And sure thing. It was unlocked."

"That had to be Carlos. Yasmin wouldn't do that."

"Well, of course. But now we know the secret."

"That won't happen again," Roberto said, looking towards Yasmin. She smiled back.

"Well, hello there, ladies and gentlemen," said Mr. Moza's raspy voice.

He and his handyman Prieto were headed for their table. Mr. Moza took pleasure in announcing himself. He always did.

"Mr. Moza," Carlos said, standing up to greet him.

"How are you, my boy?"

"I am all right, and you?"

"We are all fine, thanks. Now, let me talk to this lovely woman who is sitting next to you and who is the whole reason of our being here. She's also the whole cause for your happiness and the positive changes she has had on you."

He paused and gasped as he bent forward to hug Yasmin.

"What happened to your hair?" he whispered in her ear."

"They gave me a haircut," Yasmin answered, smiling at him.

Mr. Moza smiled back. Something had struck him, something unexpected that had shown Yasmin in a different light. Perhaps this was the connection between Carlos and her. Behind that blanket of humility, there was something daring and stormy in her character that suddenly flashed past him. She had just been through a horrific experience when all of her newfound happiness had been threatened and her very own existence placed at the edge of disappearance. For anyone else the effects could have been devastating. But here she was, making light of it all, bouncing back like a heavenly star.

"How did they treat you?"

"Not bad. The judge was courteous."

He pulled back from the table to allow his friend Pietro to step in and shake her hand.

"Mr. Moza, will you join us?"

"Yes, we are, of course. But no supper for us tonight. We are due somewhere else in a little while. We are here to celebrate Yasmin's victory. She is the girl at the winning line. She beat the feds."

"It's not over, Mr. Moza. It begins now," Carlos pointed out. "In fact it is the beginning. Tomorrow we are meeting Mr. Kline to start working on our petition."

"It's paperwork, Carlos. Just paperwork."

"Not really, Mr. Moza. Yasmin needs a waiver to get her visa, and it requires that she prove hardship through me."

"Oh, do not worry about that," Roberto interjected. "That's been going on for years."

"We have to prove there's something wrong."

"Everybody does, Carlos," Roberto added. "Who can say that there is nothing wrong in their lives?"

"Me and Yasmin."

Roberto made an attempt to answer but held back. Amelia smiled cunningly and took a sip of her drink. Mr. Moza raised both hands as a sign for silence. The waitress arrived with Carlos's and Yasmin's order.

"Do not despair, my boy," he said. "Do not rush making a judgment about something that you are about to start on. Be positive."

"We are, Mr. Moza, but when they tell you that you need to show a health condition, it's pretty dire. What health condition am I going to show? You know, it's me. I need to show that there is something wrong with me and that I need Yasmin here to take care of me. Imagine, what am I going to say about my health when we are headed for the beach in a little while to swim a marathon. She and I are in perfect health."

"Thank God. And may it remain so. But that is not the only reason, Carlos. It could be economic issues too. Emotional issues also play a part."

"We are good in all of those. We just bought a house. We are making progress. We just got married; we are moving up."

"That's all good, and let it remain so. This is a new venture, my boy. Think of it that way. You must first leave it to your lawyer. Let Mr. Kline tell you what you need as far as records, and he will do the rest."

"That's it, Carlos," said Roberto from across the table. "Let yourself be guided by Kline. He's an expert. He has done many of these cases."

"Of course," said Mr. Moza.

"Carlos, he's been around," Roberto reiterated.

Carlos nodded and smiled at Yasmin. She began to cut half of the sirloin steak the waitress had brought them. Carlos used an empty plate to place her half of the rice and some ripe plantains.

"Well, I want you to make some time for me," Mr. Moza said. "I want to take you out to meet a fellow from the city administration and have a talk."

"For what purpose?" Carlos asked, checking his plate momentarily and then turning towards him.

"Oh, the future, the opportunities."

"Mr. Moza, I am a truck driver. I love what I do. I don't have the brains to do anything else."

"That's where you're wrong. We see something in you, am I not right, Mr. Prieto?"

Mr. Moza turned towards Mr. Prieto, gesturing for a sign of approval.

"Absolutely."

Carlos turned to Yasmin and kissed her on the cheek. Their relationship had blossomed for the eyes of the world to see. She leaned over his shoulder for a moment then sat straight.

"If someone wants to meet Carlos, then he must meet him," Yasmin said.

Everyone in the group, Roberto especially, looked stunned. Yasmin was speaking out. Had a few days in detention changed her that much?

"That would be for you too, Yasmin. I would like you to come with Carlos."

"It would be my pleasure," she said.

"That's great to hear, ma'am. The pleasure would be mine. When could we meet to see this gentleman?"

"Sometime next week," Carlos replied. "It's been the heck of a week for us, and we are going to try to relax and catch our breath tonight."

"All right, that's perfectly understandable. Let's say middle of next week, Wednesday or Thursday?"

"Yes, I should be back by Tuesday from the next trip."

The waitress came around the table and served Mr. Moza and his handyman with a small cup of espresso coffee each.

"Thank you, dear. You are always a blessing, God sent."

"Does that mean she's flying on her wings tonight, Mr. Moza?" Roberto shot from across the table.

"No, every word of it is true. She's a fantastic waitress. And I know she deserves to hear it more often. But I want you to know that we appreciate you very much."

He was now looking up at her, giving her his ever-present smile. He gulped his coffee and said thanks again.

"Thank you, Mr. Moza," the attractive brunette replied.

"Well, gents, it looks like Prieto and I have to get going. There is a council meeting going on at the City Council tonight. It should be just about over now. We need to catch the culprits before they leave."

He placed some bills on the table and stood up. He shook everyone's hand, and he and Prieto made slowly for the door. The waitress returned with a bottle of red wine and four cups. She poured everyone half a cup.

"Thank you," Roberto said. "Your timing was perfect. I just finished my dinner."

"I cannot have that much, Roberto," said Carlos. "I have to drive."

"Did I hear you say you guys are going to the beach tonight?"

"Yes, we are going for a swim."

"Oh, Carlos," Amelia commented, "with such a beautiful pool at home?"

"It's not ready," Yasmin said. "Plus we both love the ocean."

"Yeah, there's something magnetic about that heaviness of the sea water."

Carlos looked at his wife. They both connected as if there was no one else in the room.

"The sudden push and pull of a wave as you try to stay on a straight line," Yasmin described.

"Above water, no cheating."

"No, no cheating," Yasmin answered. "The sea is our way of life, my love."

They both moved forward and kissed each other. Roberto turned to Amelia.

"Here she is," Roberto said to his wife, "out of prison, and she's acting as if nothing ever happened, and they are moving on with their honeymoon. I think we should drink to that."

"Yes, we should," Amelia asserted. "Let's have it."

She lifted her cup, and her husband followed. Carlos and Yasmin raised theirs and clinked them together, laughing as if they were schoolchildren.

"To you both," Roberto said.

"And do not worry about a thing," Amelia added, taking a sip of her wine. "It's gonna turn out all right."

"How are you driving to the beach?"

"Oh, you know the way. I pick up 826 then 836 and then 95 to South Beach. We are going to Lummus tonight."

"The park you mean? You are going to the park at night?" Roberto said, nodding his head to stress his point.

"We are not going to the park," Carlos laughed. "Right, Yasmin? We are going to walk past the volleyball courts and the tennis courts and the outward fitness gyms, and jump in the water and swim."

"But why Lummus at night?"

"We love the birds," Yasmin said. "*Las gaviotas.*"

"Yes, the seagulls that come close, looking for food."

Roberto drank his wine and looked at them, puzzled. Yasmin and Carlos clicked their cups again and drank their wine.

"We really appreciate what you did for us today," Carlos repeated again. "Amelia, you picked up Yasmin when she was a broken woman this morning, but look at her now."

"No," answered Amelia. "I picked up a brave woman this morning, one that seemed sure of herself, determined to win."

"Yes," they all agreed.

Ralph and two other men came to their table. They looked like typical truck drivers, wearing their baseball caps down tight and cowboy boots, anxiously extending their hands to Carlos and Yasmin.

"Carlos," said one of them. "Is everything all right?"

"Yes, everything is fine. Thanks for asking."

"We heard what happened," Ralph said. "How're you doing, Yasmin?"

He leaned towards her and embraced her, patting her back.

"I am fine," Yasmin replied. "Thank you."

She shook hands with the other two men.

"Anything you need, just call," Ralph said. "We are all here for you."

"Thank you," Carlos said. "We really appreciate it. Will you drink with us?"

"Thanks. But we don't want to disturb you."

"We are leaving in a few minutes," Carlos said. "We are driving down to the beach. We'll join you at the window for a cortaito."

"Deal. We'll meet you outside."

They headed out, and Carlos and Yasmin stayed with Roberto for a few more minutes, savoring the wine. Carlos was disciplined enough about his driving habits that he only had two sips. They bid goodbye to Amelia and Roberto, and then joined Ralph and the others outside for coffee.

CHAPTER 51

The Chevy headed down the highway to Miami Beach. Yasmin held Carlos's right hand, commenting on the beauty of the ocean. She had missed this scenery so much when she was detained and wondered constantly whether she would see it again with Carlos. Now her questions had been answered. Carlos was here next to her, and the black blanket of the ocean on both sides of the road was as beautiful to her as always.

"I think we have only been once at this part of the beach," Carlos said. "It's good that you chose it this time."

"I did not choose it alone. We chose it together," she answered.

"Did you notice Roberto's reaction when I told him?"

"Yes, they are not as fond of the beach at night as we are. But it's become our habit."

"It's called an idiosyncrasy, love."

She was quiet for a few seconds.

"It could be called that in error," she corrected him. "Maybe that is how Roberto sees it. But it is not strange. It is a perfect fit for us. To be at the ocean at night and hear the waves splashing is a love experience for us. We see our love splashing with the waves."

Carlos turned for a moment and kissed her. They were now entering the city of Miami Beach, and the neon signs lit up the streets. Groups of youngsters cluttered up the South Beach area, some walking, some skating, and some riding in convertible jeeps. Carlos and Yasmin were heading in a different direction tonight. They were on Ocean Drive and drove past Lummus Park while looking for a spot to park their car. Finally, Carlos stopped at a parking garage open twenty-four hours but a ways from Lummus. He and Yasmin parked the car and walked the long stretch, entering the sandy area.

They were dressed casually. He wore shorts and sneakers, and she wore a one-piece black swimming suit and sandals. Both carried a towel on the shoulder.

They passed the gym area where even at this late hour of the day, they found some fitness lovers using the pull-up bars and even two full-blown volleyball teams exchanging shots.

"Who would have thought they'd be playing in the dark?" Carlos said, holding her hand.

"I'd have trouble finding the ball," Yasmin answered. "But the fun makes up for it. It's late, and if you had an early supper, you'd want to wear your body down a little."

"Oh, no, they'll have none of that. Did you see the coolers on each side? That's where they're hiding the beer. Every once in a while one of them pulls out a bottle and drinks up. Then they will pass it around. Past a couple of games some of them will be dragging their feet, and the games will be over, but then they'll hit the bars really hard."

"How do you know so much about it, my love?"

"I have been here enough to see it. I've always come to the beach, even if only to sit down in the sand and watch the waves."

"Well that's what we do now," she said.

Yasmin stopped to take her sandals off, and Carlos followed and took off his sneakers. He knotted the laces together and carried them in his left hand.

"Now it's much different," Carlos added. "Much better."

"It's never been like this for me," she said softly.

"Really?"

He turned, stopped, and pulled her towards him by the hand. She let herself be led and kissed him.

"See a spot yet?"

"I haven't looked. It is all too beautiful for me. It doesn't matter where."

"Can we go forward a little more?"

"I'll follow you."

They settled at a spot where the sand was damp. Neither one of them cared that their clothes might get wet, sparkled with the foam of a wave. They could not think of missing that airy feeling that arrived when the water reached a certain point in the sand, then pulled back with ease, as if tugging the earth and everything on it back to the ocean.

"I know," she whispered.

She spread her towel on the sand. Then she gathered his towel, sneakers, and her sandals and placed them together neatly at a corner. He handed her his shirt.

"Let's sit down and watch," Carlos said.

"Forever," she answered, then sat next to him and hung her head on his shoulder.

In a moment, they felt infatuated by the sound of a new wave rushing to the shore, and they both smiled at each other as the water raced closer and closer to their blanket.

"Let's go swim," said Carlos.

"Wait," Yasmin responded.

She grabbed his hand tight as the water almost reached them and then pulled back, and they had that dragging feeling again, and Yasmin gasped in excitement.

"Let's go!" she yelled.

Holding hands they ran towards the water and both dove in as the next wave rushed in. They submerged to the bottom and a moment later surfaced together. They turned and headed south, swimming head to head, with beautiful arched strokes that swept the water in perfect timing with each other. They went a long distance, not giving up an inch from each other, even as a wave enveloped them and pushed them closer to the shore, then pulled them back. They had gone about three-quarters of a mile when Yasmin grabbed Carlos's hand and stopped stroking. They both floated on the surface, and Yasmin got in front of him and kissed him. She pulled him towards the shore.

"What happened?" Carlos asked, as they both got on their feet.

Dripping water from her hair and looking somber, she led him to dry sand. They suddenly heard clapping from some passers-by, who were still enjoying the evening. Others, scattered around and joined them. They all had been watching them as they swam majestically. It was a beautiful thing to see.

"Bravo!" they yelled in unison. "Man, that was terrific," someone said.

"Thank you," Carlos replied.

He and Yasmin walked away waving at them.

"Carlos," Yasmin began, "when does Gordon want you back?"

"Oh, I haven't asked, darling. He knows that you just got home, and I think he will give me some time so we can be together."

"How long will he give you?"

"I don't know. A few days maybe. He's real busy. Why? Do you already want me to leave?"

"No, darling. I just want to plan our time. I will work on the pool tomorrow morning and then inside the house. Later maybe we can go see some furniture?"

"Yasmin, that was a big fright we just went through when you got arrested. I blamed myself. I should have known better. I don't want you to travel with me in the truck again until you have your Immigration papers, at least a work permit or something. I don't want anything to happen to you."

"No, Carlos, how could you think of going alone? I am going to be with you in your travels. I won't let you go alone."

"You can't, Yasmin. It's too risky. You saw what happened. If we get stopped again, the first thing the police will do is ask for your papers."

"I don't want you to drive alone. You know how much I would miss you if you left me. I would be always waiting for you."

Her beautiful black eyes seemed to glow as she stared at him. He responded and held her face with his two hands and kissed her.

"Besides, I have papers now that I can show them if they stop us," she added.

"They are papers that show you are in deportation. Not much help."

"They show that I am in process. They can't arrest me if I am in process."

Carlos seemed taken aback by her comment. How much knowledge had Yasmin absorbed in the past few days of her ordeal. Then he realized what a smart woman he had married. Quiet and apparently shy, but quick in digesting everything she saw around her and applying it to good use.

"I actually don't know the answer to that. Let's ask our lawyer."

"So, I can go with you then, right?"

"No, Yasmin. I will suffer as much as you not having you, but we can't take a risk like that. A trooper may still decide to take you, and we could not have that again. Why don't we wait a little bit before we decide on that? There's a lot to do in our house. It needs you here. Let's wait till you get it all together first. Then we will see."

She got as close to tears as she had ever been, and she showed it.

"I will miss you terribly, Carlos."

"But I am right there at your fingertips all the time. Just one phone call away."

"It's not the same, my love."

She took his hand and rubbed her cheek with it.

"Come on, let's keep going."

"We are already known in these parts."

"So no one is surprised to see us," Carlos said. "You know that we are not supposed to swim here at night. If the police saw us, they could issue us a summons."

"Stop worrying," Yasmin replied, yanking his arm. "We have to live our lives."

"But we have to be careful, follow the rules."

"We follow the rules."

"No, we don't. Swimming here after 6:00 is illegal."

"But we are daring, honey, because we are in love."

They slowly walked back in the water, holding hands and whispering to each other. Then Yasmin leaned her head on his shoulder and spoke to him softly.

"I know why you worry about me. You don't want anything to happen to me. But it's okay, Carlos. Nothing will happen here. We are not going that far from the shore. If you want we can come earlier, before 6:00, but it's nothing like being here at night, right?"

"Right, but it's too dangerous for you right now. You just got out of detention, and you're already playing with fate. Imagine if a cop shows up here and wants to play hard ball. He could arrest us both."

"All right, nothing like that will happen."

"I'm not worried about me. What do I care? I'm worried about you, darling."

"All right, well, there is no police around here now."

The two looked at each other and dove in, came out a few feet farther into the ocean, then floated and turned west, their bodies aligned parallel with each other, and then they began stroking, moving forward in a straight line, swayed upwards and downwards by the oncoming waves but never losing an inch of space between them. To anyone watching them, it would seem they were professional swimmers, perhaps lifeguards practicing their coordination and freestyle swimming. No one could guess that only weeks before, they had never swum together, and that relying on their swimming skills, they had bonded to form a perfect duo whose virtuosity came naturally to them, like a pair of restless dolphins that crossed the murkiest waters together.

CHAPTER 52

That night at home, they showered together, and the fatigue brought by their long stretch in the water drove them to bed. They both embraced each other without saying a word and quickly fell asleep, resting in each other's arms. Right at the moment when the sky began to lighten up, Yasmin pulled gently away from Carlos's arms. She decided to start her day in the kitchen first. She had planned to clean the pool but realized she did not have a net. She needed Carlos to go with her and buy supplies. They needed almost everything.

She straightened up the kitchen in no time. Carlos had given her notes with numbers of who to call about furniture, and she was tempted to do it, but she did not want to buy anything without him. Later, when he woke up, she would convince him to go out and pick some furniture.

She went to the utility room, a small structure at the end of the yard, and tried to clean some of the leaves from the pool. The water was still clear, but having no cover, it attracted anything that the wind carried. She found a pool rake for the leaves and a long rod with a handle, among other provisions. She was glad that the previous owner had not taken everything. She connected the rake to the rod and began the tedious job of gathering the leaves and papers that had accumulated on the surface and bottom. Cleaning the water would be another matter, and she would have to teach herself how to do it. She would ask Carlos later.

She got breakfast ready. She was already used to the soft bread that her husband preferred, bathed with butter inside and scrambled eggs. She would have the same. She prepared two plates and left them covered on the electric stove. It would be another hour before Carlos gave any signs of life, and she decided how to use her time. She worked on the parquet floor of the dining room. It needed a shining. She thought she would make it the pride of their home.

Right around 10:00, when she was down on her knees rubbing the floor with rags, she heard the rustling of sheets coming from the bedroom, which could only mean that her husband was finally awake. She climbed the stairs hastily to the bedroom and found Carlos with his midsection wrapped up in sheets.

"It's time for breakfast, my Carlos. Come on," she whispered in his ear.

He opened his eyes, looking straight at her.

"What do you have planned for me today?" he asked.

"Let's go look at furniture. We need a dining table and chairs."

He sat up on the bed and spoke softly.

"We need a whole dining room set. I know a good place. They will throw a nice painting and maybe a serving cart with wheels for when we have guests."

"I don't think I've ever seen one."

"It's for drinks. You and I will use it for holidays when we have friends over."

"Isn't this going to cost a lot of money, Carlos?"

"I have saved for this moment, Yasmin. It's for our home. As a matter of fact, we have to go to the bank to add your name to the account."

"What for?"

"Just in case something happens to me. You are going to need access to the account."

"Let's not do that, Carlos. We will be inviting trouble."

"Oh, come on, let's not get superstitious now. Your name needs to be on the account."

He tossed the covers aside, kissed her, and got up from bed.

"Wash up and come down for breakfast now," Yasmin said. "It's ready."

Carlos heard the vibrations of his phone from the night table and stopped walking.

"That must be Gordon. I have to answer that."

He touched the phone screen and clicked on his boss's name.

"How is it going over there?" came Gordon's voice. "Are you up?"

"Yes. I know you want to set me up for a trip, but I need today and tomorrow. Just two days."

"It's okay. I am just checking. Don't forget you have to see Norman today. Around 5:00 p.m., he told me."

"We know. We will be there."

"All right. I leave you then. Enjoy the day with Yasmin, and I will call tomorrow night."

CHAPTER 53

That evening Carlos and Yasmin sat in the red soft cushion chairs across a large mahogany desk. Mr. Kline had been giving them a detailed explanation about the requirements of their upcoming applications. He pointed to several forms that Lucrecia, Mr. Klines's able secretary, had placed across from them.

"Those are the basic ones that get the process going. For now, all you need to worry about is to show that you are living together. You share your assets, home, bank account, utilities. You are both young, about the same age, and obviously in a good-faith relationship, so I do not see a problem. There might be an interview which, if it happens, should not be that hard for you to overcome. Once this application gets approved is where the real battle begins."

He looked at them and smiled. He had a way about him. He conveyed a sense of security that made his clients feel that their future was in good hands. Yasmin was the quieter one of the two, and she had hardly any questions. Carlos was concerned about the requirements of hardship as to Yasmin's petition for a waiver later on.

"The real battle," repeated Carlos. "That is what I am worried about, Mr. Kline. How are we going to be able to do that?"

"If the application was to be submitted right now, it would be based purely on economics. The question would be whether you need Yasmin's help to maintain your financial status here."

"Yasmin does not work," Carlos replied. "Yasmin depends on me."

"True," Mr. Kline said. "At the present time that is how it stands. We will have to make some changes in order to present a solid case of hardship, even if only based on financial factors. But look, you have to take it step by step. Right now your situation is changing very rapidly. You just bought a house, and as I understand it, Yasmin's name is on the deed to the property. That is an equity issue that can affect your case positively. She may need to work to help out with the bills and the upkeeping of the house."

"I thought Yasmin is not supposed to work."

"That's true too. And if she works, she will have to use her true name, remember that. Then she will have to report her earnings to the government with what they call a PIN number. The point is for her to show some income to demonstrate that she is a breadwinner in the home and that she contributes to its support. We have to start building a scenario from now."

"But no one is supposed to hire her without authorization to work. That's my understanding."

"True, but do you really think that the undocumented population does not work? They work just as much and even more than the rest of us. They have to in order to survive."

"Won't that hurt her in the future?"

"It's a chance we have to take. In the next few days, have her apply for a PIN number. You can do that through an accountant or one of the many tax preparers that we have around this area."

"Man, I wish there was something wrong with my health so I could help Yasmin."

"No, you don't want to wish that. Let's do it this way now. Get her a PIN number, and then you will have to find her some type of employment. She could be a waitress at a restaurant or a housekeeper at a hotel. Anything to show she gets some income and that she contributes towards the home."

Carlos looked thoughtfully at Yasmin. It was the last thing he wanted for his wife. He was a thrifty young man who had used his time wisely and had saved his money. When purchasing his home, he had made a large down payment. He had paid half of its price up front, and his mortgage was low, and even after it, his savings account reached past two hundred thousand, all from his years behind the wheel. He had planned his future well and wanted his family to enjoy the fruits of his labor, but now fate had played a fast one on him. His wife needed to work for her to gain legal status.

Almost reading his thoughts, she responded, "It's all right, Carlos. We will manage. I will get a job."

Carlos did not answer. They both got busy signing the forms that Lucrecia had placed on the desk.

"We now put the whole bundle in an envelope and send it out," Lucrecia said. "That's how the whole process gets started."

She worked fast, positioning each signature page in front of them and then moving on to the next one. She collected all the forms and put them together into one bundle and clipped them. She placed them inside a Federal Express envelope, sealing it, and walked away with them in hand.

"I know you have questions, and I will be glad to answer each one of them. But the idea is that we have to do this one step at a time. Try to take care of some of the things I mentioned, and let's keep moving forward. We have our hurdles to cross, but we will deal with each one as we go along."

"Have you ever seen a case like this?"

"Of course I have. It's a very familiar scenario that couples face today."

"And how do they do?"

"Some struggle and get through. There are no easy ones."

"And some don't make it, right?"

"There have been some that have had setbacks, and we have had to refile until they have been approved."

Carlos looked briefly sideways at the large window at the end of the room. The early evening sun was filtering through the partially open blinds, giving the room a golden aura of light. Carlos and Yasmin stood up to shake Mr. Kline's hand. He was impressed by their physique, both looking fit and athletic, giving an impression of readiness that he himself could not convey. No client he had seen in his office for a long time had seemed as prepared and resolute as they were.

"We will start working on some of these things tomorrow," Carlos said. "We just need a little bit of time, but we will do as you say."

"Good," Mr. Kline answered. "It helps to be positive about these things. They just don't happen by themselves. We have to see them along."

"Yeah, I know."

Carlos smiled at him, and so did Yasmin. They said their goodbyes to Lucrecia and walked out of the room and took the elevator to go to the parking lot.

CHAPTER 54

After leaving Norman Kline's office, Carlos and Yasmin stopped at their house. They had bought some furniture in the afternoon that was going to be delivered the next morning and checked the room to make sure everything was ready. They had been at the bank and made the arrangements to add Yasmin's name to the account. Now they sat by the pool with their feet in the water, making lover's talk and little reminders here and there.

"I did not see you call your mother," Yasmin said. "Have you?"

"She calls every morning, and I always call her before I go to sleep. You see me."

"Sometimes you just slump into bed, and I pick up her call. We have gotten to know each other this way."

Carlos smiled at her.

"She would never hurt a fly. She's that kind of person who finds good in everyone. She already loves you to death. I have not mentioned anything about what happened with you."

"Why not?"

"She's going to worry unnecessarily, and then she'll tell my father, and then he will be calling me, looking for answers. They are not going to understand what's happening. Have you mentioned anything to your parents?"

"No. They definitely will not understand."

"Let's hope we don't ever have to mention anything to them."

"Eventually my parents will have to know. I will have to travel there."

"And so will I. I will not let you go alone."

Yasmin smiled and hugged him.

"You are all set with everything now. You know where the money is, how to pay the bills, everything."

"Are you planning to go somewhere?"

"Only driving to Phoenix."

"Not without me."

"I thought we settled that."

"No, I don't want you to go alone."

"And I don't want you to get arrested again. Come to think of it, I should have asked Norman. I am sure he would have said no."

"I don't want to be alone, Carlos. And I don't want you to be alone."

"But we are never alone anymore, not even when we are not together, we are not alone."

She smiled and closed her eyes. It was true, and she felt it too.

"Let's go and pick up a cup of coffee outside of the restaurant. Want to? Then we'll go for our swim."

"Let's go!" she said happily and quickly stood up. "Dinner with my Carlos, how could I miss that?"

"Who said anything about dinner?"

"If we are going to be serious swimmers we have to eat."

He hugged her and grabbed her hand.

"Let's not hang around too much," Carlos commented. "Maybe we should not go after it gets too dark.

"Come on. Let's go."

They put on their shoes. She ran inside, grabbed the keys, then came back outside, and took his hand to go to the car.

"Are you driving?" Carlos asked.

"No, not yet. But I have my own professional driver."

"I have to see about getting you a license."

"I heard that we are not allowed in Florida."

"Where did you hear that, darling?"

"At the prison," Yasmin said.

"Oh, that place is a big source for immigration news."

"I heard so much in the few days that I was there."

They got inside the car and drove off to La Carreta.

CHAPTER 55

The evenings had gotten warmer, but tonight a gentle breeze seemed to freshen the traces of a long and humid day, making high the demand for outside dining. Carlos and Yasmin tried to get a spot at the front terrace of the restaurant, but there was not a single chair available. They had no choice but to move inside. They checked with the cashier before picking a table.

"We do not intend to stay long," Carlos said. "We are only going to have a light meal. Where should we sit?"

"I think you are out of luck," said the cute brunette, smiling. "Roberto is at the end of the aisle."

Carlos eyed the last table in the center aisle, and a hand went up immediately. Roberto and Amelia were sitting next to each other at the end, with an additional four empty chairs. Roberto kept waving at him, and Carlos waved back. Just then his phone vibrated, and he took a moment to look at the screen. Gordon's name was spread in wide letters on the face of the phone, and Carlos quickly picked up as he and Yasmin headed towards the end table.

"I thought you were going to give me more time," Carlos said.

"I will. I promise. But something's come up, and only you are qualified for the job. I've got an emergency drop in Phoenix, then pickup and drop-off in Mobile and drive without a wagon to Orlando. The problem is the time. It's gotta be there before the weekend. The pickup from Phoenix to Mobile is easy. There is no rerouting to Atlanta."

"When?"

"Tonight."

"Gordon, that is a stretch. I need some sleep."

"You can leave at two in the morning. I will pay double. It's an emergency."

"What kind of an emergency? A Gordon emergency."

"No, for real."

"Hold on."

Carlos put the phone down to greet his friends as he and Yasmin sat down at the table.

"All right," Carlos said into the phone. "I'll call you back later."

He ended the call and joined the chatter between Yasmin and his friends. It surprised him to see how fluently Yasmin handled the conversation. She did not show the slightest trace of timidity, and he actually waited before breaking in.

"Is that your boss calling you?" Roberto asked. "Already trying to put you back on the road? But you just got here."

"My boss lives in a different world. Everything is an emergency when it's not."

"It's a tough business to be in," Roberto said. "Ask Amelia."

"I will vouch for that," she said. "We had the opportunity to own a business like that, and I totally refused. I put my foot down, as they say, and I told Roberto that I would not do it."

"She's right. Everyone who owns a business like that lives in full-time anxiety, in a sense of pending disaster. I saw it. I drove for a living, and I had offers to have my own routes and my own truck and start my business. But no, I decided not to. I do not want a life like that."

The waitress was next to them, tablet in hand.

"Anything to drink?" she asked.

Carlos waived his hand in deference to Roberto and Amelia.

"Just water for us," Roberto said.

Carlos pointed to Yasmin.

"We both want guarapo," she said. "We could order the main course too."

"All right, what will you have?"

"Carlos and I will share," she said. "A congris and a steak."

"Oh, that's easy."

The waitress turned to Roberto and his wife, and took their order.

"Is Mr. Moza around?"

"No, he's at a meeting. He has been at meetings all day long. I couldn't even get ahold of him."

"Oh, I hate those political meetings."

"Don't go on hating them too much," Roberto said. "You might be involved."

"Me? Never. Politics would be the last thing I would ever do, even if I was broke and could not find a job. I'd crawl for a living, sweep the streets, but politics, never."

"It seems to me that you have a knack for it, Carlos."

"A knack for it? How did you get that impression, Roberto?"

"Sometimes the skills of a person are notable, even if they do not practice them."

Yasmin leaned over and kissed Carlos.

"Carlos is happy driving. That is his passion."

"Not quite, darling. You are my passion."

"That's a good answer," said Amelia.

"So what is the plan tonight for you guys? It sounds like you two are going away again."

Carlos shook his head in the negative.

"I don't want her to travel anymore, Roberto. It's too dangerous after what's happened."

"That's understandable. You should follow your instincts always."

"Oh, Yasmin," Amelia cut in excitedly. "That means you'll be home. I will come and help you set up the house."

"I do not want him to drive alone," Yasmin said.

"Oh, Carlos is a professional driver," Roberto explained. "You can rest assured. You can go to sleep on that one."

"Still, I'm used to keeping him company on the road."

"But you need to spend some time at the house. How are you ever going to get it in order if you're not here?"

"Yasmin's getting it all set up. We did a lot today, and tomorrow, some furniture is coming."

"All of the furniture?" Amelia asked.

"The dining room set," Yasmin replied.

"I gotta work my way to your house," Roberto said. "I still have not seen it. I'll wait till you come back from this trip, and then I'll come over."

"You can come anytime," Carlos said. "My house is your house. *Mi casa es tu casa.*"

"That's right," Yasmin repeated. "Anytime."

The waitress returned with some of the food. She served Carlos and Yasmin, then turned to Roberto and Amelia and said she would be right back.

"And where are you two going after this?" Roberto asked, looking at Carlos.

"We're going for our swim of the night," Carlos said.

"Again?"

"It's our daily routine."

Yasmin placed her head on Carlos's shoulder and chuckled.

"We are getting better," she said. "You want to join us?"

Roberto seemed utterly surprised by her question and was going to answer but was interrupted by the waitress, who had returned with his order.

Amelia laughed out loud.

"We could never keep up with you. One short lap maybe, and we'd be done."

"So the two of you just swim together at the beach?" Roberto asked.

"We do more than just swim. We've been practicing our freestyle swimming together. Since the first day we swam together, we clicked. Yasmin competed at tournaments in Guatemala."

"Really?"

"Yes, out in her west coast there. But we are just enjoying it right now. We swim together side by side in a straight line, as a team. It's a lot of fun."

"And you do it right after dinner. You ought to go earlier."

"No, we can't during the day. We are too busy."

"But what about your pool?"

"It's not an Olympic pool, Roberto. You're wrong on that one. We can't train there."

"We would need more space," said Yasmin.

"We are going to try to go far tonight at the beach," Carlos said. "I need to be real tired so I can sleep well before I leave."

"Roberto and I will come one of these nights to watch you," Amelia said.

"We can't tonight though," Roberto said interrupting her. "I just got back from Orlando, and I need some rest. We'll wait till you get back."

Yasmin cut their steak in two pieces. Then she chopped each half into square bits and slid Carlos's share onto his plate.

"I should be back in four days," Carlos said.

"Four days. Wow. You're really going far this time."

"We will be back in less time," Yasmin said.

"We?" asked Roberto. "I thought it was settled that he's going alone, no?"

She shook her head.

"Let's leave it at that," Carlos said. "We will talk more about it after our practice swim. All right?"

She nodded, and Carlos looked towards Roberto and Amelia.

"Yasmin, stay," Amelia told her, "and I will help you with the house. You know my number, right?"

Yasmin showed her the phone. Her name was in the contact list.

"Of course I have it. You saved me. But I don't want Carlos to drive alone."

"Let him go just this one time," Amelia said. "We need time to work on the house."

Yasmin nodded in agreement, knowing full well that she had no intentions of letting Carlos go alone. She and Carlos ate their dinner and exchanged more pleasantries with Amelia and Roberto, but for some reason, it seemed to them as a sad moment. The four of them became silent when the waitress returned one last time to check up on them, and Carlos and Yasmin both asked for a coffee, a cortaito. Roberto did also, but Amelia commented that one cup of coffee now would spoil her sleep.

The waitress returned shortly with three cups and laid them on the table. All three of them drank in silence, and Amelia went on talking about her plans of decorating the house. She had so many ideas. She thought that a china closet would look great in the dining room. What did Yasmin think about that? Yasmin nodded. She had never thought of that. And then they would have to work on china selection, Royal Albert, Lennox, Wedgewood English. There was no limit. Yasmin smiled, and then Carlos announced they had to leave. The beach was waiting.

"Are you sure it's all right to go in the water right after dinner?" Roberto asked. "Don't you worry about that? Remember that where we come from, that was prohibited. It was considered lethal to swim after having eaten. Don't you remember?"

"Yes, that may have been before my time. Now Cubans are more concerned about finding something to eat than when to swim. The needs control now. Well," Carlos said standing, "we have to go now. You are welcome to join us."

"No, thanks," Roberto replied. "Amelia needs her sleep. By the way, dinner was on me. You be careful, and we will see you by the end of the week. Do not worry about Yasmin. We will take care of her."

Carlos shook his hand and hugged Amelia. They were off to the beach.

CHAPTER 56

After their swim at the beach Carlos and Yasmin headed back home. The night had set in, and as they got on 195 from Alton Road, once again, Yasmin felt that buoyancy in her brain that made her feel as if she was in a dream. The wonder of nature and the agility of man working together and creating a passage of road that defied nature and defined true beauty. She was looking for the silver reflection of the moon on both sides of the highway, as she had seen them before, but oddly, there was no moon tonight. Was it the clouds? Or was it because it was a new moon, and its dark side was facing the earth? No, that could not be. The moon did not turn. She almost blurted out the question to Carlos, but she could not utter a word. What did it mean? Was it a bad sign? And then to her surprise, it was Carlos who chimed in.

"Don't you feel that there is something different tonight? Do you see it? Do you feel it?"

She did not speak, but she moved her head close to him and nodded. Carlos saw the gloomy look in her eyes, and he wanted to hug her tight and kiss her to make that feeling go away, but he couldn't while driving.

"Oh, it's only the light of the moon, darling. That's all. It's a moonless night."

"I know," she finally said.

They both knew it was not the same. Darkness set in the ocean on both sides of the highway, except for the faraway reflection of the hotel lights. Neither one of them said a word for the rest of the drive. Yasmin just gripped his arm with her left hand until the car pulled into the driveway.

"What time are we leaving?" she asked.

"Darling," Carlos replied. "We know you can't go. It's too much of a risk. Now that we seem to be getting closer to our goal. Now more than ever we have to be careful. If we get stopped and they arrest you again, that could set us back. We don't want that."

They went to the door, and Carlos opened the door for her. As they walked in, she pointed to the dining room.

"It's all ready for tomorrow. Look at the painting."

"Oh, you hung up the painting before the furniture got here. Yasmin, you are so talented. It's just perfect where it is. When did you do that?"

"While you took a shower before."

"But how did you know where to put it? How did you do it?"

"Oh, I measured. The table will go in the middle so that part is easy, but we have that chest coming, and we already decided that it will go on the other side, so that leaves this side for the picture. Do you like it?"

"It's perfect, Yasmin, just perfect. Everything you do is perfect."

That night Yasmin did her best to convince Carlos that he should not drive alone. That was in the old days, before they met, but now he had started a new life with her, and they were a couple. They needed each other and should not be apart.

But Carlos resisted her pitch. It was unthinkable that he could put her in danger. He fell asleep with her arms around her. A few minutes before 2:00 a.m., he was up. He brushed his teeth and got ready to leave. He came back to bed and leaned forward to kiss Yasmin and met her stare. She had not slept a wink. She hugged him before he did.

"Promise me that you will call me," she said.

"And you promise me that you will be careful. Amelia will be here in the morning to help you, and if you need anything, you have her. Maybe you should take a Uber car and sleep there at night until I get back. I should be back in four days. You know how it is."

"I know," she said faintly and hung onto his neck.

She got up and went to see him off at the front door.

"I will miss you terribly," Carlos said.

"I will miss you twice as much," she answered.

CHAPTER 57

Carlos picked up his truck and was at the loading dock a few minutes after 3:00. It felt strange driving alone. He already missed Yasmin when he got behind the wheel. But regardless of the pain he felt, he needed to get on the road; the sooner he went, the sooner he would be back. This was just another load, he thought, another pickup, and all he had to do was to drive, drive under the rules as he knew how, steady and forward and stop only when he had to as mandated by the feds. There was nothing to it. His wife was back home guarding the house. Nothing could be wrong.

He got on Route 95 North, maintaining a moderate but steady speed. He felt fully awake and in total charge but avoided looking towards the right side of the seat, where Yasmin normally sat. He knew she was an early riser but also realized that she had trouble falling asleep last night, so he decided not to call her until late in the morning. By then he would be near Jacksonville, where he would pick up Route 10 West, heading towards Alabama.

The way that Gordon was planning his driving calendar, it seemed he would have to avoid the twenty-four-hour restart that drivers were subject to. To do that, he would have to plan ahead carefully, putting in a number of hours every day so that he would not fall into the restart cycle. That meant working steadily every day without taking a day off. Because of the recent purchase of the house and other expenses that had come up, Carlos felt he had no choice but go that route. He needed a steady flow of income now to replenish his resources. Yasmin could perhaps join him again if things looked right. He would have to see.

By 6:00 a.m., Yasmin was calling him. She had slept only after he left the house, but she was up already. She found it hard to sleep past six.

"I wanted to give you more time before calling you," Carlos said. "Did you sleep?"

"I slept after you left. I decided to trust you and rely on you. That gave me peace of mind, and I went right to sleep. I'm up now. I have a lot to do in the house. I miss you so much, Carlos."

"Me too, my darling."

"Where are you?"

"I'm an hour or two away from Jacksonville."

"I'm going to learn how to track your travels on my phone. I am going to do that today."

"It's easy, darling. You can do that from your phone. If it makes you feel better, do it."

"I need it for my own state of mind."

"Can you go back to sleep a little more? You have not slept enough."

"Maybe after the furniture gets here, darling. See what happens when we are not together?"

"I know, I know. I am having a hard time too. I figure that I will stop for rest after Mobile, Alabama. You know, that is the state after Florida, going west."

"I know. I learned it from you."

"In no time I will be back, and we will be going back to the beach. We will be so good swimming together that we will draw a crowd to watch us."

"Don't. You're going to make me cry."

"They will be tears of joy, but I don't want you to cry. We are going to be so happy."

"Aren't we already?"

"Yes, but it keeps growing. It's like that song says."

"What song?"

"It's an American song. I first heard it when I came to America. It's called 'More Today than Yesterday.' I liked the music, and at first I did not know what the words meant, but eventually I learned them, and now I like it even more."

"What do the words say?"

"That I love you more today than yesterday but only half as much as tomorrow."

"Oh," Yasmin said and stopped. "Can you send me the video through the phone?"

"As soon as I make a stop I will."

"Okay. We can go even earlier now to the beach if it makes you feel safer."

"I just want us to be safe. We can't afford to get into any hassles with the police now and run the risk of being arrested. They can ticket us for swimming after dark."

"Well, maybe. But as long as we are together."

"We will always be regardless."

"Promise?"

"Yes," he said.

CHAPTER 58

Carlos dropped the load in Phoenix and made his pickup, pulled into another gate, where a loaded trailer waited for him, and was on his way east again. Being in the vicinity where he had met Yasmin made him nostalgic. He wanted to go back and stop at the restaurant where Yasmin had worked and where she had cultivated a garden, but if he did, he was sure he would have to face the old cook now. He'd probably get arrested for having threatened him. No, it was not a wise choice. He needed to get back to drop the load and move on. He would make memories in Miami with his lovely wife.

He got on Route 10 East and immediately felt relaxed. He asked himself why he would have felt stress to begin with. What reason was there to feel stressed? Yasmin was out of detention. The case was moving, and yes, there was a long bridge to cross and a high obstacles to jump, but Mr. Kline was right. Things would fall into place. He looked at the road ahead and had the urge to call Yasmin. She would brighten anybody's day.

"Hello," she said, answering his call.

"I'm on the road again," he told her. "It's early afternoon, and I thought I'd get an early start. I am on my way to Alabama and then home. How are you doing?"

"I'm finished setting up the dining room. Now I can send you a picture of it."

"What else did you do to it?"

"I could not get to do it right away. There were other things, as you know. I am done, though. I've started with our bedroom already."

"Are you going to change the furniture in that room?"

"No, not for now. But I'm changing a few things. Wait till you see the picture I am going to send you. You are going to be surprised."

"I know it's gonna be fine like everything you do."

"How does it look there? Is it sunny?"

"Oh, yes, it's a beautiful day."

"When will you stop for your rest?"

"Early evening. Early in the evening. I should be in Mobile midday tomorrow, and then I will unhitch the trailer and leave without a load, heading home."

"You never traveled without a trailer with me. You always had a load."

"That is how these companies make money. They lose when they send you out on the road empty. I think Gordon could not get another load from Mobile to Florida. He needed to get the first load out to Phoenix, and that became his priority. I won't mind traveling without a trailer for a few miles though. It's fine by me."

"Yeah, I feel better knowing you don't have that weight behind you."

"It's a little bit strange. I feel more on course with the wagon behind me. Without it, I feel like I am just going to drift away at any moment. It feels too light, like I am missing something."

"After driving for so many hours with all that weight behind you, it has to feel light. I understand."

"You haven't yet traveled with me without the wagon behind us, right?"

"No, I have not."

"Wait till I do a couple of more trips, then I will bring you again, and you will see."

"You promise?"

"I have to say that it feels awfully lonely without you. I am thinking of ways on how to justify bringing you. I cannot make a mistake about that."

"You are not making any mistakes. The answer is that I am already in proceedings. The minute they check, they will realize that and not bother me."

"That is true," Carlos muttered as if to himself.

"Now you see?"

"I do, darling."

CHAPTER 59

After dropping the trailer in Mobile, Carlos disengaged the tractor and got back on Route 10 East. He had a decision to make. Should he get off Route 10 and look for a local road to reach Route I-75 South to Orlando, pick up the new load, and then catch the turnpike from there to Miami? It avoided going around Jacksonville. But the thought of traveling on a local road, even if only for a couple of hours distance, discouraged him. He would have to slow down. Most of those roads, like 301, were speed traps, where your chances of being stopped multiplied. He had about five hours to decide that, and for now he enjoyed the comfort of hauling a trailer which made the trip seem go much faster. He did not think about his choices anymore, and he was surprised how quickly he ran into a familiar section of the highway where the road split from its course and twisted left along with a protracted curve. He had passed this section hundreds of times, and today it seemed flawless as ever, not carrying a trailer.

He was in the right lane, and as he entered the curve, an eighteen-wheeler passed him on the left doing well over the speed limit. Carlos thought the driver must be on drugs. To drive an eighteen-wheeler at high speed on a sharp curve was suicidal, and Carlos felt the draft made by the passing vehicle as it moved ahead, leaving him behind. But to his horror, another eighteen-wheeler was following the first one at a short distance behind at the same rate of speed. Because he was driving only a tractor without a trailer, the draft made by passing vehicles swayed him. He was at that second entering the angle of the curve. He switched to a lower gear, but the shaking of his tractor, caused by the wind, made him lose control.

He suddenly found himself on the shoulder of the highway, headed for the ditch.

He did not know what happened next. The bumps that he encountered shook his body violently, even strapped, and the left side of his head struck the door frame. That is when everything went black, and he passed out.

Perhaps it was luck, perhaps it was a testimony to his high driving skills, but his having switched to a lower gear slowed the engine and led the tractor to a stop before causing more damage. Passing cars that had witnessed the accident could not stop but dialed 911 for help. A man who drove a sedan was brave enough to pull onto the shoulder and get out through the passenger door of his vehicle. He went into the ditch and ran towards the tractor up ahead, his phone jammed onto his ear as he yelled for help. The man reached Carlos's tractor, struggling to get a look at the driver, but Carlos's body was slumped to the right of the seat, held together only by the seat belt at shoulder length. Blood covered his head, oozing rapidly onto the seat. Something needed to be done fast, the man thought. He tried to open the driver's door, but it wouldn't give. Whether the lock was triggered by some safety device or simply that the driver had it locked, he did not know, but he ran to the passenger side, and after struggling with the handle, he was able to get it open.

It only took a quick glance to realize that the injury was serious. Blood was flowing out of Carlos's head, and that could mean a skull fracture of some kind. The man had no idea on how to render first aid to a head injury. The only thing he could do was to at least make Carlos comfortable. But how? The driver's head was hanging loosely from the edge of the seat belt. If he could only unstrap him and lay him across the seat, he could at least make him comfortable. He tried to release the belt on the side and fiddled with the retractor, but no luck. The seat belt was stuck, probably from thrust of the impact.

The man retrieved a set of keys from his back pocket and opened the leaf of a small switchblade he carried in his key ring. He cut through the belt at waist length and then slowly let the driver's body rest on the seat. He wasn't sure if what he was doing was right, but he heard the sirens of two trooper cars that had parked at the shoulder of the road. Behind them was an ambulance with emergency lights blinking. The man jumped out of the cabin and waved at them, yelling for help.

"Here, here!" he yelled. "The driver is bleeding."

The medical personnel got to work right away. Carlos's upper body was drenched in blood, and two first-aiders tried to stop the bleeding while others secured him to a stretcher. Then the others stood aside while two of them began to move the stretcher out of the cabin. The cabin was high off the ground, and it was difficult to slide the stretcher on a downward slope.

Another medic held the door open until the other two men were on the ground.

One of the troopers and the senior first-aider walked behind the men carrying the stretcher to the ambulance.

"Any chance of getting a statement from him?" the trooper asked in a low voice.

"None," responded the medic. "If we weren't so close to the hospital he would have been medevacked."

"How does it look?"

The medic shook his head.

"We'll do the best we can for him, but it's a brain injury. That says it all."

"All right," said the trooper, turning back to face the others. "Get a statement from the witness, and see if somebody else stops by. I think there is another car up ahead whose driver might know something. I'm going to lead the ambulance to the hospital and then come back."

He pointed up ahead in the distance, where a truck had pulled to the shoulder. His keen eyes had spotted the vehicle even though it was barely visible.

In a few seconds they were under way, the trooper car ahead of the ambulance with sirens blasting and all emergency lights blinking. In a few minutes, Carlos's life had changed drastically. His life was now in the hands of strangers who would toil desperately to keep his heart going and control the bleeding that oozed out of the gash on the side of his head.

CHAPTER 60

UF Health Jacksonville was home to a trauma 1 center that tended to victims of serious accidents with severe injuries and needing lifesaving procedures. A team of nurses and doctors received Carlos's stretcher at the entrance of the hospital and slid him onto a higher trauma x-ray stretcher, equipped with the latest technological features. Two of the nurses wheeled it down the corridor into an emergency room, while a doctor rushed right alongside making his first observations. He was a young trauma surgeon, viewed by those who knew him as the lucky draw of any patient who happened to fall into his skilled hands. By the time the staffers had squarely secured the stretcher into position at the trauma unit, he was ready to announce one of his fateful findings. He turned and pointed his index finger at the first aid personnel among the bundle of men and women in blue who had crowded around the patient, setting up IVs and monitors.

"Which one of you guys worked on him?"

Two first-aiders raised their hands.

"You may have saved his life," he told them confidently as he got into position by Carlos's head and inspected the exposed gash that extended across his temple.

"Let's cover that up," he told the staffers. "Let's work on his vital signs and restore his pressure. This man is going to need surgery as soon his heart allows it."

He moved to another section where he was wanted. The nurses had already contained Carlos's bleeding. They were now trying to stabilize his blood pressure.

"Does anybody have this man's ID, his wallet, anything?"

She was the senior nurse among them and had a reputation of being able to handle more than one crisis simultaneously, typical of most personnel at trauma sections. She was tall and attractive, and she turned when the trooper standing at the entrance of the section raised his voice.

"I got it here," he said.

She did not wait for him to come forward but went straight to him.

"What do we know about him?" she asked him.

"He's a truck driver," the trooper answered. "No previous accidents that we can find. He has a clean record. He lives in Miami."

"That's pretty good. Trooper," she said, smiling at him, "if you're done with his personal effects, we are going to need them here. We need to call his next of kin."

"Is language not a problem?"

"It might be," he replied. "We will get the Miami police involved."

"That's a good idea. You can do that, and once you're done with his credentials, leave them here just in case a family member shows up."

"How's he doing?"

"Right now we do not know much. We are working to stabilize his vital signs, and then the surgeon will take over."

"The surgeon? He is gonna need surgery?"

"Yes," she answered and looked at the team of nurses around the bed. "Brain injury. You might wanna hang around to give the surgeon some detail about the accident. The history always helps."

The trooper shook his head.

"We are gonna need a blood alcohol reading," he said.

"Oh?" The nurse turned. "You think there was drinking involved?"

"We don't know. There was no contact with another vehicle so we have to check, plus in an accident of this magnitude, you have to cover everything."

"I'll go ahead and get that rolling for you. We took two vials but had to stop because of the profuse bleeding. Let me check on that."

She turned from him and headed for the bed that now had been curtained off the others and disappeared inside.

CHAPTER 61

It was near midnight near the house on 125th Street. A blue Impala was parked in the driveway, and the sound of a water suction pool cleaner was evident to the two police officers who approached the front door. One of them knocked while the other one scurried aside and peered around back. The bright glare of floodlights in the rear left no doubt that someone was working in the back.

"Good evening," the officer at the front door said.

He estimated that the woman who opened the door was probably in her fifties. The fact that she was wearing makeup at this late hour made him suspect that she was not the injured man's wife who he was here to see. Perhaps she was a relative.

"Good evening, officer," she responded in English.

"We are police officers from the city of Miami, and we are looking for Mrs. Yasmin Figueroa. We need to speak to her."

"Spanish, please?"

The officer repeated himself in Spanish. The woman seemed disconcerted.

"She is in the back. I am just a friend who is helping her. Is everything all right?"

"We need to speak to Mrs. Figueroa. And your name is, ma'am?"

"Oh, Amelia. I am a family friend."

"Can we see Ms. Figueroa?"

"Oh, sure. Would you like to come in?"

Both officers went inside, and Amelia took them to the back. Yasmin was working in the pool, up to her knees in the water and cleaning the bottom of the pool with a suction cleaner. As soon as she saw the officers, Yasmin walked out of the pool carrying the hose, went straight to the vacuum, and turned the switch off. If she was alarmed by their presence she did not show it.

"Yasmin, these officers want to speak to you. I will stay back if you need me, just call."

"Actually, Amelia," one of the officers said, "can you stay with us please? This will not take long."

"Oh, sure."

"Madam," the other officer began, "we are officers from the Miami police department. We were notified by the state police that your husband was involved in an accident, and right now he is in a hospital in Jacksonville. We have contact information for you so that you can call if you want to inquire about his condition. We also brought information about the hospital's location in Jacksonville."

Yasmin had listened carefully, showing no signs of alarm. The officers had spoken in fluent Spanish, and she understood them well.

"My husband's name is Carlos Figueroa. Is that who you mean?"

Amelia came closer. She had wanted to be strong at the moment for Yasmin, but all she could do was cover her mouth to prevent her from bursting into tears.

"Mrs. Figueroa, you are absolutely right. We should have identified your husband by name. I'm sorry. Is Carlos Figueroa your husband?"

"Yes."

Still no sign of distress. It seemed as if she was in absolute control. An immigrant young woman who had just undergone such a dramatic encounter with police was facing men in blue again. They were here for no pleasant reason, that much she knew, but whatever it was she had to face them. She could not afford to lose her composure.

"Well, as we were saying, he was involved in an accident."

"How is he?"

"His condition is guarded at the moment," the other officer replied. "He is in the intensive care unit of the hospital."

"Can I go see him?"

"Yes, of course, but before you do anything like that you need to call the hospital and ask about visiting arrangements. The hospital is a long way from here. It's in Jacksonville, and that is a good six hours' drive from here."

"Yes," she nodded.

The officer handed her a sheet of paper printed offline with the hospital's information. Yasmin studied the paper and pointed to the telephone number.

"Is this the main number for the hospital?"

"Yes."

"Is there an extension to the section where they are keeping Carlos?"

"You can call that number, and they will guide you to the section in charge."

"Are they keeping him in intensive care?"

"Yes."

"Can you tell me anything about his condition?"

"You need to speak to the staff at the hospital for that, ma'am. We don't have any details other than that he is in a guarded condition."

She took her eyes off the paper and nodded, letting them know she understood their position. They were concerned about divulging information that they were not allowed to. Yasmin thanked them and walked them to the door, thanking them again.

She turned from the door, and Amelia came towards her and hugged her.

"Oh, Yasmin, I'm sorry," she said, over her shoulder, holding back the tears. "What are you going to do?"

"I am going to call the hospital," Yasmin replied, "and I am going to Jacksonville in the morning."

"No, you can't go alone, honey. You can't. Let me go with you. We can go in my car in the morning."

Yasmin hugged her tight to show her appreciation, but she had things to do. She sat down on the sofa and perused the sheet of paper the policeman had given her. Amelia sat next to her. Amid her anxiety, Amelia did not know what to do, and she watched Yasmin in awe as she went to the kitchen and came back with her cell phone. She dialed the hospital's number and asked for a Spanish-speaking person. She began to travel through the many layers of bureaucracy at the hospital until she finally was connected to the ICU unit. It took some effort to make the nurse operator believe that she was Carlos's wife and she could be told about his condition. Still, the nurse could not say much. Carlos was in critical condition, and she could not give her details. Yasmin settled for an assurance that Carlos was being treated at the unit, and that he would be there tomorrow. She was six hours away and needed to know that when she got there, she would be allowed to see him. After she ended the call, she placed the phone on the center table and got up.

"He is there," she told Amelia. "They can't tell me much until they see me, but he is being treated. He is in critical condition."

In another burst of emotion, Amelia came close and embraced her, sobbing.

"Oh, Yasmin, how could this happen?"

"He's going to be all right," Yasmin said, speaking over her shoulder. "I will be there and take care of him. It's all right, Amelia. You should go home now. It's almost midnight. I am going to get everything ready, and I will go in the morning."

"No," Amelia repeated. "No, I will not let you go alone. This is why we are friends."

"Thank you, but no, you do not have to do that. It's a long trip. I can take the bus and be there by the afternoon. I am going to shut down the pool and get everything ready."

CHAPTER 62

The next afternoon Yasmin stood at the curtained room of the IC unit in the UF Health Jacksonville hospital. The nurse had slid the curtain aside for her to enter the narrow space where machines whizzed and beeping seemed to come out of nowhere. Behind her was Amelia who, good to her word, had driven her from Miami. The nurse stood by, watching Yasmin's reaction in case medical help was needed, but Yasmin stood solid at the edge of the bed railings watching Carlos intubated body. His eyes were closed, and he seemed to be peacefully asleep.

"Oh, Yasmin," Amelia lamented behind her. "Oh, my God."

Yasmin turned and hugged her to show her appreciation. She then turned to the nurse, who was bilingual.

"Is he conscious? Can he hear us?"

"He probably can hear you, but he can't speak right now."

Yasmin moved to the edge of the bed. Carlos was hardly recognizable. His head was fully bandaged, as he had undergone surgery the night before. A tracheostomy had been performed, and a tube had been inserted in his throat to allow him to breath. Both arms had IVs connected, and the beeping sounds from the heart regulator created an aura of solemnity that seemed hard to ignore.

Yasmin leaned over and kissed her husband on the cheek. She could not see his ears, but she whispered softly to him.

"I'm here, my Carlos, and I am not going away. You need to come back, darling. We have things to do."

The nurse touched Yasmin's arm gently.

"It's better that you don't touch him just yet, honey. Everything in him is now sensitive. It's too soon after the surgery. You can talk to him in a loud voice if you want to, but stay back."

She pulled Yasmin back gently.

"What does the doctor say? How long will he be like this?"

"The doctor can answer your questions later. He is expected to stop by later."

"How did the accident happen?"

"I'll tell you what," the nurse said. "I will give you the name of this trooper who can talk to you about that. I understand it was a solo accident, meaning there was no other vehicle involved. I will get that number for you now."

CHAPTER 63

That evening while Yasmin kept a vigil on her husband in the company of Amelia, a man in uniform stood by the room and gently moved a portion of the curtain aside. He looked directly at the two women but spoke to Yasmin.

"Are you Mrs. Figueroa?" he asked softly.

"Yes," said Yasmin, turning to look at him.

The trooper removed his hat and extended his hand to Yasmin.

"I am very sorry we have to meet in such circumstances."

She nodded and spoke to him in correct English but with a pronounced accent.

"What happened? How did the accident happen?"

"I'm sorry, Mrs. Figueroa, I need to see an identification before we can discuss the case. Can you show me an ID?"

"Yes."

She reached for her purse, a brown bucket handbag resting on the arm of her chair.

"I can vouch for her, Officer," Amelia said.

"Unfortunately, ma'am, I need to see an identification. Sorry, I know this is a bad time, but it is just protocol."

"It's all right," Yasmin said. "I came prepared."

She handed him a local ID card that Carlos had gotten for her in Miami and their certificate of marriage. The trooper looked at the documents and nodded.

"You live in Miami with your husband I see."

"Yes."

"And you just got married? Gee, less than a month ago. I'm so sorry."

Yasmin nodded.

"Well, I have all your husband's papers, and I can give you all that back. I'm sure you will need them. Can we go somewhere where we can sit and discus what happened?"

Yasmin hesitated and looked towards Amelia.

"Amelia, can you watch him while I'm gone?"

"Sure," she said, getting up. "Call me if you need me."

Yasmin followed the trooper to the main nurse station of the ICU. He asked the nurses for a private room where he could speak to Yasmin. Standing next to the uniformed trooper who towered over her head, she could not help but remember when another one very much like him had handcuffed her before taking her away. Anyone who had experienced such drama such a short time ago, as she had, would not find the current situation amenable. But Yasmin was concentrated on Carlos. She needed to know as much as possible in order to set his affairs in order and most of all, help him recover his health. Right now that was her goal.

She followed the trooper into a room out of the hallway. There was a small table inside, and the trooper spread his papers on it and sat down. She sat down in front of him. She saw several pictures of Carlos's truck right away. There were lots of papers underneath it. The trooper took his hat off and smiled at her. He was a man probably in his mid-thirties with reddish-looking skin and light brown hair.

"The accident happened on Route 10 in the outskirts of Jacksonville," he began. "I do not expect you to know the area but that is very close to where we are now."

"I know where it is," she answered.

"Oh, you do? How do you know this road?"

"Traveling with my husband."

"Well, see that is very important information because it means that he had driven on this road before. And how is that?"

"He drives to Phoenix a lot, and he has to take Route 10."

"Yes, but that is going west. This was coming east. Does he ever drive east on it?"

"No because usually he has to stop in Georgia on the way back. This time when he was coming back, he had to stop in Mobile, Alabama, and then he was going to go to Orlando."

"Oh, I see. Well, that makes sense then. That's why he was on Route 10. Well, the truck is at a warehouse right now, and I will provide you with the address. You will need it for the insurance. Does your husband own the truck?"

"No. I have to call his boss still. But I do not have his number. It is in my husband's phone.

"I can give you his phone. I have it."

He retrieved the phone from inside the folder he had pulled the papers from. He handed it to Yasmin, and she turned it on. As soon as the screen lit, Gordon's name splashed all over it."

"This is my husband's boss who's calling. I did not know how to find him."

"I think you should call him as soon as we are through here. He may want to have his truck picked up."

She nodded, and he went on asking her questions about Carlos's habits, whether he drank or took drugs. She could see that he did not have much information about the accident, and he was trying to piece it together.

"My husband is the unlikeliest person to do drugs. He does not even drink. He is very much into health. We swim together every night in the ocean for stretches of one mile and back. To do that you have to be healthy. When he is not in Miami, he is driving, and I ride with him. This is the first trip he made without me since we've been together."

She raised her eyes to him, realizing that she had said too much. Now he would want to know why.

"You were very lucky," the trooper said. "Why weren't you with him?"

"We bought a house," she said. "I really did not want to stay, but he made me. I am furnishing the house and cleaning it. There is a lot do."

"Well, it is just as well that you were not with him. Fate played a hand there."

"It doesn't matter. I'd rather have it be me than him."

"No, don't say that. Your husband needs you to make things right. If the two of you had been hurt, then there would be no one to run the household. But luckily you were spared."

"How was he hurt? What happened?"

"We are still trying to piece things together. The tractor ran off the road and went into a ditch. We still don't know whether he was run off the road by another vehicle or whether he just lost control. Maybe he fell asleep. What can you tell me?"

"No, we were in contact all the time. He had slept well, and I had talked to him several times the day before yesterday. Then I did not hear from him since the afternoon, and I called him many times with no answer. When the two police officers came to my house last night, I just knew something had happened."

She looked at him with watery eyes.

"Is there anything else that could have happened? Was he upset about something?"

She hesitated, and her eyes cleared up.

"There is something. Carlos has a friend who crashed on a motorcycle in that same area. Carlos always talked about that, how the draft of a passing truck pushed him out of the road and into the ditch. His friend suffered head injuries and lost some movement of his right arm. He's gone through a lot of therapy but can never ride again."

"Do you know where that accident happened?"

"I think it was in the same area. It's a spot where the road curves."

"Your husband was heading east on Route 10."

"Yes," Yasmin said thoughtfully. "I wonder why Carlos took that route this time. He always did the impossible to avoid it."

"Maybe because you weren't with him. He didn't have to be as cautious. But what did he think was dangerous about that area? Did he ever say?"

"He said that trucks tend to speed in that area just as the road breaks, and the draft created from the passing vehicle can make your own car slide into the ditch."

"I don't know about that. I can see that happening with a motorcycle, perhaps if you are not paying attention at that moment, but not with another truck."

"Carlos was not pulling a wagon. It was only his truck."

"I'm well aware of that. Still, not enough to push it over the shoulder into the ditch. We could tell there were actually three trailers that passed your husband before his truck seemed to lose control and slid onto the side, but there was no contact between his truck at the trailers. Did your husband sleep well the night before? Did he eat that afternoon? What about the phone? Was he on the phone a lot that afternoon?"

"His phone system was fully remote. No need to touch anything."

"I know that. But still, you can use the phone excessively, and that can wear you down. You don't have to touch anything necessarily for that to happen."

"The only ones calling him are me and his boss, Gordon."

"I'm gonna need Gordon's number. Can you jot it down for me?"

He passed her a note pad, and she wrote a number on it. She had committed Gordon's number to memory.

"That's his number. His name is Gordon, and I have yet to call him."

"I will wait till you call him."

"So, how was Carlos hurt? How did he hurt his head?"

"As the truck entered the ditch, it bumped its way through. Your husband's head struck the frame, and then he passed out."

"But he was wearing his seat belt. How could that happen?"

"It was the seat belt that may have saved him. If he hadn't had a seat belt, his body would have been ejected."

She asked him about a police report, and he explained that it would take a few days to complete it. He gave her some documentation about how to contact him and also gave her Carlos's wallet. Then he asked her to contact Carlos's boss.

Yasmin retrieved her phone and got ready to give Gordon the news. That would not be an easy phone call to make.

CHAPTER 64

Yasmin sat at the side of the bed, next to Amelia, discussing the details of the accident. The trooper had left once he decided that he had obtained all he could from Yasmin. She and her husband were newlyweds who had unfortunately stumbled on a precarious situation which had probably shattered big plans in their new lives together. Like any other young couple, they had dreams.

"Have you noticed any movement in him?" Yasmin asked as she rubbed her hand on his arm.

"No," Amelia said with teary eyes.

"It's too soon after the surgery to know," Yasmin said assuredly. "I'm sure he will come back."

"Yasmin, you are so brave. God bless you."

Yasmin ignored the comment because at that moment the lead nurse came in.

"I think you may want to consider calling it a night," she said. "He is fully comatose at this point. We have to let his organs rest right now. It's best that you retire and leave us your cell number should there be a need to call you."

Yasmin did not answer. She was lost in thought, staring at Carlos.

"Come on, Yasmin," Amelia pled with her. "It's better that we let him rest. We can stay at a motel and come back in the morning."

Yasmin looked quietly at Carlos. She leaned over and kissed his forehead.

"Come on, honey," said the nurse. "We need to give him some time alone."

"What if something happens in the middle of the night?"

The nurse shook her head.

"He is stable right now. His vital signs are in the right range. Right now what he needs the most is rest. Give him some time. You get some rest and come back in the morning."

She held Carlos's hand in hers and waited a few minutes until she felt convinced that it was best to let him rest. She turned to Amelia and told her she was ready.

They both left the section and went downstairs to the lobby. They inquired as to any motels nearby, and the woman at the desk gave them a sheet of paper with several locations. It seemed that it was a common inquiry that she had handled before. Amelia and Yasmin went past the automatic doors and headed for the parking lot. It was close to midnight, and the night was fresh with a soft breeze.

"I need to call Carlos's boss again. He wants to have an update as to Carlos's condition."

"He really cares for Carlos, doesn't he?"

"In many ways he has been our savior," Yasmin said. "He found us a lawyer, he's helped Carlos so much, but it's hard to keep up with him."

"Yeah," Amelia observed. "Doesn't he ever sleep?"

"I know. Only Carlos can keep up with him. So, what do you think about Carlos's condition tonight?"

"He had surgery today. I know that he is unresponsive right now, but I guess that is to be expected."

Yasmin nodded.

"You don't have to stay, Amelia. You can go back to Miami tomorrow morning, or even tonight. You've done more than enough already."

"I wouldn't think of it. I am going to call Roberto now and tell him that I won't be back until you go back."

Yasmin waited until they checked in at the motel. Once in the room she sat on a soft chair and dialed Gordon's number.

"Gordon, it's Yasmin. Carlos made it out surgery."

"How is he?" came Gordon's hoarse voice.

"They do not tell us much. It's hard to tell. The first seventy-two hours are the most serious."

"Is he conscious?"

"No, right now, no. But the nurse tells us his vitals are good. I have to see how it goes but I wish that he could be transferred to Miami."

"Have you asked someone yet?"

"No."

"Can you get me his doctor's name and information from the hospital?"

"Yes, sure."

"Take a picture with your phone and send it to me."

"Okay," she said.

Gordon sounded determined, as always. She had passed to him all the information about the whereabouts of the truck and wanted to ask him whether he had followed up on it. As if reading her thoughts he told her that a servicer had already picked it up and that they had found hardly any damages. It was being kept at a storage facility, and Gordon has already sent a driver to bring it back to Miami. He would get back to her about a possible transfer of Carlos to a Miami hospital.

"I think it is too early for Carlos to be transferred," Amelia said after the call. "He just got out of surgery, Yasmin. We have to be careful moving him. Even with all their sophisticated equipment, they could cause him more injuries."

The two stayed up for nearly an hour talking about the events of the last two days. Then they went to sleep, each in their own beds. Yasmin thanked Amelia for being such a faithful friend.

CHAPTER 65

At the break of dawn, Yasmin was awake. She turned over quietly and looked towards Amelia. She was still sound asleep. Then she looked at her cell phone, just in case she had missed a call from the hospital during the night. There was none. She got up slowly so as not to wake her friend, brushed her teeth, and wrote her a note in Spanish. She wrote that she would be back with coffee and a full breakfast. Then she headed out the door and took the elevator to the lobby.

She asked the receptionist for directions to the nearest Dunkin' Donuts or another fast food restaurant where she could get coffee and breakfast.

The man behind the desk seemed startled.

"This early I would guess it would be a Dunkin' Donuts. But I don't know of any nearby. How are you getting there? Walking? At this hour?"

She nodded. She was dressed in sweatpants, hoodie sweatshirt, and sneakers.

"The only close thing I know of is a McDonald's right off the main road, but it's a walk from here."

"Which way, left or right?" she asked.

"Left, all the way down. Be careful with the traffic."

She was off into the highway and began walking then slowly jogging. She steadily jogged, making believe she was out in the ocean with her beloved Carlos, stroking the fast-moving currents near the shore and looking left towards her husband at every other stroke. A feeling of calmness swept over her, and she did not even work up a sweat when she looked up and saw the familiar McDonald's logo a few feet before her. She had been daydreaming. She had almost felt the sea water, smelled the salt, and it seemed as if she had been suddenly awoken from a fantasy. Right now reality was that it was questionable whether Carlos would ever swim again, but it just occurred to her that that would be an inspiring goal: to swim again. The day when Carlos and she swam in the ocean again would be the end of this ordeal. It would mean that he recovered from this tragedy.

She went inside McDonald's and asked for two breakfast specials with coffee to carry. She asked for one large bag to place the two Styrofoam trays in and jogged back to the motel with them. When she reached the room, Amelia was still sleeping on her side, unaware that Yasmin had been out. Yasmin placed the two trays on the top of the desk in the room and took the coffee out of one bag. She heard the rustling of sheets behind her and turned. "Amelia, I brought you breakfast," Yasmin said.

"My gosh, when did you get up?"

"Oh, about an hour ago."

"What time is it?"

"It's about 7:00."

"You got up at 6:00?"

"Yeah, I'm up early. I just automatically wake up at a certain time."

"Let me dress up a little and brush my teeth."

"I'll wait for you."

"Oh, no, go ahead and eat."

Yasmin sat at the table and took a sip of her coffee. She felt uneasy not knowing how Carlos had spent the night and felt the need to go. But she needed to wait for her friend. After all she had done, she could not be insensitive. Amelia sat next to her thanking her and quickly bringing up Carlos.

"I wonder how Carlos spent the night."

"When we go back this morning, you can leave me at the hospital, Amelia. You've done more than enough."

"I can't leave you like this, Yasmin. I couldn't do that."

"But you must, Amelia. Who knows how long I'm going to be here? This could take a long time."

"I will be here for a long time."

"No, you can't do that to Roberto."

"Speaking of Roberto," she said. "Here he is."

His number showed on the phone screen, and she picked up. Yasmin took a bite of her egg and cheese biscuit. She could hear Amelia talking but she blocked off the words to give her privacy.

"That man is my life," Amelia confessed. "I could never make it without him."

Yasmin looked up at her and smiled. In her own way, Amelia had described how she felt about her own husband. But now was not the time to show weakness. She needed to be there for him and be strong.

"He is a nice man, and I can tell he loves you very much."

"We go back many years."

"That's how I want it to be between Carlos and me."

"And it will be, honey. It will."

Yasmin put her sandwich wrap inside the bag and drank her coffee.

"I don't want to rush you," Yasmin said. "But can we go?"

"Sure, honey. Sure. I understand."

They arrived at the Critical Care Unit of the hospital and walked inside the room. The hissing sound of the breathing machines left no doubt in Yasmin's mind that Carlos's condition had not improved; on the contrary, it may have worsened. She kept still for a moment then reached down and kissed his hand.

"I am here, Carlos. Amelia is with me."

She looked towards Amelia. Her eyes were already teary. She could not have asked her anything at the moment. She was affected by her emotions.

"Good morning," said a nurse who had followed them inside. "Are you family?"

"Yes," Yasmin answered. "I'm his wife."

"Are you Yasmin?"

"Yes."

"It's very nice meeting you."

She was a lean tall woman with a courteous disposition who looked affably at her and Amelia. Yasmin asked her how Carlos had done through the night.

"He's stable," she answered. "We are expecting the doctor to be here at some point this morning. Then he can give you a more detailed upgrade."

"What else could you tell me?"

"Nothing more than his general condition. He is on life support at the moment, and the doctor will give you more detail."

"All right. Thank you."

Yasmin nodded. She moved closer to the bed, watching Carlos. She kept holding his hand, looking thoughtful. Amelia hugged her and spoke to her in a low, soft voice.

"Do not lose hope, Yasmin; he'll be back."

"I know he will," Yasmin replied. "It's gonna be fine."

After a while, Yasmin waved for Amelia to take the only seat in the room. She remained standing. Nothing that the doctor would tell her could change her mind. She already knew his condition. Brain surgery was as serious as it could get, but she had a feeling that Carlos's procedure had not been as intrusive as everyone seemed to think. She did not have any experience in such matters, but she just had that feeling. She had read about such cases where the brain would swell as a result of some trauma. In her rudimentary knowledge of the complexity of the human brain, she imagined that the surgeon had intervened surgically so as to release some of the pressure, creating an outlet for the swelling to decrease. When the doctor arrived and gave Yasmin an assessment of the present situation, he more or less confirmed what Yasmin was thinking. But the question remained as to how much danger Carlos was in.

CHAPTER 66

That evening one of the incoming nurses in the evening shift made an off-the-cuff remark as if to herself as she was typing notes in Carlos's chart while Yasmin was nearby. She murmured, as if reading her own mind, that there had been no movement by the patient, involuntary or otherwise.

Yasmin did not say anything to Amelia. She sensed that her friend was uncomfortable. The hours of waiting were torture on both, but the worst part was the realization that they were impotent to help Carlos. They were entirely dependent on the doctors, nurses, and probably most of all, the machines and computers that kept Carlos's lungs and heart going.

A phone call came from Gordon. He had "gone to work," as he put it, through one of his friends, a doctor, who in turn had made inquiries and had given him a decision. Carlos could be moved but not until he was off the ventilator. That could happen fairly soon, but there was always a risk that it would not take place for a long time, or, worst of all, that it would not happen at all. He spared her that last scenario, but by now Yasmin was well aware of how dangerous of a situation she and Carlos were facing.

It was past eight in the evening when Yasmin decided they should go. She did not want to subject to Amelia to any additional trauma. She had gotten assurances from the nurses that they would call her the second anything developed. Yasmin looked at Carlos pensively and kissed him. He seemed to be peacefully asleep and showed no signs of discomfort.

"I think you should leave in the morning," Yasmin said to Amelia. "It is not fair that you stay any longer. I will be fine."

Amelia had been on the phone several times with her husband, Roberto, and although it all seemed fine, she felt she needed to insist that she leave.

"I am not sure I want to drive all that way alone on 95," Amelia replied.

"That's why you should leave early. So you don't fall asleep. Drive steadily, and you will be in Miami early in the afternoon."

"I don't want to leave you," Amelia replied. "Imagine being alone in a situation like this."

"But I'm not really alone," Yasmin countered. "I always have you and your husband. And I don't know what luck I'll have, but Carlos's boss is trying to have Carlos transferred to a hospital in Miami. If that happens then we will be close by."

Amelia glanced at Carlos laying immobile in the bed, his face distorted by the oxygen mask and his head wrapped in bandages.

"Honestly, honey, I do not think that will be possible for now."

"Yes, I realize that, but I believe it will happen in a few days."

"In a few days, Yasmin?"

"Yes. I will be here all the same. But your husband needs you. And that is why I'm telling you to leave. This could go on for a long time, and it's not fair that you be here. I will be in touch. If there is an emergency and I need you, I will be calling you. You'd be the first one I call, I promise."

Amelia watched her with admiration. Family members become drained by the trauma of seeing a loved one near death. But Yasmin showed no sign of weakness. On the contrary, she seemed stronger, focused, and resolute. What a difference from the timid young girl that she had met a few weeks back. It was as if she had reached inside herself and retrieved an assortment of abilities that had been hidden from public view. Amelia drove silently to the motel with Yasmin sitting in front. Both were in silence until they were inside their motel room. Both of them sensed a dreadful anticipation as to Carlos's condition, and neither one had any desire to hurt the other one, so they kept it inside.

"I really hate to leave you, Yasmin. What are you going to do all alone?"

"I won't be alone," Yasmin replied. "I will be with Carlos."

"I know but you see his condition. What if something happens? What will you do?"

"I can always call you if I need help, but I do not want to impose. It's not right. You've helped me so much, but now I have to do the waiting alone. I came prepared. Not as fully as I should have, but I did not know Carlos's condition at the time. I may have to buy some underwear," she said smiling.

"Do you want us to go shopping for some clothes?"

"No, it's all right. You go ahead and leave and do not worry; I will be in touch. I will be calling you while you are driving in about an hour. Can you pick up?"

"Yes. You know what is like being married to a truck driver. Roberto has me all set up. I just connect to the dashboard screen, and all the calls go there. You know, like in a truck."

"Yes, Carlos does the same thing in our car."

"Do you want something to eat?" Amelia asked.

"No, thank you. I am kind of overtired and just need some rest."

"Well, you have to eat, Yasmin. Your body is drained from all the stress that you are putting it through, and you cannot forget to eat. Let's shower and rest. Who will be first?"

"You can go," Yasmin said.

CHAPTER 67

The next morning when Amelia woke up, breakfast was already on the small table in the room. Yasmin had gone on her daily jog and purchased breakfast for both. She rose from the bed and said good morning and thanked her for getting breakfast.

"Are you sure you will be all right?" Amelia asked again.

"Yes," Yasmin replied. "You have done more than enough already. You need to get back home, Amelia."

"How are you with money, Yasmin? Do you have enough?"

"Oh, yes, we're fine. Carlos left me very well prepared. Our bank accounts are joint, and I have my own debit card. The house is set up. Everything is fine. The only thing I need is for him to get well."

Yasmin crossed eyes with Amelia as she spoke. Amelia understood her. At the beginning of their acquaintance, when Carlos introduced her to their inner circle, Amelia thought of her as timid and quiet, rather typical of her culture as Amelia understood it. But she had never imagined that when confronted with a crisis such as she faced right now, Yasmin could rise and face the tragedy with bravery and in full control. She had not seen Yasmin shed one tear, not even when she sat quietly by her husband's bed, staring at him for hours, or when she kissed him good night before retiring for the night.

Yasmin seemed to be able to persevere. She was not weakened by Carlos's current condition and what seemed to be poor prospects of a recovery. She was only more determined. Amelia came close to her and embraced her. She kissed her on the cheek.

"I will wait for your phone calls, and if I do not hear from you, I will call you. I can tell you're gonna be all right, but I just need to verify it. I need to know that you are all right. This is a storm that you are going through, but remember, you are not alone."

"Thank you," Yasmin said.

Amelia drove her to the hospital, dropping her off at the main entrance. She made Yasmin promise that she would call her to keep her informed of the progress with Carlos's condition. She watched as Yasmin walked to the entrance doors and wondered where she got the strength to deal with her dire situation. Deep inside she feared that the worst was coming and whatever happened to Carlos would affect the brave young Yasmin in ways that she herself could not realize right now. What would become of her if Carlos died?

Still hesitating, Amelia wondered whether she was making the right choice by leaving. Would she not be perceived as cruel for leaving her alone? A car that had come up behind her beeped the horn, signaling that it was time to move. Amelia drove into an empty space in the parking lot and set her GPS in motion. She tapped her home address as her destination as soon as it came up on the screen. A female voice began giving her instructions, and she listened attentively. She pulled out, and a few minutes later she got on 95 South to Miami.

CHAPTER 68

For the next six days, Yasmin sat quietly on the wide leather seat by the bed, some nights even sleeping there. The nurse staff got to know her well and tried to encourage her as best as they could. They were bound by an oath of confidentiality and the directives of the lead treating doctor. He was the surgeon who had operated on Carlos and was known for his iron fist rule, demanding that no details about the patient's condition were to be disclosed to the family except by him. Yasmin had by now learned as much, and today, as the doctor came into the room at midafternoon, she noticed a trace of reservation in him, as if he had some news but news that he was hesitant to share with Yasmin.

He grabbed the clipboard at the end of the bed that held the medical chart and perused through the pages. Then he turned to Yasmin and said hello.

"I'd like a word with you," he said, placing the clipboard back in the plastic pocket at the end of the bed. "Your husband's condition has not changed since the surgery. So far he's unresponsive, and we are keeping him alive by artificial means. We don't know how long this status will last and whether he will improve or not. The longer he is in his current condition, the less likely it is that he will go back to normal. I can't tell you with certainty whether he will be back to normal at all. We are doing all we can to keep him alive, but right now his organs are working only because of the machine that is helping him breathe. Without that he would not be living."

Yasmin stared at him as she listened attentively. It was not a curious stare but a guarded one, as if she could not bring herself to trust him. It made the doctor feel unpleasant. He waited for her to respond, but hearing nothing he went on.

"There may come a point when you, as his spouse, will have to decide whether to keep him on life support or discontinue it. It is a hard decision, I know, and by all means, do not feel pressured. Everyone here will work with you at this very difficult time."

He placed a hand on her shoulder.

She did not react in any way but merely responded softly, "Thank you."

"Sure," he said.

Yasmin watched the doctor as he stepped out into the hallway and passed the nurse station, ignoring the nurse who tried to get his attention from behind the desk. Then she turned to Carlos, who lay motionless on the bed, and she imagined having a conversation with him, yearning to tell him about this strange place where nurses and doctors tried to convince you about the fragility of life. This doctor said there was no point in fighting the inevitable. It's no use. Carlos was leaving. Maybe he had already left.

"No," she told him. "It's not over." It was not just about pills, needles, and machines that blew air into your lungs. There was something much deeper, more undefined, that needed to be accounted for. No one had asked Carlos. No one had yet told him that it was time for him to go. She told him to wait, to not yet decide. She needed some time to reach that other dimension that no one had yet consulted.

She stepped forward and grabbed Carlos's hand.

"Wait," she said. "Wait."

She walked out of the room and went to the nurse's desk. The nurse sitting behind it looked up and smiled slightly at her.

"There was an older woman right behind me when I came in this morning," Yasmin said. "She wore a long braid, and I think she went inside one of the rooms. Have you seen her?"

"Oh, yes," the nurse answered, whispering. "Boy, that is some braid, isn't it? She's inside the first room, by the door. She's awfully quiet, but she's in there."

"Thank you."

Yasmin headed for the door and entered the first room. An older woman was sitting on a chair right next to the bed where a man was lying unconscious, connected to several hoses and wires. She was staring down into her lap where she had wrapped a rosary around her wrist and kept pulling each bead as she whispered a Hail Mary at a fast pace. Yasmin could spot her fellow country folk a mile away.

"*Señora*," she said to her in Spanish. "I'm sorry to disturb you. Can you help me?"

The woman stopped praying and looked up. Her face was densely wrinkled, exposing her advanced age, but her beaming black eyes still showed an intense energy that refused to let go.

"I'm not from the area," Yasmin added. "My husband is in the bed two doors down, and he is in a coma. Do you know if there is a Spanish church nearby? One where I might find the statue of Our Lady of Guadalupe maybe?"

"Yes, there is one," the woman answered. "I was just there this morning."

"I need to go there right this minute."

"Are you Guatemalan?" the woman asked.

"I am, like you. May I?"

Yasmin leaned over and kissed her.

"God bless you, my child," the woman said.

"Are you here for a family member?"

"Yes, my son," the woman said, pointing to the bed with her chin. "If you can wait, I can take you there."

"I have to go now. Something just happened, and I felt the virgin. I have to pray to her. It's for my husband."

"Oh, may the virgin hear you," the woman said. "I understand. I know. I will give you a card."

"How is your son?"

"He's very bad, but he's alive. They tell me he's dying, but I don't believe it."

"They told me that too. But I don't believe them."

The woman opened a small purse she carried on her lap and took out a small, wrinkled piece of paper and handed it to Yasmin. On it, written in small letters in Spanish, was the phrase, "Our Lady of Mary Church." An address in even smaller letters was written over it. Yasmin took the note and examined it. The location was unknown to her, but she was sure it was part of the city of Jacksonville.

"Is it far from here?"

"Oh, twenty minutes ride from here," the woman said. "If the Lord is telling you to go, then go and don't wait. I will be here. I will wait for you."

Yasmin kissed her on the cheek again.

"I won't be very long," Yasmin said. "But if you can pray for my husband, I would be grateful to you."

"Of course I will pray, my child. Show me where he is."

"I will. Let me just look at your son."

He seemed to be an older man. He lay motionless on the bed. His exposed upper body showed signs of having been exposed to the sun, and he blistered a bit around the shoulder area. He was connected to several machines, and IVs ran from both arms. The monitor by his side showed the graphical signs of a beating heart.

"What happened?" Yasmin asked. "Was there an accident?"

"He's a landscaper. He has his own business, and the sun around here can be unforgiving. You can tell from his skin. They say he had a stroke while driving one of those lawn mowers. There was no one around to help him when it happened, and he was out for a good hour before someone called the ambulance. I am afraid I'm going to lose him."

The old woman pulled a wrinkled handkerchief from her small purse to wipe off her tears. Yasmin put her arm around her and kissed her cheek.

"Come on," Yasmin said, "let me show you where my husband is. What is your name?"

"Carmen, and you?"

"Yasmin."

Yasmin waved for her to come inside. She held Carlos's hand for a moment.

"This is my Carlos," she said. "We were married only a few weeks ago. He is a truck driver, and he had this terrible accident on a highway near here. He struck his head on the frame of the door, and they had to operate on him. It's been three days, and he shows no signs of any reaction."

Carmen crossed herself.

"Do not worry, my child. I will keep an eye on him for you. Go and say your prayers. He will hear you."

Yasmin strode out of the hospital. She was in a hurry, and it seemed to her that she had found a friend she could trust. Carlos would be fine. He would hold on. She did not see any taxis around the entrance of the hospital, but she clicked the Uber icon on her phone screen and called for a car. The driver himself sent a message that he was only ten minutes away and arrived ten minutes on the dot. Yasmin showed him the address the old woman had given her and asked him how far of a ride it was.

"That's the place that is a church, right?" the driver asked.

"Yes," she replied. "It is a church."

"I know the place," the driver said. "It's not far, maybe fifteen minutes."

He drove down a narrow street with small houses on both sides and stopped in front of a tiny wooden house at the very end.

"This is it," the driver said.

Yasmin eyed the narrow sign on top of the door with small black letters that read "*Iglesia de Nuestra Señora de Guadalupe.*" It was the only clue that let a visitor know that this was the right place.

"Yes," Yasmin said, exiting the car. "This is the place. Thank you."

The driver moved in reverse to leave the area, as the street was a dead end and too narrow to turn around. Yasmin stood by the front door, hesitating whether she should knock or walk right in. It was still morning, and the door could very well be locked. She tried to turn the knob, but it did not give in. She knocked and stood back. Slowly, a woman opened the door.

"Could you let me in?" she asked in Spanish. "I need to say a prayer."

"There is no one here. I am here just cleaning."

"I will not be on your way."

The woman moved aside and let her in. Yasmin stepped forward and realized immediately she was in the nave area of the church, with a single row of benches that led to the altar. At the end of the left aisle she found what she was looking for, a small altar of Our Lady of Guadalupe. Her statue was of medium size with her green cloak running round her head and down to her feet. Yasmin walked through the left hallway straight to the virgin. She kneeled at the prie-dieu in front of the altar and crossed herself. It had been a long time since she had visited a church. But on this sunny morning she asked the virgin for forgiveness for her past sins and begged her for Carlos's life. She implored her not to take him yet, to heal his wounds and bring him back to her. That was all she wanted, she said. She wanted her husband back. Then she asked for forgiveness again. What form of penitence did Our Lady want from her? She would do anything, anything for her husband. There were no limits.

She remained quiet, with downcast eyes, as if waiting for a reprimand from the virgin, but nothing came. Then suddenly she felt it in her chest. There was no reprimand, only a feeling of energy, an abundance of joy that kept reaching her inside, telling her to have faith, not to ever forget that the Creator could do anything. To him it was all easy. His beauty was his power. She could smell the flowers in her mind, God's pretty flowers, and she began to sob.

"Do not take him away, please, Mother, I beg you. He is my sunshine now. How could I live without him?"

She raised her eyes to the solemn lady with the tranquil eyes. Perhaps they were a message to her that she must be confident. Everything would be well. She did not know how long she was there, what had transpired. It was only when the woman janitor came quietly behind her and touched her on the shoulder that she realized she had been in a long trance.

"Are you all right?" the woman asked behind her.

"Yes," Yasmin replied without turning. "I will be going now. I'm sorry I took so long."

"Nothing to be sorry about. I know our virgin is very powerful. Believe in her."

In one last thought, Yasmin promised the virgin that she would always be a good Christian from now on and that she would never forget Our Lady again. She made the sign of the cross and stood up. She could hear the virgin's voice inside her mind, telling her that she was blessed and to go in peace, everything would be well.

Yasmin walked back to the front door and met the cleaning lady at the small foyer.

"Thank you for letting me in," she said.

"Oh, it's no trouble. There is service tonight at 7:00 and then every other day as usual."

"Thanks for telling me," Yasmin said.

The woman handed her a brochure.

"Go in peace. The virgin is helping you."

"Thanks."

CHAPTER 69

When Yasmin returned to the hospital, she found Carmen on her knees by Carlos's bed, praying. She reached down and kissed her on the cheek. But Carmen seemed to be concentrated on her prayers and showed no signs of being deterred. She merely nodded her head in acknowledgment and went on with her prayers. Yasmin held Carlos's hand and watched his demeanor.

"Carlos, I'm back. You are going to be fine, my darling. You only have to wake up."

She stretched her body over the bed to reach him and kissed him.

"I was at church, and I spoke to the virgin," she said. "She is going to help us. And look, we now have Carmen here. Her son was hurt in an accident, and he is also unconscious. Carmen is praying for you."

One of the nurses from the station walked into the room.

"Is everything all right?" she asked. "You were gone for a while, and this lady kept trying to come inside the room, and I tried to keep her away, but now she's come in again, and she's praying. I saw no harm in letting her do that."

"No, of course not," Yasmin said. "I told her she could come in and pray for my husband."

The nurse smiled slightly and looked towards Carlos's immobile body on the bed.

"Has anything changed with my husband? Has the doctor said anything else?"

"The doctor will be here later," the nurse said. "He's scheduled to pass by in the evening. But no, everything is the same. His vital signs are good."

"I think something has changed," Yasmin said, and the nurse shifted her gaze to her.

"What do you mean?"

"I can feel that something is changing in him."

The nurse looked over the monitors, searching for any shifts in the numbers. She took a few seconds and turned to Yasmin again.

"Well, it's good to be positive," she said. "It helps. The doctor will be here later to talk to you, okay?"

"Okay," Yasmin said.

The nurse left the room, and Yasmin sat on the chair behind Carmen. The hissing sound made by her prayers blended in with that of Carlos's breathing machine, and Yasmin leaned her head back and closed her eyes.

CHAPTER 70

Yasmin dozed off for a short while under the background whispering sound made by Carmen as she continued her prayers. An hour later, Carmen arose, and seeing that Yasmin was asleep, she walked quietly to her son's room. Yasmin needed her sleep after all. She, on the other hand, could not bring herself to sleep, and for the past two days she had only been able to doze off for two or three hours. It was brutally painful. She felt the agony in the side of her eyes, as sourness seemed to spread around them, and she blinked to keep the light away. She leaned over the bed and kissed her son and then resumed her old posture, kneeling down on the floor as she went on with her prayers.

Dr. Meese came inside the room and stared down at Carmen on the floor and asked if she was all right. Carmen did not move but kept saying her prayers. He moved closer to the bed to check on the patient, and after a short exam he turned around and walked back into the hallway. He raised his arm to get the nurses' attention at the station. One of them walked over to him.

"You need to talk to this lady," he said. "This can't go on. This is a hospital, not a church."

"Doctor, we allowed it under the circumstances only because of her son's condition."

"Yes, but this is a little bit too far, and it interferes with the care we provide. I cannot even get in close to examine the patient. Talk to her or get someone who speaks Spanish fluently and let her know she cannot do that here."

"All right, Dr. Meese, I will talk to her."

The doctor went to examine another patient. When he reached Carlos's room he was surprised to find Yasmin asleep in the chair, her hand holding Carlos's own. He stood still for a moment assessing the scene. He turned back towards the nurse station and called on them.

"This is unacceptable," he said. "Why is this lady sleeping here at this hour of the day?"

"Oh, all right," the nurse said. "Let me wake her up."

"Go ahead and do that so I can examine the patient."

The nurse walked towards Yasmin, but she was already awake.

"Are you all right?" the nurse asked.

Yasmin turned to Carlos first to check on him.

"Yes."

"The doctor is here. He wants to talk to you."

"All right."

Yasmin got up and gazed at the doctor, standing a distance away.

"Yes, Doctor?"

He came towards her slowly.

"Could you give us a few minutes, Nurse?"

"Sure."

The nurse walked back toward the station, and the doctor turned to Yasmin.

"Have you given any thought to our discussion?"

Yasmin felt startled. She did not know what to make of his question. It sounded so crude.

"What discussion?"

"About your husband's condition and whether you want to continue life support."

"Doctor, I thought you were going to examine my husband."

"Nothing has changed."

"And how do you know? You haven't even looked at him."

"I know his condition."

"I'm not going to allow him to be disconnected."

The doctor dropped his hands and approached Carlos, passing Yasmin by.

"Leave him alone," Yasmin said. "Just leave him."

He was about to lean over Carlos's head but pulled back. He turned around and stared her down, as if in disbelief.

"Just leave him," she repeated. "He does not need you right now."

He walked back, reached the nurse station, and whispered something to one of the nurses, then headed out of the ICU unit. As soon as he went through the double doors, Carmen walked hastily out of the first room of the section and went into Carlos's room, holding her rosary in her left hand.

"What did the doctor say? Any good news?"

"No, just the usual," Yasmin said. "But I know he's gonna be all right."

Carmen reached out towards her with her arms open. She was of such short stature that she barely stood up to Yasmin's chest. Yasmin too embraced her and kissed her head.

CHAPTER 71

Late in the afternoon, while holding Carlos's hand, Yasmin dozed off again. Carmen had been in and out of the room, and Yasmin had mentioned getting something to eat for the two of them. But the stress of that day wore off on her, and now she thought she was merely going to take a catnap, and she would be back nice and fresh. She suddenly felt the slight tug of a hand on her left shoulder.

"Excuse me," said a nurse staring right at her.

She was very slim and looked like a teenager.

"It's Yasmin, right? You're here for him. Your name is Yasmin?"

Yasmin nodded.

"I'm covering for the second nurse this evening. Nurse Jones asked me to let you know that another doctor will be covering for Dr. Meese. His name is Dr. Garland. He might be here tonight but for sure in the morning. Ms. Jones just wanted you to know that. Okay?"

"Okay, thanks for telling me."

"All right."

"And how're we doing over here? Everything okay?"

She looked towards the bed and took a step to get closer. Carlos seemed to be sleeping peacefully, and Yasmin turned towards him after noticing the nurse's steady gaze. She saw it right away. His cheeks and even his lips had picked up some color. Yasmin sat up straight, enlightened by this redness that had spread out through Carlos's face. The easy explanation was that the blood was circulating. Something positive was happening.

"Something is happening," Yasmin said.

She got up from the chair and bent towards Carlos. She touched his cheeks, trying to get a feel for his temperature. The young nurse did the same.

"Sit down," she said. "It's nothing to worry about. Let me work on him and try to figure out what's going on."

The nurse beeped the station for help.

"He's going to come back," Yasmin said. "He will be back."

The nurse turned to Yasmin in silence and then to the two puzzled nurses who had rushed to the room from the station.

"What's going on, Norma?" one of the two said.

"Temperature is normal," she answered. "His cheeks were blushed all of a sudden. I thought it was his temperature, but all vitals are good."

"You want to call Dr. Garland?"

"I think we should," Norma said.

As Norma moved aside Yasmin moved in. She held Carlos's hand tightly.

"It's okay, Carlos. It's okay to come back. Don't be afraid. I'm here waiting for you."

"Ma'am," one of the nurses said. "Can you move back for a second? We are checking with the doctor."

Reluctantly, Yasmin let go of Carlos's hand. She realized she could not be disorderly or the nurses could have her removed. Besides, she was convinced Carlos was about to come out of his comatose state. There was no point in trying to convince the nurses. They did not see what she saw.

She sat back in the chair, leaned her head back, and closed her eyes. She could hear the fuss the nurses were making, moving around the bed and checking the monitors. Norma kept going in and out of the room while on the phone with the doctor. She was obviously following instructions as she read him Carlos's heart rate and the rhythm of the breathing machine.

"No, there are no changes," she said. "The rate is the same."

Then there was a pause, and Yasmin heard Norma say that she'd see him in a few minutes. Yes, the doctor would interrupt whatever he was doing to check on his new patient at ICU. He would probably peek in the room, shake Yasmin's hand, and introduce himself, then check the readings of the machines and say that Carlos was in an irreversible coma and there was nothing to do but wait. Yasmin had learned the routine. They were so far away from the truth, she thought.

"Okay, Yasmin," Norma said. "Dr. Garland will be taking a walk through in a few minutes, just to check, but he thinks we are as before. Nothing has changed. I understand you are concerned, but just sit tight, and he will talk to you more."

"All right, thank you."

Yasmin leaned over the bed's guardrail and held Carlos's hand tight. She knew it would be all right but in a different way than what Norma considered normal.

CHAPTER 72

It was close to midnight, and Yasmin lay quietly in the chair, close to the bed. The doctor had been by earlier in the evening and, after examining Carlos for a few minutes, turned to say that his condition was irreversible. He was familiar with the charts and had read the reports. There was permanent damage, and he could not breathe on his own. Yasmin had listened attentively and nodded as he spoke but gave no opinion nor asked any questions. She had taken Carlos's condition to another level. The doctor had mentioned that it was her decision how long to keep Carlos on life support.

After that predicament, now by a second doctor, even the nurses' attitudes seemed to change. Gone were the pleasant smiles that they all seemed to wear on a permanent basis. They were now somber, quietly walking back and forth from the station, as if anticipating the end and feeling pity for Yasmin, an emotion that they could not show in their professional capacity.

Yasmin felt it all, but there was a larger force that kept tugging her and keeping her close. She must not let go. She must hold steady. There was another outcome. Was it fate? His time had not yet come. Or some of the other common expressions that she had heard?

No, she thought to herself. It came from a higher power, something that was not in the reports nor in the chart, not even in Carlos's body signals. It was something that she had felt that morning when visiting the virgin, something so powerful that she could not question it. It became true the second she felt it, and now she only needed to wait. She must rest and clear her thoughts, rely on what had been revealed to her. It would happen. Carlos would come back. She would never have to make any life-or-death decisions over him. The decisions had already been made by some power which could not be challenged by any physician or any human mind. She only needed to rest and stay close. She lay still, her head resting on the back of the chair, and she dozed off.

It did not seem like a long time when she opened her eyes again. She heard the whispering sound of Carmen's praying as she knelt on the floor, by the foot of the bed. But there was something else. It was not a sound. It was the sensation of someone else's presence in the room. She stared at Carmen. The old woman was speaking softly, uttering the words of her prayers without stumbling a word, her eyes closed. Then she turned to Carlos and noticed his body, motionless as before. She leaned over him and kissed his cheek. But as she pulled back, she met his eyes, wide open and staring right at her under the dim gleam of the overhead light.

"Carlos, you are back!" she cried. "You're back!"

She moved quickly back and kissed him again, extending her arms to embrace him, but then realizing that her movements might hurt him, she pulled back and held his hand with both of hers. By then the station had been alerted by the sound of her voice, and Norma and another nurse rushed into the room.

"Move back, Yasmin," the second nurse said. "Don't touch him."

"Why not?" she asked. "I'm his wife. He needs me."

"No, honey," Norma said. "You could hurt him. What's wrong anyway? Why the yelling?"

"You can't tell? Can't you see?"

"No, what?"

"He's back. My husband is back!"

It was only then that Norma and her coworker looked towards Carlos and noticed his hand being held by Yasmin's but slightly moving, as if trying to close a grip on hers. Then they looked at his eyes and saw them, looking at the ceiling but slowly moving, trying to see those who were in the room.

"Oh, my God! Oh, my God!" Norma yelled. "Sara, please," she told her companion. "Tell them to call Dr. Garland. Quick!"

In a few minutes Sara and another nurse were surrounding the bed with Yasmin, standing next to Carlos and holding his hand.

"Yasmin," Norma said, "why don't you move back, honey? We need the space to work on him."

"No," she said. "I'm not leaving my husband again. And what are you planning to do to him?"

"We need to check his vital signs, to examine him."

"Well, then go ahead and do that. Check his vital signs. I don't think you even have to do that. Look at the monitors. There are his vital signs."

"We need space to work. Dr. Garland will be here in a few minutes. He's coming up."

"So, let him. What is he going to do? Is he going to try to convince me to disconnect my husband from life support? Or is he going to try to do it himself?"

"Oh, come on," Norma said. "This not the time for such nonsense. We are trying to help you out."

"All the same. I'm not leaving my husband alone for a second. I'm staying right here."

They all could hear the flapping sound of the double doors being opened and closed, and the fast footsteps approaching.

Dr. Garland was a lean man of short stature, wearing square black glasses; he came near Carlos in the other side of the bed. He glanced briefly at Yasmin but spoke to no one and came close to Carlos's head, staring at one side and then the other. He retrieved a penlight from his white coat pocket and examined both of Carlos's eyes.

"Nurse," he said without looking back. "We need to order a head scan immediately."

"Yes, Doctor, sure," said Norma. "What about his breathing, Doctor? Are we changing anything?"

"No," he answered. "We need to make a full assessment of his respiratory system. We don't know whether a sudden awakening is transitory or permanent. I need to check his lungs and heart. Can you have this lady move out? I need space to work."

He started to step over to the other side of the bed, and Yasmin moved aside to give him room, but she did not walk away. She stood at the foot of the bed watching Carlos's eyes as his pupils began to move about, as if he had just been born.

"Can you tell her to step out of the room for a few moments?" Dr. Garland said to Norma. "Tell the praying lady to also move out."

Norma came to Yasmin, but she voluntarily had stepped back, bringing Carmen along. The two went out into the hallway, and Norma closed the curtain all around the bed to give the doctor privacy.

"What is happening, my dear? What are they doing?"

"They're examining him. I think they are trying to make sure that he can breathe on his own, without help from the machine."

"Oh, Yasmin, that is so great. The virgin is answering your prayers, honey. She heard you."

Yasmin had to bend a little to fully be able to hug her. She fought the tears, but her eyes were watery when the short lady looked deeply at them.

"I am still praying for you and him, darling. He's come back, and he's going to be fine. I wish my son would come back. Oh, dear God, how I wish that. Let's go and see him, darling. Let's say some prayers for him."

Carmen grabbed Yasmin's wrist and brought her along to the first room in the hallway. She was emotional as she entered her son's room and saw his immobile body on the bed. The whooshing sound of the breathing machine let them know that things had not changed.

"Oh, my Lord," Carmen said, looking up at the ceiling and abruptly kneeling down.

She almost threw herself down, and one could hear a thud as her knees made contact with the wooden floor.

"Please, Lord," she went on. "Have mercy on my son. Do not take him yet. Please let me see him with his eyes open one more time, just one more time. Please, Lord."

In support of her new friend, Yasmin knelt next to her, and in a low whisper, she too began to pray.

CHAPTER 73

That night Yasmin did not leave Carlos's bedside. She kept talking to him, whispering at times, holding his hands, and thinking of ways to bring him back to normal times. Carlos hung on for a while, but close to midnight he closed his eyes again. Yasmin moved her head down in disappointment. Had it all been in vain? Did he go back to being unconscious? She watched him for a good half-hour before she decided to sit back on the chair, holding his hand. She did not notify the nurse station. Why should she? She had now lost trust in them. If Carlos was only asleep, he would wake up again. She felt the warmth in his hand and knew he was there. His heart was beating, and there had been no alarm signs from the monitors. She dozed off in the chair, waking up every few minutes to the hissing sound of the breathing machine. Well into the early hours of dawn, she was awakened by an unmistakable voice. It was a voice that she loved, one that she would never forget no matter how long she lived.

"Yasmin, where are you?"

She immediately was on her feet, holding both of his arms and looking deep into his eyes.

"Yes, darling," she said, "I am here and have never left you. How do you feel?"

She was surprised by her own composed reaction. She had not broken down in tears as she expected to do.

"What happened to me?" Carlos asked coherently.

"You were in an accident. You've been unconscious for over a week."

"Oh," he said, looking straight at her. "And you've been here the whole time?"

"Almost. Not the first day. I had to hitch a ride with Amelia here."

"Where are we?"

"We are at a hospital by Jacksonville."

"How long have I been here?"

The emotion finally got ahold of her, and she leaned forward and sobbed on his chest. It was then that Norma, the head nurse, became alarmed and ran behind her and pulled her back.

"No, honey, no," she said. "You can't pull him like that. You may hurt him."

"No, I can't. He's back. He's talking to me."

"What do you mean he's talking to you? The doctor said there would be these short episodes. He opened his eyes, but then he closed them again."

"Look at him," Yasmin said and reached out for Carlos's hand. "Carlos, please talk to her."

"What's wrong?" Carlos asked the nurse. "Why am I here? I feel fine."

Norma let out a shriek. In her nursing career, she had seen some fast recoveries, but this was astonishing, a total surprise.

"Girls, girls," she called the nurses behind her. "Call Dr. Garland. Whoever is on call, fast, please!"

Yasmin made a gesture as if to lean forward, but Norma stopped her by placing her extended arm in front of her.

"Let's not do that now, honey. Do not touch him. Let's wait till the doctor examines him."

"Yasmin," Carlos said. "Have you called Gordon?"

"Yes, darling. He knows everything. He knows everything."

"How long are they going to keep me here?"

"I don't know, darling. They did surgery on you. It's only been a few days."

Norma placed her index finger in front of her lips as an indication to keep quiet.

"Let's wait for the doctor to be here. He will examine him and give us a full report. I am glad he's talking, though. That's a good sign."

Yasmin turned around and saw Carmen, standing right behind her, with her arms open wide.

"Let's thank the virgin, honey. Let's thank her."

"Come," Yasmin said, taking her hand. "Now you can look at his eyes. He can hear you."

Carmen stood next to her and spoke to Carlos in a low voice.

"God bless you, Carlos," she said. "I know all about you from your wife. We are both with you, and so is the virgin. You are going to be fine."

"All right," Norma said, as the two other nurses walked in from the station. "You are going to have to stay out of the room for a few minutes. I have to prepare him for the doctor, who is on his way. I'll let you know when you can come back."

Yasmin and Carmen pulled back as the nurse closed the curtains all around Carlos's bed. Yasmin took one last peek at Carlos before his face disappeared behind the curtain. She went hand in hand with Carmen to her son's room. She was so thrilled inside. And the first thought that came into her mind was Gordon, Carlos's employer. She must tell him. She must tell him that Carlos was back and maybe he could now have him transferred to a hospital in Miami. She was still deep in thought when she stood by the edge of the bed of Carmen's son. His body was laying there, immobile, and breathing through the respirator.

"Look at my poor son," Carmen said. "Just look at him. He hasn't moved, but I have faith in the virgin. She will bring him back too."

Yasmin made the sign of the cross and laid her arm around the small woman's shoulder. Quietly, she said a prayer to the virgin, pleading that she would not forget her friend's son, that she would bring him back as she had done with Carlos.

CHAPTER 74

Dr. Garland showed up a few minutes later. He always seemed to be at the hospital, and Yasmin saw him walk in the room and give a sweeping glance that captured the full scenery. He asked the nurse to tell Yasmin to clear the room. Yasmin had anticipated the move and was already on her feet, ready to walk out. She held Carlos's hand in a tight grip and stepped back.

"I will be back soon," she said to her husband.

The nurse slid the curtains closed and stayed inside with the doctor. Yasmin took advantage of the moment to call on Gordon, who answered the phone on the first ring.

"Yep," he said, "I'm here."

"Hello, Gordon, it's Yasmin."

"I know. How are things up there?"

"Carlos woke up," she said. "He's talking normal, and I don't see any memory loss in him. The doctor is looking at him now. I suspect they're considering taking him off life support, probably gradually."

"All right," Gordon said in a cheerful mood. "That's my man. I'm gonna start making some phone calls then. Let's see if we can get him moved to one of our trauma centers down here. Jackson Memorial has one, and there are others. But I've got to call the doctor and see."

"Do what you can for us," Yasmin said.

After his call, Yasmin dialed Amelia's number and gave her the big news. She was thrilled and passed the phone to Roberto, who happened to be home.

"Hi, Yasmin, what is happening?"

"He's back, Roberto. He's back!"

"Completely? Is he talking?"

"Yes, he's talking. The doctor is evaluating him now to see whether they are going to be disconnecting him from the machines. But I wanted to know if you and Mr. Moza can help me have him transferred to a hospital near Miami."

"We are working on it. It's been hard because of his condition. But with this breakthrough we have a much better chance. Mr. Moza has contacts at Jackson Memorial. You know, if the director makes the move to have Carlos transferred here, there is a much better possibility of success. I will call Mr. Moza now. He may be calling you, so answer his call. We will get him here. It's terrific news though. The best news we could hope for. I am going to pass the phone to Amelia. You talk to her while I call Mr. Moza."

"Yasmin!" said Amelia's excited voice. "I can't believe it. He's fine?"

"He woke up this morning and looked at me and asked me how long he's been here. It was as if nothing had happened."

"Oh, thank God, thank God. Does he remember everything?"

"I did not get to talk to him a lot. The doctor came in, and they are looking at him now, but he seemed totally normal to me."

The nurse had gotten ahold of Yasmin's arm and whispered for her to follow.

"They're calling me, Amelia. I will call you back."

The nurse walked her to Carlos's bed, where the doctor was waiting. He was standing at the foot of the bed. The curtains had been closed again.

"It looks like your husband is making a recovery," he said.

The doctor looked at her through his black-rimmed glasses as if he were reading a book. Yasmin looked directly at him.

"Does he have any limitations from all this? Are there things that he cannot do anymore?"

"We don't know that yet. As far as I can tell right now, he can move his arms and legs. I do notice some loss of motion in his left arm, but to what extent, I am not sure yet. The big question right now is when we can stop providing him with life support. Let's wait for now, and see how he does. We will have to run some tests. For now the first one will be a brain scan. But I do not want to do that tonight. Let's see how he sleeps tonight and how he does with his vitals. Then we will decide on that."

The doctor nodded, and Yasmin knew then that he was calling for an end to the session. He tapped the rail of the bed with his clipboard and walked towards the nurse station.

"You have to give your husband a sign instead of words," Norma said. "Even though he is awake, you can't let him speak too much. He needs rest."

Yasmin nodded in agreement, but she got closer to the bed, and Carlos turned his head towards her. He slowly raised his right arm, and Yasmin realized that he was trying to raise his left arm also but couldn't. Did this mean that his whole left side was paralyzed? She leaned over to him and grabbed his left hand. She watched his reaction as she tightened the grip on his hand, and he pulled slightly back. He did have feeling in his hand, she surmised.

CHAPTER 75

All through that night, Yasmin kept a vigil on her husband. She could not even think about sleeping because Carlos would not take his eyes off her, and he kept on talking and asking questions about his release. He wanted to leave the hospital and go home, and he kept asking her why he couldn't just leave.

"Because it is dangerous, darling," she said, holding his hand tightly and watching out for his movements.

She wanted to learn as much as she could about his limitations. The doctor had said there would be some, especially the left side of his body, and Yasmin needed to know what that was all about. She had determined that it was only his left arm, as he had shown normal movements in both legs.

Well past midnight, a male nurse walked into the hallway and headed directly to the nurse station. He showed them a slip with Carlos's name on it and asked them to direct him to his room. One of them came around the counter and walked with him across the hallway to the open curtained room, where he immediately noticed Yasmin sitting on the lounge chair next to the bed.

"Good morning," he said in an upbeat tone. "It's still dark out, but it is a new day."

"Good morning," Yasmin answered back.

"Good morning," Carlos said unexpectedly.

"Wow!" the young man replied. "We have an energetic patient here. How are you this morning, sir?"

He came to stand near the edge of the bed, broadly smiling down at Carlos, and Yasmin immediately sensed his affability and bedside manner, something that she had found lacking in the doctors treating her husband.

"I'm feeling fine," Carlos said.

"Well, I'm glad to hear that. My name is Sam, by the way, and the reason I am here so early is to prepare you for the CAT scan that we have scheduled this morning for you. Now, your doctor has not authorized the disengagement of the respirator that you now are using, although that may be in the works. So, we have to plan in advance how we can get the scanner here in the little room that we have. That's why I'm here, to plan ahead. I hope I did not wake you up, sir. I actually did not think you would be awake this early, but it's all well and good. I'm very pleased to see that you're doing better."

"Thank you," Carlos said.

The other nurse came forward and stood next to Sam, still feeling the bafflement that prevailed among her crew in regards to Carlos's amazing recovery. Another nurse come from the station to join them, and Sam retrieved a regular Stanley tape measure from his pocket and began to measure the width of the bed and the free space on the sides, writing the numbers on the screen of his phone.

"You don't mind me," Sam said, as he kept on.

The other two nurses were keeping their eyes on Carlos. His name had become popular in the hospital. He was the miracle man who had awakened from a coma against all probability. The two nurses came near him, one on each side.

"I think you should try to get some sleep. Don't force yourself."

"That's right, Carlos," the other one said. "You should rest, don't force yourself. You should have complete rest now."

Yasmin's phone lit up. There was a call coming, and it was barely 5:00 a.m. Yasmin had a suspicion that it was Gordon, but when she picked up she heard the unmistakable voice of Mr. Moza.

"Good morning, lovely Yasmin, good morning. Tell me, how is Carlos?"

"He's awake, Mr. Moza. He's fully awake. He's made a terrific comeback."

"Roberto told me, and I am meeting tonight with a doctor at Jackson Memorial. I'll need some medical reports about Carlos's condition for the doctor here. Can you get them to me?"

Yasmin looked up at Norma, the head nurse. She thought of her as the only one who could help her, and she seemed more friendly than any of the other ones. She finished her call with Mr. Moza and decided inside what she would do. She would take help from whoever offered to her first.

"All right," Sam said, coming close. "You are his wife, I am told."

"Yes."

"I am really glad to hear that your husband has made such a rapid recovery. It really is remarkable. I am all done with the preparation, and I will be back probably in two hours to do the scan. Will you be here?"

"Yes, of course."

"All right, well, see you then."

Yasmin shook hands with him and watched him leave the room. The nurses were close by, and she could tell that they wanted to say more but were being cautious. They were bound by the doctor's orders.

"Is Norma around?" Yasmin asked.

"She will be on at 7:00."

CHAPTER 76

The CAT scan went through rather routinely, and Sam's comments remained resonating in Yasmin's head after the crew left the room.

"In this business, when something is routine, it means good news," Sam had said smiling as he left.

The biggest challenge to her remained on how to approach Norma. Should she just level with her and tell her that she was trying to have Carlos transferred to another hospital? Could that not be taken wrong by her and the staff? After all, they had been very helpful to her. After some debating she went to the nurses' station and asked Norma if she could have a word with her. The two met inside the room, and Yasmin poured out her feelings to her. She was immensely grateful to her and everyone, but she was trying to have Carlos transferred somewhere near Miami, closer to home, so it could be a little easier on her.

Norma said she understood. She saw nothing wrong with it, but on the issue of getting her a report, it would be a little more difficult. She would need consent from Carlos, and she could only give her a short summary of his condition. It would have been best if Dr. Garland himself who wrote out a note. Yasmin said she thought that he would never do it. Norma remained quiet after, and Yasmin understood. She was bound by her profession not to discuss the flaws of her coworkers, least of all the doctors.

Carlos had had a busy morning. The people who took his CAT scan were fast. They were professionals who knew what they were doing, and they got to work quickly, bringing the scanner right over the bed and above Carlos, who remained awake throughout the whole process. They were done in ten minutes and wheeled the machine away after they were done.

Carlos kept talking. He had talked so much since early morning, and Yasmin could see that his speech was improving. He was speaking in long sentences and discussing topics that only she and him knew about. Someone who heard him could not have imagined about the trauma he had been through.

Early in the afternoon, Yasmin kept falling asleep then waking up. She had not moved from her chair all night and constantly held on to Carlos's hand. He was now more responsive and receptive to her touch, and he softly rubbed the top of her hand as she dozed off.

Suddenly, a scream came from the end of the hallway that startled them both. Yasmin sat up on her chair and stared at Carlos.

"That sounded like it came from Carmen's son's room, and it sounded like Carmen. I should go see. I will be back."

She got up and went hastily to the first room in the hallway. There she found Carmen bent over the body of her son in bed, while a nurse held on to her shoulders. Yasmin sensed the worst. She became aware of the deep silence around them. There was no beep from the heart monitor, and the hissing sound of the respirator was gone. She tried to make contact with her friend, but Norma waved for her to stay put. Two other nurses came in the room and looked towards Norma.

"Don't do anything yet," she told them. "Dr. Garland is on his way."

Norma moved back, allowing Yasmin to move in. Yasmin moved next to Carmen and placed her arm around her shoulder. She said nothing to her, but her presence made a difference to the old woman.

"He's gone, my child. My son is gone."

"He'll never really leave you, Carmen. He'll always be right next to you."

Carmen opened her arms wide, in a childlike motion, and Yasmin bent down and embraced her. Carmen's sobs reached a crescendo as she held on tight to Yasmin's embrace.

"He left so quickly," Carmen said. "I did not even know when. When I saw the nurses right by me and realized the silence, I knew he was gone."

Dr. Garland walked into the room and went to the other side of the bed to examine the patient. He asked Norma to take everyone out of the room and close the curtains. Yasmin held Carmen's hand and walked along with her to Carlos's room.

"What do you think they'll do?" Carmen asked, in between sobs.

"The doctor is examining him. They will call us."

They both had reached Carlos's bed, and he looked inquisitively at Yasmin.

"This is Carmen," Yasmin said. "We are waiting to hear about her son."

"What happened?"

"I'm not sure. They are looking at him now."

"Carlos," Carmen said. "Forgive me. I think I lost my son."

"No, you haven't," Carlos replied. "Have a little faith."

Carmen smiled amid her watery eyes and flushed face. Yes, there were miracles, and yes, someone was in control. What could possibly be more proof than Carlos himself? Her son did not really go away. He would always be with her.

Carmen extended her hand to him and held his tight. Carlos seemed touched by the gesture, and his face lit up. He had never been a pious man. But he hadn't been facetious in his assessment of Carmen's situation. Call it fate or call it godly, her son's body may have left but something of his would always remain in the petite woman who now knelt on the floor beside him as she began to pray. Her whispers filled the room again until Yasmin tapped her on the shoulder and told her to stand. Dr. Garland had entered the room, accompanied by Norma.

"You need to come with us," Norma said to Carmen in Spanish.

She was proficient in the language and waited for the doctor to begin. The doctor spoke to Norma directly, as if she had been the patient's family. Norma translated his comments almost simultaneously. Her son had passed, he explained. He had been on life support, and actually he had been kept alive by artificial respiration, but his heart had stopped, and nothing else could be done. He left it to the nurses to explain to her what she needed to do to claim his body. Then he nodded and went on his way, walking out of the section through the hallway. The nurses took Carmen to the station to make the arrangements, and then one of them took her to her son's room to see him one last time.

CHAPTER 77

Late that afternoon, Norma handed Yasmin a large envelope that contained several sheets of paper summarizing Carlos's condition and history. It was enough of what she needed to send to Mr. Moza to make Carlos's transfer happen. She made inquiries from the guard downstairs, and they allowed her to scan the documents and email them to Mr. Moza's email. She had called Gordon previously and asked him if there was any news. She did not want to slight him, and if he had any definite way to make the transfer happen, she would go with him, but at the moment, he had said, he had not been able to convince any doctor to take Carlos's case.

She felt satisfied. She never thought much of Mr. Moza. In her mind he was someone from a different era, with archaic ideas, but slowly she had discovered that the old man was incredibly adaptable, and now she would not be surprised that he could make Carlos's transfer possible.

She smiled at Carlos and leaned over to kiss him. Then she held his hand and sat down on the chair next to the bed.

"Mr. Moza has your papers," she said. "I'm hoping that he can make the transfer happen. Do you think Gordon will mind that we are doing this without him?"

"I would not worry about that, darling. Gordon is a very practical man. He's like an eighteen-wheeler on the road that does not stop at anything. He was made for the trucking business."

"You don't think he'll mind?"

"Not at all. He wants me there. That's so."

"He's a good friend."

"The best. When are they going to take all these wires off me?"

"We are waiting for the doctor to decide. I think it's going to be gradual process."

"What's he waiting for to decide?"

"They have to take more tests. They have to see what is the nature of your problem. You can hardly move your left arm. They have to find out what's causing it and then set up a treatment plan for you. It's going to be therapy and that has to start right away. If you don't do that, then there is danger that your arm could stay like that. We don't want that."

"I want to be disconnected from all these machines. This is no way to live."

"Carlos, we are extremely lucky that you are not more seriously hurt. Many people do not come back from an accident like that. You know, it's your brain. That's what was hurt. Any injury to your brain is serious, and we have to be cautious."

Carmen walked in silently, holding her rosary in her left hand and bowing as she spoke to them.

"Excuse me, Yasmin. Excuse me, Carlos. I am so glad that you are doing so well. I came to say goodbye. I am going to be leaving now."

"Leaving? No," exclaimed Yasmin. "I won't let you leave."

Carmen came close. She reached up and hugged Yasmin.

"I have to take care of my son. I have to find a plot to bury him."

"Oh," Yasmin said, realizing that she had momentarily overlooked the woman's plight. "What can we do to help?"

"Nothing. Just be my friend."

"That we are. But how can we help?"

"There's nothing you can do. I don't know what to do myself. They told me I should cremate his body because it's very expensive to buy a cemetery plot."

"Do you have a place to stay?"

"I lived with my son, but now that he's gone, I don't know what I will do."

"Do you have a family?"

"My son was my family. He was all I had."

Yasmin turned to Carlos.

"Can we take her?"

"Sure we can," Carlos replied. "She can come with us to Miami."

"No," Carmen answered. "I can't do that. I can't be a burden to anybody."

"You are not going to be a burden to anyone," Yasmin said. "You're coming with us."

Carmen shook her head and silently walked to the end of the bed and knelt down on the floor to pray. Carlos and Yasmin continued their conversation, both realizing that they had been extremely fortunate. Carmen's son had died of a brain failure, a total shutdown of his organs, and Carlos and Yasmin felt incredibly guilty. Why did her son die and not Carlos? Did the virgin play a fast one on Carmen by choosing Carlos to survive and not her son? As they stared towards the diminutive lady, hardly visible at the end of the bed, they thought the only way to make things right would be to take her with them. She had no other relatives, no one who could fix her a meal, offer her a bed. She needed them.

CHAPTER 78

By the end of that week, things began to move rapidly in domino fashion. First, came the medical team that disconnected Carlos from the respirator. He was kept on watch to see how his body would react when breathing on its own. Then came the news that the transfer to Jackson Memorial in Miami had been approved and that a new doctor had agreed to take Carlos's case. Pending an assessment at arrival, he would be going to a regular room. When Yasmin told Carlos the news, he merely looked at her and smiled.

"I have good insurance," Carlos said.

She came close and kissed him, laughing.

"Have we paid the insurance, by the way?"

"I don't know. You are in charge."

"Please, Carlos, don't say that to me. How would I know anything about that? We've never talked about it, and I could not ask anyone."

"It is okay, darling. My memory is good. I make yearly payments. I pay ahead. All the records are at home. Besides, do you think the hospital would be treating me if my insurance was not covering?"

"They have not asked me anything. I tried to bring up the subject with Norma, remembering that it needed to be discussed, and she said they had all the information, that they had gotten it from you."

"They got it out of my wallet when I came here. That's what happened."

Carmen had been standing at the end of the bed. They had had a service for her son the day before at the church where Yasmin had prayed so desperately to the Virgin of Guadalupe that morning. There was no casket. Carmen could not afford even a flimsy one.

Due to her vigil watching her son at the hospital, she had lost her job. She only had a room at an apartment that she shared with other men and women, where her son had lived too. His body was cremated and brought to the church in a gold vase, encased with a picture of him, smiling broadly. Only a few people had attended the ceremony where the minister gave a short sermon, the focus of which was that migrants who came to America were poor but honest and welcome in the house of God. Yasmin held Carmen by her arm as she shivered as every attendant embraced her. It was at that point when Yasmin made her sit down.

After it was over, it was Yasmin who picked up the vase with Carmen's son's remains and carried them. She took Carmen with her to stay at the motel. The two had been inseparable since Carmen's son's death.

***

Carmen kept standing there at the end of the bed, still quiet.

"I have your wallet," Yasmin said to Carlos. "I wonder if we should be carrying it during the trip, just in case we get separated."

"Aren't you coming with me?"

"Of course, I am coming with you, darling. Whatever gave you the impression that I wouldn't?"

"It sounded like you were planning to go separately."

"That's not happening, Carlos."

Yasmin sounded resolute, leaving no doubt that she would not leave Carlos alone under any circumstances.

"Do we know anything yet?"

"We know that there will not be a helicopter transfer. They made that clear since the first day. The question is between an ambulance and a private car with a driver. I was told yesterday that it seemed almost sure that it would not be an ambulance. I think because of the long distance involved, they would use a private car. The question is now with the insurance company of who pays for what?"

"You mean we could get stuck with the bill?"

"It would be a big bill."

"Why don't we just pack up and leave?"

"You can't do that, honey. You are doing great with the therapy sessions, but you can't risk it. We can't go on our own."

"We can too. We can fly out of here."

"No, darling. We can't go on our own."

Carlos's phone buzzed, and he tried to grab it with his left hand but couldn't. Yasmin took it quickly and pressed down on the screen to take the call. It was Gordon. He had been frustrated that he had not been able to make the transfer possible himself, although Yasmin assured him that all had worked out, and they were just waiting to hear.

"Any word yet?" he asked.

"No, we are waiting," she said.

"Well, let me know as soon as you hear."

He clicked off, and Yasmin put the phone by Carlos's right-hand side.

"When you pick up a call, use your right hand," she said. "Don't try with the left because it's still slow, and you might lose the call."

"Okay."

Before it was her quitting time, Norma came into the room to give them the good news. They had been approved for the transfer in a private van. They were leaving early in the morning, around 7:00 a.m.

They were all elated and then discussed how they would spend that last night at the hospital. Carlos wanted Yasmin and Carmen to go back to the motel and sleep there through the night, but Yasmin wouldn't hear of it. She would not leave Carlos alone ever again. She would sleep on a chair, a chunk of the bed, or on the floor. She would make room for Carmen at the bottom half of Carlos's bed.

CHAPTER 79

They arrived at Jackson Memorial by the afternoon, around 1:30. The trip had been rushed because of the need to get Carlos to the hospital as soon as possible. The driver made stops for gas during which Carlos used the bathroom under Yasmin's watchful eye. As soon as they entered Jackson Memorial Hospital and checked in, a nurse brought a wheelchair, and they all went in the elevator to bring Carlos to his room. In no time, he was in bed. Yasmin waited until he was settled in and then she called Uber for a car and went home to pick up Carmen.

She had been away for more than two weeks, and home never seemed so sweet. She showed Carmen around the house and made her feel welcome, telling her to choose which bedroom she liked best. The small woman was in awe, impressed by the beauty of the house she found herself in. She had never been in a house of such beauty, and yet, she was even more impressed by the simplicity of its proprietor, who strode back and forth arranging pots and pans in the kitchen and, incredibly, mopping the floor.

"Yasmin, leave that. Tell me what you want me to do. I will do everything."

"No you will not. You have to rest. Get some sleep. Pick the room that you want, and we can build a little altar for your son there. I know you want that. I'm just doing some basics, but I have to get back to the hospital to meet Carlos's doctor. I can order some food. No time to cook now, but I do not want you to go hungry. There are a few restaurants from our country here. What rules here is Cuban food. I've gotten used to it now. It's quite good. Here's a menu."

She handed Carmen a flier with several entries on both sides.

"It's a small place," Yasmin added. "But as always, that's where the best food comes from."

Yasmin smiled at her, hoping Carmen would respond, but she just stood there, frozen, looking at the flier and looking back at Yasmin.

"Ay, I'm sorry, I just remembered you don't read. Give me, I will tell you."

"No, Yasmin. I don't want anything."

"You have to, Carmen. You have not eaten, and all you had was a lousy coffee, which was not really coffee, just colored water. So, now we will order, and you will try the Cuban coffee. It's a lot like ours but stronger. But what would you like to eat? Steak with fried potatoes? That's very common here, but there are other things. How about tamales?"

"No, Yasmin, I'm not hungry."

"You have to eat. If I order something, then you might not like it."

"Some soup?"

"Okay, I will order that and some other things for both. Would you like that?"

Carmen nodded. She was still too amazed to sit. Yasmin approached her and took her by the hand, sat her down on the sofa in the living room.

"We are still not fully furnished here but we are getting there. Sit and relax. I don't have much to eat here. We had barely moved in when Carlos had the accident. But let me order."

She got on the phone and ordered several entrees and drinks. Then she remembered and ordered coffee and several bottles of water.

"I'm going to set the pool a little bit, take the cover off and set the timer on so the lights come on at night. Carlos loves the pool, and so do I. Then I have to go back. Come with me if you want. Come on."

She opened the sliding door to the pool and went outside. There were no leaves on the cover of the pool, and she got busy rolling the cover back manually. The water seemed clean, and she thought about turning on the vacuum cleaner but then changed her mind. She sank her hand in the water and deemed it still chilled. She thought by tonight it would be warm and perfect for a swim, but no, she could not see herself swimming without Carlos next to her. She went to the shed and flipped the switch for the underground lights on and off. Everything seemed to be working just fine. She looked around to see if anything needed tidying up. It was all in order.

"I'll be back tonight after Carlos falls asleep," she said to Carmen. "You need to get some rest. You hardly slept last night. Food is coming. I need to bring one coffee with me for Carlos and two sandwiches I ordered, one for Carlos and one for me. The rest is for you. Eat whatever you want and put the rest in the refrigerator."

Yasmin walked ahead of her and went inside. She turned the large screen TV on. It was the first time she had watched it. It was delivered a few days after Carlos's accident, and Amelia had received it. She had been making rounds to the house daily and keeping everything intact for Carlos's return. Now Yasmin hurried. She needed to get to the hospital and fidgeted with the monitor until she found a Spanish channel for Carmen to watch. She did not know how long she would be at the hospital and wanted the poor woman to have entertainment that she could understand at least. There was a knock at the door, and she hastened to answer.

A young man dressed in casual clothes held a paper bag that seemed to be full to the brim and read from a slip.

"A steak well cooked and fried potatoes—"

"It's okay," Yasmin answered. "How much do I owe you?"

He showed them the bill, and she paid him with two twenty-dollar bills and gave him a five-dollar tip.

"Thank you."

She handed the bag to Carmen and quickly got on the phone to call for a Uber.

"I will be just taking the sandwiches, one soft drink, and two of the small coffee cups. I need to get going, Carmen. If you have any questions just call me from your phone."

Carmen made her a bag. The car was outside in the less than ten minutes. She kissed Carmen on the cheek and walked hastily outside.

CHAPTER 80

Yasmin was unable to get a pass at the hospital's reception desk, but she showed the nurse her identification card and gave her Carlos's name. The receptionist remained still on her chair, as if she had been hit by a thunderbolt.

"They are looking for you on the fifth floor," she said, looking at her. "I just got a call from them upstairs. Here, I will print you a pass. Go to room 503 as fast as you can."

Yasmin ran to the elevator and pressed the button for floor 5 and darted out as soon as the doors opened. She rushed through the corridor, counting the room numbers as she went by. But she didn't have to count anymore as soon as she saw a group of people gathered in front of the room ahead. Had something happened to Carlos? She focused her gaze on the man standing right at the door, aside of the group. She knew instantly he must be the doctor, and she went straight to him.

"I'm Carlos Figueroa's wife. Is everything all right?"

The doctor gazed at her up and down, and gave no hint.

"Well, I am Dr. Sanders, and I am going to be treating your husband, as you know. Let's go inside."

"Yasmin, we are all here," Amelia said, tapping her shoulder. "Everyone's here."

"Hello," Yasmin replied, waving at everyone, and followed the doctor.

She was so anxious that she could hardly speak. She had thought that something had happened, that Carlos had gone back. But there he was, eyes wide open, and she leaned over and kissed him.

"I love you," she said to him in Spanish.

Hearing the words, she felt so good, and she held onto his hand.

"I think that the first issue is whether your husband should at this point be without any breathing support. I think I would have preferred that he stayed with the support for a little longer, but overall I think it was the right call to make. His organs are all working, and I do not see anything in his body functions that call for artificial help. He has been doing therapy already, which again is a little bit of a jump too high, too soon. But I am not going to disturb any of the actions by the Jacksonville trauma center. I think they did a fine job there and really brought your husband back. We are going to do a series of tests to assess your husband's injuries. After trauma like this it takes the body some time to find itself, so to speak, and I already see some effects from his head injury."

"He cannot move his left arm fully," Yasmin said. "And he walks very slow, favoring his right leg."

"Yes, I'm aware of that. We will learn more about that in the next few days, and I think what I will do is to continue with the therapy but at a slower pace until we know in depth the nature of any injury from the accident."

He nodded and smiled, as if to indicate that that was all. Yasmin liked his approach. He was much more personal than any of the other doctors who had treated Carlos before, and she suddenly felt her anxiety decline to a minimum level. A few moments ago her heart was racing, thinking that the worst had happened.

"Thank you," she said.

The doctor walked away, and almost immediately, Mr. Moza and Mr. Prieto walked in. Mr. Moza opened his arms and embraced Yasmin. He was wearing his white guallavera and black trousers. He held her by the shoulders and smiled broadly at her.

"Didn't I tell you that it would be okay? Didn't I? Carlos is going to be all right, and he is with us now, where he belongs."

"Yes, thank you so much for all your help, Mr. Moza. We will never be able to repay you. Thank you."

335

She reached out to Mr. Prieto, who was behind Mr. Moza, and embraced him. Then came Roberto and Amelia.

"I knew that Carlos would come back, I knew it," Roberto said. "He's going to be fine. What did the doctor tell you, Yasmin?"

"Oh, he wants to keep him in a regular room, out of ICU, and have him take some tests. He is doing fair, but he has some limitations. It's all on his left side. He can only move his left arm a little bit, and he drags his left leg."

"So, he takes therapy. Isn't he doing that already?"

"A little. I think the doctor wants to do it at a slower pace."

"But why? It's the opposite. The sooner you start with the therapy, the more chance of a recovery."

"Well, the doctor is not going to stop it, but he wants to take tests."

"Oh, that's all right," Amelia said. "Naturally, they have to take tests, Roberto. They have to see what is wrong."

"All right, so what is the prognosis? What did the other doctors say in the other hospital?"

"Well, he suffered a concussion in the accident and damaged his skull. They had to operate to release the pressure. His brain was swollen."

She took a few steps back to get closer to Carlos. She held his hand, trying to make him part of the conversation. Mr. Moza positioned himself at the other side of the bed, close to Carlos. He also did not want to miss out on anything.

"And it's amazing that after something like that, Carlos, you have made such a comeback," Mr. Moza observed, "and you have come back strong, haven't you?"

He laid his hand on his shoulder with affection.

"I wouldn't say that, Mr. Moza."

"Why, Carlos? Look at it this way, realistically you cannot be on the road driving as you used to for a while, maybe quite a while. But here is your opportunity to pursue other interests, which may be your actual calling. Maybe, although hard to admit, this may be a hidden opportunity for you."

Carlos smiled and turned to Yasmin. They both knew where Mr. Moza was going. Politics again.

"I was born to drive a truck."

"No, you were not. I want you to put all your efforts, as much as you can, into making yourself well again, to try to recover most if not all your physical abilities because mentally, you have no deficiencies. Give your max during the therapy, especially now, at the beginning. That is when you set the pace of how the rest of your life is going to be. This is pretty important right now."

"I've been giving it my best shot every day," Carlos said.

"Good, Carlos." Mr. Moza said, tapping his shoulder. "Let's see how fast you can get out of this hospital now and be on your way home."

"I wish," Carlos said.

"Have you heard anything from your lawyer, Yasmin?" Roberto asked.

He and Amelia had been standing at the other side of the bed, next to Mr. Moza.

"I don't know," Yasmin replied. "I was in such a hurry to get here that I didn't even check on the mail."

His look across the bed towards her seemed somber.

"Dear, I know how busy you are right now and the load you are carrying on your shoulders, but I think you ought to call the secretaries to inquire. This is just too important for your plans and those of Carlos to not follow it. Give them a call, Yasmin."

"I will, Mr. Moza, No worries. But I assure you that I am certain that if something had happened, Gordon would know, and he would have called us already."

"Right," Carlos said. "Gordon doesn't miss much."

"I know. You're lucky to have him as a boss and a friend. But still," he insisted. "Just check up on it as soon as you can, honey."

Mr. Moza looked down towards Carlos, to carry his point across to Carlos too.

"We will," Carlos said. "Yasmin will call tomorrow."

"Do not forget," Mr. Moza repeated. "Something new may be cooking in the stove, and it's good."

Yasmin and Carlos crossed glances. They had no idea what the old man was talking about. But Yasmin suspected it. She caressed Carlos's left arm that was resting awkwardly on the bed. She made it seem as if Carlos's limb had an entity of its own, that it was a loose part of its body that had been hurt in the accident, and it needed petting, stimulation, to feel he had to jump back into everyday living and perform his functions as always. His role was vital. Carlos needed him.

"It's only your left hand that you are having problems with, right?" Roberto asked.

"So far," said Carlos.

"What's that supposed to mean? You expect more?"

"No one knows for certain," Carlos added. "With injuries of this magnitude, you can never tell."

"I don't think it's that bad, Carlos. It could have been, but it wasn't. You just have to follow the therapy, and then you will be out of here in no time. I'm planning to have our first meeting two weeks from now. So please, Carlos, stick with that therapy. What's happened has only been a test. You are now back on track but not on the road. You should never think about driving for a living again."

"All right," Carlos said. "It will be as you say, Mr. Moza."

"We need to talk. We need to talk a lot, but I know that now is not the time. I know that."

"Are you tired, Carlos? Do you feel all right?"

Roberto was close to him also, and perhaps his questions were a signal to the others. Carlos needed to recover.

"I feel fine. I do not have any pain. I feel great. They want me to rest, and that is why I am laying here, but if it was up to me, I'd be swimming already."

"No," Mr. Moza said. "Let's not overdo it. An error like that can set you back."

"And how do you feel, Yasmin?" Amelia asked.

She came around and put her arm around her.

"I am glad to be back," Yasmin said. "I actually brought something for Carlos, and I am afraid it's getting cold in the bag. But I only have two cups. Sorry."

"Oh, go ahead," Roberto said. "We should have brought him one."

"Is it okay for him to have that?" Amelia commented.

"It will do him no harm, perhaps stimulate him a little bit. But that is all right."

"Should we ask the nurse?"

Yasmin had taken one cup out of the shopping bag she carried and carefully placed it in Carlos's right hand. Then she leaned over and kissed him. Everyone applauded.

At that moment, Carlos's phone went off, and Yasmin picked it up.

"How is Carlos?" said the voice, and she immediately recognized Gordon.

"He's here," she answered. "I will pass him on."

She grabbed his right hand and made him hold the phone.

"It's Gordon, Carlos. Just talk to him for a minute."

"Hello," Carlos answered.

"Are you ready to come back to drive?"

"Oh. I don't know that I'd be of much use. I could crash another tractor for you."

"You never crashed anything. It was another truck driver. I'm still looking for him."

"You'll never find him. There is something sinister about that curve on Route 10."

"There is no such thing," Gordon said. "All these guys have to do is slow down."

"Maybe they have a boss like you who hustles them."

"Come on, Carlos. How do you feel? Yasmin says you are completely fine. No leftovers."

"Not really, Gordon. I can hardly move my left arm. I am going to be like an invalid."

"No, you're not. Therapy will take care of that. Listen, you're gonna have to go see Mr. Kline as soon you feel a little better."

"Why?"

"Well, it's nothing bad. On contrary, you've had an accident, and you were seriously hurt, and I think that counts in your favor. But get well first. Once you are out of the hospital and you're fully charged, then I'll remind you. You have to go talk to him. How do you feel?"

"I feel great."

"That's fantastic. Keep up the good work with the therapy. That is what you need now. These first weeks are the most important."

CHAPTER 81

After two long weeks of therapy and multiple tests, Carlos's doctor came to the sound conclusion that he was out of danger and that there was no purpose in keeping him in the hospital. The doctors who had treated him had served him well by surgically intervening early in the process. They had saved his life, but there were consequences. The damage was permanent, and Carlos's use of his left hand was impaired. It would always be. Therapy would serve a high purpose by enhancing Carlos's degree of movement. But he would never be the same man, and how far his new limitations would interfere with his daily life only time would tell. Among the factors playing a role in his future lay a very special one, and that was Yasmin. She was the star that shone his path, and she showed her prominence with amazing dexterity.

One afternoon, they both sat on folding chairs by the pool. Carlos had come home the day before, and Yasmin had immediately gone to work. There was a schedule for everything: his medications, his therapy, his meals; every aspect of Carlos's life was controlled by Yasmin.

"Did you call the attorney yet?" Carlos asked.

"Actually," she said, "there is call that came from his office this morning. They left a message."

"And you haven't called him back?"

"No, not yet."

"Why not, Yasmin? This is so important for us. What are you waiting for?"

"I've been pretty busy setting you up. I haven't had time."

"No, I don't think that's the reason. You are afraid of what the news might be."

"A little," she said, tightening the grip on his hand.

"Give me my phone. I will call him."

"No, Carlos. Let's wait. Didn't you see the letter that came in?"

"The letter. What letter?"

"I found it in the mailbox when I came in with Carmen. It was from Mr. Kline's office."

"And what did it say?"

"It's just a copy of a receipt, as I understand it. They sent us a copy of the receipt of the application we filed."

"Are you sure about that? Let me have a look. Let me go get it."

"No, stay. I will get it. Talk to Carmen for a minute."

Carmen had just pulled another chair in front of them and was about to sit down.

"Yasmin, do you want me to get anything?" she asked.

"No, Carmen, you just sit down and talk to Carlos."

Carmen had fit in right into the family, and though she insisted on helping out, Yasmin turned her down. She made it clear that she had not asked her to come with them to become a maid. She was family. But Carmen was skilled in housekeeping, and no matter how Yasmin resisted, she followed her around and helped in any way she could.

"Here it is," Yasmin said, handing Carlos a torn envelope and its contents.

Carlos studied them for a long time, reading every detail, especially the official receipt from the Immigration service.

"You were right," Carlos said. "This is a receipt from Immigration letting us know that they got our application. I think we should still call Mr. Kline's office. I think Mr. Moza was trying to tell us something."

"Like what?"

"That we should call Mr. Kline. Something's up."

"If there was something going on, Mr. Kline would have called us."

"Do you remember the name of that secretary?"

Even Yasmin hesitated. She looked up, trying to jolt her memory.

"I can't remember. She has an unusual name."

"Lucrecia," Yasmin snapped.

"Let's call her now," Carlos said.

Yasmin did not move, so Carlos grabbed his own phone from her lap. Yasmin even kept his phone to keep him from being burdened with the constant phone calls.

"Hello," Carlos said as a voice picked up. "Can I speak to Lucrecia? This is Carlos Figueroa. I'm calling about my wife's case."

"Oh, Carlos," she said. "How are you feeling? I understand you were in an accident. But wait, you are not supposed to be talking. Am I wrong? Are you okay?"

"Yes, I know," Carlos said. "I was supposed to be dead, but my wife saved me. I came back from the dead."

"Oh, nonsense, you are too young. Don't think about that."

"I just wanted to let you know that we got a letter from Immigration. It's the receipt of our application."

"Actually, I am very glad you called. I was getting ready to call your wife, Yasmin. Something has come up with your application. Are you okay to get around? Could you come here to have a meeting with Mr. Kline?"

"Yes, I can do that. Has anything happened?"

"Well, it's nothing bad with your case. But Mr. Kline wants to talk to you and Yasmin now that you are out of the hospital. I mean, you are out now, right?"

"Yes, I'm out. Live and sound."

"Well, I'm so glad to hear that. When would you be available?"

"Oh, anytime. We have lots of time now."

"All right, well, how about tomorrow, late afternoon?"

"That would be fine."

"How is 3:00 p.m.?"

"That's okay."

"So, can you be in our office around that time, and then Mr. Kline will sit with you to discuss your case. Okay?"

"Yes, sure."

"I am very glad to hear that you are much better and out of the hospital. That is really great."

Carlos thanked her and ended the call. He handed his phone back to Yasmin, reaching out to her with his right hand. This was one of the changes in his new life. He would now favor his right hand.

"Tomorrow at 3:00 p.m.," Carlos said.

"Why do you think they want to see us?" Yasmin asked.

"She says it's not bad news. Mr. Kline just wants to bring us up to date on the case."

Yasmin looked pensively at Carmen, sitting across from them.

"Good news?" Carmen asked.

"I'm not sure. The attorney wants to talk to us."

"It is good news, Yasmin. Remember that the virgin looks out for her sheep," Carmen said.

"We are due at church tonight. Do you want to stop at the restaurant before we go to Mass?"

"Yes," Carmen said. "I want to ask about the job."

Carmen had quickly adapted to her new life. Every day she showed her gratitude by helping out in whatever chores came along in the house. But Yasmin kept her at bay. She did not want her to become her maid. She had offered Carmen their help in exchange for nothing. Carmen had quickly become part of the family.

"Carlos, is it okay if we stop at the restaurant before we go to church? Carmen really wants that job."

"If we run into Moza there tonight, maybe he can help us. We stand a better chance doing it through him."

"Mr. Moza will only be happy to participate."

"That, he always does," Carlos said laughing.

CHAPTER 82

It was supposed to be a quick stop at the restaurant, but as usual, any visit there was compounded by the many friends who knew Carlos and who wanted to share time with him and his faithful companion, Yasmin. Everyone's impression was that they were inseparable, and that now that Carlos had been injured, she had shown her devotion to him even more.

Roberto and Amelia caught up with them at the little window, or ventanita. They said they were not even planning to eat dinner tonight but only wanted some coffee. They would sit with them at a table and chat.

But such plans of trading dinner for coffee never quite worked out. Yasmin chose a table at the rear of the restaurant as usual. She let Carlos sit first and helped him move his chair forward. They were sitting at the last table in the restaurant's long corridor, and they were facing the back window. Carmen sat next to them, and it was Roberto who broke the silence.

"So, Carmen, how do you like it so far? Do you like Miami?"

"Yes," she said in a soft voice.

"Isn't it comfortable? Everything is in Spanish. You could live your entire life here without speaking a word of English."

"But that's not a good thing," Amelia added. "You should try to pick up some of the language."

Carmen nodded her head but said nothing.

"Carmen has lived in the US for some time. She was living in the Jacksonville area with her son," Yasmin said. "He was hospitalized with Carlos during the same time. After his passing, she had no other relatives, and we brought her with us."

"Oh, she's the one looking for a job?" Amelia asked.

"Yes," said Yasmin.

"I think Mr. Moza has that all wrapped up already. He spoke to the owner."

"What kind of work will she do here?" Amelia asked.

"We are not sure," Yasmin said. "Probably dishwashing, taking out garbage. She is good with anything. She is a good cook, but she doesn't know this menu."

"She will learn in no time," Amelia said. "Our menu is easy."

"Yes, you might say that."

Carlos seemed quiet, and he leaned against Yasmin's shoulder, something that Roberto and Amelia took notice of.

"Her only difficulty is with her short height. When she cooks, she stands on a short ladder so she can reach. She actually has her own at home, and she used to work in a small restaurant by Jacksonville, and that's how she would do it. They really liked her there and did not want to let her go, but we couldn't leave her alone at a time like this. She just lost her son."

Carmen made the sign of the cross and pressed her hands together with her fingers pointed up, in a perfect praying emoji. The waitress arrived at the table, ready to take their orders.

"It's great that you are out of the house, Carlos," the waitress said. "You look so much better. I bet Yasmin had a lot to do with that, right?"

"She does with everything," Carlos said. "She's my guardian angel."

"Do you want to see a menu?" the waitress asked.

"No, we're fine," Yasmin said. "Carlos and I are going to have soup only. And maybe a steak, Carlos?"

"Yes." Carlos smiled at her. "I am hungry."

347

"That is a good sign," Roberto said. "Could you bring us one menu, please?"

The waitress tapped her foot on the floor.

"Now, what's that all about?"

"I know Amelia is not saying it, but she wants to make this a special night."

"Oh, really? Shall I get the candles and some flowers?"

"No, it's a private affair," Roberto said, laughing.

"Oh, okay."

The waitress turned to Yasmin.

"And what about Carmen? What will she be having?"

"Carmen, will you tell the waitress what you want?"

"I'm just gonna have the thick broth soup and one tamal," she said.

"And to drink?" asked Carlos.

"A bottle of water," she said.

"We're good then," Carlos observed.

"We're going to go to church after this," Yasmin said.

"What church?" asked Amelia.

"The *Ermita* on South Miami Avenue."

"Oh, really? You're going there tonight?"

"Yes, we have a lot to be thankful for."

"I know."

"It's different," said Roberto. "It's the shrine right by the bay. All you have to do is sit outside on one of the benches, and you can feel the peace in the wind."

"Have you been there before?" Amelia asked.

"No, I haven't. But we are hopeful that Carlos can get us there."

She squeezed his left shoulder and rested her head on it.

"Do you expect to see Mr. Moza here tonight?" Carlos asked.

"I am not sure," Roberto said. "He's quite busy these days. The election campaign is on."

"And they're starting already?" Carlos asked.

"Yes. We're in the middle of summer. November is right around the corner."

"Who's running?"

"For community council members there are many."

"That is good, I guess, but somehow it does not interest me."

"It should interest you. We should all be interested."

"I've never been convinced. I find it a dirty business."

"It doesn't have to be. You can actually do a lot of good as a politician."

"I don't know about that. I know that some of these positions are thought of as reputable, but look at a politician's life, look at the cycle. A politician wins the election. There might be a party that night, but the next day he already has to start his next campaign to be re-elected, and the things he said today that are praise to some of his colleagues he might have to take back tomorrow, when he finds out that some of them are running for office in the next cycle too. It's the most hypocritical job on earth. You and I can be friends right now, and when you go to the press tonight, you can say awful things about me because I might be running against you. Tomorrow you will see me and shake my hand as if nothing has happened."

The waitress arrived with their orders on a large tray. She served them quickly. She knew exactly what portion everyone was supposed to get, such was her familiarity with them. She served the food first and then the drinks.

"Anything else? Is everybody okay?"

"Perfect," said Roberto.

Carmen came back to the table slowly.

"Is everything all right?" Yasmin asked.

"Yes, I start tomorrow," she replied smiling, taking her seat at the table.

"At what time?"

"They told me 11:00."

"Oh, that's great. You can sleep till late. I will bring you."

"Will you be here?" Carlos asked the waitress.

"Not at that time, but I will keep an eye on her for you. She's gonna be all right."

"Please," Yasmin said. "She's been through so much."

"I know," said the waitress. "But no worries. She is gonna be all right."

"Till when is her shift?"

"Probably till the early evening, but I could be wrong. Carmen, till when did they say?"

"They said I have to do lunch and supper."

"Oh, that sounds like a long day. That means we will be leaving together. I will come in to see you when I get in."

"I'm so glad that you took an interest. We really appreciate it."

"It's fine. Does anyone want anything else?"

"No, we are all fine."

"Roberto, you said it's a special occasion. Do you want wine?"

"No. Unless Amelia wants some."

He turned to look at his wife, and she smiled at him.

"When you have time," Amelia said, "bring me a cup of red wine. I will drink to Carlos's comeback. Doesn't he look great?"

"He does," the waitress answered, nodding her head. "Carlos, you must keep that up. Get better and better."

She went back up through the ally carrying her tray in one hand and surveying the tables as she passed.

"Carmen has landed a job," Carlos said proudly.

"Let's drink to that," Amelia said.

They all clinked their water glasses and laughed.

Left of Yasmin, quiet as a mouse, the tiny lady gave them a slight smile, and she began to dip into her soup. She was too shy to express any sentiments of joy. The recent loss of her son and Carlos's own delicate health issues had shaken her and made her even more secluded. Only secretly, and as if in an afterthought, she gazed towards Yasmin in silence. No one could ever know the intensity of her love for the beautiful young woman who had come to enlighten her soul, just when she felt it was buried by her tragic loss.

CHAPTER 83

It was a windy night, and the three of them felt it right away, as Roberto had predicted. It was in fact so peaceful that the three of them sat down on one of the benches right across from the church. Some of the congregation were arriving in droves, and families greeted them as they passed them by. Still, Carlos and Yasmin sat back, enjoying the cold breeze. It was only Carmen who remained standing, holding her rosary in both hands and gazing at them.

"We are coming now, Carmen," said Carlos. "I just couldn't pass this up. This wind is holy."

"Let's go, Carlos," Yasmin said, taking his hand. "The Mass is about to start."

The three of them walked inside. The door was wide open as a welcome sign. Right across from them was the bay and the open ocean, beginning to be blanketed by the night's black veil. They entered the beautiful chapel with its white sparkling floor and its artistic walls bearing the paintings of historic heroes of the Cuban island.

"This is so beautiful," Yasmin whispered. "Were you ever here before, Carlos?"

"Once right after I arrived," Carlos answered. "I wanted to give thanks to the virgin for getting me across the ocean from the island. She's known for saving the lives of many shipwrecked sailors."

"How is it that you never told me?"

"We never talked about it. It's a new church. It's the shrine of Our Lady of Charity."

Carlos and Yasmin came to the middle aisle and genuflected in front of the virgin's altar. They walked towards one of the front benches and sat down, saving space for Carmen. She had lagged behind them and made the sign of the cross at the altar and sat next to them.

"I'm really happy that you brought me here," Carmen said. "This is a beautiful church."

She crossed herself once more and knelt down to say a prayer.

"The murals are so beautiful. They are historical figures of Cuba, right?"

"Yes, they are patriots of the island. One was a priest, and the others are war heroes."

"They are so striking."

They stood up as the priest came to the altar, followed by two altar boys. He said good evening and announced the passage of the Bible he would rely on for his sermon. Then he moved to a side of the altar with the altar boys. A deacon came forward from the front row and walked behind the lectern to read the Holy Word.

Yasmin could not get over the setup. She had never been to a church like that. She could smell the sea water and feel the breeze, even after the doors were closed. Carmen held onto Yasmin's arm, sitting next to her. Despite her grief she had a lot to be thankful for. She had met Yasmin, her guardian angel. She concentrated on the deacon's reading of John the Baptist as he preached to the crowds the upcoming of another prophet whose sandals he was not even worthy of tying. Brimming with devotion, she knelt to pray and remained in that position for the remainder of the Mass.

At the conclusion of the Mass, the three of them moved to the front row to face the statue of the virgin. Yasmin especially needed to thank her. A miracle had happened that had brought Carlos back. She would have preferred to give thanks before the Virgin of Guadalupe, but Carmen had whispered that it did not matter. She was watching all the same. Yasmin reached to her side and kissed Carlos on the cheek. She gazed at him for a few moments, trying to transmit to him the joy that she felt at having him back. She thought that he could never know the depth of her happiness and that someday maybe he could. She held his hand tightly and thought that she wanted to convey her gratitude to the virgin. He was her trophy that the virgin had given her when he so remarkably returned from his unconscious state.

CHAPTER 84

The next afternoon found Carlos and Yasmin sitting at Mr. Kline's conference room looking into the suburban streets behind Coral Way through a large colonial window. Lucrecia had come in with them and stayed for a few minutes, conversing mostly about Carlos's injuries and commenting how well he was recovering. Then she excused herself and assured them that Norman would be joining them momentarily, after he finished his first appointment. Then she returned again shortly after.

"Still nothing?" she asked from the door.

"No, not yet," Yasmin answered. "But it's okay. We are in no hurry."

"Oh, let me try to find out what's going on."

She closed the door behind her and no more than five minutes later, Mr. Kline came in the room. He came close to them and shook their hands.

"How're you feeling?" he asked of Carlos. "You are doing some therapy, I assume."

"Yes," said Carlos.

"And how is that going?"

"He's doing much better," Yasmin interrupted. "He's making progress each day."

"With you at the lead, right?"

"Oh, yes. I am there."

"That's what I expected to hear," Norman said, shaking his index finger at Carlos. "You need Yasmin at the helm, right? You could not do this alone, right?"

"That is true. She is what guides me now."

"That is very important for our goals," Norman said. "Extremely important."

Yasmin and Carlos both turned to Norman with inquisitive looks, and he smiled at them.

"There has been a change in circumstances," Norman said. "It's because of what happened to Carlos in the accident."

"What do you mean?" said Yasmin.

"As you know, because of your entry into the country through the border, you are required to return to Guatemala for the final interview for your resident visa. And because of that requirement, you will need to get a waiver here before you can travel to Guatemala. The waiver requires that you show an extreme hardship that your husband would experience if you are removed and not allowed to stay in the US. I think we can now prove that hardship through Carlos's condition as a result of his accident."

Carlos and Yasmin looked at each other.

"Could you repeat?" Carlos asked. "We don't quite follow."

"Okay," Norman said. "Let's start by you telling me about your condition. Are you seeing your doctor right now?"

"Yes, of course. I see the doctor on a monthly basis, and I see the therapist three times a week."

"Do you have any impairments from the accident?"

"Yes."

"It's all on his left arm," Yasmin said cutting in. "He cannot make a full swing with his arm. He cannot make a fist, and he cannot lift his left arm above his ear. They are telling us that he will gain some of his abilities back, but he won't get all of them."

Norman quickly assessed that Yasmin had taken over. She was now in charge of Carlos's health, and there was no way that he would miss out on his treatment. She would make sure that he would make as full of a recovery as medically possible and more. Norman smelled victory.

"I am going to make an expedited request to US Immigration Service for a resolution of your I-130 petition. That is the first petition that you guys made. I am going to need copies of Carlos's medical records immediately to support that request and additionally a short letter from your treating doctor explaining his condition, his diagnosis, and the consequences for the future."

He reached forward and tapped the intercom line.

"Lucrecia," he said. "I need a letter to Carlos's doctor to be hand-delivered by them tomorrow. We need an opinion to support an expedited request for their I-130. Can you come over for a moment?"

"We need your doctor's name and address," he said to Yasmin after ending the call. "I want you to give it to Lucrecia now. She is coming."

"Don't worry, Mr. Kline," said Yasmin. "I will make sure he gets the letter tomorrow morning."

"You have to jump on this," Norman said. "I know you will, but I can't stress its importance enough. We have to move quickly."

"I think I understand but why the urgency?"

Yasmin looked at him inquisitively.

"He may get better," Norman answered, pointing at Carlos. "And let that be the case, but we need to show the need for expediency to have Immigration decide the petition quickly, and that is not easy to do. We need records of his condition now in his present state."

The door opened and Lucrecia entered the room, pad in hand.

Yasmin gave her the name of the doctor and the address.

"Don't you want to check your purse to make sure?" Norman asked.

"I don't carry a purse," Yasmin said. "But that's the address. I drive there to all of his visits."

Lucrecia smiled at her and turned to go back to her office. Mr. Kline stopped her.

"I need an additional letter to the hospital," Mr. Kline said. "We can then have Yasmin take it to patient's records at Jackson Memorial Hospital and see if they can give her copies of the treatment records from there. Give her the letters, and we will have her deliver them tomorrow. See if you could start working on a request for an expedited proceeding. The reason will be Carlos's medical condition."

"But I will need at the very least the doctor's response."

"Agreed but just get it started and save it for the record. We can follow it up once Yasmin comes back with whatever they give her at the doctor."

Lucrecia left the room, and Norman went on to explain the need for records to show joint residence.

"I have quite a few already," Yasmin said. "We did the joint utilities, bank statements, the mortgage statements for the house, deed."

"That's good," Norman said. "You're right on target. Remember that we may get the petition expedited, but there will be an interview slated, and we have to be prepared for that."

"I know," Yasmin answered. "We really appreciate what you are doing."

Her admiration for Norman was visible. In a flash of a second, she imagined a large thank you sign that she handed to Gordon. She decided that Gordon was the type of man you wanted on your side. He had led them to an energetic attorney who knew how to cut corners and take advantage of whatever chances were favorable to his clients. Norman knew how to play his hand. Gradually, and as they prepared to leave the office, she became more and more confident. Removal from the US was now a deadly word to her. One year ago, it would not have mattered. She had been at a dead end. But now she had Carlos, and she could not imagine for a second that she could ever leave her husband, even if they ordered her to do so.

"The next step after our petition is approved will be to move to dismiss the deportation proceedings, but we can't do that yet. We need to get an approval of the petition first. You understand?"

"I do," Yasmin said, followed by Carlos.

CHAPTER 85

In the next few days, things unfolded rather fast and very much as Norman had predicted. He pursued with intense perseverance his request for an expedited process. The waiting period had happened to decrease in the last few months, and incredibly, his request for expedition was granted. The next thing that Carlos and Yasmin knew was that they were sitting at a small office with a middle-aged Immigration agent on the other side of a desk who kept asking them unpleasant questions. But not once did any of the two hesitate in answering back. Their case was obviously meritorious. Two people in close age range who met each other at a restaurant in Phoenix where the husband had stopped for a quick meal on his way back East after having dropped his truck load. Things had moved quickly from there, and the wife came to live in Miami with the husband, and the couple married days later. Then came that fateful morning on Route 10 East when Carlos was severely injured when a passing truck brushed him off the highway. The injuries were serious and undeniable. They had changed his life forever, and Yasmin had stood there by him, supporting him and keeping him positive despite it all.

When asked what was his biggest regret from the accident, Carlos answered how he and Yasmin had become a passionate swimming team who practiced in the later evenings by the shores of Miami Beach, side by side, like two high-spirited dolphins which could not lose sight of each other for very long. In fact, it was rather miraculous that they could maintain the same distance from each other, tossing aside the upcoming waves with natural skill. That was his deepest regret. There was a moment of silence after that, and the agent looked Norman in the eye.

"I don't have a problem with an approval. I'll pass it on to my supervisor. He will act on my recommendation, and you will probably have the approval in a few days."

"I didn't think you would," Norman said. "It's an easy case."

The agent smiled at him and wished good luck to Carlos and Yasmin. They walked out of the office and into the hallway, led by the agent who led them to the exit door.

They left the building, and once outside, they both shook hands with Norman, thanking him deeply for all he had done.

"We are not done yet," Norman quipped. "This is the stepping stone into something much deeper. We are just toeing the waters, but yes, it is an important starting point. You have an approved alien petition, and the case will not be sent to the National Visa Center. It's there that we need to be in order to process the waiver. We have a court hearing coming up, which is also good news. A motion will now be filed once we have the approval of this petition in our hands. We should have that in about a week, and I will do that on my own."

"We are following you," Yasmin said. "We are, and we thank you so much. Can you come with us for lunch? We want to invite you either now or tonight. Can you?"

Norman remained silent for a few seconds. He was thinking that it could not hurt although he did not make a habit of eating out with his clients. He liked to keep work disconnected from his hours of pleasure. But it happened that tonight he was meeting with Gordon for a light dinner.

"Yes, perhaps we could," he answered. "I am going to be seeing Gordon later."

"Oh, that would be perfect," Carlos said. "I will call Gordon. We always go to La Carreta, over on Bird Road."

"I don't think I've ever been there."

"I will call Gordon and tell him. If you want to join us, it will be a pleasure."

Norman nodded.

"Okay, I will call Gordon in a little bit. We will work it out for tonight, somewhere in Miami."

Norman smiled at his own joke and turned to go. As usual, he was under pressure to move on.

"I hope the other cases you have today will not be so challenging," Yasmin said.

"They all are. I have to get going. Congrats. You guys did well, and that's the key to everything, how the applicants perform at the interview."

"We will see you hopefully tonight."

Norman was off to the parking lot, and Carlos retrieved his phone with his right hand. He could not quite dial with his left hand but pressed the button for Gordon's line. The line clicked on, almost immediately.

"How did it go?" said his raspy voice.

"We made it," said Carlos, "thanks to you. How will we ever be able to pay you?"

"No payment is due. Just be my friend. You and Yasmin just be cool. I will take care of Norman, don't worry. He will be with me at La Carreta tonight."

CHAPTER 86

Carlos and Yasmin stopped at the window of La Carreta that evening. The two of them were holding hands. There was a crowd of people ahead of them, some waiting to be helped and some holding cups of coffee and chatting. One of them was Ralph, Carlos's friend, who immediately came over to shake Carlos's hand.

"How're you doing?" he said.

"I'm doing all right. Coming for some supper."

Ralph nodded towards Yasmin, and she said hello.

"Are you going to order?" Ralph asked.

"We were going to, but I think we will go inside."

"Sure? I can get it for you."

"No, it's all right. We will go inside."

Carlos and Yasmin checked with the cashier inside, and she directed them to one of the tables, midway towards the rear.

"There is your friend, Roberto, and his wife," she said, pointing.

"Hello," Yasmin said as she moved a chair back for Carlos.

"Hello," responded Roberto and Amelia.

"We may need some extra chairs," Carlos said. "Gordon and our lawyer are going to be joining us."

"Oh, no problem," Roberto said. "I think we can make room."

"What about when Mr. Moza arrives?"

"Yeah, that might be a problem."

Roberto called the waitress and let her know they needed a bigger table. She said she would be back. Amelia rose, came around the table, and embraced Yasmin. The two women had spoken earlier, and Yasmin had given her the good news of her approval.

"You did it, honey," she said. "You did it. Congratulations, Carlos."

She turned to Carlos and shook his hand.

"Thank you," Carlos said. "We still have ways to go."

Roberto followed, embracing Yasmin and kissing her cheek.

"That was fantastic," he said.

"We still have ways to go," she said.

"Yeah, but look at the speed of how this was done. That was amazing."

The waitress came to their table and said another table was ready. She took them to another section and seated them at a table for eight. It was Yasmin who spotted Gordon, followed by Mr. Kline, standing by the entrance. She waved at them.

"We will need to switch to English," she said.

"Gordon understands everything in Spanish," Carlos said, "but he can't speak a word."

The two men introduced themselves, shaking hands with Roberto, and Gordon made a move to glide behind Roberto and Amelia to take seats next to them, but Roberto had already stood and asked Amelia to move over.

"It's okay," Roberto said, signaling to Gordon to take his seat.

Gordon let Norman go first. Yasmin and Carlos extended their hands over the table.

"Thank you for this morning," Carlos said. "We owe you."

"You don't owe me. I just did my job, and you guys did the rest. You batted a home run this morning."

"Norman is just being humble," Gordon said. "But he deserves a hand."

He was the first to applaud, and the others followed. Roberto signaled the waitress to come.

"What would everybody like to drink? Wine, beer, champagne?"

"Wine would be fine," Gordon answered, pointing to Carlos. "I have a trip for you outside."

"How much do you value your truck?" Carlos asked in jest.

"He will soon be ready," said Yasmin, leaning towards Carlos.

"You two batted a home run," Roberto said. "But your lawyer made the pitch. He made the home run possible."

Everyone at the table applauded again, and just then the waitress arrived with cups and a bottle. She filled the cups halfway and passed them one by one to everyone. She then kept one for herself.

"With everyone's permission," she said. "I want to wish congratulations to Yasmin and Carlos too."

"And so be it," said Gordon. "To a great driver and a great friend."

Everyone leaned forward to clink their glasses.

"To two great people," Roberto added.

"Yes," repeated Amelia. "To two great people."

"To a great lawyer," Yasmin said.

"Yes, to a great lawyer," Carlos repeated.

They all emptied their glasses, even the waitress.

"Shall I collect your glasses, or you want to keep them?"

"You can take them," Roberto said, "I think the first two gentlemen will need menus."

"All right," she said.

She passed a menu to Gordon and Norman.

"I will be back when you are ready," she said and headed towards the front.

"What do you recommend?" Norman asked Carlos.

"Excuse me," Roberto interrupted. "If you are a first timer, I need to have the privilege of helping you. I've been around for ages here, me and my lovely wife."

Norman nodded towards Amelia.

"Are you familiar with the Cuban menu?" Roberto asked.

"Well, yes. Who isn't in Miami? But only as to basics, not too profound."

"Well, pork is the ever presence, but that's not kosher food, so we'll skip that. But we have a section of fish entries that you can pick from, and then if you want to stay safely away from some of the meat entries, you can pick from some of the typical vegetables or plantains. I highly recommend the ripe ones. They are delicious, and as far as the grain, they can be cooked in many different ways, and then you have the soups, which are Carlos's favorite, by the way, and the bean soups are good too."

"That was a heck of an introduction," Gordon said. "I am listening too. And I'd just want something not too filling."

"Gordon, you are a glutton, and you know it. I think you need the jerked beef. You will love it."

"It's called *ropa vieja*," said Yasmin. "That is filling though."

"I think I had that once," Gordon said. "It's a great dish."

Next to him, Norman had made his pick. He delved into the seafood, being a conservative follower of kosher.

The waitress returned, and surprisingly, Gordon went first, and then Norman followed. Roberto and Amelia went with seafood, and Carlos and Yasmin ordered soup and a steak that they shared with plantains.

The waitress did not take long to return. Instead of making two trips, she pushed the silver-plated cart with the entrees sorted out on each shelf.

Everyone turned to the sound of a familiar voice,

"How are you, my dear?" Mr. Moza muttered as he came close to the waitress and hugged her.

"Well, Mr. Moza, where have you been?" Carlos said. "We have been missing you."

"I know you have, son, I know you have. And how is your lovely wife?"

He first shook hands with Carlos and then reached Yasmin, who stood up to greet him. The two embraced. Then he turned to the others and moved quickly to shake hands with Gordon.

"We never formally met," Mr. Moza said, "but you were at the wedding reception, and I have seen you so many times in City Hall. It's time that we get acquainted. You are Carlos's friend, and that means you are mine too."

"It's funny. I was thinking today of who I could talk to in City Hall, and I thought of you, but I did not quite know how to get ahold of you. May I?"

"Of course, of course."

From inside his jacket, Mr. Moza retrieved a card, which he handed to him.

"Anytime after 11:00 you can reach me there."

He smiled as he turned past him to speak to Norman, and he extended his hand to him.

"Mr. Kline, it's a pleasure to see you here. It's been a while since we've seen each other. But what a pleasure. I understand that there is good news about Carlos and Yasmin, right?"

"Yes, there is," Norman said, standing to shake Mr. Moza's hand.

"Please sit down, sit down," said Mr. Moza. "There is no need. I am a little late and cannot stay long, but I could not let this opportunity go by without coming to see Carlos and his lovely wife, and thank you for your efforts with them. We all appreciate it so much."

"He's the best," Gordon said from his chair.

"I know he is," Mr. Moza replied, waving to Prieto, his eternal companion, to come in.

Mr. Prieto shook hands with the men and squeezed himself behind Mr. Moza, who was moving to other side of the table, past Roberto and Amelia.

"Amelia and Roberto," he said, "stay put, we are only going to be here for a few minutes. We have a long meeting tonight."

"About elections again?"

"No, this is work. Meetings with the Urban Development Review Board."

That remark did not escape Gordon, who flirted a smile at Mr. Moza as Mr. Kline looked on. Both men were involved in the real estate world of development. Carlos nodded at Gordon. A few years back, Gordon had persuaded Carlos to join in a real estate venture with him. After days of coaxing Carlos finally gave in and made a large deposit of hard-earned savings into Gordon's account. Gordon had not steered him wrong. In a year's time his investment was doubled. Carlos thanked his boss and friend. The transaction had served to solidify their relationship beyond boss and employee.

"But not again," Carlos had said. He was no speculator.

"What can I do to have a meeting with this man?" Gordon said.

"I will talk to him," Carlos replied. "He will see you. He relishes the attention."

"Can he deliver?"

"I don't know. He is an aide to the mayor, among other things."

"I'm interested. Will you help?"

"Of course. I'll get you his card before he leaves."

"I have his card," Gordon said. "I want you to recommend me."

Carlos laughed it off.

"What will my recommendation count for, Gordon?"

"You'd be surprised, Carlos. Don't underestimate yourself. I know how men like him operate. They do not easily trust. But you are part of his crowd. He knows you are for real, and when you tell him that this guy or that one is trustworthy, he listens."

"I will do that for you or whatever else you ask to, but you see how me and Yasmin bought our house recently, right? We did not ask for his help. He could probably have gotten us a cheaper deal and a bigger property. I think he might resent that I did not consult with him. But I do not like any of that Godfather stuff. I want to remain simple."

"That's fine. I respect that. But I'm asking you to put in a word for me. Will you?"

"Well, of course. Consider it done."

Gordon pulled back on his chair, and Norman shifted his gaze. Carlos knew he had not missed a word of the conversation and was not surprised. These two were a team.

The waitress served Mr. Moza and Pietro two small cups of espresso. Then she went around the table and swiftly served everyone else.

"If there's any problem with the orders, please let me know."

"Everything is perfect," Gordon said.

Later in the evening, after Mr. Moza had left and they all prepared to leave, Carlos slipped Gordon one of Mr. Moza's cards with Mr. Moza's cell number scribbled on it.

"Don't tell me you two are going to the beach tonight," Roberto said to Carlos and Yasmin.

"No, we are going to our pool tonight," Yasmin said.

"You are not going to swim yet, Carlos, right?"

"No, I want to watch her. She's magical."

Gordon and Norman shook hands with Carlos and hugged Yasmin. Roberto and Amelia walked with them.

"Aren't we forgetting something?" Yasmin asked.

"Carmen, right?" Carlos said. "No. I was going to ask."

"Oh, is she all right?"

"Today was her first day at work," Yasmin said.

"Shouldn't you let her be? They might not like that here."

"We'll just ask," Carlos said.

"Okay," Roberto said. "We are gonna get going. I'm really glad everything is working out for Yasmin."

"Thanks," Carlos and Yasmin replied.

They stayed by the cashier, who told them to wait. She would bring Carmen to see them.

"Just for a minute," Yasmin said. "It's her first day. We want her to know we are thinking about her."

CHAPTER 87

Carlos sat on one of the two chairs by the edge of the pool. He had taken the one closest to the water, and he had tested his reach by sweeping through the water surface with his right arm. He wanted to make sure he could touch Yasmin when she swam by.

They had talked about going to the beach, and he suggested he could watch her swim back and forth as the two of them used to do, but Yasmin declined.

"It was too spooky," she said. "That's something that we did together. If I do it alone it will feel like you are gone, and I don't want to feel that. Let's go the opposite way. Let's work with the therapy to make sure you gain full swing of your left arm. Then we can swim in pairs as we used to do."

But Carlos wanted to see her swim. It inspired him. It energized him and gave him hope that someday the two of them would again cross flawlessly through the incoming ocean waves, side by side, and kiss each other on every three strokes.

"That is our goal," Yasmin said. "We will swim like that again. People will come to see us as they used to. And who knows, we might even get arrested for going in the ocean so late at night."

"That would have to be after we get back from Guatemala and you are a permanent resident; otherwise, they could throw you in prison and try to deport you again. Or, we could wait three years till you are a citizen."

"I will take my chances. I don't want to wait that long."

"Neither do I. Besides, that would only be a city ordinance violation. They don't put people in jail for that."

"They could if you are a second-time offender."

"Which we likely would be."

Carlos turned to her and slowly and with some difficulty moved his left arm towards her lap, until he could grab her wrist. It was not a full circle grab, but it was the first time he had been able to move his arm that far down and make somewhat of a fist.

"See what I mean? See what I mean?" Yasmin said, excited. "You can do it, Carlos, you can!"

"Let me not try too hard, Yasmin, because then they'll say I am not disabled enough and I don't have a severe hardship which could affect your waiver."

"I don't care," Yasmin said. "I'd rather have you come back to full health even if it means that I'll be an illegal immigrant for the rest of my life."

"No, darling. Never. You will be a US citizen."

"I don't want it at your expense."

"It's not, darling. I did not hurt myself on purpose. It was an accident."

Yasmin gave him a quizzical look just as Carmen came striding softly through the patio tiles.

"Carmen, you just got home?" Yasmin asked.

"Yes."

"And you came in a Uber?" Carlos said. "Why didn't you call?"

"No, Uber only charges me ten dollars."

"Yeah, but that's another ten dollars that leaves your pocket. Tomorrow you call us when you think you are getting out. We will pick you up. We are home."

"Sit down," Carlos said to Carmen. "Pull up a chair. Let's watch Yasmin swim."

Yasmin rose and handed Carlos her towel.

"Come on, darling, let's see you swim. I need it so much tonight."

Yasmin reached down and kissed him.

"Okay, darling. Only for you."

Carmen brought in a small folding lawn chair and placed it across from Carlos.

Yasmin walked towards the diving board at the other end of the pool. She was wearing a blue one-piece swimming suit, and her hair seemed to be growing fast. The clumsily chopped ends from the prison had disappeared. She stood at the tip of the board, both arms extended, balancing her stand. She dove in gently, in Olympic fashion, as Carlos looked on. Her figure moved swiftly under the water, quickly reaching the bottom. Then slowly she turned and came up on the other side, by her husband. He reached out with his right hand and took hers.

"Will you swim a few laps for me, please?"

"As many as you want," she said and let go of his hand.

She did not want him to see her tear up. The sight of him sitting there, feeling incompetent, was too much for her to bear. Of course she would swim for him but felt weird on her right side, where he would usually position himself stroking the water.

"Yasmin is such a good swimmer," Carmen said. "She looks as if she was floating on the water."

"She does," Carlos said. "She barely has to move her limbs to get ahead because her body floats on its own. She is a natural."

"You know, Carlos, that people in my country do not swim that well. Yasmin must have had private schooling to learn to swim like that."

"No, she didn't. She spent a lot of time near the coast. Her parents would send her with relatives there, and that's how she learned. She learned on her own."

"She did?"

"Yes. My Yasmin is the most beautiful thing ever made."

He rubbed his hand over her shoulders as she halted her lap near him.

"What could Gordon want with Mr. Moza, Carlos?"

"Some influence in town. Mr. Moza works at the right place, and Gordon is probably involved in some real estate development. He needs someone like Mr. Moza to help him with his deal."

"I didn't know Gordon was involved in things like that."

"He is when the situation is right for him. He's careful and bides his time. He's a speculator. I guess that's what they call it."

"That's a little scary," she said.

"He's shrewd. He knows how to do it. What he does is not illegal but risky."

"You did well with him."

"It was only one time, and I'll never do it again."

She smiled at him and kissed his hand.

"We are cowards," she said.

CHAPTER 88

Weeks went by, and Carlos's therapy sessions began to pay off more noticeably. He gained more movement in his left hand, and it almost seemed he was back to normal. But not exactly. The injuries were internal, and Yasmin knew it. The doctor had shown her. If she had Carlos hold out both hands extended and had him make a fist with each one, the left one always lagged behind. If you asked him to move the fingers of each hand, the ones from his left were way behind. The signals from Carlos's brain were not reaching his left hand as fast as they did the right.

Thankfully for Yasmin, Carlos had taken his loss rather well. Driving was all he knew, and if he had not had Yasmin, his life would have been over. But his life had been changed forever when he met Yasmin. The thought of not being able to drive again was not as catastrophic now as it would have been before. She now was his lifeline to the outside world. It did not matter so much that he could not drive a truck. He had Yasmin. She could face any crisis that came their way.

They had gotten a call from Lucrecia, Mr. Kline's secretary. It was time to proceed with their waiver application. They again found themselves at the big conference table across from the large window overlooking the suburbs. Lucrecia came in and placed a large stack of papers in front of them. She handed each of them a highlighter.

"This is what they call the waiver application. It was completed based on our discussions over the phone. I need you to review it and mark any corrections with the highlighter. I am going to get on the NVC website now and pay the visa fees online. The money will be deducted from your checking account. So, take your time reading the application, and I will be back."

They both went through the application page by page, discussing the data and reviewing the declaration at the end of the form. With the exception of a misspelling in Yasmin's city of birth, everything was correct. Lucrecia was known for her neatness. Everyone around Mr. Kline shared the same quality. Neatness was the firm's business.

"Everything all right?" she asked as she returned.

"We found only one misspelling," Carlos said. "We highlighted it."

He pointed to the page, and Lucrecia called another secretary through the intercom and instructed her to make the correction directly from the uploaded document in her computer screen. A few moments later, another young woman came in the room, greeted them, and handed Lucrecia the corrected form.

"We are going to need your signature now, Yasmin," Lucrecia said pointing to the page.

Yasmin signed, and Lucrecia handed her two pages generated by the payments she had just made.

"These are receipts for the payments we made for the issuance of your visa to travel to Guatemala and payment for the affidavit of support which will be the next document we will be completing. Both of these forms show that the payment is in process, which means the bank has not yet transferred the money into the NVC account. I have to hold your application until I can show a receipt which says that the funds have been paid, which will be a couple of days. I always do it this way because I now have your form and supporting documents ready to go. I just need the final receipts. Understand everything?"

"Yes," Yasmin replied. "It seems like we are moving fast now, ah?"

"We are, yes. But processing this form can take a little time. That is the last hurdle right now. Mr. Kline has reviewed all your documents, and he thinks you have a high probability of being approved."

"That's good to hear," Yasmin said. "What else do we do now?"

"Now we wait," Lucrecia said.

"Just wait?" Carlos asked. "How long do you figure?"

"A few months. Unless Mr. Kline gets it expedited. He is trying to do that. A written request is going with this package, based on Carlos's medical condition."

Carlos and Yasmin looked at each other, not sure how to react.

"Your removal process was dismissed last week, as I told you. Mr. Kline was able to get that done through the head prosecutor of DHS. Now because of Carlos's medical condition, we are going through with the waiver. Things are starting to look up."

"Right," said Yasmin. "Right."

"But we needed the removal case dismissed before we could move on with the waiver. One has to be done before the other."

"Mr. Kline does fine work," Carlos said.

Lucrecia nodded, smiling.

"You guys have come a long way."

"Thanks to him," Carlos said.

Yasmin had grabbed a checkbook from her purse and tore off a check that had already been prepared. She handed it to Lucrecia.

"Is it correct?" she asked.

"Perfect."

Carlos and Yasmin got up, ready to leave. Lucrecia shook hands with each one of them.

"I will call you once those payments have cleared and then this application will go out."

CHAPTER 89

Accustomed now to a routine, Carlos entered the therapy room in the large upgraded office building in downtown Coral Gables. He was accompanied by Yasmin, who took his gym bag and laid it on one of the comfort chairs. After signing in, Carlos met Clark, his therapist, who came eagerly to greet him and Yasmin from the back of the room.

He was a tall, lean black man who seemed satisfied with his line of work, smiling broadly at Carlos and Yasmin.

"How are you doing today, Carlos?" he asked. "Are you ready to shake hands with your left yet, or you need a little more time? You're afraid my grip might send you gasping to the floor, maybe? How about it, Yasmin?"

"I think if you shake his left hand, he'll hold up. You taught him how to do it, and now you can't take it back."

He let out a loud laugh and tilted his head back, as if he enjoyed the moment.

"How're you doing there, Clark? Are you ready for another session?"

Carlos shook hands with him, and the three of them started walking towards the rear of the room.

"I'm always ready, Carlos. What kind of a question is that? Come on, let's get going. I'm just waiting for that one day when you tell me that you and Yasmin are going to that interview in Guatemala City. You won't forget to take me, right?"

"No, you're invited," Yasmin said, from the rear.

"That's actually beginning to climb up," Carlos said. "Or so it seems. It's gaining steam now, and it does look like it's going to happen."

"Really, Carlos? That's so good to hear, man. It's so good to hear. The two of you deserve it. You've earned it. You both earned it."

He stopped next to a weightlifting bench and signaled for Carlos to sit.

"Do not worry," Clark said. "I won't have you lift the bar yet. But I want you to sit near it. I want you to start feeling confident close to it because that is next in the program, assuming that you get to thirty pounds with the dumb bells. Okay?"

"I'm up to thirty pounds already," Carlos said.

"You are. But we need to go through the repetition phase," Clark said. "We need to have you build up some muscle. Let's get the swing part perfect first, and then we can think about increasing the weight. Let's go."

Clark grabbed two dumb bells from the stand and placed them at each side of the bench. He put himself in the back and gave the thumbs-up signal. Part of his job was to build up confidence in the patient, and he needed a little bit of luring to achieve that. Dare the patient as one would do a pet. Let him see the prize and then pull it back to build up some intrigue. Yasmin watched them from a distance. Usually, non-patients were not allowed to be involved directly in the sessions, unless the therapist determined they could be of help to the patient. Clark felt that Yasmin's presence was crucial to Carlos's recovery. He wanted her to be present and considered her to be part of the team.

"Let's go, come on," Clark called as Carlos began to lift the weights.

He was always slower with his left arm, and it took him longer to make a full swing with the dumb bell. Clark egged him on but guarded him closely. Any notable failure to make the lift would spring him into action, and he would grab the dumb bell from him.

"All the way," Clark yelled. "All the way, big boy. There you go, there you go. Now I need you to do that again. Move your right arm, make the full swing, and then come back to your left. Come on."

Yasmin approached, but Clark's extended arm let her know that she needed to stay back.

"Now, we need your cooperation here, Yasmin. Tell your husband to move. He's looking a little sissy today. What did you give him to slow him down like that?"

"Nothing," she said.

"Nothing? What happened, Carlos? Why are you so slow today?"

"I'm not—"

"Never mind with that. Let's go with the left arm again. Let's go!"

"Let's go, Carlos," Yasmin cheered from the back. "Show me what you can do."

"Whoa! Did you hear that, Carlos? Do it for Yasmin. Come on, show her what you can do with that left arm. All the way up to the chin."

Slowly and wisely, Clark built up Carlos's confidence, making him struggle to achieve a full swing. Soon Carlos built up a sweat and complained of pain to his left shoulder.

"It's gotta hurt, Carlos. You're in new territory. That's what it means. Think of it like that. You're moving up, Carlos. You are winning, babe."

Clark's approach was much like that of a physical trainer, someone who spends his time at a gym, guiding athletes to build up their muscles and maintain body tone. Clark had to play that role many times. But his function in the recovery process of a patient went much further than that. Clark's true target was to help the patient recover the use of limbs that had been harmed by sudden trauma. His work could prove vital to overcoming paralysis and a future sedentary life.

At the end of the session, Carlos appeared worn out. His T-shirt was soaked with sweat, and Yasmin helped him walk to the men's room to change.

"Can you go in with him?" she asked Clark.

"Sure," he answered, throwing his arm around Carlos's shoulder. "Okay, old man, come with me."

"You almost killed me today, Clark," Carlos said.

"No, Carlos. We broke new ground today. You are regaining use of most of your left arm."

Yasmin felt a little teary about Clark's prediction, now knowing fully well that it would prove to be right.

CHAPTER 90

Carlos was on the phone that evening with his mother on a routine call to keep her abreast of his progress in his therapy sessions. Yasmin had informed his parents about his condition, and she had toed the line during those early dark days after the accident. As a result, Yasmin and Carlos's parents had become close. Carlos's mother, Magaly, was eager to know about her son's condition, and she was elated when she heard Yasmin tell her the story of how Carlos came back from unconsciousness. Yasmin said it was a miracle, and Magaly promptly agreed. They had now become very close, and Magaly was constantly singing praises about her daughter-in-law, who she had never seen in person but yet she admired her like a daughter. She was precisely doing that when Carlos heard the sound of another call coming in the background. He took the phone off his ear to check the screen and saw Mr. Moza's number flare up. He excused himself from his mother to take the call.

"Hello," he said.

"Hello, young man," came the all-too-familiar voice. "How has your day gone today?"

"It was my usual, Mr. Moza. Just me and Yasmin going to my therapy session, and that took our whole morning, then we have been home for the rest of the day."

"Very well, Carlos, very well. Oh, that wonderful Yasmin is such a jewel. How did you get so lucky? You realize that, right? You are a wonderful young man too, and you are worth the prize, of course, but you were darned lucky to have found her. Gosh, so lucky. Incidentally, I have something of interest to you that I would like to discuss. Do you think you and Yasmin could work your way down here tomorrow to see me?"

"Where, Mr. Moza?"

"Oh, when I say here, I mean the same place where you and Yasmin were married not that long ago, at City Hall, where I work."

"Oh, yeah, of course. Is everything all right?"

"Everything is wonderful, Carlos. I want you and Yasmin here in the early afternoon, at about 1:00. Be on time, Carlos, because I have to leave by 2:00."

"What's wrong?" Carlos said.

"Nothing is wrong. Do you trust me?"

Carlos looked at Yasmin, who was sitting on the long lawn chair next to him. He shrugged his shoulders to show his lack of knowledge. He had no idea what the old wizard was up to. What mysterious web had he suddenly sewn to try to ensnare Carlos in it? He did not want to know, but at this point in his life, after he had almost lost it all, he felt more than ever that nothing could make him divert from the path he had chosen. But courtesy was a grace that paid off. He would listen.

"Yes, of course."

"Then I want you and your lovely wife here tomorrow, at one o'clock sharp."

"We'll see you then, Mr. Moza."

Carlos turned the call off.

"He wants to talk to us," Carlos said to Yasmin.

Yasmin was standing next to him, wearing her one-piece suit readying herself for a dive in the pool.

"What about?"

"I am not really sure. I think he is getting ready to offer us something."

"You get the feeling that Mr. Moza exaggerates his role?"

"Probably. I think it makes him feel powerful to be able to control people's lives."

"He's probably going to offer you a job with the city."

"Do you think so? I think it has to do with politics."

"That might be too, but you are not interested. Or have you changed your mind?"

"No. I do not want to do anything that would keep me from you. Besides, that is a business that I hate. It's such a rotten business."

"But even if you wanted to do it, how would he be able to help you?"

"I think he likes to play the strategist, someone who makes plans and uses people he knows to carry out those plans. He wants to be the man behind the scene; that way he can control the fate of many people. I think if you do it long enough, you get to be bigger than the people you appoint."

"Do you think he's honest?"

"Nobody in that business is honest."

"So why is he interested in you? What do you think he plans to do with you?"

"Probably appoint me to some low-level job with the city to gain experience and then run for office."

"Run for office as what?"

"Some low-level position that he can control."

"And how do you know all this?"

"I watched him do it to others. It's how he operates. Do you see Roberto? He took Roberto under his wing, but things did not exactly go as planned, and Roberto ended up in a semi-executive job but not as an elected official. He did not make the votes for treasurer and had to settle for a plain job. But it's not too bad actually. He did not do bad at all, just not what Mr. Moza had wanted for him."

"At least he got a job."

"Mr. Moza got that for him to save face. But I have to say that he was loyal to him. He stuck by him even though he lost the election."

"So when do we see him?"

"Tomorrow at 1:00 p.m. He wants us both there."

"But why me? I do not have status and no work permit. There is nothing I can do."

"That's not why he wants you there. He wants to let you know that he respects you and he wants you to hear what he has to say to me. He is telling you that he sees us as one."

Yasmin leaned over and kissed him then she let herself go and fell softly on his lap.

"I am so glad Mr. Moza sees that. I must say he is a very observant man, witty and attentive."

"He is," Carlos said, kissing her back.

"I'm going to do my laps now so you can watch me, and I will pass near you, and you can brush my back."

Carlos remained wistful for a second, and she quickly questioned him.

"I think I want to give it a try tonight, you know, swimming."

"Doesn't your left arm feel painful?"

"It does, but I still want to try. I haven't been in the water for so long."

"We have to stay shallow. I don't want you swimming in the deep end yet."

"Yasmin, I could swim with one arm."

"No, let's stay in the shallow end and see how you do."

The two entered the pool from the other end, and she held his hand as he descended the short stairs into the pool. Carmen had come to the area and waved at them then sat down to watch them.

"I will hold you by your stomach and keep you afloat, and you can swim from side to side and see how you do."

In his first attempt, Carlos could not make a full stroke with his left arm, and he struggled to reach the other side stroking with only his right arm.

"I'm in too much pain from the workout this morning. Clark really worked me today."

"It's okay. We will go slow and see how far we get. It's our first time."

"I know but I want to make a full stroke."

"Maybe we shouldn't, Carlos. We might overstrain the muscles in your left arm."

"No, let me try a few times. Don't hold me. If I get in trouble I'll yell."

"Yes, but don't go to the deep end. Stay here."

"All right."

He tried as vigorously as this morning. But still, his left arm would not make a full stroke. They both got intensely involved, wondering why they had not started therapy in the water before. They went on for a good fifteen minutes, and then Yasmin stopped him.

"That's enough for now. It's our first time. Let's ask Clark whether it's okay to do this. I'm afraid we might overdo it, and you could hurt your left arm."

"All right."

CHAPTER 91

Miami City Hall was located in Coconut Grove at the former Pan American Airlines terminal. The building was historic in that sense but not as roomy as one might have expected. But the newly restored lobby was impressive for its elegance, and the main interior space had been restored to its original appearance with ceiling panels depicting the signs of the Zodiac. Not long ago, Carlos and Yasmin had exchanged vows here. But it seemed like ages ago. So much had happened in this short span of time.

They both walked inside with a guarded sense of foreboding. Why were they here exactly? They were going to meet with Mr. Moza, who had been a trusted friend to Carlos, but what was he about to offer them? Was it some charitable act like a job offer or some sham performance of courtesy shrouded by his embellished compliments? They both suddenly began to feel uncertain about their presence there.

They checked with a clerk at the main desk and gave her Mr. Moza's name. She made a call from her phone and told them to sit for a moment. Someone from his office would come to get them. No sooner had they sat when a young woman appeared from one of the interior doors. She seemed to recognize them and came straight to them.

"Hello again," she said and stretched out her hand. "You are still on your honeymoon, right? It will never end for you."

Carlos and Yasmin stood to shake her hand.

"Thank you," they both said.

"We are here to see Mr. Moza," Carlos said.

"I know," she said. "Let's go inside to meet him. He is waiting for you."

They followed the attractive brunette through an interior door that she held open for them, and once inside she led them through a hallway, stopping at one of the turquoise-colored doors, archetypal for this county.

"Come on in," the clerk said. "Have a seat. He will be right with you."

Mr. Moza was on the phone, and he waved for them to sit down. Carlos and Yasmin sat next to each other in the upholstered red chairs right across from his oak desk. All the paperwork was neatly packed on one side, while the other had a phone, a rotating pencil holder and pen organizer, with pencils of various colors standing in a bundle, a legal pad, and several files lined up in perfect symmetry across the front of the desk.

"I am honored that you are here," he said as the clerk stepped out. "You make such a gracious couple, for which there's no comparison in today's world. And how're you doing, my boy? Is the therapy going well?"

"It is," Carlos said. "We are starting to work out in the pool also. I swam yesterday for the first time since I had the injury."

"Well, that is great to hear. I actually knew. You have a great doctor there, don't you agree?"

"Yeah, I think so. He sent me to a good therapist. At this point, that seems to be the key. It's all about how effective your therapist is."

"But that's working well for you, right?"

"Oh, yes. Very much so."

"And what about you, dear?" Mr. Moza said, addressing Yasmin. "Do you think Carlos is making progress?"

"Oh, yes," she said. "A lot. But it's like Carlos just said, Mr. Moza, much depends on the therapy. Carlos works hard on his therapy, and that's why we are seeing results. He's getting a lot of the motion on his left arm back."

"Really? Well, that's great to hear. So, are you ready to go back to work, my boy?"

"I don't think I can ever drive for a living again, Mr. Moza," Carlos replied. "I'm getting most of the motion of my left arm back, but my left hand does not move as fast. If I drive an eighteen-wheeler again, I'd putting myself in danger as well as the public. It's not the same."

"I didn't mean working as a driver but another type of job."

"Driving is all I've ever done."

"I think I have a position for you with the city. I will get right into it. It may involve some driving but only within the bounds of the city. And that is Code Compliance. I think it would be a good start for you, a promising young man with a predictably good future in politics. I am talking about a career in politics. But for now, let us get to a good start. Let's start there, and then in the near future, we will go further. I will guide you. You know I am never going to steer you wrong."

"Well, I thank you, Mr. Moza. I am afraid you are seeing way too much in me. You are really a good friend."

"There's no need to thank me. By the way, I want to thank you for that referral that I got from you recently. That was very nice. This fellow was your employer, and he owns a trucking company, right?"

"Yes, his name is Gordon. He is a great guy. He has been an asset to Yasmin and me during these difficult times. And he's very smart. He is involved in developments, and maybe you can refer him to other investors where he can thrive. He is good at that. Actually, he is good at everything he does."

Mr. Moza nodded.

"I see that. I think I spot in him a very shrewd man who knows how to make his choices. Shall I say more? No, I think he's gonna be all right. All right, so I want you to work even harder with your therapy. The position will come to life in about one month. By then I think you should be ready. What do you think?"

"You better ask Yasmin. She knows more about my condition than I do."

"I apologize, my dear. You are sitting there being quiet, and I'm sorry for not letting you speak. Now, we need your take on all this. What do you think?"

"I think it's very nice of you, Mr. Moza, to think of Carlos at such a crucial moment in his life. He's right when he tells you that his driving days are over. It's too dangerous, even if recovers the full swing of his left arm, which is most important to him. But driving trucks requires fast impulses, and reaction time, especially, is crucial That is where he lacks at this time."

Mr. Moza nodded.

"To tell the truth, I have not noticed that in him, but that is why we need your take. You know more about your husband than anyone else. Do you think he will make a full recovery?"

"In the sense that his movements will go back to normal, yes. But his reactions may not. The doctor tells us that it will all improve, but right now they are not what they used to be. I will not let him drive for a living again. If we need to, I will learn how to drive a truck myself."

Mr. Moza smiled broadly.

"Why is it that I'm not surprised at your reaction, dear? But you won't need to drive a truck. Carlos has a good future. Let me work on it and see. For now, he's gonna have a job. That's a good start and one that he needs."

He got up from his high-back executive chair and came around the desk to shake Carlos's hand, then approached Yasmin and kissed her on the cheek.

"Let's give it around two weeks," he said. "Then you'll come around and start training. I will take care of the big boys upstairs. They already know that I have the best candidate for the job. You will begin training and getting to know the people you will work with. That's important. But for now, let's keep it quiet, my boy. After you are completely in, we will have a nice welcoming party and inform everyone."

He retrieved an envelope from his inside breast pocket and handed it to Carlos.

"That is just a form for you to fill out. Let me have it back by the end of the week. It has to be fed into the computer programs, and then you will be officially a candidate."

Mr. Moza shook Carlos's hand again. He turned to Yasmin and kissed her on the cheek again.

"Goodbye, my dear. Remember that you are in charge. Make sure that Carlos keeps up with the therapy."

"Will we see you at the restaurant tonight, Mr. Moza?"

"No, not tonight, my dear. We have too many meetings going on. It's the busy season now, you know, pre-elections. Maybe later in the week."

"Thank you, Mr. Moza. Thank you so much."

CHAPTER 92

Carlos and Yasmin sat by the pool, engaged in their collective thinking and pondering about their meeting with Mr. Moza. Yasmin reminded Carlos that they had time.

"Two weeks," Carlos said. "That almost makes it clear that I must take the job."

"Why?"

"Who else would hire me?"

"Gordon would."

"You're not thinking as a driver, are you? You said yourself that I would be a menace to the public if I got behind the wheel."

She held his arm affectionately.

"Carlos, I meant it for your own protection, darling. You have taught me how dangerous an eighteen-wheeler can be. Putting yourself behind the wheel of one could be disastrous. You know how unpredictable it can be. A delayed move on your part, and it could be deadly. Over my dead body you would drive a truck again."

Carlos sensed her determination and slowly leaned forward to kiss her.

"You are my guardian angel. What do you think about the offer?"

"I think it's a great opportunity. The job is exactly what you need. There is no physical requirement. It's almost like a supervisory job."

"I wouldn't go that far. If any of my responsibilities fall on construction sites, there may be some physical labor involved. Not that I would mind."

"What does a code enforcement job involve?"

"You have to inspect the conditions of the work site or the house that's being inspected and report whether it's in compliance or not."

"That doesn't sound too strenuous, Carlos. I think the job might be a good thing for you, Carlos. It's good that he's giving you some time. I don't want you to go back to work just yet."

"We do not know enough about it yet," Carlos said. "We don't know what the pay is. I am sure the benefits are good. But what's even more important is what comes later."

"You mean, the plans Mr. Moza has for you?"

"You are very perceptive, darling."

"I'm with you, my husband. You know that."

"Where does it say that a man can plan another man's future? What gives him the idea that he can do that?"

"He can only if others let him."

"I am not going to let him."

"You shouldn't, darling. Even if it means not getting the job, you can say no to him."

"That is probably what will happen if I take the job. I'm not going to get politically involved, as he is expecting me to, and there the honeymoon will end."

"Then you should let him know since the beginning, Carlos. Honesty pays."

"Darling, every time he has mentioned politics to me, I have refused. But you know he is one of those people who will not accept no as an answer."

"He's used to pulling the strings from above."

Carlos pointed his index at her.

"Now you got it, honey."

"We both got it, Carlos. You want to practice some more now?"

He nodded. The two of them walked hand in hand to the low end of the pool, and they positioned themselves a few yards from the stairs. Yasmin kept her hands underneath him, holding his upper body. He floated and slowly began to move forward, with free strokes. He made a full swing with his right arm and struggled to come up half the distance with his left. She egged him on, and he kept trying, improving slowly until he reached the other side of the pool.

"Don't worry about Carmen," Yasmin said. "We can pick her up from the job another time. Let's give it a good try going back. Come on."

They were working for a good hour, and Carlos did seem to improve, but the effort had made him weak. He needed Yasmin's hand to help him get out of the pool.

"Why don't we cook tonight?" Yasmin suggested. "We haven't done that in a long time."

"Okay, what shall we make?"

"We could make soup."

"Do we have chicken and noodles? Potatoes?"

"All of the above. I can use the big kettle, but it will take some time."

"No, honey. It comes out too watery Guatemalan style."

They both laughed at his wisecrack.

"So are we going to make it thick?"

"We'll cut up the potatoes, marinade the chicken, wet the noodles, and toss them in the pressure cooker."

"Carlos, pressure cooker? We bought one, yes. But do you have any idea how to use it? I know you wanted one very badly, but we haven't used it. Do you know how? I don't. I had never even seen one until we got it."

"Well, they say that from under any rock a frog may leap out when least expected. You are just about to discover my cooking skills, honey. You didn't know?"

"No. I have never seen you even turn on the stove."

"Aha! You will see."

Carlos got right to work. He opened the refrigerator and grabbed a package of fresh chicken fillets and put them in the sink under hot water. He opened a cabinet door and took out the pressure cooker she and Yasmin had recently purchased.

"Here, let me help you," said Yasmin. "Let's do it together. Remember? We promised each other we'd do everything together."

"I know, but I wanted to show you."

"But you could get burned, Carlos. Your arm is still weak. Please, let me set up the pressure cooker. Let's make enough for three. Carmen will be here shortly."

"I've never cooked since we have been together, but I can do it. I'll use the pressure cooker, and it will come out dense, just like in La Carreta. So, you can set it up while I cut up the potatoes."

They both got to work, he peeling the potatoes and she filling the pressure cooker with water and dipping noodles inside. They were a team.

CHAPTER 93

Mr. Moza was right after all and true to his word. Two weeks later, Carlos drove to City Hall along with Yasmin, who accompanied him to the minutest detail.

"Maybe you should take the car and come back, Yasmin?" Carlos asked Yasmin inside.

"No, what if something happens to you? You have not been alone yet. This is the first time."

"But you are going to be all alone, darling. How about if I call you?"

"No, I'll wait."

"But it might be a long time."

"It's all right. I'll wait."

She sat in the reception room while Carlos went inside to meet Mr. Moza. She knew he would be awhile, but she still did not know how he would react to instructions. This would be the first time since the accident that he would be under some degree of pressure.

After greetings, Mr. Moza assigned Carlos to a Code Enforcement officer who was visiting City Hall this morning. He asked him to stay with Carlos and take him to the Code Enforcement facility on Second Avenue and show him the ropes for a few hours. Carlos could get an idea of the particulars of being a code enforcement official. It was a rather delicate position for someone who had no experience in dealing with such issues, such as exercising authority over homeowners who would be bound by his recommendations. They also would be in a position to complain about him and question his decisions.

The middle-aged man who was assigned to him was an ideal candidate for the task, having had years of experience. He extended his hand to Carlos.

"My name is Mark," he said.

"It's a pleasure," Carlos said.

"We are going to make a few stops in the building, then we will head out to the main office. I have a home inspection scheduled for 10:00. It would be a good idea if you come with me. Let me just clear that with my supervisor. You just wait in the reception are. I will be right back."

Carlos went out and spotted Yasmin, sitting on a bench across from the door he had just exited.

"They're gonna take me on an inspection of a house. I don't know how long it will take. Maybe you should call a Uber and go home."

"No, I will wait here. How are you feeling so far?"

"Yasmin, I feel fine. Why would I not? We've been everywhere since I came out of the hospital. And what about the therapy sessions? That's more pressure than any of this, and I think I handle that well."

"Yeah, but that's physical. This is mental pressure. I want to make sure that you do not overreact and get sick."

"Come on, Yasmin, you're being ridiculous. You can't drive the car without a license, so let me call a Uber."

"No, you go and learn all you can. I will take advantage of the downtime to call your mother and my family. If there's a problem with you, call me right away."

The officer came out through another door and stopped by Carlos.

"Ready?"

"Yeah. This is my wife. She is going to stay around for a while."

The officer extended her his hand.

"It's a pleasure meeting you," he said. "You sure you want to hang around here? We might be awhile."

"Yes. I don't mind."

"We'll be back," Carlos said.

They went outside and got inside a four-door car bearing the seal of Miami Code Enforcement on the driver's door.

"Mr. Moza mentioned that you are recently married, and it shows. You have a very beautiful wife there."

"Thank you," Carlos answered. "I can't get her to stay home."

"That's all right. Enjoy it while you can. It's not always like that, you know?"

"I can imagine."

"Good though. No harm done that she wants to follow you. She is showing you that she cares."

"Yeah, we are very close."

"That's good to hear. So, this is a private home. It's a small house, one family, and it got sold, so the closing is coming up, and we have to do an inspection and report any violations. If everything is okay, we will issue a certificate of code compliance. If not, we give the homeowner a list of the discrepancies and some time to correct them."

"What happens if the owner does not fix the discrepancy?"

"Then we have to issue a summons. Sometimes we have to appear in court. It's part of the job."

They pulled up in the driveway of a duplex. They both got out of the car and walked to the front door. There was no sign of life around the home, and the inspector knocked on the door. After repeated tries, he placed his card in the crack of the door and turned to Carlos.

"In cases like this when no one is home, we want to leave a card to make sure they know we were here and that they should call the office. If they don't, then the office will call them and set up another date."

They headed for the main office at Southwest Second Avenue. The location was on the seventh floor of the Miami Riverside Center, a state-of-the-art building that provided access to the latest technologies. Mark walked with Carlos around the floor, introducing him to some of his coworkers.

"I just have to make several phone calls as follow-up on other cases," Mark said. "If you want you can hang around the reception area, or you can come with me to the office."

"I'll go with you."

Carlos followed him. He felt the vibration of his phone and looked at the screen. It was Yasmin, so he picked up.

"Are you busy?" she asked.

"No, not really."

"Lucrecia from Mr. Kline's office called. She said we need to go see her as soon as possible. Any time after 3:00 p.m."

"What is it about?"

"She wouldn't tell me. She said it was important. It sounds like good news, though."

"Okay. We'll head out over there as soon as I'm done."

Carlos ended the call. They went inside an office, and Mark took a seat behind one of the two counters in the room. He waved for Carlos to take a seat in one of the other chairs.

"Is everything okay with your wife?"

"Yeah, she's fine. She just called me to see how I'm doing."

Mark looked at him and smirked.

"Still living in the honeymoon, right?"

"Pretty much, yeah."

"That's great to hear," Mark said. "Let's keep it that way now, right?"

"I think we will," Carlos replied.

Mark nodded.

"I'm glad to hear that. Sorry for busting your chops."

"Oh, it's quite okay. We are good. We are happy."

"All right. So, what I do is answer calls in regards to some of the cases I have pending. You know, just follow up with the Realtors involved in some of the transactions. Usually, they call looking to see if a certificate of code compliance has been issued. They are always in a hurry to close the deal. We answer them, but we can't let them put pressure on us. You gotta keep them at bay. The main thing is that no certificate can be issued until a full inspection has been done and any irregularities found have been corrected. That's a very basic rule you gotta follow. As long as you stick to that, everything will be fine."

Carlos nodded and watched him as he made several calls, writing notes in the files. They later took a walk around the floor, stopping at several offices and chatting with other officers.

"I have another inspection this afternoon, but I will be passing by City Hall to drop you off. I think Mr. Moza wants to see before you head out. He just wants you to get a feel for the environment, which is the right thing to do, I think."

"Okay," Carlos said.

CHAPTER 94

Late that afternoon, Yasmin and Carlos walked into Mr. Kline's office and checked at the reception window. No sooner had they sat down to wait, when the door opened and Lucrecia appeared, smiling as if she had terrific news.

"Come on in," she told them.

She stood aside to let them in. Carlos and Yasmin went into the conference room and took a seat. She was right behind them.

"Mr. Kline is not here right now, but he told me to let you know that your waiver has been approved. That is the last application that you filled out. Now, that means that you now can travel to your country, Guatemala, to have your interview, which is how it's done. So, I have already started working with the visa center to try to get you an interview date, but we have to finish the paperwork that they require. We have already started to fill out the I-260, which is the questionnaire for your visa application. I need you to help us with that. I will need you both to sit with Sonia, who is working on the form, but we need you to give us the information. So, can you follow me? I will take you to her office."

They went to a small office next to the receptionist's, where they sat next to Sonia, a young woman who greeted them without leaving her seat.

"Hi, how are you?" she asked. "Congratulations, by the way. That was a hard application to get through. But you made it. You proved hardship. I am now filling out biographical details, and that is why we need you both here so we can email the form and the other supporting documents to try to get you an appointment at the embassy in Guatemala as soon as possible."

"Wow. That seems to be moving fast," Carlos said.

"Well, Mr. Kline had requested that the file be expedited, and that seemed to do the trick. So, now that we are almost at the end, let's hope that we can have a smooth ride. Are you ready?"

"Yes," Yasmin said. "This is what we've been waiting for."

"All right," she replied.

She read the questions from the form on her screen and wrote the answers from Yasmin as she gave them. It was a tedious process, requiring dates as far back as birth, including all the addresses where she had lived during her lifetime. Surprisingly, Yasmin had all the details and recited them from memory, which was remarkable. Sonia also had some questions for Carlos. It took them a good one hour to complete the form that Sonia finally saved to Yasmin's file and filed the form at the National Visa Center website. Sonia took a moment to clip her long hair into a ponytail and exhaled.

"This is not an easy form to fill out. We will probably hear back from them if they have any questions, but I do not think so. This form, if accepted by them, means that we are good to go with the rest of the documents that I am ready to file now too. I will need your signature, Carlos."

She spread each page for Carlos's signature on her desk, pointing to each signature page, which Carlos quickly signed.

"Well, that is pretty much it for you. I will have to scan these documents now and forward them to the website. This means that we have now complied with all the requirements, and we are waiting only for an appointment. That may take a little while, depending on the consulate, but probably not."

"We thank you," Carlos said. "You've answered all our questions before we even asked them."

"It's a pleasure," Sonia replied. "We hope that we have good news for you very soon. Then we will have to schedule an appointment for a physical in Guatemala for you, and then you are good to travel. But you do not go without picking up a package first. Remember that. As soon as we call you, you both come in one more time."

"Okay, thank you," Carlos said."

CHAPTER 95

That evening Carlos and Yasmin arrived early at La Carreta. They both felt satisfied. It seemed as though their dream was going to come true after all. They were there to celebrate together before their friends arrived. But even if they wanted to share the good news with them none had arrived yet. They went near the open counter, and Yasmin ordered two small espressos. Yasmin had by now joined Carlos in his coffee cravings.

They both eyed each other as Carlos handed her a cup. It was such a transition, they both thought. Such a long journey that the two had endured and how did they do it, they wondered. Then Yasmin lifted her Styrofoam cup, raised it, and tapped into his.

"Let's drink to the world," Carlos said. "We are going to conquer it."

"We already have, my love."

"No, it is only the beginning."

They both laughed and took a sip.

Someone slapped Carlos in the shoulder. It was his friend Ralph.

"How are you, Carlos? How are you feeling?"

"Doing well, thank you."

Carlos shook his hand and so did Yasmin.

"Yasmin can tell you better than me," he said.

"He is doing great," Yasmin said, smiling. "He still cannot run a marathon, but we are working on it."

"I want you to know that the roads are not the same without you. For one, your boss is losing his hair since you've been gone. Any driver you see here will tell you about that. He calls everyone for help.

He has tried to hire me for so many trips. At weird times of the night he has called me. But you know, I can't, I can't take his trips. I don't want to go that far."

"He has local trips too. All throughout the state. You just have to tell him that you want only inside Florida, right? That's what you want, no?"

"I do. I can't be traveling three thousand miles on a single trip. It takes too much out of me."

"I think he'll work with you. One thing about Gordon is that he will back you up."

"I know. I happened to pass by that tricky portion of Route 10 the other night, where you had the accident. Man, it's spooky there, how the road twists. It's freaky how that happened."

"I am not the only victim, by the way. Someone else was hurt there."

"Yes, I know."

"Stay away from that passage if you can, Ralph."

"It's not worth the risk," Yasmin said. "Even if you have to put on an extra fifty miles to avoid that section, it pays to do that."

"Well, I used to always go past there because there are not many other major routes that take you to the east of Florida. Route 10 is very popular with the truck drivers."

"There are other routes," Carlos said. "They are just not as fast."

"What are some of the other routes?" Yasmin asked.

"You can take Route 10 up to a certain point and then go south on 75. You can avoid that section but then Route 75 throws you to the west. Well, the other option is just to be careful."

Another tap on Carlos's shoulder. This time it was Roberto and Amelia.

They were dressed for the evening. Roberto seemed as if he just had had a shower. They greeted everyone.

"What is new with you two?"

"Good news," Carlos said. "Yasmin's waiver got approved."

"No way!" Amelia said. "Yasmin, congrats, my dear! How exciting!"

The two hugged each other, and Roberto waited for his chance to embrace her.

"Great news, Yasmin," he said.

Then Ralph joined them, and he shook her hand.

"Congratulations," he said.

"So, Yasmin, this is now the end, right? There are no more applications, no more interviews, right?"

"Right," she answered. "We now have to travel to the embassy in Guatemala City, and I have to be interviewed there."

"Let's go inside, come on," said Roberto.

They all went inside and greeted the cashier. She told them to pick their table, wherever they chose. There was plenty space, as the night crowd had not arrived yet. They went to the end of the middle aisle as usual and all sat down at the last table.

"Well, now," Roberto began, "Carlos, you are not needed for that interview, am I not right?"

"I think that's right but—"

"Please don't even mention that. Carlos is coming with me," Yasmin said, holding his hand tight.

"Of course, darling, I would never let you go alone."

"Okay, that's fine but technically, you don't have to go, right?"

"I think Lucrecia said that in Mr. Kline's office because the real interview was done here. This is only the visa interview. They look at her past record to see she has been in the US before, if she has any record, things like that."

"I think he might not even be allowed inside," Yasmin said. "But I want him there."

"Of course," Amelia added. "Roberto, what does it matter? They both want to be together anyway. They've been through a lot."

"I know that, Amelia," Roberto said. "I'm not talking about that. I'm just curious about whether his presence is mandatory."

"Well, I will be going anyway. I would not miss that."

"You know, perhaps you should ask your doctor about that," Roberto added. "If it's all right for you to be flying, I mean."

Carlos and Yasmin eyed each other. It had not occurred to them that that could be a problem.

"Okay," Carlos said. "We will ask, but I think that it will be all right."

"You ought to make sure. The difference in pressure could be a factor."

The waitress had come towards their table and stood at the middle, smiling.

"Hey," Roberto said, "we definitely could use some wine tonight."

"That's right," Ralph seconded.

He had taken a spot next to Yasmin, by the middle of the table, remaining silent as he did most times.

"Okay," said the waitress. "Do you want a whole bottle or one glass per each."

"Roberto, let's leave it at glasses," Carlos said. "We are driving. We cannot drink more than one glass."

"Yes, but I think Mr. Moza will be joining us soon."

"So he gets a glass too," Yasmin said.

"I understand but let's get a bottle. All right, waitress?"

"Okay, and what else?"

"You guys go first," Carlos said. "We're deciding."

He and Yasmin began talking in a low voice. The others placed their orders, and the waitress came back to them.

"Can we get an order of *picadillo* and the individual salad for each and some rice and *maduros*."

"Wow!" Roberto exclaimed. "I can't remember the last time you two ordered real food. What's going on?"

"It was Carlos's first day of work," Amelia said. "Didn't you hear?"

"Oh, that's not work. Mr. Moza has him being shown around. He's just watching others work. By the way Carlos how'd you like it?"

"It was all right."

"When does he have you coming back?"

"I have to go back two more times. We have to work on my application which has not yet been filed. Then, I am supposed to check again in two weeks, and that is really when the application process begins."

"But that sounds all good though. That really means that you're going to get the job."

"When do you think I would start?"

"Only Mr. Moza can answer that question. Let's hope he can give you that information tonight.

"I am going to be traveling to Guatemala soon so I want to work it out in such a way that I do not have to miss any days from work."

"I see what you mean. Well, you can tell Mr. Moza. He can work your schedule out even before you start. He has those qualities."

Roberto gave a short laugh, and Amelia followed.

"Everyone knows Mr. Moza and his wonders," Amelia said.

"Oh, I hear him," said Roberto. "Here he comes now."

Mr. Moza's voice was hard to miss as he worked his way inside the restaurant, stopping and greeting acquaintances. He was followed by his faithful companion, Mr. Prieto, also dressed impeccably as Mr. Moza.

"Good evening, everyone," Mr. Moza said. "Why is there something in the air, as if there were good news coming? Could it be what I think?"

He pointed towards Yasmin, and he quickly bent forward to kiss her on the cheek.

"You are looking as beautiful as ever, dear, and your smile gives you away. Can you share the good news?"

"Yes, Mr. Moza. Our waiver was granted."

"How did you know, Mr. Moza?"

"Well, you can't trick an old dog, let's just say that."

"Congratulations!" Mr. Prieto said.

"We are going to drink to that," Mr. Prieto said.

"Sit down, Mr. Moza," Roberto said. "There's room. We will slide to the next chair."

Mr. Moza nodded towards Ralph and Amelia.

"That is fantastic news," he said to Yasmin. "If you think about it, it has been a smooth ride considering. I tell you what, you really have to give it to Mr. Kline. That man knows his business."

"I agree. I've never heard of any application moving so fast," Roberto said.

"Me either," Amelia added.

The waitress returned with a bottle of wine and cups.

"Hello, Mr. Moza and company," she said. "You're just in time for the celebration."

"I never miss," he said, laughing. "How are you, dear?"

"I'm great, Mr. Moza."

"What kind of wine do you have there?"

"The brand you guys always drink, Vran."

"Okay, that is just what we need."

"Will you and Prieto have something to eat?"

"No, I'm afraid not. We have to move on to a meeting. We came only for the toast. It's Yasmin's celebration."

"I will drink to that myself," the waitress said.

"So, pour a glass for yourself," Roberto said.

She quickly filled cups for everyone, and they all clinked their glasses in unison.

"To Yasmin," Mr. Moza said. "To her and her husband who are going to be the most successful couple ever."

Yasmin pulled her cup back and raised it next to Carlos's. Then they kissed and drank.

"So, tell me," Mr. Moza asked, "what are your plans now?"

Carlos did most of the talking, with Yasmin adding some details. They wanted a start date for the job far enough so they could travel before. Mr. Moza assured them that it would be all right.

CHAPTER 96

Yasmin and Carlos met with Sonia at Kline's office several times in the next few days. They kept gathering documents as she requested them. Then they would meet with her and fill out some forms, but shortly thereafter she would call them back. Summer had passed, and they both felt like they were on the verge of success.

"What was that form we filled out last week?" Carlos asked Yasmin that night as they swam back to the shallow side of the pool.

The bluish pool water seemed to sparkle from the underwater lights. It was past 10:00.

"I think that was DS-260, Sonia said," Yasmin answered. "It's a very tedious form to fill out."

"Yeah, mostly for me, more than for you, darling. But it's over. We did it."

"Can you imagine, Carlos, what it would be like for someone older?"

"Yeah. It must be terrible remembering all those previous addresses."

"We are young, and it was hard for us."

"But it's over now," Carlos said. "We are all done."

"I am not sure, darling," Yasmin said, coming close to him and throwing her arms around him. "Whatever comes next, I am sure we will face it."

They went straight to the pool after leaving Sonia's office. It was still early, and Carmen had just arrived from work. They each grabbed a glass of cold orange juice from the refrigerator and went to sit by the pool in lawn chairs holding hands.

"You look thoughtful, darling," Carlos said. "What is wrong?"

"Nothing," she answered. "Perhaps you should stay, darling. I will only be gone for a few days."

"We don't know that, honey. It could take a few weeks, Sonia said."

"That's only if there's a problem, but our records are very clean. She said that herself."

"No, I'm still going. I don't want to leave you alone at the most important moment. That would be nuts."

"Yeah, but I don't like you to exert yourself. Even the doctor said that we ought to be cautious."

"But we are. What exertion am I going to be doing? I will just be with you."

"I know but the flying and the traveling there could be stressful."

He moved strands of her hair back from her temples and smiled.

"Your hair is growing, my angel. It's past your shoulders. Soon you will be able to make that braid. Have you forgotten about that?"

"No, I have not. I know it's what you want."

"It's what we both want."

"I think I would probably not do it again if it wasn't for you."

"Why, darling?"

"Because it's different here in America. It's more suitable for our cultures."

"And you hastily want to become an American, darling?"

"No, I just want to be with my husband and make him happy."

"Well, you know that I love that braid. I still think that those folks who cut your braid should have been shot."

"No, they were only practicing safety. Imagine what a depressed prisoner could do with a long braid of hair."

"I know, but I still think it was a crime to chop it off."

"It's growing back," she said, shaking her head.

He kissed her and leaned his head on her shoulder.

"I wonder what they did with that shock of hair."

"Yeah, I wonder that too. What do you think? Any guesses?"

"For sure I don't think they would have dumped it in the garbage."

"But there are legal issues as far as using a person's body parts, which hair is one. So, what could they do with it?"

"I've no idea," Carlos finally said. "They could have given it to me. I would have either hung it as a prize or put it to good use as added cushion to the soft bottom of a couch. We would be sitting in our sofa in the living room, keeping comfortable on bundles of your hair."

"You have such an imagination, darling," she said and laughed.

Just then, Carmen came from the Florida room of the house, carrying a round tray in her hands, with a full assortment of empanadas that she had prepared the previous day. She came by their chairs holding the tray at chest level.

"I made these last night," she said. "Take some."

"You made these?" Yasmin asked. "You shouldn't have. You work so much, Carmen."

"How did you make them so fast?" Carlos said.

"I had them prepared in the refrigerator. I just needed to cook them in slow fire. That was all."

Carlos passed one to Yasmin and took one for himself.

"They're delicious, Carmen," Yasmin said.

"I will leave them here for you. I brought some tamales from the restaurant for dinner for you, and I could steam some potatoes and rice for you inside."

Carmen lay the tray on a small plastic summer table, dragging it near them.

"No, Carmen, sit down and talk to us," Carlos said. "Sit down and rest. We already had some supper."

"Really? Oh, I was going to cook for you."

"No," Yasmin said. "No need. Your empanadas are great though."

"Thank you. Have them all. They are for you. I will be back," she said and quickly returned to the house.

"She does not stop," Carlos said. "She's like one of those wind-up toys from the old days. I'm amazed at how much energy she has. What drives her?"

"It's genetics, dear. Add that to a harsh childhood where daily misery was part of your life, and that's what you get. You rush because you think the food might not last. Your brain tells you to rush."

"I guess that is engrained in your brain. What a shame that people have to live like that."

"It's poverty that does it. In some cases it is extreme."

"Did you ever experience anything like that?"

"No, it did not quite get like that, but it was close. But then, as you know, my parents sent me to the capital because they saw something in me, and they wanted me to get an education. Had they not done that, who knows what might have happened?"

Carlos nodded and rubbed her hair then looked at her pointedly.

"I think we should start planning our trip. Where will we start first in Guatemala?"

"We have to start in Guatemala City because of the interview, which is at the embassy. Then we can go visit my parents in Xococ. They want to meet you. From there we can decide where to go. We can go to the beach if it's not too cold."

"What about the beaches on the Pacific coast?" Carlos asked.

"The waters can be rough to ride there. I used to go to Monterrico in the summers and practiced swimming there for hours, even at night sometimes."

"A lot of surfers there?"

"Some. They come from here. There are not too many tourists. Some days you can have the beach all to yourself. I'd love to go back there with you, Carlos."

"So, we'll go there, darling. I'd settle for that. We go to the big city first, take care of our papers, then we visit your parents, and then we hit the beach."

"I'm worried about you running into too much stress, Carlos."

"But that's not stress, darling. We will be relaxing."

"Come on, let's go inside. Let's see what Carmen is cooking now."

"I'm done eating, babe."

Carlos picked up the tray with the few leftover empanadas and headed for the house, holding Yasmin's hand.

"If she is cooking tamales, you might change your mind, Carlos."

"I might, but you've already made up yours, Yasmin."

"I have, yes. I love those things."

CHAPTER 97

Carlos was at City Hall a few weeks later, finally getting a decision on his job application from the city. The answer was affirmative, and Mr. Moza did not mince words that morning when he told him so.

"You've been accepted, Carlos," Mr. Moza said. "You're going to be a home inspector for the city of Miami. It is a delicate job that carries with it a lot of responsibility. Inspectors are the voice of the city they work for, so you can imagine the responsibility that you carry. Whatever you say in a certificate of inspection, it is as if the city of Miami had said it. Should you be right, as you are expected to, the city will shine. Should you be wrong, the city will be held liable for your actions."

Carlos listened attentively. The last thing he wanted to do was to fail Mr. Moza. After all, the man had gone out of his way to help him, and if he now could breeze with ease, it was because of him. Carlos's life had been shaken by a tragic accident and his future put in question. But Mr. Moza had changed all that. He had obviously worked to make sure Carlos had a job suitable for someone with a disability. He had a brain injury, and it was practically a miracle that he had been hired for such a job.

Carlos was a man of deep integrity. What would he not do to make sure that Mr. Moza looked good to the establishment for having helped him secure this position? He would work tirelessly to provide the best quality performance in his new job.

"I want to thank you, Mr. Moza," Carlos said. "I am indebted to you forever."

"No, you're not, my boy. I just happen to spot good people among a crowd when I see one. I've always been good at it."

Carlos smiled at him in silence. He did not think of himself as anything special, but he agreed that Mr. Moza had an eye for people who fit the role for his political plans. He was skilled in arming his machinery.

"So you are going to join your lovely wife in her trip to the consulate in Guatemala, right?"

"Yes."

"Are you sure you're okay to go? It can be a very strenuous trip."

"Perhaps," Carlos said. "But I can't let Yasmin go on her own. I am going to meet her parents and keep her company during a very crucial time."

"I understand, of course, and your wife needs and deserves your company. I am just concerned that your health could be affected. One thing that bothers me is the flight. I am not sure if it's safe for you after all you've been through."

"I think I will be okay."

"All right. Well, that is a good sign that you feel sure of yourself. But we just have to make sure. So, I can have them issue a reporting date for you. When can you start on the job?"

"I wanted to be sure that I would not have to travel after I start working, Mr. Moza. So I've been waiting for Yasmin's interview date, but so far we have not gotten it. When do you have me starting?"

"They really want to fill this position, and they are telling me around two weeks. You think you can handle that?"

"Yes, I think so. If it came to be that the interview comes right after, I would need a couple of days. Would that be all right?"

"I am sure it will be, Carlos. If something happens and you have to be out, I will talk to the department."

"Thank you so much, Mr. Moza."

Carlos stood from his chair and came around the desk to shake Mr. Moza's hand. No matter how odd you felt about the man, you had to extend him a courtesy. He was kind and had a conscience.

"No worries, Carlos. You are going to be fine. It's the beginning of a career for you. Bigger things will come your way."

Carlos was not sure what he meant, but he had a feeling that it was best not to ask. Not now anyway.

He stepped out of the office and went towards the general area. Not far off, he saw Yasmin sitting in one of the row seats reserved for customers who were waiting on city personnel to see about their various affairs. She was on the phone and waved at him with her free hand.

When he got close, she removed the phone from her ear and whispered to him, "It's Mr. Kline's office. We got a date."

CHAPTER 98

Yasmin and Carlos relaxed by the pool that night. They had already done their daily ten laps in the pool and had been debating on whether to go on to the beach to face the waves. It was now early October, and it was unthinkable to go swimming in the ocean in the dark.

"We can't go this time of year. The water is too cold, Carlos," Yasmin said.

"But we can beat the cold, Yasmin. I've done it before."

"Why do we need to do that, Carlos, if we have our pool with heated water? Remember what you just got through. Who knows what effect the cold water may have on you?"

"None, Yasmin. It will have no effect on me at all because we will moving. Our bodies will generate heat."

"No, I'd rather take no chances. Let's not jeopardize all the improvement you have made for something that is outright silly."

"What's the weather now in Guatemala?"

"It's hot, very hot."

"We are going to the beach there, right?"

"Yes, darling, we are going to Monterrico."

She leaned over from her chair and kissed him.

He looked at the copy of the email that Sonia had given them. They would be traveling in two weeks. They needed to return to her office tomorrow to pick up a package of documents and Yasmin's medical appointment.

"We need to make our flight reservations tomorrow," she said.

"We need to call your parents," Carlos said looking her way.

"I know. As soon as we go inside."

"How about if we order over some dinner from a restaurant. La Carreta does not make deliveries."

"All right," she said. "Come on, let's go in."

She took his hand, and they walked inside together.

"We have to make our hotel reservations too."

"We can do that tomorrow," Yasmin said. "No need to stress, my love."

"All right, you know, I just want everything to be perfect."

"I know, darling. It will be."

She kissed him, and he held her in an embrace.

"We can see the sights in the city of Guatemala, no?"

"Well, I don't know how much it's changed, but it's not the place where you should be exploring too much. The bad elements are everywhere, and they spot tourists right off the plane."

"Yeah, I know all about that, but we still need to see some sights."

"We have to dress casual. Anybody dressed up formal is a target."

"Neither one of us has that problem. If anything, we underdress."

"I am dialing my mother's number now. She will pick up for me as soon as she sees my number on her screen. After this call, I'll calling your parents."

"I'll wait here."

"Do not go far."

CHAPTER 99

Carlos stopped to see Mr. Moza the next day and got him to extend his starting date by four weeks. It was an amazing gesture because he was a brand-new hire and was expected to show up as scheduled. But the man did wonders. He was in control. Carlos was accompanied by Yasmin, and the morning turned quickly into a toast (without champagne) upon hearing the news about the upcoming interview.

"Dear," Mr. Moza said getting up from his chair, "you have come a long way, and it all has happened so fast."

He came around the desk to hug Yasmin. The scene turned emotional, and Mr. Moza held her tight and then turned to Carlos.

"Do not worry about the job, Carlos. It will be here when you get back. But you have to promise me to be careful down there, right? I wish you did not have to go."

"It will be all right, Mr. Moza. We will be back in less than a month."

Mr. Moza nodded and walked with them out of the room. They agreed to meet at La Carreta that evening. The occasion could not be ignored. Carlos and Yasmin were about to turn when a familiar voice held them up. It was Gordon, dressed in casual jeans and short-sleeve shirt.

"I am here to see Mr. Moza too," he said, shaking Carlos's hand. Then he turned to Yasmin and kissed her on the cheek.

"Gordon, we love you," Yasmin said.

"Tell him," Carlos said.

"We got an interview," Yasmin said.

"Oh, wow!"

Gordon shook Carlos's hand and then hugged Yasmin.

"This means victory. You won."

"You didn't know?"

"No, Kline would not tell me ahead of you. He's strict about clients' confidentiality."

He turned to Mr. Moza and shook his hand.

"Gordon, how are you doing, my man?"

"I am doing all right, just seeing these two out. I think we will celebrate tonight. You are welcome to come if you are available."

"I can always make the time for these two."

"Well, then, we should all meet in the evening, as always."

Yasmin and Carlos bid them goodbye and left the building. The events had rapidly unfolded. There was no doubt now. They got in their car and headed to see their travel agent to discuss the trip. Neither one of them felt secure enough to make the transaction themselves off a computer. This was too delicate of a matter for them to do themselves.

CHAPTER 100

At La Carreta that evening, it was all well-wishing to Carlos and Yasmin, the couple that had come out of nowhere, like something never seen. The atmosphere was one of happiness for the couple that had fought so hard to be together. Now their final hurdle was about to be crossed, and they were going on this voyage that was going to decide their fate. It had been a hard trip getting here. Roberto raised his wine glass, and Gordon, in faithful attendance, raised his also.

"To the loveliest couple I ever met," Roberto said.

"I second that," Gordon said. "If I can elaborate, this union happened during my watch. I was chasing Carlos at all times. He always answered me and put up with my insistence. He joked about it and never seemed to mind. Then suddenly, out of nowhere, came this beautiful girl with the long braid who seemed to take control of his life, and from that moment on, they have been together, always together, and I think it's only fair that they be given the opportunity to stay that way. They've earned that, and to their triumph over circumstances, I drink."

It was an unexpected speech, much unlike Gordon, who was a very practical man who loathed speeches. But this was his way of showing how much he cared and appreciated Carlos and now Yasmin. He gulped his drink down before anyone else could. In the distance, they all heard that distinctive voice of Mr. Moza, greeting everyone at the main entrance.

"Here he comes," said the waitress. "Anything special going on this evening?"

"Yes," Roberto said. "Carlos and Yasmin have their interview."

"What? You're kidding."

"No," Carlos cut in. "We will be leaving you for a few days."

"Oh, congratulations."

"Hello," Mr. Kline said after her.

He had made it to dinner tonight. He had fallen into the encircling group's web after all.

"Good evening to all. I am here to wish my clients a nice trip."

"Is that all?" asked Roberto. "You are the one who made it possible."

"That's not entirely correct," Mr. Kline said. "I would not have been able to do it without my clients."

Everyone laughed, and it was Gordon who quipped that you needed two to tango.

"I need to move you all to a bigger table," the waitress said. "There are more of you today than usual."

While she cleared a table for them, Mr. Moza greeted everyone, with Mr. Pietro following him shortly. Everyone stood to switch places, and Gordon, Mr. Kline, and Mr. Moza made it a point to sit next to one another. In answering Roberto's questions, Carlos revealed that he and Yasmin would be leaving for Guatemala this weekend. They had decided to jump ahead of the interview date to visit Yasmin's parents. Amelia was filled with emotion, and before sitting down again, she came and hugged Yasmin tightly and kissed her on the cheek. This pretty much would be a farewell dinner, and everyone knew.

CHAPTER 101

That weekend, Yasmin and Carlos flew out of Miami to Guatemala City. They took seats by the middle of the cabin, with Yasmin sitting by the window. Yasmin was feeling somewhat apprehensive not knowing how Carlos would react to the change in pressure. She had taken every possible precaution and asked advice from their doctor and the therapist. Everyone concurred that there would not be a problem and that Carlos should avoid exerting himself, smoking, and other activities that neither she nor he practiced. They both lived a very clean life and exercised daily. But there was always that doubt in Yasmin's mind. She had lived through his brain trauma and knew that a repetition of that could take him down. She was his watchdog, always alert as to any abnormalities.

Carlos now held her hand tightly as their aircraft headed for takeoff. She kissed him, and she smiled and then placed her head back on her seat.

"It's my first time flying," Carlos said. "And I know it's your first too. We are both new in the flying business."

"We are new at many other things, and we keep discovering them together."

"Don't you get a sense sometimes that we are like two children who are beginning life together?"

Her black eyes gleamed at the thought.

"Yes," she said. "I think about that many times, like now for instance. Here we are, flying for the first time. It's like a game."

"But we are not children," Carlos said, smiling.

"No, we are lovers, intimate companions, friends until death, husband and wife."

"And we fulfill all our roles perfectly."

"Yes, we do, darling. Is there anything that you find where one of us lacks?"

"I'm lagging behind in the swimming."

"No, you're not," she said emphatically. "You were hurt, and the accident took a lot out of you. My gosh, Carlos, you have come back so fast that it's unbelievable."

"I have tried to return to the same point I was before the accident, as far as swimming anyway."

He chuckled mischievously at her, and she smiled back.

"You're back in every way," she said, and the two laughed out loud.

They had developed an uncanny, parabolic way to communicate that was suggestive but not quite literal in meaning. It was pleasing to them because it made them feel that only they knew their true meaning, and then it became comical. The stewardess interrupted them and offered them a drink. They both chose Sprite.

"We will be there in the late morning, right?"

"Yeah, I would say so. It's two and one-half hours," Yasmin said.

"Can we sleep?"

"Of course. People sleep when flying all the time I hear."

"Let's hit the sack then, darling. I was really tired waking up this morning. You think I can get a pillow?"

"We can get one from the stewardess."

The stewardess returned with the drinks, retrieved a small pillow from the luggage bin, and handed it to them. Carlos placed it smack in the middle of the two seats. They drank some soda from their glasses and put them in the cup holders. Carlos laid his head on the pillow, Yasmin came close and did the same, next to him. The flight was steady without any disturbances. For new fliers, they were notably daring. They were in a limbo status, half-asleep and dreamy, all the way through, until they felt the rough scraping of the landing gear on the ground, and they both looked through the window. It was so sunny and clear outside, as if a new day had arrived in their lives.

CHAPTER 102

Yasmin had made preparations for their traveling inside Guatemala. As soon as they gathered their luggage, they were met by a driver she had hired who would take them from Guatemala City to Xococ, the village where Yasmin's parents still resided. They were scheduled to spend three days there in what would prove to be a very emotional gathering. Their driver was the son of a man who had known Yasmin when she was a schoolgirl in the city. His father had also come to meet the couple. He went straight to Yasmin and hugged her. In a very emotional voice, he held both of her hands, telling her how grown she was.

"You turned into such a young woman, now," he said in a shaky voice that seemed about to break down. "I am so happy to see you, Yasmin. We will be delighted to take you to the village. Your parents are going to be really happy. They might be very emotional. Do they know you are coming?"

"Oh, yes, we are in contact."

"How long has it been since you saw them?"

"About three years."

The man suddenly responded in the Achi dialect, which she couldn't speak well but could understand.

He was asking who the man next to her was. She knew enough to respond in the dialect: "He's my husband."

"Oh, God," he said in surprise. "I did not know. Sir," he said in Spanish, "I am so pleased to meet you. You are Yasmin's husband. I have known her since she was a little girl. I am so pleased to meet you."

He bowed his head as he reached out to shake his hand.

"So pleased to meet you," Carlos replied. "Was Yasmin a quiet girl when she was younger, or was she always this bold?"

The man worked up a smile. His hair was totally silver, and he spoke fast, with a grim expression on his face.

"I'm Reynaldo," he said, smiling. "Yes, Yasmin was quiet. Well, you know, Achi people are quiet. But she was also bold, very smart, and very studious."

"Yes, I've noted all those qualities, but especially the bold part."

He turned to Yasmin, and they both smiled at each other.

"Well, my son and I are going to take you to our village. It is not like the city; it is simple and poor, but her parents are there, and they will be very happy to see her."

"I am anxious to meet them. I have not seen them yet."

"They will be very happy to meet you. Let's get going now. We have three hours to go."

He waved for them to get in the back seat through the open door; his son was holding it for them. Once inside, he asked them if they wanted him to drive them to the city, but Yasmin told him they would do that on their return. The car took them through a new highway, from which they overlooked the new buildings that had sprung up in the distance. Then the road narrowed, and they were suddenly traveling on a one-lane road with few houses on the sides. The trip was rigorous, and they only made two stops to fill the gas tank and then continued without having eaten anything.

The road turned narrow and unpaved ahead, and at several points they were driving through narrow straights that edged rocky abysses. They passed near Rabinal, a nearby city, and finally arrived at the cluster of adobe houses that was the village of Xococ.

"We can drop you right at your parents' house and wait to make sure you get in," Reynaldo said. "The neighborhood has not changed much since you were here last, Yasmin. The old people are here, and they will be glad to see you. The young ones are different than before."

Yasmin took Carlos's hand and stepped outside through the passenger door, tugging him behind her. She stood on the soft ground that had been sprinkled by recent rains and stared at the wooden porch with empty seats.

"This is my parents' house," she said to Carlos, grabbing his hand as she made a move to get out the car.

Carlos followed her, his arm now stretched from her tugging it.

"Wait, Yasmin," he said, "wait for me."

Reynaldo was standing behind them.

"Let me get them," Reynaldo said. "They are probably inside waiting."

"No," Yasmin told him. "We'll walk in."

"I should announce you and your husband," Reynaldo said. "These are different times, Yasmin. You can't just walk in unannounced."

The front door suddenly creaked open, and a short, thin woman with long gray hair looked curiously at them. She was brown skinned and looked frail but immediately smiled broadly upon recognizing Yasmin.

"Yasmin! You're here, my child!"

A man appeared at the side of the house and stopped walking at the very edge of the front wall. He was rather tall, light skinned, and with gray hair. He stared silently at the group.

Yasmin moved hastily towards her mother first, with Carlos close behind her. She threw her arms around the small woman and held her tight towards her chest. The woman sobbed softly on Yasmin's shoulder, and Yasmin patted her in the back.

"It's okay, Mama," Yasmin said comforting her. "We are together now. Look, this is my husband, Carlos. He has been waiting to meet you."

Carlos got close, and the old woman reached shyly towards him to shake his hand. Her face was wet with tears, and Yasmin came behind them with a tissue to wipe them. Then she looked ahead towards the man standing a few feet from them, broke off the group, and rushed to greet him.

"How are you, Papa?"

"I'm well, Yasmin. I'm happy to see you."

They both embraced and stayed in that position for a few seconds.

"I see Reynaldo brought you."

"Yes," she said, "he was right at the airport just as he promised. Come meet my husband."

He waved at Reynaldo and his son as he followed Yasmin.

"Carlos, this is my father, Geronimo," Yasmin said to Carlos.

"It's very nice to meet you, sir," Carlos said, shaking his hand.

Geronimo made a slight nod of the head and shook his hand. Yasmin asked Reynaldo and his son to come inside with the group.

"It's not safe to stand outside now," Yasmin's mother said once they came inside. "It's dangerous now. Someone could be watching us, and they will know right away that we have visitors."

"I know, I know," Reynaldo responded.

"So what shall we do? We had to come in from somewhere, Mama," Yasmin said.

"Don't stand outside, daughter," the old lady repeated. "It's too dangerous."

"Has it gotten that bad, Papa?" she asked her father, who was standing a distance away.

"He doesn't go to the fields anymore," Yasmin's mother said, interrupting. "It's not worth it anymore. They will steal our harvest anyway."

"Oh, so what are you supposed to do? How can people survive?"

"Many don't. We don't have hope. We live one day at a time."

"Cecilia, it's not that bad," Geronimo said. "We are old, and that's why they haunt us."

"No, Geronimo," she shot back. "It's very bad."

Geronimo nodded.

"It's all right that you don't go to the fields anymore, Papa. It's better that you stay home."

He seemed quite disconnected. It was evident that he had white blood in him, perhaps even all. His wife Cecilia was obviously of Achi blood, and Yasmin had her features except that she was taller than her mother. Cecilia was slim and her face ragged by years under the hot sun of the countryside, where she had toiled the ground along with her husband.

"He does," Cecilia said. "It does not pay anymore. We are renting the land now."

"Cecilia, have them sit down," Geronimo said.

"Yeah, yeah," the old woman said, turning rapidly around and taking Yasmin by the hand. "Sit, Yasmin, sit and your husband too. Come, come."

She pointed to the green painted cushioned chairs, set in a row in the dining room area.

"No, thanks," Reynaldo said. "We will be leaving now. We have to get back," he said in pure Achi dialect, addressing Cecilia.

She waved her hand down.

"Ah, no, you are not. Not without eating something first. Look at the time, it's past noon. You cannot leave with an empty stomach."

She waved for them to sit and quickly walked away to the kitchen in the adjacent room.

"Geronimo, sit them down," she said on her way out.

"Reynaldo, sit," Geronimo said. "It's no use resisting, and she's right. You must eat. How could you think you could leave without eating?"

Reynaldo and his son nodded and sat next to Yasmin and Carlos. Yasmin got up and took Carlos's hand.

"Come, Carlos, let's look at the house," she said.

The floor was tiled throughout the entire house, the result of Yasmin's financial help from the US. It had two bedrooms and only one floor. The terrace was reachable through back and hardly used now by Yasmin's parents. It was a lonely room with small wooden chairs with faded green paint. For the most part, its purpose had passed. Gone were the days of improvised music by local musicians and dancing by women dressed in typical Guatemalan dresses. The glass door to the house was now covered with green curtains, and hardly anyone ever crossed into the terrace anymore.

Carlos and Yasmin hugged tightly in the room.

"There is not much vegetation in the patio anymore," Yasmin said. "It used to be beautiful in the old days."

"Why is that?" Carlos said.

"Everyone is afraid to call the attention of the gang elements."

"Have your parents ever had any problems? You never said."

"No, not quite, but as you can see, my mother makes sure not to attract anyone's attention."

"Yes."

The door opened, and Cecilia called them to come back in.

"Are you ready to eat?" she asked.

"We are not really that hungry. We wanted to take you and Papa out to dinner."

"We can't do that now," Cecilia said. "Come and sit. We have some food ready. Geronimo is setting the table."

Yasmin turned to Carlos and kissed him on the lips. The two held hands as they walked towards the dining room and sat across from Reynaldo and his son. Cecilia came behind them and sat at the table. Geronimo had made two quick trips to the kitchen and filled the table with tamales, black beans, and enchiladas topped with sliced boiled eggs.

"That is a large amount of food, Mama," Yasmin commented. "How did you make this?"

"I made it early this morning, daughter. Have you forgotten? This needs time to make."

"Oh, you must have gotten up very early then."

"No, I left everything ready to be cooked last night, as usual."

Finally, Geronimo sat at the head of the table, and they all drank a sip of artesian water that came from a local well. They ate as they talked, discussing local events as Yasmin and Carlos stayed close, eyeing each other and sometimes tasting each other's food as Cecilia watched.

CHAPTER 103

Carlos's and Yasmin's stay in Xococ extended to five days, but by then it was Carlos who began to get edgy about the proximity of Yasmin's medical exam, scheduled dangerously close to her interview at the US Embassy in Guatemala City.

"We have to go, Yasmin," he insisted. "It's getting too close to the medical exam."

"But you saw how close we are to the capital," Yasmin said. "We are only a couple of hours' drive from here. We have time."

"You've read some of the papers we've picked up. Every day there is some horrific event happening and people dying. The roads are a horrible place to be. Yeah, we're a couple of hours away if we don't get pulled out of the car by some thugs on the way there. It's happening all the time here. I don't want you to miss your medical appointment. Not after what we've been through."

"We won't, Carlos. We will be fine. It's still two days away."

"It doesn't matter. We are leaving in the morning. Let's call Reynaldo tonight to take us back to the city tomorrow morning."

"All right, love," Yasmin said. "Let's keep my parents company till later tonight. Who knows when I will be able to see them again?"

"It will be soon, darling. We just have to get through this."

That afternoon, Reynaldo and his son were back in the village to pick up Carlos and Yasmin. Their car stayed running, with Reynaldo's son behind the wheel as Reynaldo got out to bring the luggage in.

"I am sure they will be back soon," Reynaldo said to Cecilia, who stood by the front door with Geronimo at her side. "Once Yasmin has her interview she will keep coming back."

Yasmin leaned over to kiss her mother. Then she hugged her father, and Carlos followed suit. There were no tears, but everyone felt the anticipation. The medical interview was not worrying, but only the concern that they would not arrive at the embassy in time for the interview. It was a concern they had shared with their attorney's office but had decided one week away was safe enough.

"Mom," Yasmin said from the car. "We will be back. We both will be back."

"Be careful in the city," Cecilia said, waving at them.

The car got under way on the dirt road out of the village and towards the capital. She looked towards her husband, who suddenly seemed to tear up.

CHAPTER 104

Reynaldo and his son were reliable people, Yasmin thought. There was no one else she would have trusted in this trip. Reynaldo's son did all the driving, and as soon as the car got on the road back, the conversation flared, with Reynaldo doing most of the talking.

Carlos and Yasmin had chosen the Hotel San Carlos, mainly because of the availability of a pool which they both wanted to sharpen Carlos's swimming abilities and keep up with his rehabilitation exercises. It was a bit pricy, but Yasmin had made reservations way before the scheduled date of the interview. She had to renegotiate the cost each time that their itinerary had changed, but still the price seemed fair.

They settled in a room with a good view of the foliage in the center of the hotel, reminiscent of a plaza. The room was comfortable and homey. They wasted no time, and that same night they practiced their daily laps in the turquoise water of the pool. Carlos had by now regained much of his strength, although he still had a lag in the strokes with his left hand.

They paused by the middle of the pool and went up the stairs from the bottom and sat down at the only table under a cantilever umbrella.

"What do you think?" Carlos asked. "Am I caught up?"

"To me you never have been behind, darling. It was only a temporary state. But remember, Carlos, that you must not overdo it. We can't abuse your body. We increase little by little."

"I know," he said and kissed her.

A waiter dressed in a hotel uniform came up to them, tray in hand, and served them water. He made an effort to speak in English, and Yasmin stopped him.

"It's okay," she said. "We speak Spanish."

"Oh, great," he said. "Do you want a drink? Something to eat?"

"The restaurant is open inside, right?" Carlos asked.

"Oh, yes. This is only for the pool area."

"I think we'll just have a drink," Yasmin replied. "We will go up and change after, Carlos," she said. "Then we'll eat and rest. We got to be up early tomorrow."

"What kind of drinks do you have other than alcohol?"

The waiter hesitated then gave them a list he had obviously memorized. Yasmin turned to Carlos and explained.

"The fruit punch is great, Carlos, especially the pineapple one. There is the apple one also, and with warm drinks, they have the *atol de elote* and *rompope*, which is like eggnog. Those are warm."

"Don't you feel like drinking something warm after the pool?"

"I think we should, yeah."

"You want to try the rompope? I think you'll like that one."

"Okay, let's go with that one."

Yasmin asked the waiter for two, and he asked them if they wanted some pastry but both declined.

"Let's leave that for dinner," she said.

"Not that we are so fond of pastry, right?"

"No," she said agreeing.

They each got a small glass with the yellow thick liquid inside, and they drank it in short gulps, savoring the creamy custard and taking small bites from the stick of cinnamon on the side of their plates.

"It's really delicious," Carlos said.

They talked about Yasmin's parents' village, Carlos lamenting their seclusion and inability to move around.

"It's the tragedy of the times," Yasmin said.

"And the government seems to do little about it."

"They are corrupt. They're in it for the money they collect from the gangs."

"Are other towns in Guatemala affected?"

"It's all over, darling."

She went for his hand and held it tight and kissed him.

"Now, darling, it's getting late. Let's get something to eat. We have to be up early."

"What do you feel like eating?" she said.

"Some soup," he replied.

"You have to eat something solid, my darling. We both need some protein."

"Soup will be a starter. I think a good steak after will be good. Is that an entree in the menu here?"

"I'm sure it can be worked out. Let's move over, my darling."

They left their seats and told the waiter they'd be going inside to have some dinner, and he followed them. Holding hands, they walked inside the dining room and sat at a table on the first row. There were not any guests yet present. The waiter brought each one a menu, and Yasmin read hers first as Carlos watched her.

"Yasmin, your hair is growing fast, darling. It's now about shoulder length. You are so beautiful, honey. Can you do your braid yet?"

"I can but it would be a short braid, my love. Don't you want to give it a little more?"

"I can wait," he said.

They both looked at each other with an intense tenderness that only they appreciated. Tomorrow would be another step towards their goal, and they expected that the medical exam would be uncomplicated. In a few more days, they would have the final interview, and the embassy would tell them the results. If approved, Yasmin would be a legal resident of the US.

CHAPTER 105

The morning of the interview Carlos and Yasmin were up early. It was too important of a date for their lives. Each of them hugged as soon as they opened their eyes, and both got up immediately and washed their teeth together. They usually dressed together, and both did it with the same speed. Yasmin rarely needed more time once Carlos was done, but this morning, he coached her and made suggestions about her makeup and her clothes.

"Carlos, you never cared about makeup, honey. Are you worried?"

"I want you to make a good impression, my angel. You have worked too hard for this day. Remember that I probably won't be allowed inside. You will be on your own then, darling, but I will be with you even if not in the room."

"I know. So what would you suggest I wear?"

"Light makeup but enough to see you shine."

"Lipstick, cream?"

"I'd say, go easy on the lipstick, and definitely do not wear a bright color. Something like lilac or brownish."

She searched in her purse and retrieved a bar of lipstick and showed it to him.

"Do you think that will do? I will wear no other makeup. It's a light brown shade."

"I would think so. I did not think you would wear some crazy color anyway, but it's always good to check."

She kissed him in front of the mirror, and they then finished dressing and got ready to leave. They had been advised by Sonia, their attorney's secretary, to dress casual but elegant. She wore light brown slacks and a light blue blouse. Carlos wore blue jeans, a white shirt, and brown moccasins.

It was barely 7:00 and they stopped downstairs for a coffee and waited for Reynaldo outside. His son, Marcos, was the driver as usual, and Reynaldo rode in the passenger seat. The car beeped the horn as they reached the front of the hotel.

"Good morning," Reynaldo and his son said as Carlos and Yasmin came in.

"Good morning," Carlos and Yasmin said back.

Yasmin crossed herself.

"That's always good to do, Yasmin," Reynaldo said from the front seat. "But you are going to be just fine."

They sat in the back seat, and Marcos drove them past the historic center of the city. The US Embassy was located in zone 16 of the city, and the high building with rows of windows sparkled in the distance with the morning sun. The car dropped them off right at the entrance and then headed for a commercial parking lot nearby. Reynaldo had agreed that he would wait for them until they were done.

Carlos and Yasmin went through the entrance The agent inquired what was Carlos's relationship to Yasmin. He then told them that Carlos would not be involved in the interview, and he asked him to wait outside.

"I will be outside waiting," he said to Yasmin. "You will be fine."

He said it loud enough for the agent to hear. After all, there was nothing dishonest about their marriage, and if they did not want him to be present at the interview, then they ought to know how he felt about his wife. He turned to leave, and Yasmin held his arm, as if she did not want him to leave her alone at that very moment, so important in their lives. He turned back to look at her. There she was, holding steady, and it seemed that her moment of weakness may have been over in seconds, just a fleeting moment that dissipated into space. She stared straight at him and leaned towards him to kiss him, but he met her halfway. They kissed passionately, and then he patted her back.

"Be strong, darling. We both need to be strong," he whispered.

Then he finally turned again and walked away towards the door without looking back until he was outside. He turned to look at her through the glass doors, but she was inside, walking towards the main lobby to sit and wait for someone to call her case.

CHAPTER 106

Right at the end of the tiled passageway, past the embassy's American flag, Carlos began to realize that he did not know where Reynaldo and his son Marcos might be waiting. He thought about retreating his steps and sitting in one of the benches but then that might not be a good idea for security reasons, and he might be asked to leave the grounds. He kept walking forward not knowing exactly in which direction. Then, to his surprise, Reynaldo and Marcos were whistling at him from the sidewalk.

"What happened?" Reynaldo asked. "Where is Yasmin?"

"They did not need me for the interview," Carlos said. "Yasmin is inside being interviewed right now, I think. I can't call her. We are not allowed to bring a cell phone inside."

"That is a good sign," Marcos said. "When it's a couple, and they only want one inside, that is a good sign."

"Yeah, our attorney told us that I would not be needed, but I did not want Yasmin to be alone."

"That's good, that's good," Reynaldo said.

"And where are you parked?"

"We are not far. In a commercial parking lot. We are not allowed to park in the consulate grounds."

"Do you come here often?"

"Occasionally. When someone calls us."

"You get many interviews like ours?"

"Once in a while. We mostly transport people who arrive from the US to visit family here, and they call us to take them to see their relatives. Sometimes we travel far from the capital."

"So, you know your way around the country, right?"

"He does better than me," Reynaldo said, pointing to his son.

"What do you know about the beach in Monterrico?"

"It's very nice," Marcos said. "Some people go to see the sand. It's black sand."

"What about the waves? Do they have big waves there?"

"Yes, they surf there."

"It's about two-and-one-half-hour drive."

"Oh, that's what Yasmin and I thought. I think we are gonna want to go there. It depends on the outcome of the interview."

Carlos looked back at the entrance of the embassy. Something seemed incredibly serious about it. If America built such a gallant building, it must be because she cared about the region very much, and right now, inside of it, his fate and that of Yasmin was being decided by someone who had no clue about how much it meant to them. Would this person, man or woman, know the importance of their decision to two people who were so deeply in love? Would they care? He and his friends walked away on the sidewalk deciding to just stroll around. Carlos was afraid that Yasmin could walk out and not see them and panic. She did not have her cell phone on her.

CHAPTER 107

By midafternoon, Carlos was getting restless. He, Reynaldo, and Marcos had strolled by the sidewalk a few times since this morning, having heard nothing from Yasmin. He was walking ahead of the other two and stopped by the entrance to the consulate. Carlos turned back in frustration. As if by magic, he saw Yasmin suddenly make the bend from the embassy's driveway. Yes, it was Yasmin, coming towards them. She had appeared from the embassy's grounds, walking hastily. Reynaldo was the first to react.

"Yasmin, what happened?" he asked.

"I was approved," she said in a soft voice, smiling at them.

Carlos came towards her and hugged her.

"Congratulations," they all said.

"You did it, Yasmin," Carlos said. "You did it."

"I could not have ever done it without you," she said.

Carlos held back the tears as he clung to her in a tight embrace. Reynaldo came close behind them and tapped Carlos on the shoulder.

"Let's go, Carlos," he said. "It's better that we do this in the car. They do not like gatherings outside."

Carlos and Yasmin held hands, and they walked forward behind Reynaldo and Marcos. Yasmin retrieved her passport from her purse to show them.

"They sealed it inside. They only asked me if I was married to Carlos."

They all laughed.

"That is what I thought this was about," said Carlos.

"No, Carlos," Yasmin said. "We passed that part in the first interview. This is about whether I am qualified."

"Yeah, that's right," Reynaldo said. "Some people fail this interview because they have a criminal record, or they have other entries."

"We made it," Yasmin said, now fully realizing what had just taken place.

Carlos hugged her and lifted her up high then turned her around in circles several times. Reynaldo and Marcos watched them curiously. They seemed as happy and carefree as two children at play.

"I hate to break this up," Reynaldo said."

"No, let's go," Carlos said, putting Yasmin down and walking ahead with her, hand in hand.

"When can you take us to Monterrico?" Carlos asked, still ahead of them.

"Whenever you want," Reynaldo replied. "We are at your service."

"We have a few more days left before we leave. We'll rest tonight, and we will call you tomorrow," Yasmin said. "We need at least a night before we go. We have to call and make reservations for a hotel."

"Maybe the day after tomorrow?" Carlos asked.

"We will see if we can get a reservation. Do you know of a good hotel there, Reynaldo?"

"What price range?"

"Something modest," Carlos replied, adding, "as close to the beach as possible."

Yasmin nodded approvingly. She held onto Carlos's arm and walked with the others to get in the car. She felt as if she needed to sit at the hotel and rest for a few moments, travel in time to wrap up all the events that had brought her and Carlos here. It all had taken so much time, so many hurdles, and then suddenly it all had ended. They were going to have a normal life after all.

CHAPTER 108

The afternoon went fast after Reynaldo and Marcos dropped Carlos and Yasmin at the hotel. They sat by the pool and had a light lunch then discussed their future. It seemed bright. Yasmin would be a resident and legally able to work. Perhaps she could work for the city of Miami too. They debated that, understanding it might not be possible because they were husband and wife, and that might not be allowed. They did not know. But their lives would change. Now Yasmin would be able to drive, and she could move around without a worry. They then concluded that it may not change much after all, that their highest interest in life, their most intense passion was to be together, and that everything else seemed behind them. Then Yasmin brought up the subject of their trip to Monterrico. Was it really that important?

"Do you really want to go?" Yasmin asked him.

"Why? Don't you want to?"

"I do if you want it," she said while softly running her fingers through his cheek. "If you want it, I want it."

"But you were there already, darling. Maybe that's why it's not that important for you. But I have never seen it. I'm curious about the sand."

"You are right about that. I guess it did not make such a great impression on me at that time. I was much younger. Maybe that is it."

"You did not find the black sand peculiar?"

"Yeah, sort of. But not that much. I was there on a weekend while in school, and I got there by bus. Really it was all about swimming in a different beach, at a different ocean."

"But that's it. I had never swum in the Pacific. Then I came back a few times. The waves were great."

She laughed and touched his chin.

"It would be my first too because you were not with me in the past. So, this would be my first time, my first time with you."

"It's a memory, darling. We can always tell our children someday that we swam in the Pacific together."

"And when do you think that will be?"

"Ah, who knows, right? Now it's all green lights for us. We can have children. We can swim in the Pacific. We can do anything."

She suddenly looked aghast.

"We can, but remember that you still have not swum in the ocean since the accident. It will be your first time."

"Does it worry you? I feel strong as ever."

"Still, it's the first time."

"You could always drag me out."

"I mean it, Carlos. I am concerned."

"Let's do something, darling. We have been so consumed with ourselves that we have forgotten about our parents. Let's call them both. First your parents, then mine."

"Carlos, you are right. How could we have passed that?"

Her eyes brightened as she grabbed the phone. It was a moment they both had dreamed of.

CHAPTER 109

Carlos and Yasmin arrived at Monterrico in late afternoon. Reynaldo and Marcos dropped them off at a popular hotel, and they quickly checked in. They took a glimpse at the distant beach through a window, and both were stunned by the size of the waves coming in the horizon. Yasmin grabbed Carlos's wrist.

"I don't think we should go in the water now," she said. "The sea is too rough."

"But that's what we want, darling. That's our game."

"No, it's not, Carlos. Not like this. Look."

"We can handle it, Yasmin. We've done it in Miami."

"Let's look around first. Let's have a drink and talk to some of the tourists. Besides, if the waves are too high, there's not going to be any swimming allowed. You know that."

"These waves are not so large, Yasmin. Look."

"It's too big a step for you, Carlos. You are hardly coming back to form, and you want to jump and try your skills in a rough sea. No, let's wait. Let's go down there and find out what's going on."

They were both dressed in shorts and T-shirts. Yasmin wore reef water beach sandals in white and Carlos wore fiber summer ones. The two were obviously connected and could be spotted as husband and wife at a glance. They sat near the beach and watched several men play volleyball. A crowd had built up around them.

"Let's go down there, darling," Carlos said.

"No, Carlos. Let's get something to eat."

She grabbed his hand, and they went back inside their hotel. They sat at a table for two and ordered sandwiches.

"You know that in Cuba there was a belief that you could not bathe after having eaten, and that's what we are about to do."

"Yes, I've heard about that. But we are not going to the beach just yet. Maybe not at all tonight. Let's find out if we are even allowed to swim today."

Their waiter came to their table holding a tray, two sandwiches, and soft drinks. Yasmin quickly asked him if the beach was open for swimming.

"Sure," the waiter said. "We could not keep people from swimming here."

"But the waves are so big. It's dangerous."

"This is not that bad," said the waiter. "There are times when the waves are over 3 meters."

"I know," Yasmin answered. "I've seen them, but today is close to that."

"Well, there is a lifeguard on duty. That means the beach is open."

"Thanks," Carlos said.

"There is no one at the beach, Carlos. We should come back in the morning. Let's just sleep tonight."

"I want to at least touch the water, honey. Let's just get our feet wet."

She did not answer. She was not thrilled about the idea. After their meal, they made their way past the group gathered by the volleyball court. Carlos was impressed by the black sand, and he kept grabbing fistfuls and sifting it through his fingers.

"Let's just go in a little bit," he said.

"Watch, Carlos," she answered. "Here comes a big wave."

The wave came in with a thunder, and Yasmin grabbed his hand and pulled him back gently.

"Yasmin, what are you afraid of all of a sudden? We swam through bigger waves than those."

"I'm a little nervous about them today. They are really large. The beach should have been closed."

"Darling, what is happening to you? Come on. Let's swim together by the shore. Look, it's not bad after the wave passes."

He suddenly let himself go and floated. She reached his hand and held it.

"No, Carlos, not tonight."

"Come on, Yasmin, just a little."

She lay next to him on the surface, floating. The two began stroking freestyle. They were inches from each other, and she kept watching for the next wave. Carlos's safety was her deepest concern. They swam side by side in shallow water. When the next wave came close, the sea would recoil and pull back, dragging them. They knew about this effect. They were after all experts and knew how to reverse the drag, but it required strength and an able body that could fight the current. As far as timeliness, they were both impeccable, and they both tipped their heads under simultaneously, turning towards shore. They raised their heads at the same time and checked to see how far they had been dragged back.

"We are back at the same spot," Carlos said. "We are perfect."

"You feel all right?" she asked.

"I feel fine, darling. How about you?"

"All right, but watch for the next wave, Carlos."

"Oh, we can handle them. That one was not so big."

"Here comes the next one. It's building up."

"No worries. I see it."

They repeated the same procedure, dipping under just as the wave came in and then turning at the bottom towards shore. Each time they did it, their timing was right on target, and they would come from under just at the same time.

"I love this water, Yasmin. Isn't it good?"

"It's a little cold."

"What about the sand? Don't you think the sand is amazing?"

"Yeah, it brings back memories. I remember being here and being so young."

"Since what age?"

"I started coming at about ten with my aunt and cousins. Before that I had never swum in big waves."

"I see the lifeguard walking on the beach, Yasmin."

"We have to get out, Carlos, come on."

She turned towards the shore to look at the lifeguard, and suddenly she heard the roar of the next wave. She felt the water under her feet being swept back and momentary lost her balance and fell back, but she quickly recovered and saw the massive wall of water coming towards her.

"Carlos, go under," she yelled and submerged head on, just at the moment when the wave hit.

She swam towards the bottom, but the current was so powerful underneath that it carried her back in a straight line towards the shore. She could not tell how long it took, but she felt dragged until she hit dry sand. She quickly stood up, looking for Carlos, who should have been behind her. But she could not find him.

She quickly plodded back towards the sea, anxiously calling his name. She ran until she could not run anymore and then dove deep as the next wave came in. In her haste to find him, she did not realize the danger she was entering. She felt in a daze that she needed to hit bottom in order to avoid being smacked unconscious by the impact of the wave. She did not wait long to swim back up and found herself in a tumultuous ocean. She saw no sign of Carlos.

"Carlos, Carlos! I am here, please come out, come out!"

She turned her head towards the shore and saw the lifeguard standing in about a foot of water and yelling at her.

"Come back," he yelled.

"Why can't you help me?" she yelled back at him. "You're supposed to be a lifeguard. Can't you swim?"

She turned away and swam farther away from the shoreline, meeting the next wave and then the next one without finding him. She began to lose strength. She realized that she could no longer handle any big wave. She was out of breath. But she must keep trying, no, she could never give up. Then she suddenly got struck again by another wave, and everything went black around her.

She went under in a last-ditch effort to keep trying. She was dragged underneath towards the shore, and as the wave broke off, she came up floating on the surface, breathless. The lifeguard hurriedly dragged her out of the water and quickly lay her down on the sand and began administering first aid. From afar the crowd around the volleyball court rushed to help, but no one seemed to notice that another person was missing until the guard agitatedly spoke.

"There is another one! There is another one out there!"

He continued giving Yasmin mouth-to-mouth resuscitation, and in between breaths he kept yelling at the crowd to look for a man in the water. Yasmin moved her head slowly, coughing up water.

"I got her!" the lifeguard yelled. "I got her!"

He pulled Yasmin's upper body towards him, and she continued to sputter, spitting big slumps of water.

She opened her eyes, muttering her husband's name.

"First Aid is here," the waiter who had helped Yasmin and Carlos at the restaurant said.

He had run from the restaurant's terrace to the scene upon hearing the commotion. "I called them. They are here, they are here."

Two men dressed in blue pants and white shirts rushed over to the scene, carrying a bulgy bag with medical equipment. They knelt down next to Yasmin and quickly got to work. Seeing that they had control of the situation, the lifeguard got up and ran towards the shore.

"Has anybody seen anything?" he asked in broken English.

"No!" the men said. "There's no one out there."

"All right, everyone stay put," he said, now in Spanish. "No one should be in the water unless I call for help."

He went in and walked until chest length, keeping a vigil eye on the horizon. Then one of the men in the crowd yelled out.

"There's someone out there!" he yelled pointing towards an incoming wave. "He's on top of that wave!"

"Let's go in!" another one said. "Let's go in!"

"No," said the lifeguard. "No, no one comes in! Stay put!"

A young boy came rushing in from the lifeguard shack, carrying two life ring buoys and other floating gear. Someone from the group rushed in to help him. They went quickly in the water and swam over to the lifeguard. He turned to them and ordered the young boy to get inside a ring buoy and follow him. He grabbed a float belt from him and put it on. The two moved forward, fighting the incoming waves. It took him a good twenty minutes before they could make contact with the man, and the lifeguard quickly slipped the other ring buoy around him.

The man slumped his head forward while the lifeguard tried to keep him afloat as he and the boy fought their way to shore. By then most of the people who had gathered in the shore were stepping in the water, moving slowly towards the three figures. They waited for the right moment, and after a sweeping wave bolted them forward, several of them rushed in and grabbed the ring buoy carrying the man inside, and all moved towards the shore.

"We need you here!" they yelled to the First Aid men who had been working on Yasmin.

"We need you!" the others repeated.

"Carlos, Carlos!" Yasmin yelled from her spot on the sand.

She tried to get up but was held back by one of the First-Aiders. One of them quickly rushed towards the lifeguard and the others, and began to render mouth-to-mouth resuscitation to the man. Everyone stood silent as they watched. For a few minutes, it was only Yasmin's screams that broke their silence until the First Aid men took turns, and the second one stood back and shook his head.

"We've lost him," he said.

Yasmin was finally able to get up and walked towards them, slapping away the hands of those who sought to stop her.

"My Carlos! My Carlos!" she yelled, falling on her knees by his side and then throwing her arms around his lifeless body and sobbing uncontrollably.

CHAPTER 110

The evening was fresh at La Carreta restaurant this evening, a few days after Yasmin's return from Guatemala. Most of the regulars seemed to gather outside by the counter, engaging in low conversation. The events of the last few weeks had unsettled the mood of many, having learned of the tragedy of Carlos's passing at a moment when his future and that of his wife had just become brighter. Carlos's funeral was held at a local funeral home on SW 40th Street, a few blocks away. It was an unforgettable event, attended by local people and overwhelmingly by the trucking population, who seemed to come from everywhere to pay their respects to one of their most likeable comrades. The pinnacle of the affair happened at the burial, when a long line of eighteen-wheelers remained with their engines running at the curb of the road and then all beeped their horns in unison as the casket was lowered into the grave. There were no dry faces after it.

Today's dinner had been arranged by Amelia, who had made sure that their table was the same as it had been in the past. Roberto, Amelia, Gordon, Yasmin, and Carmen sat across from each other, and only two spots remained vacant, as everyone waited for Mr. Moza and Prieto. They heard Mr. Moza's voice in the distance. It seemed like a whisper of his old self, and it was evident to everyone that even he in his everlasting cheer had been affected by the tragedy. As he made his way to the table, Mr. Moza approached Yasmin and hugged her tenderly.

"How are you, dear?" he asked. "Your hair is almost shoulder length. Soon you will wearing your braid again."

Yasmin smiled lightly.

"I'd like that very much," she said.

Mr. Prieto then made his way to Yasmin and kissed her. Meanwhile the waitress posed herself in front of the table and addressed the group.

"Have you all decided or will you want to see a menu?"

"We know," Gordon said. "I want the ripe plantains. Those things are great."

Gordon had given Yasmin a job at his dispatch office. This was his gesture of gratitude to the late young man who had served him so well, and now his wife was in need. Carlos's life had ended young but he had been a very thrifty young man who had never given into bad vices. He lived a rather frugal life and had saved a large amount of money for his age. Still, his young widow was now facing a mortgage payment and the support of a home with no one to help her. Yasmin had just received her driver's license from the state of Florida and took Gordon's job.

"And what else will it be?" asked the waitress. "The bananas never go alone."

"I will try the chicken and rice."

The waitress looked towards Moza, waiting to hear his order. He never let her ask."

"My dear," Mr. Moza began. "I must say that for this occasion I will try something out of the ordinary. Prieto and I will have that famous chicken soup that you have here. And that would be all."

Mr. Moza sat next to Gordon. The two had developed a quite intense business acquaintance that grew more into a friendship each day. Rumors began to circulate about Gordon's thirst for challenging ventures and Mr. Moza's willingness to feed them. Amelia was the first one to pick up on these developments, and when alone with her husband at night, she commented to Roberto about her observations. They both agreed that Gordon, as a newcomer into their circle, was moving pretty fast. It remained to be seen what the future would bring between Mr. Moza and Gordon. Both were astute men who made a living taking risks. Nevertheless, Roberto frowned at the prospects of seeing Gordon get hurt. To him it seemed that Gordon was moving too fast.

"Very well, Mr. Moza," the waitress said, now moving to Yasmin.

She quietly wrote on her pad as Yasmin softly asked for chicken soup and one tamal, reminiscent of the days when she and Carlos ordered together. Then it was Carmen's turn, and she asked for the same. She had been Yasmin's constant companion since she returned from Guatemala.

"Did you get your green card all right, Yasmin?" Roberto asked.

"Yes," she said. "About two weeks ago."

Roberto was going to propose a toast but quickly changed his mind.

"Congratulations," he said. "I take it then that that is it, you're legal."

"Mr. Kline called me, and I went to see him. He says there is a technicality involved because Carlos passed on right before I returned, which means I was not supposed to have received my card."

"What?"

"He said he is going to fix it because it could become an issue in the future. He is going to file a petition of status for me as a widow."

Yasmin shifted her body on her chair and stared quietly at Amelia. She no longer could ignore the dizziness she had been experiencing lately and only Amelia, her trusted friend, knew. She could no longer attribute her symptoms to her husband's death. She was with child.

"I'm not sure I understand," Roberto said, turning towards Amelia.

"Mr. Kline is right," Mr. Moza said in the background. "Mr. Kline is a fine lawyer. Your status is locked at the time you return, not at the embassy. If the conditions have changed, then the procedure is faulty and that could prevent Yasmin from becoming a citizen later. Mr. Kline will fix it, Yasmin, no worries."

Yasmin nodded. She had made peace with the past. Strangely, it did not matter to her as much as anyone might have thought. But part of the reasoning for her following up was that this was what her late husband had wanted. He had sacrificed so much to make sure that she became a legal resident. It was what maybe even he had given his life for. She would follow his wishes.

Everyone became quiet.

"He said he is going to fix it because it could become an issue in the future. He is going to file a petition of status for me as a widow."

Yasmin shifted her body on her chair and stared quietly at Amelia. She no longer could ignore the dizziness she had been experiencing lately and only Amelia, her trusted friend, knew. She could not attribute her symptoms to her husband's death. She was with child.

"I'm not sure I understand," Roberto said, turning towards Amelia.

"Mr. Kline is right," Mr. Moza said in the background. "Mr. Kline is a fine lawyer. Your status is locked at the time you return, not at the embassy. If the conditions have changed, then the procedure is faulty and that could prevent Yasmin from becoming a citizen later. Mr. Kline will fix it, Yasmin, no worries."

Yasmin nodded. She had made peace with the past. Strangely, it did not matter to her as much as anyone might have thought. But part of the reasoning for her following up was that this was what her late husband had wanted. He had sacrificed so much to make sure that she became a legal resident. It was what maybe even he had given his life for. She would follow his wishes.

CHAPTER 111

Just as the next year's summer receded and the traces of a light Florida autumn set in, an eighteen-wheeler rolled down Highway 95 South, past the city of Jacksonville, having made its way through Route 10. The driver was a woman, dressed modestly in a man's flannel shirt and wearing a baseball cap, from under which darted a long black braid till the middle of her back. It was Yasmin. Another woman sat on the passenger side, and both were engaged in friendly conversation.

"Do you think we could visit the church of the Virgin of Guadalupe since we are now in the Jacksonville area?" asked the passenger.

Her short stature made her seem appealing. If facing her from the back, one could have mistaken her for a teen.

"I think that would have been very appropriate. Frankly, I did not think of it before. Since we had dropped our load, I think we could have managed to get to the church from Route 10. But I can't go back now. Next time we will do that. But I need to get back to Amelia's house and pick up little Carlos," said the driver.

"All right then. We should not try that tonight. We need to pick up that beautiful baby. He's the spitting image of his father."

"Do you really think so?"

"Of course I do. He's got his arms, his face, his eyes. Everything."

Yasmin smiled at her. She was always gentle with Carmen. To her, the poor woman had lived a deep misfortune, left abandoned by the death of her only son, having no means of survival and portraying such humility. She had become Yasmin's constant companion, her most zealot pillar of survival. Carmen was now the official nanny of her newborn son, also named Carlos, like his father.

There had been many reasons for Yasmin's early withdrawals from life as she had known it. Losing Carlos had been a blow that left her blind, without any desire to go on. She had wanted to relive those happy moments with her husband and desperately clung to anything that sparked his memory. She had kept on living but only for him, as if he were still here, and she would follow his steps. And so he had been a truck driver, and she had become one too. He had been a family-first person, and she was one. She would trace his steps. It was the only way she could entertain living without him until one month ago, before her son was born. But help had arrived with her beautiful baby.

She had rigorously completed her truck driving course after Carlos's death and gained her commercial license, then turned to her husband's boss for a job driving a truck. Gordon did not blink. He was a man who welcomed new ideas and knew how to pick his gambles. He had never before employed a woman as a driver. But to him, Yasmin reminded him so much of his one favorite driver ever, Carlos Figueroa, that it was freaky. What had been the purpose of all that had happened and why? Gordon had wondered.

The eighteen-wheeler moved flawlessly on Route 95, leaving the city of Jacksonville behind, and remaining in the right inner lane. The rain was overwhelming. Not far behind them was the site where Carlos had lost control of his truck and slumped into the ditch. Maybe Carmen was right. They must go back to the Virgin of Guadalupe church and thank her for having given her Carlos for just a little bit more time. And now their baby.

About the Book

The story begs the question of whether fate is a manmade concept, a product of the human imagination, or a reality. Whichever side the reader favors, the story of Carlos and Yasmin can make him a believer or not one at all. The question of what role this concept plays in the daily lives of the characters in the story, and beyond, hangs on feverishly throughout its theme. It in fact controls it and makes it inevitable that such question be answered. Carlos and Yasmin possessed the ingredients for a long-lasting love, one that could be truly exceptional, one that could never have been if not for fate, or perhaps one that never was because of it. An intriguing story.

www.ingramcontent.com/pod-product-compliance
Lightning Source LLC
LaVergne TN
LVHW021754060526
838201LV00058B/3084